CHARITABLE TRUST
By Marlene Browne

Copyright © 2015 by Marlene Browne

Half Court Press Publishing
PO Box 590
Lavallette, NJ 08735
www.halfcourtpresspublishing.com
Ordering Information: Quantity sales: Special discounts are available on quantity purchases by corporations, associations, and others. For details, contact the publisher at the address above.

Charitable Trust is a novel. As a work of fiction, names, characters, places, events, businesses, and incidents are either the products of the author's imagination or are used in a fictitious manner. Any resemblance to actual persons, living or dead, or actual events is purely coincidental.

Printed in the United States of America
Name: Browne, Marlene
Title: Charitable Trust / Marlene Browne

Description: Half Court Press Publishing, 2015. | Summary: After a divorce, a single female attorney, also a commercial pilot, returns to Cape Cod to find she's been named as the trustee in a secret codicil prepared by her ex's very wealthy father; a legal mystery with a romantic subplot and strong comedic undertones features Kate, a likable, flawed, warm and capable pilot and attorney in pursuit of what is fair and just and contentment, too.
Identifiers: Library of Congress Control Number 2015920043 (print) | ISBN 978-0-9970829-0-6 (paperback) | ISBN 978-0-9970829-1-3 (epub)
Subjects: LCSH: 655 _0 Legal stories—Fiction | 655 _0 Love stories, American—Fiction| Cape Cod and Aviation—Fiction. | BISAC: FIC044000 FICTION / Contemporary Women / Legal / Mystery & Detective /Action & Adventure / Romance / Clean & Wholesome/ Suspense/ Aviation / Cape Cod | GSAFD: 655 _7 Mystery fiction | Romantic suspense fiction | Legal stories
LC record available at http://lccn.loc.gov/2015920043

Dedication
To M.H.B.

"Make yourself necessary to somebody."
The Conduct of Life
Considerations by the Way
By Ralph Waldo Emerson

PROLOGUE

I have always thought of courthouses like churches, holy and sacred, offering judgment or mercy—punishment or reprieve—according to circumstance. I arrived early today and took my time surveying the gray stone Greek revival building on Foley Square in lower Manhattan. No matter how familiar it had become, the structure remained for me a striking monument to civic order and pride, a place of righteousness, for rich and poor alike. I was proud to work here, mostly.

I'd been practicing law in New York for more than a decade, appearing in this cathedral of justice at least once a week for the last five years; but today this building felt both awesome and foreboding. I climbed the granite steps to the Roman temple portico and entered the rotunda through the main doors. Like many times before under the 75 feet dome, I flashed my ASP (Attorney Secure Pass ID), to enter the expedited check point. Once cleared, I admired the depression-era murals, as I always did, and headed down the second radial corridor, taking the stairway up to the courtroom on the third floor. I entered the empty room and sat in a back row of the sparse and solemn space. Soon, the lunch break would end and court personnel would enter through the side door, to the left of the judge's bench at the front.

Despite my litigation experience, I felt queasy as I waited to hear the caption. Today, it was my case and I was the defendant. The matter of Ethan v. Ethan was the only divorce on the docket for this Friday afternoon session, a professional scheduling courtesy, no doubt, to me with hugs and kisses from Frankie, the court's clerk, who I knew well and much esteemed.

Ruminating about my marriage and the twelve years spent with Rick—and his father—I felt sad that we wound up here. Rick's

1

dad, Warren, and I shared interests—aviation; Rick; business—and chemistry. Warren, born Werner Eidenberg, in the Lower East Side of Manhattan, from an immigrant family of humble means, was a self-made man by necessity. At age seventeen he joined the Army, becoming a fighter pilot serving in the European theater. Upon returning from the war, Warren bought and sold airplane parts, until he had enough cash to buy a single-engine plane to ferry the affluent between New York and various playgrounds along the New England Coast, from Newport to Kennebunkport. With a reliable stream of income, Warren qualified for credit, got a loan, and bought two more planes, forming a small commuter airline. After developing vertigo that grounded him as a pilot, Warren sold the airline and used the proceeds to purchase the next big thing: raw land in New Jersey, Connecticut, and New York.

Warren built his empire by developing plots of dirt into finished apartments, hotels, residential communities, and shopping centers; and then selling them to syndicates for enormous profits— again, and again. Warren had the feel for the deal and worked alone. He knew what he wanted and often got it, on his own terms. He was not a team player. His transactions were conducted through Ethan Enterprises, his privately held company. There were no partners, not even his son, just an intimate circle of long-time trusted subordinates to run his day-to-day operations. When Warren grew sick of the cold and snow and ice of the East, he moved West. The California real estate business was more lucrative than anything he'd touched before and he became an immensely wealthy man.

Waiting in the courtroom, I reminisced about my past. I realized that I would miss Warren as much as anything else from my marriage. I wondered if he felt the loss, too. As the back door opened, I startled just slightly when I noticed my soon-to-be ex-husband enter the courtroom with his dad's lawyers in tow—two of them. I wasn't sure what purpose they would serve here, today. Rick was leaving our marriage with his bond to me in tatters, but his dad's fortune intact. His father's attorneys had accomplished that goal through intricate financial planning long before Rick and I were wed.

The Ethan legal team was already mobilized, protecting Warren's wealth from the claims of his second wife, who was on her way out of the family, as I was on my way in. Ignoring the outcries of my then new legal colleagues, I signed an iron clad prenuptial when it was presented. When you lack a family of your own, attachment to

2

someone else's can be emotionally appealing. Executing a document to fill an emotional void is nothing, or at least that's how I saw it. Besides, when you're young, you're mostly optimistic.

Soon after signing the prenup, I received a six carat diamond solitaire selected by Warren's personal assistant. I teased my husband about the engagement ring that his dad bought for me, but Rick was unfazed. His detachment should have concerned me at the time, but didn't. My attachment to his father, and his to me, Rick viewed as helpful. It all seemed to work.

Warren's fondness for me grew as his dearly departing second wife fought a public legal battle for half of the community assets and property, in the absence of a contract limiting her marital rights. Sitting in the courtroom this afternoon, I recalled how all those years ago, Warren would ask for my advice and show me the pleadings and papers that each side had filed in his messy divorce litigation. I offered my opinion, confirming that his army of attorneys was serving him well. Warren appreciated the reassurance and once told me that I was like the daughter he nearly had. Whatever that meant. Now some of those very same attorneys were plying their professional skill to erase me from the family register, only with far less effort thanks to the prenup I executed and would not now contest.

Feeling worse this afternoon than I anticipated, I changed my focus to the better times. I recalled Warren's East Coast trips. He'd call to invite us on his jet to join him for lunch in Nantucket or for supper on the Vineyard, or wherever else he wanted. During these aerial jaunts, Rick appeared disengaged, bored by his dad's memories and experiences, remaining silent and sullen as he gazed out the windows into the ether. I'd sit next to Warren, and listen closely to his stories and insights.

Today, I gazed at Rick sitting on the far side of the courtroom, with his dad's attorneys beside him. My soon-to-be ex, now thirty-nine, looked a little older with less hair; but still handsome and well-dressed. He had the same entitled bearing as the day we met at one of New York's premier society galas at the Waldorf Astoria. I don't recall the charitable cause, but I do remember the nude-colored, tissue-crepe Donna Karan slip gown that I wore. Warren was the chairman, hosting the luxurious event attended by the great and the good of the City. When we were introduced, Warren looked at me, paused, and said I could be the twin of Katharine Ross, only much younger, of course. "Did I know who she was?"

Yes, I did. She was a film actress from the later 1960s; a natural, all-American girl with long chestnut-brown hair, big wide-set dark eyes, a square face, and a slightly dimpled chin. My late mom was her doppelgänger, often confused for the actress. When we were out and about on the Cape or in Boston, strangers would approach my mom and ask for her autograph, mistaking her for Ms. Ross, in her prime. Of course my mom complied, signing Ms. Ross's name. This was long before eBay so there were no repercussions and no disappointments. Everyone was happy.

"But your eyes turn up at the end, like a cat's." I recall Warren commenting all those years ago.

"More hazel than feline. See." I replied as I leaned in and looked directly into Warren's lean, tan face and round blue/gray eyes.

"Very nice." He remarked then introduced me to his son, Richard, "Rick," who was seated beside him.

That much was seared in my memory and the rest, well, led to today in this courtroom.

I caught Rick looking in my direction and responded by lifting my hand in a slight wave. He nodded in acknowledgment and remained still in the pew-like bench across the way. I was thinking that this just might be the last time I would lay eyes on him. Despite a marriage of more than twelve years, we had no children. There was no support to be paid. Our marital assets, including our co-op, were sold and the proceeds were divvied up fairly between us. According to our settlement agreement, each of us would pay our own attorneys fees, which was beside the fact. Rick's lawyers were on Warren's payroll and my lawyer was my law partner, Mike, working gratis.

Mike Fortune had been my colleague at my Manhattan law firm. He was an expert in corporate taxation and helped me and my clients from time to time. I was glad to have him here beside me. Mike was investing my share of the marital proceeds and I trusted him. When he said he'd take care of me and asked for my limited power of attorney, I obliged without hesitation. In return, Mike assured that I'd be all right so long as I worked and wasn't careless with money; but the lavish and privileged lifestyle I'd led was a thing of the past. So be it. Que sera, and all that.

At the conclusion of today's legal proceedings, Rick and I were poised to make a clean, polite, and final break from each other. Rick would walk away with his dad and his dynasty to himself; and soon, I would fly from New York to Cape Cod, where my parents were buried and a part of my heart remained attached since childhood. With my new Massachusetts Bar admission and an ATP (airline transport pilot) license, I was ready for the next chapter in life. Recalling that old Harry Chapin tune, with the taxi driver pondering his youthful dreams to become a pilot, I became calm and hopeful. I wasn't young, but I wasn't old either. Time hadn't ruined me yet, though it had made me wiser, and just a touch winkled around the corners of my hazel eyes. In a matter of days, I'd be off to find the sky and rebuild my life in the place I left behind long ago, on that spit of land that first nurtured me and my soul.

Recognizing that I was lost in reverie, Mike gently placed his hand on my wrist and whispered, "Hey Kate, ready?"

I nodded and spoke. "Yes. Let's get this over with."

Frankie, the court clerk, called the docket and read the case caption out loud to the five of us present in the room. We approached the front tables set before the bench for counsel and their clients. The plaintiff, Richard Ethan, and his lawyers entered their appearances. Attorney Mike Fortune followed for the defendant, Katharine Ethan. The combination of words startled me. I'd never been a defendant before.

We followed the liturgy required to confirm our legal residency and identify our divorce settlement agreement as an exhibit. After acknowledging my signature on the document, including a stipulation inserted at Rick's insistence that I drop the Ethan surname, the judge declared us divorced. I bowed my head in silent prayer after these last legal rites were administered—a Viaticum for my failed marriage. I thought of my long-dead parents who never saw their only child as a bride or a wife. No matter now. From today going forward, I would be known once more by my birth name, "Katharine Bergin," and that was fine. Trying to be more positive, it occurred to me that I'd just had a baptism in reverse, which might qualify as a sacrament and cause for celebration; but I wasn't feeling festive or full of the Holy Spirit, just depleted and sad. Stunned, really.

Standing at counsel table as the proceeding ended, I watched as Rick promptly left, leaving his, or rather his father's, attorneys to gather up the paperwork. I heard the senior counsel, Thomas Beck, ask Mike if he could speak with me privately. I looked up at my attorney and nodded "yes."

Mike passed on my assent, "She'll speak with you. I'll wait outside."

5

Thomas Beck, who knew me as Rick's wife, but was never particularly warm or welcoming, solemnly walked towards me. "Ms. Bergin," I have something for you."

I looked at him, still processing the use of my natal surname as he addressed me, a now single, thirty-eight-year-old woman.

"Mr. Ethan wanted you to have this." Mr. Beck handed me a sealed ivory-colored envelope that I recognized as Warren's custom stationery.

"What is this for?"

"Mr. Ethan wanted you to have something from him."

"Thank you." I stated flatly, as I took the envelope from his hand.

Thomas Beck added, "He wanted me to make sure you received it."

"Thank you." I repeated and added, "Please, give Warren my warm regards."

"I will be sure to do that, Ms. Bergin."

We walked down the center aisle of the empty courtroom, toward the exit, somberly, slowly, a funeral march in my mind.

I made my way to my soon-to-be former partner, Mike, who was seated in the hallway. I watched as my ex, Thomas Beck, and the other lawyer exchanged some words and then departed. They seemed relieved that all went as planned.

"What happened back there?" Mike was curious.

"Beck gave me an envelope from Warren."

I pulled it out of my purse and showed Mike the engraving on the finest handmade linen paper.

"What's inside?"

I shrugged. "I don't know."

"Well, aren't you curious?"

I paused. "Not at this moment. I'll open it later."

At some point, I thought to myself. But not now. Today, I had endured all I could. I was sure Warren's note thanked me for honoring the prenuptial and wishing me well in my future flying endeavors, as he'd done so well with his. I just didn't have it in me to read it in the courthouse. I tucked the envelope deep into the Chanel handbag Warren had given me a few years back as an anniversary gift.

Mike invited me to join him and his family for dinner that evening, a kind gesture from a good, dependable friend. I thanked him, but declined. I was okay on my own and ready to begin anew. I'd been living in a hotel since Rick and I sold our co-op and I needed the time to pack my personal items and clear out.

CHAPTER ONE

I moved from Manhattan to Barnstable County, Massachusetts, my native land, in mid-November, just before Thanksgiving. Like every child growing up on the Cape, I had a special relationship with this New England/American holiday. Any first-grader from Falmouth to Provincetown could tell you that a place called "Pollock Rip"—southeast of Monomoy Point, where the Nantucket Sound tears into the Atlantic—made it impossible for the Mayflower to sail south towards her goal: the chartered lands in "Virginia" (now New York) near the mouth of the Hudson River. Forced northward and looking for a natural harbor, the Pilgrims made first landing down Cape, in Provincetown, past Race Point and leeward round the hook of the peninsula.

Without Pollock Rip and those treacherous shoals off the Chatham shore, there'd be no Pilgrim story in New England, let alone Plymouth. Even so, the Pilgrims—William Bradford, William Brewster, Myles Standish, and the rest—didn't step foot on that famous rock in Plymouth for more than a month after signing the Mayflower Compact in P-town Harbor on 11 November 1620, using our calendar. And for the record, the Pilgrims' first encounter with the Cape's natives wasn't all that friendly either. The Indians attacked the Pilgrims at Eastham, but the plucky (new) Englanders fought back. Over the next year in Plymouth, the Pilgrims and the Wampanoag learned to cooperate and by October of 1621, they celebrated for three days with a harvest feast of shellfish and eels, waterfowl, wild turkeys, venison, and corn. The yams and mashed potatoes came much later and I for one was grateful for that, too.

So, it's understandable, considering the history, that we Cape Codders embrace this feast and its menu. Nearly four-hundred years later, a Thanksgiving spread reminds us of our special part in the national narrative and remains a blessing; even if you eat it by yourself, as I would this year. But besides the native fare and Pilgrim lore, there's something nearly mystical about New England in the fall—or any time. Read Henry David Thoreau's "Cape Cod" and you will understand what makes this "bare and bended arm" of Massachusetts not simply a place; but a compulsion.

I rented a little house in South Yarmouth on the Bass River, not too far from Wellfleet where my parents were buried, but not too close either. Shingles and shutters and gables, my little cape on the Cape was adorable and quaint and tiny compared to the size of the co-op I shared with Rick in Manhattan. Fulfilling my frugal New England heritage, I was learning to do more with less and mastering the art of living as if in a lighthouse—or a sailboat. There's a place for everything and everything in its place. Organization is the key to happiness when your interior is less than 1,000 square feet, and a good deal of that is attic and dormer. Yet, my little New England cottage with its whitewashed ceiling rafters, vanilla-colored beadboard, and walls of bluish-green Nantucket gray felt just about perfect to me now. It was home.

I was also the founder and proprietor of "Katharine Bergin, Attorney at Law, LLC." Hanging my own shingle as a solo practitioner, after being a lawyer in large New York law firm for most of my professional life, was quite a change. I had traded complex commercial transactions for simple lawsuits, some real estate work, and drafting wills and trusts. A lawyer will always have work when there's land at stake, taxes to pay, or someone dies. But my change in legal diet wasn't the most drastic adjustment to my professional daily routine.

After leaving Manhattan for Barnstable County, I became a commercial aviator, too. Ever since I was child, watching the jets pass over Otis Air Force Base, and my parents flying their Piper Cub along the coast, I longed to be in the sky, at the controls. Until Rick and I wed, the closest I got to the professional aviation world was working during summers off from college as a gate agent for a small airline at Boardman/Polando Field in Hyannis (HYA). After that, law school beckoned, tragedy struck, and I left the Cape behind after burying my parents and selling their home. Life, as it does, took a different course.

But my love for flying never waned and was something I shared with Warren, who nurtured my aviation interest. My first

9

flying lesson was a birthday gift from Warren many years ago. When Rick and I travelled in his dad's jet, the pilots were kind enough to answer my questions, sometimes even letting me don a pair of headsets and place my hands on the control column after we'd reached cruising altitude. I watched and listened, mesmerized by the pilots' mastery, their technology, and their inscrutable verbal exchanges with the controllers. These verbal transmissions were crucial, yet clipped and cryptic, nearly unintelligible to the initiated. New York Center "Gulfstream 6RE, descend to 8,000 feet, squawk 174 niner." I wanted to comprehend and speak this lingua franca proficiently, if not fluently.

Every day these controllers were in charge of thousands of flights. They protected the flying public by giving pilots headings and altitudes that prevented them from playing bumper planes in the skies above you. The verbal dexterity and alertness of the air traffic controllers awed me. I doubted the best litigator could process as much information, as quickly and concisely as the average, say, Boston Air Space ATC. And NY control, they were the best of the best. You wouldn't think about flying into Class B controlled airspace over Manhattan without being on top of your game. Just "fa get a boud it."

During longer flights on Warren's jet, in less congested skies over the vast country west of the Mississippi, I would venture up to the fight deck and ask the pilots to handle the radios, for practice. What a thrill to get it right. When I failed, the guys helped me. Unlike the terse and unforgiving controllers of Class B airspace over New York, those in charge of the air over North Dakota were accommodating and good-natured. I made a mental note to visit North Dakota some day because the controllers were patient and courteous.

When I would return to the cabin, Rick's displeasure was clear. He'd complain that I'd lost my dignity by mixing with the help. He told me that it was like jumping in the front seat of his dad's limo and asking the chauffeur if I could take the wheel. I didn't see it this way, nor did Warren, who encouraged my interest and participation from his base in L.A. Back on the East Coast, Rick's different perception on matters such as flying and fraternizing were among the causes of our divorce—well that and his mistress from Los Angeles.

During my marriage, I indulged my need to fly at a fixed base operator (FBO) across the Hudson, in Essex County, New Jersey, just like J.F.K. Jr., had done. Years of flying lessons, ground school, paper tigers, and simulators made me a pilot. By the time I was a Bergin again, I had gained enough time to qualify for an airline transport pilot (ATP) rating. That rating allowed me to fly a single pilot twin engine for hire. Good enough to work for a small air carrier on the Cape.

So, these days, when I wasn't fighting for my clients in the local county courthouse, I was in flight, operating charters for people who demanded convenience, privacy, and speed when traveling to the Cape, Nantucket, or the Vineyard, or anywhere else within my plane's range. Shortly after the New Year, my first professional trip was to LaGuardia (LGA) carrying a woman and her pet poodle. As we flew over Manhattan on a left downwind for runway 4, I felt a twinge of nostalgia for my old Ethan life. Yet everything was different now. You learned quickly when you operated a small charter. You were not only the captain; you were the flight attendant; the customer service representative; and the baggage handler all rolled into one. Because of the multi-tasking required of you, your passengers tended to think of you as their factotum, the gofer who gets their stuff off the plane, not the professional whose aviation skills brought them safely through the atmosphere at 180 knots in a small metal tube.

Once we arrived at the Marine Air Terminal, I helped my human passenger out of the plane and removed the poodle's carrier, strapped in the back seat. While I was at the cargo hold, fetching the lady's luggage, her doggy pooped on the ramp upon exiting its crate. When I appeared with the portmanteau, the woman looked down at the poo, then up at me and barked, "You'll take care of that." Then, she lifted the nervous pet into her arms and walked away towards the waiting limo, leaving the baggage standing on the ramp where I'd brought it to her. Stunned into immobility for just a moment, I soon grabbed her Taiga leather LV Pégase rollabout and towed it over to the driver who had the limo trunk open. As he took the luggage from me, I asked him for a plastic bag to complete my next task. That's when I fully understood my place in the aviation charter universe.

No wonder Warren's pilots were so nice to me. I treated them with dignity and respect and even a little awe—not like the hired help who were to be endured, sometimes ordered, but never acknowledged. But I wasn't flying for admiration. I would do whatever was required till I could leverage my charter pilot job into a legacy carrier position. Meanwhile, I was patient and fortunate to be in a position to do the two things I enjoyed and did well: flying planes and arguing cases. For the present time, one day I was appearing in the Barnstable County Courthouse, the next, I was running a charter to Nantucket (ACK), or wherever.

The day had gotten by me and I was running late to my law office. It was time to call my legal controller, my assistant, my angel, my friend from the heavens, my sister from another mother—eight years my senior, the noble, the wise, the witty, and the wonderful, Ms. Celeste MacKinley.

"Hi C-Mac, I'll be there shortly, are we still on for the hearing this afternoon?"

"Yes, Mrs. Hoffman is already here, waiting for you to drive her to court."

"Okay, how does she look?"

"Nervous. She needs your reassurance, that's all."

"Fine. I can do reassurance. If you have the file ready for me, I'll meet with her for a few minutes in my office before we leave for the courthouse. How is everything else? Are you managing to put out all the fires?"

"As much as I'm able without having passed the bar."

"Oh Celeste, no excuses, you're a better lawyer than most lawyers."

"Thanks, Kate. Time to talk to you about that raise?"

"Okay, Cel. Put it on my 'to do' list."

We both chuckled.

I pulled up to a parking spot flanking my office, a nice storefront in a strip mall on Route 28. Nothing like the luxurious digs I had when I worked for a large firm in the City, but life is different now. I'm different now and that's okay. For one thing, there are few opportunities for strutting about in Armani and Chanel, which I now stored in mothballs, along with the matching shoes and purses for each outfit. Half the year on the Cape requires practical clothing as spring, summer, and fall last only six months, roughly April to October. The other half of the year, you have to be prepared for inclement and disagreeable weather. High heels, dresses, skirts were not optimal as you dug out of the snow, or trudged through the mud or cold or fog so common on the Cape. Today, however, was a clear, temperate mid-May morn which allowed me to dress like a proper lady lawyer.

The doorbell jingled as I opened the front door to my storefront practice in the strip mall.

"Hi, Cel, is Mrs. Hoffman ready?"

"She's in your office, waiting. Hey, you look nice."

"Thanks."

I grabbed the file on the corner of Celeste's desk and entered my office.

"Good morning, Miss Bergin. Do you think we'll win today?"

"Morning to you, Mrs. Hoffman. I sure hope so. Let's get in my car and we'll talk more on the way."

Sometimes, even moderate reassurance can afford great relief to the recipient. We left my office and headed for my Hybrid Ford SUV parked outside. I helped Mrs. Hoffman up into the vehicle and buckled her in for safety. In springtime, the pot holes are sizeable out here and unexpected turbulence was a possibility. The seat belt sign was on for the duration.

Driving along, we both felt hopeful and the law, I reminded her, was on our side. These days, my practice was more hands on than what I knew in the City. Back in the day, I wouldn't have much client contact unless I was taking a deposition or preparing someone for testimony. Staff handled most of the touchy-feely stuff. Up here, much like my life as a charter pilot, I wore many hats: lawyer, therapist, and chauffeur. Payment on the Cape was a different matter, too. In the city, I billed 900 dollars an hour. On the Cape, folks balked at 200 dollars. Even then, some couldn't afford to pay in cash. Instead, they offered homemade candles, cranberry sauce, oysters, quahogs—whatever they could make or catch that was valuable.

Out of respect to my clientele and Yankee tradition, I accepted it all as legal tender for my debt. Mrs. Hoffman paid her bills in cash, in increments of twenty dollars per month. I figured at that rate, her invoice would be satisfied in 300 years, but that wasn't the point. I enjoyed helping those whose limited means left them generally unable to hire a good lawyer. And I was a good lawyer, becoming a very good person.

Today's court appearance was for a summary judgment. A big bad developing company had filed an action to take a quarter of Mrs. Hoffman's property on the basis that it needed an easement to reach the rest of the parcels it had accumulated by similar unsavory means. Mrs. Hoffman was served with legal process just after Thanksgiving last year and didn't know to whom she should turn for help. Hearing of her plight, her neighbor suggested that she see the "flying lawyer" who'd just opened an office nearby. The "flying lawyer" reference

13

tickled me, as I vaguely recalled the reruns of the 1960s television show about "the flying nun." Helping people like Mrs. Hoffman, made me feel good and there is nothing better than that, except maybe the perfectly executed spin, followed by a smooth recovery and safe landing.

Pulling up to the courthouse, I could see that Mrs. Hoffman seemed nervous again. I reminded her that we were prepared, our papers were excellent, and that today's appearance was merely to hear Judge Snyder's decision. There really wasn't much left to do unless he required additional argument. I exited the SUV and walked over to Mrs. Hoffman's side. I unbuckled her seatbelt and helped her down. Then I took her arm and we walked, side by side, through the parking lot towards Main Street where the classic Greek revival structure, replete with pediment and pillars, stood as it had since 1831—sort of like Foley Square, but older and more quaint than grand.

As we passed by, for luck I rubbed the petticoat of Mercy Otis Warren's life-size bronze statue. We entered this traditional New England courthouse and waited in the reception area till it was our time. I saw my adversary and noticed that his clients, brothers who amassed cash from several restaurants on the Cape, were there as well. Good, I thought. It's always easier for us lawyers to explain court decisions when our clients are present to hear them from the judge, first hand, themselves.

Today, Judge Snyder would decide the ultimate issue in the case. If he decided for us, Mrs. Hoffman would leave the courthouse with her property intact. If he decided against us, she'd face a trial at worst. At least that's how I would frame it. For now, however, we'd sit.

"Kowalski Bros. v. Hoffman" the clerk called. I took Mrs. Hoffman's arm again, and this time led her up to the front of the room. We sat at the defendant's counsel table, the one farthest away from the jury box. Mrs. Hoffman asked where the people were, and I explained, again, that this was just a motion and not a trial. Mrs. Hoffman nodded. We were instructed to rise. We did and I looked to the judge who had just appeared on the bench before us. My adversary and I entered our appearances on the record and the court asked that we all be seated.

Judge Snyder began to recite the facts of the case. I sat and listened, trying to detect if the court was reciting my version of the facts, or my adversary's. So far, it seemed fair and balanced. Though

14

attorneys must present the facts as they are, we are trained to present them with a bias slanted towards our client's view of the case. This is not being dishonest, this is being an advocate. After all, facts look different depending upon your perspective. Mrs. Hoffman's reality was different from my adversary's clients. Right now, I was listening closely to the court's recitation, trying to detect if my version of events prevailed.

After five minutes of reading from the bench, I heard Judge Snyder say: "And what the plaintiffs could not gain by contract, they sought to take by litigation."

Bingo. I nudged Mrs. Hoffman, smiled and whispered, "We won."

Her eyes brightened and she took my hand and gave it a good squeeze. Judge Snyder continued reading from the bench and when I heard my legal analysis coming through his mouth, I could barely contain my joy. Several more minutes and the judge announced his ruling, which by this time, I could predict.

"For the reasons aforesaid and the cases aforecited, the Court grants defendant's motion for summary judgment. The plaintiffs' complaint is dismissed, taxed costs for defendant."

I turned to Mrs. Hoffman and confirmed her victory. "It's over, you won. You can go home and not give this case a second thought." Mrs. Hoffman was delighted and expressed it in that distinct, understated Yankee way: she invited Celeste and me over to her home for a celebratory dinner. I accepted and left the details for her and Cel to confirm.

Mrs. Hoffman relaxed on the ride back to my office as I made several calls: first to Cel (We won!), and the second to Cape Air Charter to confirm my departure time for a flight that evening to the Vineyard.

CHAPTER TWO

After such a great day in court I was flying high on the win. Soon, I'd be literally at 3,000 feet between Barnstable Municipal Airport—HYA and Vineyard Haven—MVY. I was informed that this trip was on the Bain Capital Private Equity account and, given the client, the destination surprised me. Bankers usually preferred the posh and preppy Nantucket (ACK), with its busy social scene and seaside shingle estates, similar to those on the south eastern end of Long Island; to the groovy, laid back Vineyard with its artists' colonies and cottages filled with writers and editors. The Vineyard even had a nude beach beneath the beautiful clay cliffs of Aquinnah—or Gay Head, as we used to call it. It piqued my interest that a Bain Capital person would prefer the Vineyard.

As I prepared the plane for the short hop to Vineyard Haven, I glanced at the manifest and noticed the lone passenger's name was Mr. Steven Philips. Didn't ring a bell. First time with us, I guessed, or at least with me. Before I could meet and greet Mr. Philips in the lounge, and inspect the private equity banker/Vineyard koan more closely, I had to complete my preflight chores. I was carefully checking the flight control surfaces—I think I had made it to the ailerons, or maybe the flaps?—when a man approached me.

"Are you the mechanic?"

"No, I'm the pilot. Are you the passenger?"

"Yes, ready to go."

"Welcome to Cape Air Charter. You can board in approximately ten minutes; we're scheduled for an 1800 departure."

"I'm early."

"You're fine. I'll complete the walk around and I'll be with you soon."

"Your name's not Amelia is it?"

16

"No, she was a lousy pilot. They haven't found her yet."

"So what is your name?"

As a female pilot, I generally discourage passengers from becoming too familiar with me, at least initially, so I don't share my first name. I replied, "Captain Bergin, I'm your P-I-C."

"Pilot in command?"

"Yes. You've done this before?"

"Many, many times. And you, Ms., pardon, Captain Bergin?"

"A time or two, but I'm feeling lucky. Have I flown you before?"

I gave Mr. Steven Philips a scrutinizing stare, pretending to squint at something past him towards the setting sun. He was tall and wore his expensive clothes easily and without fuss. His handsome, strong features were framed by thick, wavy dark hair, worn inches longer than most bankers. He was self-assured, but not arrogant. Polite and approachable, I liked this fellow.

"I don't believe I've ever had the pleasure," he responded.

"I…uh…It should be a smooth ride. Free from turbulence."

"Well, now I feel lucky, too." Mr. Philips replied in good humor.

"Let's get aboard." I suggested in a mildly authoritative tone.

After leading him up the airstairs and entering the plane, I gave Mr. Philips the required passenger briefing, pointing out the exits and how to operate them in case of emergency. I also showed him where we stowed the life vests. I asked him to buckle up and put his smart phone in airplane mode. Then, I climbed into the cockpit. I clamped on my harness and ran through the cockpit preflight items and completed the checklist. I yelled outside through the open window beside me, "Clear!" and started the engines.

In minutes, we were taxiing to the runway. I closed my window and we took off, headed into the evening clouds. I had filed an IFR flight plan and was busy communicating headings and altitudes with the controllers during the brief flight. Though fluent in aviator-speak, it's not my native tongue. So I have to really listen. Under these circumstances, when you are the only pilot on board and you wear your seafoam green David Clark headset, mic at your lips, you can't communicate with your passenger unless he chooses to plug in with his own headset, which my banker did not. So, the flight was silent, smooth, and from my point of view, too short.

After we landed, I completed the postflight checklist and was ready to leave the cockpit. I turned back to see what my passenger was doing in the small cabin. He didn't seem in a hurry. He'd pulled out his phone and was engaged in conversation. He might have been talking to his ride, or his wife. Whatever. I liked this slightly rumpled banker.

I unbuckled my harness, walked aft, opened the airstairs door and exited. He rose and followed behind me down to the ramp.

"Have a pleasant evening, Mr. Philips. Thanks for flying with Cape Air Charter."

"No, Captain Bergin, thank you. Hope to fly with you again."

"Likewise."

I watched him traverse the apron like a pro. As he walked towards the general aviation lounge door, I could see a tall, dark, attractive woman waiting for him. Figured, he was taken. C'est la vie. Per my paperwork, I was to pick up a couple to fly back to Hyannis. It was nearly time to meet them and I had pilot duties to fulfill.

Nearly three seasons had passed since my divorce on that damp, drizzly November day in Manhattan. Summer time was approaching on the Cape and I yearned for a romantic companion. Throughout the late fall, winter and most of the spring, I surveyed my new surroundings—the courthouses, the airports, the supermarkets, and the restaurants—searching for possible new partners. But so far, I saw no one I fancied, until last month. That Mr. Philips intrigued me— was a good sign; that he was spoken for—a bad omen.

Yet my karma was good and I kept it that way. I was single and hopeful, practicing law and flying, eyes wide open. Meanwhile, at my law office, to support the local publishing industry and inform my clients, I subscribed to area newspapers, the *Cape Cod Times*, the *Nantucket News*, and the *Vineyard Gaz*ette. To entertain my clients, I had the *Robb Report* and *Town & Country Magazine* delivered. Old habits die hard. Sometimes I fetched the mail before Celeste could get it and I'd take the new magazines to my desk to gaze at what was happening in the old proverbial neighborhood.

I was at the office early this mid-June morning and saw that the mail included the new *T&C* issue. I flipped through it and the social pages caught my eye. A two page spread in the July volume announced that Mr. Richard W. Ethan, son of Mr. Warren Ethan, had married. The bride wore a white Monique Lhuillier and looked radiant, and not a day younger than 40. She wasn't a natural beauty, but she might turn a head if you went for that sort of stick-in-your-eye obvious gorgeous. It wasn't everyone's aesthetic ideal to have a perfect, inflexible face.

The photos revealed that the wedding was an elegant affair held last February at Warren's country club in Los Angeles. Most of the pictures focused on the bride, as they should, and some of the bride and groom and their small wedding party. There was one with Warren and his latest companion, showing him looking off in the distance, distracted. Rick and his bride, Tiffany—what else would she be named—reportedly honeymooned in Fiji—where else would they go?

I had every reason to expect this day would come, that I'd receive my monthly *T&C* and open it to see photos of my ex and his beautiful, blonde, buxom, Californian wife in my storefront office in Hyannis; but really nothing prepares you for it. Good thing I was sitting down. If I had to put it into words, or word, I think I would say I was "stunned." I didn't want Rick, but like nearly every divorced woman in the world would tell you, she might not want her ex; but she really didn't want anyone else to have him either. Tiffany was about to live a life with my name and my former husband, with my ex family. But no matter how that marriage turned out (and I gave it five years, tops); I would always be wife number one and I would always be Warren's first, and in my mind, favorite daughter-in-law. I wondered if this wife was the mistress from L.A. I doubted if I would ever know, and really, what did it matter anyway?

I had to stop ruminating over this wedding. When I heard Celeste enter the office I called her in, to confirm or deny my assessment of the situation at hand. Celeste was reliable that way, and many more.

"Hi, Cel, I got the mail already. When you can, would you come in here? I want to show you the future mother of the children I never had."

Appearing at my threshold, still wearing her raincoat, Celeste asked, "What are you talking about? Did you put vodka in the coffee again?"

"No, the chief pilot hates when I do that, but today I might." I replied, pointing to the magazine splayed out on my desk.

Celeste walked over and took a look. "Pretty. Nice dress."

"Wrong answer, Celeste. You, my friend, are fired." I replied, very good-naturedly, given the circumstances.

"Who are they?" Cel ignored my comment. She did that regularly, in a practical and good way.

"They are the new Mr. and Mrs. Richard W. Ethan." I sounded surprisingly proud.

"Oh my God. That's your husband with a new wife."

"Well, my ex and his new wife. Tiffany."

"Oh, you didn't want him anyway...You know it's just the shock of seeing him in the photos." She took off her coat. "What's this about children? Is she pregnant?"

"I don't know. Crazy talk." I responded.

"There, there, Ms. Kate." Celeste was appeasing me.

Rick and I talked about having a child, but it never was the right time, and when I thought it was, after five years of marriage, he didn't. Though we wed, Rick never really did commit to me. After all, if you mixed blood and produced a child, you became a shear-proof branch in that family tree, for good or ill. Having a kid in most cases required a permanent connection, at least for as long as you and your child lived. Rick obviously didn't want this. At least with me—for whatever reason. But enough of these disquieting reflections. I had clients to work for and adversaries to browbeat and that's how I would distract myself till I could put this *T&C* issue behind me.

This morning I got to be both boss and employee for a client, which is unique. Sean, my Cape Air Charter (CAC) boss, otherwise known as "chief pilot," sat across from me to hear the latest about the case involving the local airport. I represented CAC, the Hyannis company for whom I fly. The same developers who'd pestered and sued Mrs. Hoffman and lost were now trying to stop local and state authorities from improving the Hyannis Airport so it could accommodate larger jets and more traffic, all good for us.

If people could fly to Hyannis directly from, say Chicago, or even Florida, instead of coming via connection from Logan in Boston, it meant more feeder traffic for all airlines and charters, not to mention the ferries, the buses, the rental cars, the hotels, the restaurants, the lawyers, the charter pilots, and so on. By having temporarily enjoined this expansion, the development brothers were preventing economic growth and tourist development. But they had a reason. Highway access to one of their real estate holdings would disappear with this new expansion. The injunction put the new terminal on hiatus until the trial court in the Land Division could rule, which could take months.

Since I would be working with attorneys for the local government, the state, and even the feds who were footing the bill, I was not in any way lead counsel. I told Sean, boss/client, that we were simply supporting the larger effort. It was cheaper this way, and besides, we had no choice. This was the hierarchy. Cape Air Charter was merely an interested party, along with the rest of the local businesses. My boss/client understood the strategy and our position and place in this litigation.

"Okay. Thanks for the update," he stood to go. "By the way, you're on the schedule tonight for a Vineyard turn, 1900 show time, 2000 depart."

"Fine," I said, knowing that I could leave my law office early and rest before I had to sign in at 7 p.m.

The forecast predicted fog at the Vineyard before nine in the evening. In an instant, I recalled the images of the boats looking out for J.F.K. Jr.'s Piper Saratoga the day after it disappeared, not far from Gay Head en route from New Jersey to the Vineyard the eve of 16 July 1999. But I was a trained aviator, with 3,200 hours, whereas J.F.K. Jr. had been an amateur with far fewer. Besides being over planed, private pilots like him, with less than 350 hours of flight time are famously in danger of crashing because they feel comfortable, when they shouldn't. I knew better. I was never relaxed in a plane that I was flying because you never knew what dangers lurked behind you, let alone ahead.

Tonight, I would be checking the ATIS (Automatic Terminal Information Service) for weather forecasts and status reports frequently. If the Vineyard was below minimum visibility I would not go. As pilot in command, if I say no go, the plane stays grounded. I set that parking brake and my metal does not move. My boss can say or do whatever, it doesn't matter. The FAA gives me the final word on safety, because it's my neck and my license on the line. A late night turn (when you fly out and back to your local base in the same day) to the Vineyard would be dicey tonight, and without knowing more, all I could do is show up, be ready, and determine whether or not the weather permitted flight. If not, we'd stay put. Like they say, there are old pilots, and there are bold pilots, but there are no old and bold pilots.

21

After a cat nap at home, I felt refreshed and checked the weather reports. Though the air was thick, it was not pea soup. If it got no worse than this here in Hyannis and at the Vineyard, my charter would depart and return as scheduled. I pulled into the nearly empty parking lot at 1845. Visibility was decent and it seemed that the weather was clearing as the time passed.

Entering the terminal, my first stop was always the ladies room. You must be physically comfortable when you are a pilot and our planes lacked lavatories. My next stop was generally to the office to collect my paperwork including my routes and my weather reports. After that, I filed my flight plans and checked my V-file for updates on anything I might need. I reviewed my documents and rechecked the weather before this instrument flight rules (IFR) nighttime charter flight. It seemed to be getting thicker again. I consulted with a fellow pilot who'd come in from Nantucket. He assured me that it was fine, but Nantucket was further east out in the Sound. Sometimes the weather would be clear there and socked in at the Vineyard and vice versa. Bellwether or red herring? I couldn't tell, so his info wasn't that helpful.

I was left to my reports and my judgment. I needed a minimum runway visual range (RVR) of 1,800 feet to shoot an approach and for now, the report gave me RVR of 4,000 feet. That was plenty. If my passenger arrived early, we could depart sooner than scheduled and we should be fine. I made final marks on my charts, checked the weather again and was off to do my walk around. Passing me on his way out, one of our mechanics told me the aircraft was just serviced and ready to fly. Satisfied with that, but still having to inspect it for myself, I thanked him and walked toward the plane on the ramp.

The Cessna 402 is a stable airplane with dependable engines, nice handing, and is easy to control, even in shifting winds and variable conditions. I was getting in the mental zone, one with the plane, when I heard footsteps and then, "Captain Bergin. Are you still feeling lucky?"

"More than ever, Mr. Philips. Nice to see you again." As the fog and wind were my primary concerns, I hadn't reviewed the manifest, knowing only that I was taking the 402 with one passenger outbound and empty on the return leg. This was a pleasant surprise.

"How's the weather at the Vineyard?" Mr. Philips asked.

"It's reporting strong gusty winds out of the south; 2,000 feet partially obscured; RVR 4,000 feet for runway 24 with RVR 1,800 feet minimums."

"Translated to mean we're on schedule?"

"For now." I replied in a light tone, laced with confidence.

After completing my final inspection, I asked where Mr. Philips would like to sit, front or back, this evening.

"Front this time." He responded.

"Very well, after you."

Like a pro, Mr. Philips climbed the airstairs while ducking for the low headroom. He moved gracefully forward through the small cabin and seated himself in the copilot's seat. I glanced around the aircraft, then climbed in securing the airstairs behind me. I walked forward and took the left seat. Mr. Philips had already buckled his seat belt and reached up above for his shoulder harness.

Comfortably positioned in the captain seat, I tended to the final items on my preflight checklist. Fuel, flaps, radio, lights, etc., and we were good to go. My final weather check revealed that visibility was down to RVR 3,000 feet, but that was still 1,200 feet more than I needed. My calculations had me landing back in Hyannis long before visibility diminished along with the cooling southerly Atlantic wind. I started the engines and called for the taxi clearance. We taxied to the runway in clear but heavy humid air. Soon, we were airborne.

The takeoff was normal. V1, rotate, I was making the call outs to myself with the object of my recent interest beside me. But this was not the time or situation for small talk or distraction. Though I'd be using the autopilot tonight as soon as my flaps were up, I would remain vigilant and ready for the worst, ahead of the airplane at all times. It was not a "set it and forget it" kind of night.

As we climbed out of Hyannis through the low clouds to a star-filled dusky sky above, I remained concerned about landing conditions at the Vineyard. Contrary to weather reports and best efforts at prediction, twenty-two nautical miles southwest from Hyannis, conditions could deteriorate rapidly at the Vineyard. After Hyannis Tower switched us to Cape Approach, I asked for conditions at the Vineyard. After an unusual pause, the controller replied. She said they were busy. The Vineyard weather was "up and down," we were number three and a couple of aircraft had already diverted. She cleared us up to 4,000 feet and told us to hold at the intermediate approach fix (IAF) called "CHOPY." She said she'd "get back to us" and ended her transmission.

This controller sounded harried and that was not a good sign. As a pilot, you like normal conditions, nothing out of the ordinary, and a controller who was rock steady and confident. The thing about controllers is that they are the calmest sounding set of professionals that you will ever encounter. They make world class poker players seem nervous by comparison. So, her anxiety put me on high alert.

Meanwhile the ambient sound in a small airplane can be a distraction if you're not used to it. In most small planes, if you don't wear your headsets, there is little communication between the occupants. It's just too loud up there to discern the normal range of the human voice above the roaring engines, propellers, gyros, and air noise. Plus, you cannot clearly decipher the radio over the cockpit speaker unless you plug in a headset; never mind the ATC language barrier. Unlike the first flight with Mr. Philips, when he sat in the back with no headset, he seemed interested in tonight's operations and wanted to see and hear what was being communicated, or not.

As we entered holding, we joined the other wonderers revolving like planets over the non-galactic milky way covering the Vineyard Sound. Mr. Philips donned the headphones stored in the pocket beside him and plugged in. I could tell by how he knew which headphone plug went into which jack on the instrument panel, that he'd done it before. I asked Mr. Philips if everything was all right. He didn't react. Surmising that the volume on his headset had been turned down and he didn't realize it, I tapped him on his arm and motioned to my volume control knob on the right ear of my headset. Mr. Philips got the idea. He turned his own volume knob up.

"Thanks, Captain Bergin. How long will we be holding?"

"Not sure. There's a pocket of bad weather over Vineyard Haven. The controllers are busy dealing with diversions and they don't want us in their hair right now. We're in a holding pattern over CHOPY just northeast of the island, but we have gas on board and they know we're here."

"CHOPY? Do you mean turbulence?"

"No, well, it may be, but 'CHOPY' is a designated fix, a defined location on the airport's approach plate."

"Okay. Do you mind if I ask questions?"

"So long as you're quiet the moment you hear the controllers speak. I'll use sign language by raising my hand like this (I raised my

24

hand, palm towards the instrument panel), to indicate that we need to be quiet momentarily to hear what is going on." I was blunt, but it was necessary.

After several turns and two step-downs in altitude in the holding pattern, I heard our call sign, our plane's manufacturer (Cessna) and the last three identifiers of our airplane's "N" number. "Cessna Bravo Charlie One, Runway 24 RVR 2,400, cleared for the ILS 24 Runway approach."

"Cessna Bravo Charlie One is out of 2,000, cleared ILS 24." I reported.

"So we're in?" asked Mr. Philips.

"We'll see. If we're planning to visit the Vineyard this evening, we're going in now." I said curtly.

We descended to 1,700 feet. Turning inbound, I engaged the approach mode for the instrument landing system (ILS). Observing the passage of CHOPY, I reported leaving the holding. Cape Approach switched us to Vineyard Tower, which reported strong gusty winds from the south, 200 feet obscured, RVR 1,800 feet, and cleared us to land.

The autoflight system captured the glide slope and we continued to track inbound on the localizer as we descended. From my instruments, I knew where we were; but outside it was dense white when I checked with the landing lights. To reduce the water vapor reflecting in my eyes and blinding me with glare, I shut off the landing lights to more readily see the approach and the runway lights. We were cleared to land, but I still couldn't see anything. We were at minimums and I missed the approach; power, flaps, gear and we were ascending again.

My passenger appeared calm and remained silent. His arms folded in front of him, there were no death grips on the handle or armrest or me during this go-around. So far, this would be just another foggy night trying to get into the Vineyard.

"Cessna Bravo Charlie One, missed approach." I used my very serious pilot voice, much like my lawyer voice, only a tad nicer.

"Cessna Bravo Charlie One, fly the published missed approach and change now to Cape Approach on 119.7."

I checked in again. Cape Approach broke us off the published missed approach to the south with radar vectors to the northeast and a climb to 5,000 feet. When asked my intentions, I requested the MVY weather. She reported 100 feet obscured and RVR 1,800 feet for runway 24—minimums, but still good enough to try again.

I glanced at Mr. Philips for a decision whether we should try again to land at the Vineyard. He nodded approval and I requested another approach. In response, we were brought back to CHOPY and stacked again at 5,000 feet.

"Will we return to Hyannis if we can't land in the Vineyard?" Mr. Philips was as matter-of-fact as any passenger I've ever carried who'd just experienced a missed approach at minimums.

"Not sure yet." I was clipped, attentively listening to the controller.

As the preceding aircraft shot the approach, we descended in turn. Again, we were cleared to land on runway 24. Out my side window, through a break in the clouds, I detected the shore lights below us illuminating the low scud and fog, but nothing else. These were windy variable conditions, but there were some breaks in the weather. Now we just needed a break at the airport, because this ride wasn't getting any smoother.

Turbulence and shearing had dramatically increased along with the surface winds on this second approach. The minor airspeed fluctuations indicated possible wind shear conditions. The aircraft interior was starting to resemble the inside of a washing machine during the spin cycle. I glanced at my passenger and noticed his face was now perspired and his complexion was grayish in color. His right hand was clamped tightly around the grab handle on the forward right window pillar, trying to steady himself from the rocking and swaying motion of the cabin. As we continued down the glide slope, the wet night air was condensing and streaming off the windscreen. The ride inside was becoming seriously rough, even for me. It felt like I was strapped to a wild bronco bucking through the air in an effort to dislodge me. I was relieved we were both secured by our harnesses.

Landing at the Vineyard this time was not an option. I executed another missed approach, and as we climbed, the ride improved. Cape Approach again asked my intentions. The Vineyard weather was becoming "socked in" and during the time we'd been flying around, only one Vineyard landing was successful out of the last ten approaches.

I glanced at Mr. Philips. Sometimes, body language and facial expressions convey so much more than words. He was not comfortable, perhaps even terrified. Many passengers don't realize that so long as the aircraft is sound, and there is plenty of fuel, staying airborne is much safer than a risky approach and landing. What's more, the aircraft itself endures turbulence much better than its human occupants. So, we were fine.

I was about to explain all this to Mr. Philips, who was silent throughout, when I heard my call sign again. In response I informed Cape Approach that we were done with the Vineyard and wanted to return to Hyannis. Cape Approach gave us the Hyannis weather, which was now even lower than the Vineyard's, with stronger winds. No one had gotten in to Hyannis in the last hour. The other aircraft were experiencing the same problems and had started to divert. The door was closed on Hyannis.

Next, Cape Approach came back and informed us that all the airports on the Cape had gone down along with Nantucket, but New Bedford was still good. I looked to Mr. Philips, who appeared nauseated and a putrid shade of green. He barely, but clearly, nodded his approval. I requested a clearance to New Bedford, 23 miles to the northeast.

There was no cause for alarm, but diversions are busy times for both the controllers and the pilots involved. Cape Approach gave us our clearance to New Bedford via radar vectors and then, after a few minutes, switched us over to Providence Approach for more delaying vectors to accommodate a couple of aircraft ahead of us. When our turn came, Providence Approach cleared us for the LOC BC (localizer back-course) RWY 23, and switched us to New Bedford Tower. The tower gave us the ceiling, visibility, winds, and cleared us to land. Finally, after our third approach for the evening, we had an uneventful landing in New Bedford. What should have been less than forty minutes total out and back for me was now nearly double that, with a diversion. Not a good night.

After landing, I taxied to my favorite fixed base operator (FBO) at the far end of the ramp. I pulled into a tie down spot, set the brakes, and shut down the engines. When you are flying charters from Hyannis to the islands (what we Cape Codders call the Vineyard and Nantucket), you get to know the surrounding mainland airports and their FBOs very well as divert stations. New Bedford was one of many alternates when the Vineyard was socked in. Though its three private fixed base operators were closed after 2000 (8 p.m.) to the general aviation public, they were always open, in a sense, to the professional charter pilot. We know where the ties downs are; we know how to get access to the fuel; and at some FBOs, we know where the car keys are stowed.

The strengthening wind and wet misting conditions kept us inside the aircraft while I tended to my pilot duties. First I needed to figure out if we were done for the night, or if the weather might break-up out at the Vineyard, allowing for another try. I turned on my cell phone and called the flight service station (FSS) operated by Lockheed Martin. The forecasts for our area had finally caught up with what was happening over the Cape and the islands, giving us no option but to remain where we were. Our FAA IFR flight plan was closed when we landed. No worries there. Now, my immediate concern was executing my postflight checklist; securing the aircraft for the night; finding accommodations for my passenger and me; and finally, contacting my employer to update our status.

When he sensed that my work was finished inside the airplane, Mr. Philips asked if it was okay to exit, as he needed fresh air. I could see he was not well.

"Yes, follow me. Do you need an airsickness bag?" I asked with earnest concern.

"Not yet—thanks." Though still polite, Mr. Philips appeared uncomfortable.

Unbuckled from my harness, I made aft for the airstairs exit with Mr. Philips close on my heels. When I opened the passenger door and lowered the stairs he seemed relieved to see the tarmac. Upon reaching the ramp, Mr. Philips walked a few paces then stood motionless. I felt bad for him. I used to succumb to air motion sickness and there's not much worse than feeling like you will vomit at any minute. It nearly makes you wish for death.

I grabbed the lines and began to tie the plane down for the night. After several minutes, I spied Mr. Philips watching as I chocked the wheels. I was relieved to see that he was looking better, not so green and sweaty.

I asked him, "Have you ever diverted before?"

"Not like this."

"Me neither." I replied and smiled as I completed my walk around, making sure the plane was secure. When I was satisfied, I dug my phone out from my ditty bag and called the crew hotel. Relieved that there was vacancy on a bad weather Friday, I made reservations for two rooms, one night.

After making a call to my employer and updating our status, I suggested to Mr. Philips that we leave the ramp and head towards the closed terminal building. As we walked in the mist and the wind, I apologized to him for the bumpy ride and the added inconvenience of laying over in New Bedford. I offered consolation by advising that we'd overnight at the Marriott on the Acushnet River, a decent place, considering it wasn't where he was supposed to be; but, I hoped we'd be on our way early tomorrow to the Vineyard, weather permitting. If not, high speed ferries to the islands were available at the sea terminal across the road from the hotel. If a boat could operate in the morning and my Cessna and I could not, Mr. Philips would cruise to the Vineyard, care of Cape Air Charter.

Mr. Philips nodded his understanding and then asked, "Did you call for a cab?"

"Not yet."

As we walked on the sidewalk between the building and the parking lot, I was relieved to see the old blue, beaten up Chevy parked in the first spot, near the entrance to the terminal. That it had not already been taken this evening by an earlier diverting pilot was a piece of good luck. When we reached the car, I politely excused myself and went off to the hiding place where the car keys were kept. I returned to the Chevy and opened the driver side door.

Mr. Philips, who appeared completely recovered, inquired as he approached the passenger side, "Captain Bergin, we're not stealing an automobile are we?"

I laughed, "Nope. This is our car for the night. My friend, Rob, the manager, leaves the keys to the pilotmobile in a special place for contingencies, like this."

Mr. Philips nodded his approval at the old beater with an automatic transmission. I unlocked the door and entered. I opened the door for him from the inside and he entered as bidden, throwing his luggage in the back seat. Like in the plane a few hours before, we both buckled up in the front for safety.

"This car is an improvement over the last one." I told Mr. Philips.

"Hard to imagine." He responded with a smile

"At least I can drive this one. I never learned how to drive a car with a manual transmission." I said.

Mr. Philips, object of my recent interest, began to grin widely.

"Are you laughing at me, or with me, because I'm not laughing?" I offered.

"Captain Bergin, you are a fine pilot, but it strikes me funny that you cannot drive a stick shift. I would have thought you could drive a tank, if you had to."

"Given a few hours, a handbook, an instructor and a simulator, and I'm sure I could; but I used to live in Manhattan and was driven by... Never mind." I paused. "Mr. Philips, I'm ready to motor. Shall we go?"

I knew the way to the hotel and reported that we'd arrive at our destination in less than ten minutes. I was on autopilot as I welcomed Mr. Philips to New Bedford, which, I explained, rivaled Nantucket as the capital of the country's whaling industry back in the mid-nineteenth century, when Herman Melville wrote *Moby-Dick: or The Whale*. Mr. Philips nodded his head in acknowledgment and surveyed what little he could see past the fog as we drove south towards New Bedford's wharf area near the city center.

"Captain Bergin, what is your first name?"

"Katharine," I replied, and after a pregnant pause given circumstances, added, "call me Kate."

"Not Ishmael?"

"Melville fan?" I was pleased, as we were in New Bedford and *Moby-Dick* was a favorite book.

"Not really. English minor." He smiled.

I made a mental note and wondered what he majored in, but remained silent as we approached the hotel. I parked near the entrance. Mr. Philips had an overnight bag; I had my flight bag and a tote with basics—black sweater, clean underwear, sandals, lip balm and mascara—that I always bring on trips, just in case I encountered this kind of unscheduled event. We each dragged our bags into the hotel.

I checked us in at the front desk and placed both of our separate rooms on my tab. It was nearly ten p.m. and the grille across the way from the hotel on Homer's Wharf had taken its last dinner order. The clerk suggested I try the Black Witch Tavern, an afterhours pub in the center of town that served decent dinner fare till midnight. I needed to eat something and out of courtesy, curiosity, and a desire for company invited Mr. Philips to come along for a late supper. He accepted without hesitation.

"I'll meet you in the lobby in fifteen minutes." I said.

"Fine." Mr. Philips replied as he walked away, fangling with his phone as he left.

I was downstairs early, wearing my sweater, a bit of make-up, sandals, and loose hair. When I fly, I wear my hair either up in a bun, or pulled back in some fashion, away from my eyes and my face. This evening, I let it down. Dinner hair to match my less formal dinner attire and attitude. I waited just a few minutes for Mr. Philips to arrive in the lobby.

"No epaulets?" Mr. Philips commented.

"We're not supposed to wear our pilot costume in a bar."

He nodded his head in assent.

"Do you know the pilot rule about drinking, Mr. Philips?"

He shook his head, back and forth, sideways instead of answering "no," but the meaning was still conveyed, and then he quipped, "Tell me."

"Eight hours, bottle to throttle. Or... some would tell you no smoking within eight hours of flight and no drinking within fifty feet of the airplane." I smiled.

"Do you smoke?" Mr. Philips asked with interest.

"No." I answered, not wanting to offend him, in case he did.

"Good for you. I wish I never started." Mr. Philips said with regret as we left the lobby and walked toward the parking lot.

"Do you want to smoke now?"

"No."

"Okay, 'cause I can't let you smoke in the pilot car."

"Understood. I wouldn't want to spoil it. I'm fine for now, thanks." Mr. Philips was good natured about it. Then, after looking in my direction, he asked, "Has anyone ever told you that you look like that actress with long brown hair; she worked mostly in the 1960s and 70s."

"Yes." I answered.

"What was her name?"

"Katharine Ross."

"Yes, that's right. I thought she was great in that role."

"In *Butch Cassidy and the Sundance Kid* or *The Graduate*?" I asked.

"No, *The Stepford Wives*. Great movie."

"I see." I looked at him, askance.

"Maybe we shouldn't talk about it." Mr. Philips laughed.

31

We left the hotel and I drove in lighter fog for what seemed like seconds until we came to the heart of the city. There was street parking in front of the pub and I pulled in. Everything so far was nice and easy. I hesitated for a moment before exiting the car. I understood that the man beside me was supposed to be at Martha's Vineyard, doing whatever he (and his lady?) had planned; but instead he was here with me because my plane and I were unable to deliver him, after shaking him up a good bit. I felt bad.

"I apologize for this inconvenience, Mr. Philips."

He looked at me for a moment from the passenger side of the old car. Then, in a benign, kindly manner said, "I'll call you Kate, if you call me Steven. And I understand. These things happen."

With that, we left the car and headed for the pub. The hotel clerk had called ahead, so the waitress met us at the entrance and greeted us by name. Though there were no other diners, she escorted us past the long golden solid oak bar along one wall, to the last booth on the opposite wall, tucked into a corner. We sat on the benches across from each other. The room glowed dim amber and a candle flickered in the middle of our table between our paper place settings and cutlery. From where we sat, a large flat screen TV was visible above the bar. A small crowd, mostly men, gathered to watch the baseball game being broadcast. Except for the hollers and screeches occasionally erupting from the patrons when a good or bad thing happened on the screen, it was quiet enough in the booth to hear a normal volume human voice without shouting or straining.

After we were seated, the waitress asked if we'd like drinks as she handed us each a laminated single page menu. I ordered club soda with a twist; Steven went for a Johnny Walker Black, neat. After all, he wasn't flying in the morning, maybe not even as a passenger if the weather didn't improve.

"So, Kate," Steven began, "What kind of girl flies a plane but can't drive a stick shift?"

"A special girl but, I do not like to boast much, about it— thank you." I responded in imperfect haiku.

Steven nodded his head with a grin and then asked, "What was the chance of a mid-air collision with the other planes that we couldn't see flying out there."

"Low probability." I was polite and truthful, though I didn't really want to discuss that topic.

32

"You seemed comfortable up there." Steven was complimentary.

"Not bad for a girl." I replied, with graceful jest.

Steven winced in his seat, clearly taken aback by what I just said.

"Just kidding." I tried to relieve his distress.

"Were you in the military?" Steven asked.

"No." I could be laconic.

"How did you learn to fly?"

"Do you mean how or where?" I asked, because those are different questions and sometimes people confuse them.

"Both." Steven responded.

At that moment, the waitress arrived with our drinks and asked what we wanted to eat. We each ordered a salad and a shared, small thin crust pizza: half plain, for me; half anchovies and sausage for him. When the waitress left the booth, I changed the topic from my flying career and offered a toast instead.

"To Rob Russo." I held up my drink and so did Steven. We clinked our glasses and drank.

"So, why did we toast to him?" Steven was earnest.

"Rob Russo is a pilot and a gentleman and he leaves the pilot car keys where I can always find them."

"Okay, so that deserves a toast?" Steven was not impressed.

"There's more. If the weather clears, and I'm able to fly you out of here tomorrow, you'll meet Rob. He runs the fixed base operator where the plane is."

"Fine. To Rob."

"There's even more." I added.

"Oh." Steven was mildly interested.

I hesitated for a moment, thinking of the best method to tell the story. I settled on the shortest with the least detail. Sometimes, giving the bare bones version will suffice. Let the listener fill in the gaps. I began the narrative.

"Rob was a Cape Air Charter pilot."

"Okay." Steven was interested.

"A few years ago, Rob was running a short flight from Hyannis to Boston when an electrical fire erupted in the cockpit, suddenly engulfing him in smoke and flames." I paused to assess Steven's reaction. He was still with me, so I continued.

"Rob maintained control of the airplane while he was being burned and could see nothing. He landed the plane allowing his passengers to escape safely."

"That's some story. I'm not sure I want to know this." Steven looked serious.

"It's rare, but it happens. Sean, my boss at CAC, was a passenger on that plane. He was lucky. He suffered only minor lung damage from the toxic smoke, but nothing permanent, at least in a physical sense. But like me, he avoids fire."

Steven was ashen.

"That's why I offered a toast to Rob Russo. He's a hero and there are humans alive today because of his courage and flying skill."

"I don't recall reading about that accident." Steven sipped his JWB.

"Maybe you were away?" I offered.

"Probably. I travel a lot." Steven took another sip, slowly, looking directly at me.

Our meal arrived and we began to eat. I had to have nourishment. It'd been hours since I'd had any food and I was beginning to feel weak. I tried to never talk with my mouth full, especially with salad, so we didn't speak for a time. It was a comfortable silence, for me anyway, until I broke it.

"So, what exactly do you do?" I asked in a friendly tone, returning his gaze.

"Investment banking at Bain Capital, but the good kind."

"I see." I replied, knowing that he was flying on the Bain account. Plus, I was thinking of all those leveraged buyouts that went so wrong for everybody else but the bankers, or as they liked to call themselves, "private equity guys."

I thought for a moment, and asked a rhetorical question, "So you have an M.B.A.?"

"J.D.-M.B.A.?"

"Like Mitt Romney?"

"Yes."

"Harvard?" I knew that was Bain's feeder school.

"Right."

"Why not pursue a career in law?"

34

Steven looked at me after another swig of Johnny Walker Black and said, "Are you serious, be a lawyer? No way. The first thing we need to do is kill all the lawyers."

I rolled back on my bench, hitting the wall of the booth with my shoulder blades, eyes opened widely. I might have audibly winced, as I wondered to myself if Steven would have said this if he knew I was a lawyer, but I remained mum on that topic.

Our conversation turned to the superficially personal as we consumed our food. Steven commuted between New York, Boston, Hyannis, and the Vineyard, where he had a second home. His wife and two tween daughters resided in Chestnut Hill, Massachusetts, while he, separated from them, lived in Boston. His girlfriend, "Lee"—the one I saw at the airport—lived on the Cape. I listened with interest, and no visible judgment, as Steven explained that Lee was the designer who had worked with Steven and his wife on their Vineyard summer home. I simply nodded silently and took mental notes: this guy left his wife and kids for the interior decorator. Nice.

Steven never resumed his questions about my flying experience, nor did he inquire about me or my life. And why would he? I was just the pilot for hire on an unscheduled divert. For the remainder of dinner we spoke of Boston, the Cape, and the islands. Nothing heavy or objectionable. This was work after all, not a dinner date. When the bill arrived on a small plastic tray, Steven grabbed it. I tried to retrieve it from him, explaining that it was business policy to pay for customer meals on diverted flights. Steven looked at me, smiled, and pulled a hundred dollar bill from his pocket and, placing it on the tray, handed it back to the waitress. Minutes later, when she returned, Steven told her to keep the change. A seventy dollar tip, by my calculation. The waitress looked at me, then Steven, smiled and thanked us.

I drove us back to the hotel through mist. Before we retired to our respective chambers, we agreed to meet in the morning at the hotel's breakfast room. I said I'd be downstairs by eight and would have the latest weather and flight status.

"Thanks for dinner," I said.

"You're welcome. Good night, Kate." Steven replied and left.

I slept heavily, but arose early. This was a diversion after all. I was in the middle of a trip that should have deposited my passenger an island away, a day ago. I turned on the TV and watched the local news reporting that a small single engine plane crashed at the Vineyard early this morning, seriously injuring the pilot and his passenger. The aircraft flew through the trees and partially broke-up before coming to rest on the ground well short of the runway. There was a fire and injuries. The pilot was airlifted to Massachusetts General with severe burns and the passenger was taken to Martha's Vineyard Hospital, seriously hurt. So much for feeling bad about this unscheduled layover.

The weather in New Bedford was currently clearing, but still heavy over the Vineyard. I was nearly certain we'd be wheels up by nine or so, if the wind blew the Vineyard clear as predicted. Used to being on the go, we in the travel industry pack up and leave a hotel room faster than most people can brush their teeth. Uniform on, hair bun in place, I was all systems go by seven, but didn't want to disturb Steven, who could still be sleeping on account of the agreed upon eight a.m. lobby show time. I decided to head downstairs anyway and check us both out before Steven could pay that bill, too.

When I arrived at the lobby, I saw Steven sitting in a corner chair, tapping on a tablet and talking on mobile phone. Before I greeted him, I went to the front desk and settled the bill, this morning's breakfasts included. I walked over to Steven's makeshift office where he was engrossed in whatever he was doing. Standing close to his chair, but in his blind spot, I studied him for a moment. He was clean shaven, but his shirt was wrinkled. I guessed that he did not iron and was not packed for a night away from his Vineyard home, where he probably had an entire wardrobe. His hair was wild and just barely dry. He smelled like hotel bodywash with a subtle note of tar and nicotine. I found the combination nearly irresistible, and it surprised me, loathing the smell of smoke as I usually do.

I walked where Steven could see me. I had no intention of telling him about the crash, unless he brought it up. Then, I'd answer any questions. My intention was to keep it light.

"Good morning, Steven. Weather clearing here and nearly clearing at the Vineyard. By nine thirty or so we should be fine to depart."

"Sounds good. You're up early."

"You, too. Will you join me for breakfast? It's buffet style, lots to choose from." I was lighthearted about the matter.

He nodded to me in a nearly dismissive way and said, "In a bit."

This was my not so subtle cue that Steven was involved in something far more important than my breakfast offer. I should not have disturbed him before our eight o'clock time. Humbled by the brushoff, I ambled off to the breakfast room and set my bags by a table where I could see them as I roamed the buffet area. Once satisfied with my security arrangements, I aimed for the bran cereal, eggs, coffee, milk, sugar, and orange juice. After collecting my breakfast items, my tray and I returned to my rollabout and tote.

I sat alone, in a room of about twenty strangers, sipping my orange juice and reviewing the latest weather on my phone. I was slightly concerned that the Vineyard would be socked in longer than first expected. I should've under promised and over delivered. Now, I wasn't sure what would happen this morning. Pondering my tactical mistake, I added milk and sugar to my coffee. Steven appeared as I looked up and sat down across from me.

"Leave them here, I'll watch them." I offered, seeing that he was encumbered by his bag and his electronica.

He complied and started for the buffet where he selected a pastry and a coffee, no tray required, and returned.

"You're low maintenance." I offered as he sat down with his meager breakfast.

"You don't know me." Steven said matter-of-factly and took a swig of coffee.

"Truer words have never been spoken." I admitted.

"You're different from most pilots."

"I'm not a man." I said nonchalantly.

"There's that, of course..." Steven's voice trailed off.

He began again, "Kate, how long have you been a pilot?"

"Long enough."

"You don't want to tell me?" Steven caught on.

"I'm a new hire at Cape Air Charter."

"I see, so you're new to the Cape?"

"That's not what I said."

"Great, a pilot who answers like a lawyer." Steven was joking.

"Something like that." I replied, smiling.

"Don't tell me." Steven said the three words slowly.

"Okay, I won't tell you." I complied.

"I didn't mean what I said last night at dinner about killing the lawyers." He was now slightly embarrassed and clearly apologetic.

"Didn't you?" I smiled and winked so he knew I wouldn't hold a lawyer grudge, which can be very long and horribly expensive. Yet, I had to excuse myself and take care of pilot business at a place with a printer. I gathered my things and left Steven at the buffet, promising to meet up at the pilotmobile at 0900.

During our short ride to the airport, I reassured Steven that I understood he meant me no personal insult when he said that we should kill all the lawyers. To make himself feel better, I think, Steven reminded me of the context of the quote from *Henry VI, Part 2*; that Dick, the butcher, uttered that line about killing lawyers in the context of aiding Jack Cade's rebellion. So really, it was a complement to legal advocates from Shakespeare, who was no stranger to litigation himself.

I remained silent as I listened to Steven's lawyer killing rationale. Once we arrived at the parking lot and pulled into a spot close to the terminal door I said, exhausting my memory of Shakespeare phrases, "Steven, methinks you doth protest too much. But alas, valiant, I am and able to endure much. And, in the end, all's well that ends well." We both chuckled and prepared for crosscheck, before exiting the car and grabbing our belongings.

Rob greeted me warmly as I entered the terminal building. He asked to speak with me privately. Rob wanted to know if I'd heard about the crash. I did. He knew the pilot, I didn't. Since Rob knew that horror, there wasn't more to say. I returned to the counter where Steven stood and introduced the men. Because I knew Rob well, I'd nearly forgotten that when people see him for the first time, the scars on his face and both hands and arms could be a source of curiosity—or worse—horror.

Seemingly unaffected by the skin that appeared as twisted bands of melted plastic over the bones of Rob's hands and face, obliterating his fingers and features, Steven shook Rob's right hand and looked directly into his eyes to thank him for the use of the car. Rob accepted Steven's gratitude, explaining that it was his pleasure and that's what the car was for. I gave Rob one of my new legal business cards and made him promise to call me if he needed anything—ever. Rob nodded and knew I meant it.

Steven and I were in the plane by nine thirty, ready to roll. The Vineyard airport (MVY) was open for business and Steven and I were bound for the sky. Though not perfectly smooth, it was far more comfortable than last evening. We made it to our destination safely flying at 3,000 feet, just below the ceiling. We landed and taxied to the ramp adjacent to the fixed base operator. When I finished in the cockpit, I led us out of the Cessna down the airstairs. Walking out on the tarmac, I looked over to the GA terminal and saw Lee beyond the chain-linked fence waiting for Steven. As soon as he joined me on the ramp, Steven asked if he could give me his card. I saw no reason why not and I accepted it. Then, he took it back, right out of my fingers. I must have looked puzzled so he explained that he wanted me to have his private number, just in case I needed to contact him, like, if the plane he chartered for the Vineyard was stuck in New Bedford or something like that.

I understood. That was fair, and even a bit funny, as I didn't tell him about the crash and wasn't sure he knew yet how I saved our lives, pretty much. After scribbling on the back of the card, he put it back in my hand and told me to keep it in a safe place. I nodded my acceptance of the terms and just as I was about to fish my own business card from my ditty bag, returning the favor, his girlfriend, Lee, the decorator, approached. I guessed she'd waited long enough for him, as he was more than thirteen hours later than the originally scheduled arrival time. Steven introduced us. It was a straightforward exchange:

"Lee, this is Kate, my pilot for this trip, and she's a lawyer." Lee stood, motionless, her eyes fixed on Steven.

"Kate, this is Lee, my friend."

I reached out for her hand, which she ignored. Steven looked mortified. Being subjected to hostility was part of the deal as a lawyer, so I knew how to handle an awkward moment. As if nothing happened, I retracted my hand from the space it occupied in front of Lee and reached into the pocket of my ditty bag to grab a business card for Steven. I gave it to him without a fuss and excused myself for my next leg. I liked Steven and gave this relationship with "Lee" a month or so at best. I could wait. Time and water really were on my side, as there was no swimming to the Vineyard. Besides, I moved at the speed of dreams and I was sure I'd see Steven Philips again. For now, it would have to be another day, another charter. There was a family and a labradoodle puppy that were waiting to return to Hyannis and I had a plane to prepare for flight.

The weather broke completely and the sky was severe clear. The Cape-bound family and pet were easy going and the flight back to Hyannis was smooth. When I finished my duties, I walked over to the CAC counter in the terminal. My boss, Sean, the chief pilot, asked me to follow him to his office. I did.

"Thanks, Kate. Close the door." Sean said sternly as we both stood there.

This was never a good sign. When I used to do this to an associate in my Manhattan law firm, it was usually bad for the associate. I was not prepared for my own firing just yet and didn't believe I'd earned that inglorious end on account of a righteous diversion to New Bedford. Sean soon saw that I was uneasy. In a solicitous and deliberate manner, he asked if I had heard about the crash. I confirmed that I did. Sean briefed me on the details and commended my judgment and flying skill. We were done. I was free to go and off the schedule for two days.

CHAPTER THREE

It was a beautiful, clear Saturday and I was at my little Cape Cod home early in the afternoon, eager to relax in my reading chair and catch up on the law journals that accumulate by the week. As I was prepared to sip the iced tea I'd just made and peruse the legal news, the doorbell rang. Before I could reach the front door from my living room, I heard a knock. And then another, but more adamant this time. I peered out the windows beside my front door and saw a courier standing on my porch. His truck was parked at the curb. He and the vehicle looked legitimate so I opened the door.

"Ms. Bergin." The courier used my name.

I replied affirmatively. I rarely received hand deliveries of anything at home and was caught off guard. I wondered if someone sent me a gift, or worse, if I was being sued or served with a subpoena. These days, private servers do what was once reserved for sheriffs and their deputies. So you could never be sure what to expect. In a moment of dumb, I asked the courier what this was about, as if he would have known—or would have told me. He handed me a tablet and a stylus and asked for my electronic signature and today's date to acknowledge delivery. I was no longer concerned as legal process would have required an acknowledgment of service, something more formal and still preferred in ink, not bits or bytes. I exhaled a sigh, relieved that I wouldn't be calling my malpractice carrier just yet or appearing before a grand jury or ethics panel.

After the courier processed my acknowledgment, he handed me a nine by twelve inch white wove envelope. I saw the Los Angeles return address and recognized the law firm founded by Mr. Thomas Beck, my ex father's-in-law attorney. I must have seemed startled because the courier asked if I was all right. His sincere concern surprised me. I nodded, said I was fine and thanked him. He wished me a good day, left my porch, and headed for his truck. I was inside my house by the time he reached the first paver on my foot path. I used the mail opener that I keep in the drawer in the foyer and sliced open the flap, perfectly, careful not to tear anything inside.

I figured it would be better to sit, so I returned to the reading chair and tea and sat down before removing the envelope's contents. I slid the two unattached pieces of paper out from the envelope and read the top leaf slowly. A missive from Thomas Beck enclosed a separate letter from the probate court in L.A. County. I was now officially informed that I was named a trustee in the will of Mr. Warren Ethan. Mr. Beck was representing Warren's company in what looked like a contest over this will, but I couldn't be sure from the bare bones notice and the caption. There were proceedings scheduled at the Los Angeles courthouse next week. I should be there. Thomas Beck's letter contained a number to call for more information and to confirm travel and accommodation arrangements.

At first, reacting as a lawyer, I figured that a simple mistake had been made and the wrong will was read, maybe one that was prepared before the divorce? So, I read the letters again. The probate court notice was mailed to Mr. Beck three days ago. If a mistake had been made, it was a recent one and would take a mere phone call to fix. It took me several more minutes to process what was happening, or what happened days ago. An unexpected and profound wave of grief crashed over me.

My thoughts wound around the image of Warren in the *Town & Country* wedding spread looking off in a distance, but not death-bound. It's hard to process your feelings about someone who once meant so much to you and was now no more. I felt grief and yet, I was perplexed and apprehensive. Why me? Was this a stunt or a bad joke? I couldn't shake the feeling that a terrible mistake had been made, or maybe something more sinister was afoot. Either way, Warren was gone, and I felt his loss. I liked having him in the world—when he was in it. I felt a need to get to my office, which had become my home away from home and was barely a ten minute drive with moderate traffic. If I really was required in L.A., I had to organize my files, and take what I needed with me via upload, so I could continue my practice during my trip to California.

I arrived at the strip mall quickly and opened my office. I perused my calendar. I was lucky that next week was fairly light and transportable, nothing I couldn't postpone or accomplish by telecommuting. The reassuring phone calls to clients were easily handled and Celeste would have my back, fill in any gaps, and file papers in my absence, if necessary. I had to call Celeste to tell her of my impending absence and why. Before I rang her, I searched for the old *Town & Country Magazine* to see now, post death, those photos of Warren, his girlfriend, and my ex-husband and his Tiffany bride. I wondered if I could detect any clues to why Warren named me in his will. I knew that I was unlikely to learn anything from these photos, but I wanted to see Warren again, if only in a glossy spread. It was all I had for now.

After a few minutes I located the magazine. It was nearly where I left it. Celeste had tidied up a bit and shifted my pile of pleasure reading to a lower shelf on my bookcase; but findable, if you knew what you were looking for. I grabbed the issue I wanted and opened the pages to the wedding section. And there they were. Rick and Tiffany were no longer the focus of my attention. I was fixated on Warren, looking westbound, outward, and away. Though having access to the best care and preservation techniques available, he was clearly an old man. Well past eighty years by this time, he appeared weary. Warren's gorgeous, young girlfriend seemed curiously detached from him. This was not a picture of romantic bliss.

I searched online for news about Warren's demise. The obituary was fulsome. He was a big deal in the financial world after all. Death was not the time to hide your light under a bushel. More search results revealed that Tiffany was best known for her marriage to Rick. I learned nothing at all about the woman in Warren's life.

I reached out for Celeste and told her what I received from California. I shared my sorrow upon learning of Warren's death and my discomfort and confusion at being involved in this way, at this point in my life. Why me? Why now? Why not his son or lawyer or anybody else who could serve as an administrator to a testamentary trust? Celeste was compassionate and thoughtful, and as always, indispensable.

"Kate, what about that letter?"

"What letter?"

"When you came to the Cape, you told me that when you were divorced your ex's attorney gave you a note and you never read it."

"I put it my purse and left it there."

"Time to read it, Ms. Kate."

Celeste was right. It might shed some light on the situation. In the meantime, Cel and I decided how to divide the remaining legal labor, if this wasn't all a huge mistake and I really was L.A. bound on Monday. After a few more minutes in the office doing whatever it is someone does when she's in semi shock and a bit fatigued, I was eager to return home and find that purse.

I recalled stowing it away safely with my expensive footwear and corresponding French accessories that complemented my designer wardrobe from what seemed like a lifetime ago. I am careful with my clothes and matching things. After peaking in a few of the wrong flannel pouches stacked in the back of my closet, I found the large taupe quilted lambskin Chanel flap bag I wore that gray November day. I thought hard about why I neglected to read the note back then. I didn't remember much about that day of my divorce, just my eagerness to reach out for the next and the new. I suppose I'd just answered the question, I wanted to leave the old and painful behind.

At first I didn't see the envelope when I opened the purse and was deeply disappointed, thinking that I'd either thrown it out, or put it some place I could no longer remember. Opening the wine-colored leather inner compartment of the bag, I was relieved to spot an edge of the envelope. I removed it and sat down on the closet floor. I recalled thinking that Warren probably had his secretary write it and that I was not interested in reading a "Dear Kate" letter at that time. Now, I had some trepidation. I wondered if I had missed an opportunity by failing to read the note sooner. A letter has a different meaning when the person who sent it is dead, even if the letter wasn't meant to reach out from the grave.

In law school, you read about "fertile octogenarians" and "dead hand control"—admittedly not in the same sentence—but in the same Trusts and Estates class. The former relates to the rule against perpetuities and a life in being plus twenty-one years; the latter was shorthand for the attempt of the dead to exert control from the grave upon the living, generally by how they worded wills or trusts, commonly by placing specific conditions on a beneficiary's right to receive a gift or an heir's right to an inheritance. These conditions were like sticks or carrots. Both sorts were efforts by the grantor or testator to affect the behavior of the living, but without any consequence to the departed.

I brought the divorce envelope from my bedroom, downstairs to grab my letter opener. I carried the items to the kitchen table that sometimes serves as my home office and laid them out, side by side. I sat down. When I picked the envelope up in my hands, I paused, looked up, and said a prayer. A strange thing to do, perhaps, but it's what came to mind. The "Hail Mary" gave me the fortitude to continue. I hoped Warren's soul was at peace and I wondered what he had in mind for me—both now and back then. Lost in thought, I sliced the paper open, took the letter out, and unfolded it.

Though not intended as a "if you are reading this, I am dead" letter—that was the effect, because Warren was gone. The note was composed on one sheet of his letter-size stationery written on both sides, single-spaced, in his own hand. Personal and directed to me, there was no secretary involved in the drafting. An ethical will of sorts, the contents of this epistle reflected Warren's worldview and wisdom, distilled from his lifetime experiences and offered from his unique point of view. Towards the end of the document, Warren expressed his esteem for me and appreciation for the bond we shared, broken by his son, but fondly remembered. Warren closed with, "Mostly it is loss which teaches us about the worth of things." I recognized the line from Arthur Schopenhauer and thought how it could be taken any number of ways.

CHAPTER FOUR

There's nothing wrong with the urge to pour yourself a nice goblet of a cabernet blend before you make a cross country call about the wishes of a man from the grave. In addition to the letter in my hand from Warren, I had retained some of the wine that he'd bestowed upon Rick and me—a case of Chateau Lafite—during our marriage. This vintage, a blend of cabernet sauvignon, merlot, cabernet franc, and petit verdot was supposedly an incarnation of the legendary 1959 Lafite. At the time of the gift, Warren explained in a card that I kept with the case, that it had been bottled in mid-May of 2005, after achieving the perfect percentage of alcohol and tannins that would enable this wine to age beautifully, as he hoped for us and our marriage.

I recall Warren's toast when we opened one of the bottles and drank to our health and success. After the first sip he described the garnet-purple liquid. "Dense and deep, with classic notes of graphite intertwined with melted licorice, crème de cassis, smoke and flowers." He urged us to sip again, exclaiming the elixir's viscosity, power, opulence, and extraordinary richness. Who could ask for more from a bottle, I thought at the time I first tasted it. Warren expressed his desire that we open the remaining bottles as a family to celebrate births, anniversaries, graduations, and other times of glad tidings. We never did.

When Rick and I separated, I recalled how that combination of words, "smoke and flowers" jarred me anew as I watched him remove six of the remaining eleven bottles of this superb Bordeaux blend from the home we shared. I kept my five bottles and Warren's personal note for my own celebrations and joyous milestones, confident I would have a few, at some future date. Recently, I'd read that full case of this vintage fetched over fifty thousand dollars at a

Hong Kong auction. To date, I didn't have the occasion to warrant the opening of a bottle worth 4,184 dollars. Given the events of the day, however, I figured this was the time. If not for Warren, then for whom? If not now, when?

After a few minutes of reflecting and sipping—but not enough to affect my judgment, I made the call to California. I even used the landline that I retain for times when cell coverage fails on the Cape. I was not surprised to hear a live human answer. I figured if it was important enough to reach me by courier, someone would be staffing the line all weekend. A female voice asked me to hold while she connected me to Thomas Beck. It didn't take more than ten seconds.

Mr. Beck, ever polite and direct, confirmed that I was indeed named the trustee of testamentary trust. It was not a mistake. Rather, a deliberate act by my deceased ex father-in-law. If I accepted the position, I would be needed in L.A., per the notice. If I chose to decline now, he would relay my response to the court and would have no further communication with me. I remained silent as I processed the information.

I felt strangely flattered. I'd not been forgotten and forsaken after all. I had been too involved with Warren and his family to just say "no" and move on without learning more. I wondered why I was selected and what my duties would entail. I told Thomas Beck that I didn't want to commit to what could be a long term job without having more information. Beck agreed that my approach was reasonable and advised me that I would learn more upon my arrival in California. His firm had made tentative travel and lodging arrangements for a trip west and his secretary would confirm the details if I agreed to make the journey. That was it. He was gone and a woman's voice was reciting my itinerary for the four-day trip to Southern California, to be confirmed in writing by email.

When I checked my smart phone, sure enough, the information was waiting for me. I was to be at Boston's Logan Airport (BOS) early Monday for a transcon flight on United. I'd arrive in L.A. (LAX) six hours later, but with the time zone difference, only three hours would elapse. I was scheduled for an afternoon meeting with Mr. Beck at his downtown office. My ex and his wife and Warren's girlfriend would not be present. I would have to wait till the Tuesday morning court date to deal with them. If all went as predicted, I would be back on the Cape by Friday morning after taking a nighthawk (known to the lay public as a "red-eye") to BOS, then a connecting flight to Hyannis in time for the busy weekend of charter work between the Cape and the islands.

After calling Celeste and confirming that I'd be in L.A. for a few days, I used Sunday to clean up the house and tie up loose ends. I looked forward to my upcoming flight. I hadn't flown commercially as a passenger in a long while. I wondered why I was being flown out coach. Warren would never fly coach—or expect me to. But he didn't make the arrangements, Beck did. At least my hotel was first rate. Still, I wondered what else was in store for me when the plane touched down in L.A. and my new position appeared in sharper focus.

The flight from Boston was smooth and on-time. By Monday afternoon, I was checked into the Four Seasons Hotel, rested and ready for the meeting at Beck's law office. The last time we'd met was in a New York City courthouse the day of my divorce. I wasn't exactly nervous today, but I had some reservations about being thrust into my former family's most private affairs at a most grievous time. What was happening here was not common. Previous spouses are generally anathema to estate planners, particularly if you are the ex of an adult child who has remarried.

The hired car arrived early to ferry me from my digs in Beverly Hills to the downtown tower that held Mr. Beck's law firm. Travelling east toward L.A., we passed the building where the State Bar of California was located and pulled up to a sleek granite and glass skyscraper at 801 S. Figueroa Street. I gave the driver a generous tip and entered the building and checked in at the imposing security desk. Taking the elevator up to the top floor I was wondering how secure this structure would be in an earthquake. When the doors slid open, my safety apprehensions dissolved. I stepped out into the stately marble hallway and entered the lobby of the law firm's premises.

The space was decorated to emulate the East Coast establishment from which the primary partners of this firm originated so many years ago. Not at all L.A. style. All dark green and hunt scenes; this office reeked of reliability and reassurance, all substance. Nothing here was unsettling or cutting edge or superficial. I was greeted cordially by an attractive receptionist who asked if I would care for anything to drink. I declined. She invited me to have a seat in the reception area while she contacted Mr. Beck. While waiting in the luxurious English country house-like setting, I checked my office email. So far, no calamities. Celeste was holding down the fort in Hyannis and my cases and clients were fine on the Cape.

I was feeling nearly tranquil when Mr. Beck greeted me. In the several seasons that had passed since I'd last seen him in New York he looked older, thinner, drawn. Wizened was the word that came to mind. Mr. Beck welcomed me with a handshake in a formal manner, almost as if we'd never met. Fair enough, I was no longer family, just a putative trustee. I followed him to his office. He closed the door. He walked leisurely behind his enormous mahogany desk, devoid of computer or papers, but bearing a phone, a blotter, and a pen set. Mr. Beck motioned for me to sit across from him. I complied. Once I was seated, Beck smoothly lowered his body into a great maroon leather chair that squeaked as he leaned forward, allowing his arms to rest comfortably on the blotter. He paused for a moment, as if to ensure my attention, and then commenced his address in a most formal manner.

"Ms. Bergin, I'm not sure how much you knew about Mr. Ethan's private charitable impulses."

I recalled the Waldorf gala years ago, where Rick and I first met; but nothing about that event was private. "Not much, tell me."

"Mr. Ethan had reservations about leaving the bulk of his estate to his new companion and his son and daughter-in-law in the manner structured by my firm's tax department."

"Oh." Was all I could manage.

"Mr. Ethan apparently had personal interests that took him in another direction..."

I interrupted, "You said 'apparently.' As his lawyer, don't you know for sure?"

Mr. Beck's response surprised me. "I did not counsel Mr. Ethan concerning this codicil."

So, you had nothing to do with my appointment as executor?"

"No. Frankly, Ms. Bergin, it would not have occurred to me to involve someone of your status in the personal affairs of someone in Warren's position."

This was an honest appraisal from a lawyer ignored by his old friend and longtime client concerning succession of a sizable estate.

"May I see the will?" I said with a slight edge to my voice, reasserting my position and my place as executor, wondering meanwhile who Warren had hired to draft the document to Mr. Beck's exclusion.

The chair squeaked as I watched Mr. Beck swivel back and reach behind his desk for the credenza upon which sat a red robe file enclosed by an elastic cord. Mr. Beck turned back my way, file in hand, and pushed it across the expanse of wood to my side of the desk until I could reach it. On top of this file was what looked like a sheet of Warren's stationery covered by longhand. As I inspected the file, I saw that this paper was stamped "copy" by the court, and bore a law firm receipt stamp marked 7 June.

"Is this the will?" I was incredulous.

"Not exactly. It is a codicil to revoke the existing will. You are looking at the copy sent to my office from the court after Warren died. Naturally, the probate court has the original for now."

I quickly scanned the first page of the single-spaced, two-sided epistle written in a masculine and clear continuous stroke cursive that I immediately recognized as Warren's. It was the same script he used in his "divorce" letter to me and the card he'd written with that case of Chateau Lafite. Hastily reading the letter, I realized what Warren had done. By drafting his codicil, Warren intentionally rescinded all the expensive estate planning Mr. Beck's firm had prepared for him the year before.

I couldn't imagine why Warren would do this to his estate; to his heirs. Though I was not licensed in California, every lawyer knew that Golden State residents in particular preferred avoiding probate court to keep fees down and legacies private. Generally, they accomplished these goals by establishing trusts without the need for formal probate. Why, I wondered, would Warren neglect these commonly used tools and place his private financial arrangements in a testamentary trust via holographic (handwritten) will? This self-written document guaranteed that Warren's estate would be overseen by the probate court, in full public view. It just didn't make sense.

"Why do you think he'd take this matter in his own hands—literally—and over write your work?"

"Read closely, Ms. Bergin. I can't speak any plainer for Mr. Ethan than he has for himself. He committed tax suicide with this foolishness. If his secretary hadn't sent it to the court, it would never have seen the light of day."

I didn't respond to that last comment, but I understood Mr. Beck's implicit message. He would have destroyed the sealed envelope containing the codicil had Warren given it to him. Warren was wise not to trust him.

I reread the first paragraph of the missive closely. It was full of what we lawyers call "precatory language," verbiage that expresses a person's wishes, hopes, aspirations, regrets, what have you; but, which is not binding on a probate court. Warren opened his letter with details about Tanya, his recent companion, and her on-line gambling compulsion requiring thousands of dollars a week to feed. According to Warren's narrative, while Tanya was his playmate, she was worth the cost. Warren gave her a one hundred thousand dollar bequest and thanked her for the memories, assuring her that she was still young and pretty and could find another man to fund her lifestyle.

According to Warren's codicil, my ex had recently filed for bankruptcy after over-extending himself when a real estate development deal he brokered went bust and caught him in a tight squeeze between private investors and a public bank. Rick lost to both. Warren wanted to spare his estate from Rick's blunders and future creditors' claims. Warren wrote that he had provided amply for Rick during his life and that leaving him a lump sum of one hundred thousand dollars should give Rick enough of a cushion to begin anew. Unless his executor believed differently, that was all Rick would inherit.

Rick's brand new wife, Tiffany, was the next on Warren's list. She did not gain an honorable mention in this holographic codicil. Warren simply stated that there was no reason to provide for her upon his death. (In my mind, she remained the West Coast mistress who broke the back of my marriage to Rick.) Reading on, the document evolved from one of stated preferences, reasons, and wishes—lacking the mandate and detail required to form an enforceable trust—to one of express intentions meeting the legal standard for enforcement, at least in the courts back East.

In the most important paragraph of the codicil Warren wrote:

"The whole of my invested remaining realizable estate shall be dealt with in the following way: The capital, invested in safe securities by my executor, shall constitute a perpetual fund, the interest of which shall be annually distributed to organizations across the United States and its territories and possessions to assist American Veterans injured in the line of duty and their families, with an emphasis on providing health care and rehabilitation, education, employment opportunities and even 'start up' capital for these Vets."

The next paragraph noted:

"I hereby give the executor, one, Katharine Ethan, now known as Katharine Bergin, who I knew well, loved as a daughter, and trusted as a person, unlimited discretion to provide for any member of my family, or person named herein, in addition to the bequests made in the document, if, in good faith; but in no event shall any gift to any person exceed the sum of one million dollars in the aggregate."

The penultimate paragraph of this letter described the contours of Warren's wealth. He wrote: "At the present time, my holdings are placed in the Warren Ethan Family (WEF) Trust, which is globally active and engaged in the management of a diversified portfolio of financial market instruments and real estate projects, investments in stocks, funds, and currencies, as well as residential and commercial properties. The executor will find full information regarding the holdings of the WEF Trust by contacting my longtime employee and trusted comptroller, Mr. William Chase, who has been tending to my affairs for many years."

Warren's comment on taxes and estate planning was equally clear. "Taxes are what we pay for civilized society. If there are taxes owed to California or the I.R.S., so be it. The U.S. Government fed me, clothed me, trained me, and educated me. California's been good to me, too. It's been worth every penny."

This man knew exactly what he was doing. Warren didn't require Beck's advice to write down how, or on whom, he wanted his money spent. No court would find that he lacked the mental capacity to write his own will.

Warren's final paragraph affirmed, "This Codicil is up to now the only valid will, and revokes all my previous testamentary dispositions in any form, should any exist even after my death."

It was signed by Warren and dated the first of February of this year, nearly three months after my divorce from his son. It was also around the time of Rick's West Coast wedding. I reviewed the document again, closely, this time as a lawyer, searching for a paragraph or a phrase that would prevent any of the beneficiaries from contesting this will under penalty of losing their legacy. I looked up at Mr. Beck, who had been waiting patiently for me to finish.

"Warren did not include an 'in terrorem' clause. That presents a potential complication."

I was concerned about this technical drafting flaw, but mollified by the knowledge that other wills suffered from the same deficit and were upheld anyway. Alfred Nobel's handwritten will lacked a "no contest" clause, but was famously sustained and continues to fund the "Nobel Prize."

After a pause, or maybe it was a sigh, Mr. Beck responded.

"Yes. Regrettably, Warren didn't deign to discuss the details with me."

I nodded in semi-disbelief and added, "With all his business experience and a lifetime dealing with lawyers, he omitted a simple passage that would have limited the motivation of his heirs or anybody else to contest his wishes."

Beck was silent. I sat quietly as well; convinced that Warren's big blunder all but invited a challenge to the codicil, no matter how unlikely to be successful. With only an upside, why wouldn't the heirs invest a few thousand dollars in probate litigation seeking a better result? There was literally no down side and nothing to lose.

Setting aside the possible will contest, I wondered what California required to admit a holographic codicil to the probate court for legal administration.

"Will the court recognize this document as a legitimate testamentary instrument?"

"Unless it's shown to be a fraud, or written under duress or coercion, or undue influence, or while the testator was not of sound mind—yes." Mr. Beck opined.

"So, Warren appointed me to orchestrate his charitable giving and antagonize his son, current daughter-in-law, and girlfriend?"

"Evidently."

"And what was their reaction?"

"Predictable. They filed a motion to invalidate this will, contest its contents, and remove you as executor. Tomorrow the court will rule on their applications."

"Who will defend the trust—and me—tomorrow? I'm not prepared to appear 'pro se.' I'm not sure I'm prepared for any of this."

"We call it 'pro per' in California, Ms. Bergin; but, to the point, my colleague, Mr. Gary Gensler, will appear for you."

"Doesn't your firm have a conflict of interest? Warren's handwritten testament contradicts the formal will that you prepared for him."

"That's true but it doesn't disqualify us. We checked with the ethics committee. My firm and I are following the California probate code."

"Can your firm handle future pleadings for me, or must I apply for pro hac vice admission to practice in California?"

"No need for that. We'll handle the litigation for you. Much will depend on what happens tomorrow in court. We expect the judge to uphold this will, despite the unusual origins and contents. To ensure that all rules are followed and Warren's last wishes are enforced, I will be your co-executor."

"Co-executor? That's not mentioned in the will."

"I realize that. I made an application to serve with you. You are not admitted in this state and I am—was—Warren's counsel for years before you were involved with his son and for seven months after your divorce, when Warren died."

"When did he die?" I missed the date of death and was curious.

"The second of June." Beck answered gravely.

"That was our wedding anniversary." Realizing what I said could be misconstrued, I continued, "to Rick, I meant."

"Naturally." Beck replied, dryly.

"Was Warren sick?" I wondered if he knew he was dying when he drafted the divorce letter to me.

"Not that I'm aware of, but plainly, Mr. Ethan, was not keeping me in his confidence."

I nodded and I sat silently across the magnificent mahogany desk, absorbing what had been said during this meeting.

Beck continued, "Tomorrow in court, I will confirm that you are able to fulfill your duties and will provide the added benefit of a full service law firm in California to assist."

Beck had managed to angle his way back into the administration of Warren's estate, though Warren himself took great pains to exclude him.

"I see. I'd like to have a copy of the codicil."

"Of course." Beck called his secretary in to his office. She promptly entered the enclave, took the document, and left.

"I will have a car pick you up at your hotel. Court commences at nine tomorrow morning."

"Thank you. Good bye."

As I left Beck's office, the secretary handed me a copy of Warren's codicil in an unsealed envelope. I made my way from the hallway to the elevator to the lobby downstairs. Waiting for my ride back to the Four Seasons, I was astonished by what I'd seen and heard and read. Warren fooled me. I never expected him to be so generous to strangers. But he was generous with me, too. Suddenly parentless in my twenties, Warren had welcomed me warmly, treating me with respect and fatherly tenderness. In return, I was a dutiful, daughter-like substitute. I cared for him and wanted nothing from him, other than to meet my own unrequited filial needs. I was gratified and stunned by the terms of the secret document in my hands.

Yet, the man I knew enjoyed his wealth and was not given to hidden works of charity. When Warren was philanthropic, he wanted the world to know about it. And, he knew how to enjoy all the amusement his amassed wealth could afford, like thousand-plus dollar bottles of wine; and to venture a guess, Tanya and the pageant of women who preceded her after his second divorce. But Warren was also a shrewd, self-made man.

I couldn't blame him for avoiding the trauma he would have encountered if his expected heirs were aware of his plans. Excluding his longtime lawyer from the process was probably a smart move. Next, I wondered how long Tanya would have stayed around if she'd known her dollars were numbered with her elderly boyfriend's remaining days? I doubted if Rick and Tiffany would have reacted any better. Beck certainly would have protested.

Yet at the end, Warren left a noble and honorable legacy that I was proud to execute, without hesitation or reservation. I would humbly do my best to fulfill Warren's private last wishes and see those veterans served. I might even dole out extra cash to Tanya and my ex and his wife, if needed and they asked nicely. Tomorrow, the court would make a record and Warren's remarkable largesse would be placed in the public domain. We would learn whether Warren's holographic codicil would be upheld or thrown out. I was rooting for the veterans, the charitable trust, and me, too.

CHAPTER FIVE

By Monday evening, still on East Coast time, I was exhausted by the day's events and retired to my room. My suite was uncommonly good for a business traveler. I had a big bed and a balcony with a city view. I figured Mr. Beck's firm had a special deal. After a dinner from the room service menu, I slept well. The next morning found me anxious, however. I didn't relish seeing my former husband with his new wife and Warren's paramour preparing to battle me in court over Warren's money—or control over it.

When I feel distress or strain, I try to self-sooth. It's cheaper and more convenient than psychotherapy, especially when one is travelling on business or what have you. When I'm in a place far away and feeling overwhelmed or stressed, I have a routine. I recite a favorite passage from *Moby-Dick*: "But even so, amid the tornadoed Atlantic of my being, do I myself still for ever centrally disport in mute calm; and while ponderous planets of unwaning woe revolve round me, deep down and deep inland there I still bathe me in eternal mildness of joy."

I say it sometimes more than once. Like a special mantra, reciting that passage slowly produces deep tranquility and calm inside my soul. This morning, my mantra was working for me and I was feeling more centered, if not exactly bathed in eternal mildness of joy.

My room phone rang. Once again, my hired car was early. Today we'd be headed to the Stanley Mosk Courthouse in downtown L.A. I'd never been to the courthouse in this city and was interested to see the building, to compare it to the courthouses from the East. We arrived in what felt like not enough time for me to gather my thoughts. Before I exited the car, I pushed the button to lower the window. I saw near the entrance a side yard in which a bust of Abraham Lincoln was erected. Lincoln's beardless expression was

56

serious but not melancholy or fraught, as in the images made during his presidency. Seeing Lincoln's serene, younger face reminded me of a letter in which he cautioned a young Captain Cutts, "Quarrel not at all." A perfect motto for a courthouse, I thought. It should have been inscribed over the doorways.

Having a few minutes to spare till the session commenced, I exited the car and walked over to the wall beside the Lincoln bust and sat down. I remembered another of Lincoln's aphorism: "Better give your path to a dog, than be bitten by him in contesting for the right. Even killing the dog would not cure the bite." And who could argue with that guidance when you're about to engage in a legal battle over millions. Lincoln's practical aphorisms never disappointed. No wonder he was a successful trial lawyer.

When it was time to head in, I walked to the North Grand Street entrance and noticed the carved figures on the façade above the courthouse. Similar to the courthouse on Foley Square, this L.A. courthouse featured lawgivers through the ages, only on the West Coast, they were depicted outdoors. The statue on the left was Moses. The middle character was an English knight from the era of the Magna Carta. The last one was Thomas Jefferson with the American Declaration of Independence. Representing the "Foundations of Law," these sculptures were personifications of, respectively, Mosaic Law; English common law; and our own nation's birth and democracy. Who wouldn't have high hopes of justice meted out here?

I passed the security check and remained in the lobby area for a few minutes, making sure my phone was set on airplane. I saw no one I knew and headed to the assigned courtroom. All I could do today was watch what was to unfold. The Ethan estate was in the court's hands for now. At this stage I was barely more than a spectator.

When I arrived at the hallway upstairs, adjacent to the courtroom, I spotted two tall women with long, silky, platinum-bleached hair. Then, rounding the corner, I saw Rick. It seemed weird not to go over and greet him. I'd done nothing wrong or to be ashamed of in this situation, so I did.

"Hello, Rick. I am very sorry for your loss."

He stared at me, paused and said, "Then get on the next plane to New York and leave us alone."

Well, so much for bygones and good will; plus, I hadn't lived in New York since the fall of last year. Going home meant Cape Cod, in case he cared.

"Rick, I didn't know about any of this until a few days ago. I will honor your dad's trust and do the best I can to serve his last wishes."

"It's best that you go."

I paused. Democritus wrote that magnanimity consists in enduring tactlessness with mildness; but that wasn't my nature, at least not at this moment.

"Were you aware that your dad gave Thomas Beck a note for me to read when we were divorced?" I asked Rick in the most civil tone I could muster.

"No."

"Well, he did. And I have some news."

"Tell it to my lawyer."

"It's personal—I whispered—you might want to hear this from me."

"What's your news, Kate?" He said, voice dripping with contempt.

"Your dad trusted me to do the right thing. That's probably why I'm here."

"Please go." Rick uttered as he walked away in disgust.

Just then I spotted Mr. Beck and he waived me over. I approached and he introduced me to my lawyer, Mr. Gensler. After greetings and polite banter, I was informed that this motion was likely already decided on the papers. Today's return date in the courtroom was for show and a clear record before the litigants. I understood that. He said we could confer about the ruling after the hearing and he ushered me into the courtroom. I took my seat at counsel table with him and Mr. Beck. The plaintiffs, Rick, Tiffany, and Ms. Tanya remained in the gallery behind their attorneys.

The court was prompt and we rose as the judge entered. She instructed us to sit down as she did. I saw a large file in front of her as she called the case by caption, Ethan, et. al. v. Bergin, and began to recite the facts and its legal posture. The judge noted that the case was scheduled for the return date on a motion filed under the complaint of Mr. Richard Ethan and his wife, Tiffany Ethan, and the decedent's companion, Ms. Tanya, concerning the distribution of Warren Ethan's Estate. The plaintiffs' suit named Kate Bergin, the defendant, the sole executor named in the holographic will that the plaintiffs sought to invalidate.

The judge continued to read from a multi-page typed memo, soon to be the written opinion. The official version from the bench was that Warren Ethan died at eighty-nine years old, leaving behind an estate ("the Estate") allegedly worth two hundred fifty million dollars, including real estate and all other personal property. According to the complaint, the decedent and his first wife, whom he later divorced, raised one child, Richard Ethan. The decedent was unmarried at the time of his death, but had an obligation to one Tanya, per a habitation contract.

The judge read from her notes, "Plaintiffs allege that the decedent's original will ("the Beck law firm will"), left half of the Estate to Richard and Tiffany, and the other half to the decedent's companion, Tanya. Plaintiffs also allege that the holographic codicil prepared within four months of the decedent's death should be invalidated due to his incapacitation at the time of drafting, or alternatively, because it fails to comply with the California probate code." The judge paused.

"If the court denies the plaintiffs' application to invalidate the decedent's holographic codicil, the plaintiffs request that the defendant, Ms. Bergin, be removed from the position of trustee for equitable reasons and her unclean hands."

I shuddered. "Unclean hands" means that I did something dishonest.

The court continued, "Plaintiffs allege that the holographic codicil was created by the decedent, Warren Ethan, while he was under duress, heavily medicated, and susceptible to influence, and that persons unknown, perhaps including Ms. Bergin, fraudulently induced Warren Ethan to revise the Beck law firm will, depriving his companion, Tanya, and son, Richard, and his wife, Tiffany, of all the entitlements they had reason to expect, and from Warren's lifetime assurances that he would evenly divide his estate one half to Tanya and the other half to Richard and his wife, Tiffany."

The judge paused and then began anew. "Intervenor plaintiff, Lyndsey Taylor, alleges that Warren Ethan was her biological father, and joins in plaintiffs' action to invalidate the will."

I think my heart stopped. No wonder Rick was so testy when I told him about his dad's letter after our divorce. He had someone seeking to be his long lost half-sister.

The court acknowledged the intervenor's requests for half of the estate, leaving half to the plaintiffs, Richard and Tiffany, excluding the one plaintiff, Tanya. Intervenor Taylor sought other forms of relief including the building of "a new high quality residence," as well as the costs of insuring, furnishing, and maintaining such a residence for her in Bel Air, with an "annual allowance for vacations comparable to the ones that her half brother, Richard Ethan, enjoyed during the decedent's lifetime." Plus, Ms. Taylor requested, "an apartment in Las Vegas at absolutely no cost to her; plus, one hundred thousand dollars to furnish same apartment."

Finally, the intervenor, Ms. Taylor, sought, "justice for herself as Warren Ethan's rightful heir, and a shared legacy among the other rightful heirs and/or damages awarded to her for the irreparable harm against Taylor, who was never acknowledged as a legitimate child during decedent's life, though he knew he was her father and she was his daughter, conceived in a Las Vegas high roller hotel suite."

I needed a breath. There seemed to be a few material details— like missing heirs and baseless fraud accusations against me—that Thomas Beck neglected to mention during our visit yesterday. I listened when the judge began to speak again. Now it was time for her to recount my position as the defendant. I had nothing to do with these pleadings, so I was interested to learn what had been written and filed on my behalf.

My attorney's papers addressed the legality of the handwritten codicil and the trust it created. Warren's longtime secretary filed an affidavit stating that I had no contact with her boss since my divorce from Richard Ethan. To bolster her statements, the secretary attached all of Warren's phone records and itineraries to her affidavit showing no contact between me and Warren either at the office or anywhere else. The court noted that the secretary's testimony and proofs were unrefuted and wasted no time addressing "my arguments." I was keen to hear what they were. Noticing that my lawyer appeared calm and confident, I did, too.

The judge said that Defendant Bergin raised numerous legal grounds for dismissal of the complaints. The judge went on and on. Her laundry list was just as long for me as it was for the plaintiffs and the intervenor; but my list made sense. I thought we had a winner here. And I was right. So said the judge. After reading for nearly ten more minutes, the court announced those magic words: "Plaintiffs' motion to invalidate the decedent's holographic codicil is denied.

Intervenor's motion for stated relief is denied. Defendant's motion to dismiss plaintiffs' and intervenor's complaints, with prejudice, is granted. The application of Mr. Thomas Beck to be named co-executor is granted as unopposed and for good cause. The plaintiff and intervenor will be responsible for the defendant's fees and costs incurred by the estate."

"Your Honor, I have a special request." Mr. Beck stood and addressed the court.

"What is it?" The judge replied.

"As Your Honor has upheld the codicil, I request that my firm be allowed possession of the original document and transmittals. I have never seen the original myself, as it was sent by Mr. Ethan's secretary without my knowledge. Additionally, as the co-executor of the estate and trust, I would like to place the original codicil and envelope in my firm's file for safekeeping and future reference if necessary."

"That's an unusual request. I will get back to you on my ruling."

"Thank you, Your Honor. Of course I will be filing a petition seeking an order for dual compensation; allowing my firm and Ms. Bergin to be paid for wearing two hats, as it were, attorney and trustee, and providing the required statutory notice."

"Very well." The judge replied.

Beck was civil and remained standing as the judge rose and left the bench.

No one was surprised at my counsel table, least of all Mr. Beck, by the rulings made today. The other side was less composed, and their clients were noticeably shaken. They had nothing to fear. As the new co-executor, I was much like Winston Churchill: resolved in war; defiant in defeat; and when I won, then I was magnanimous—but not a moment before. I would co-administer the testamentary trust with an iron fist, but fairly. The plaintiffs had no worries with Beck and me at the controls. Warren's wishes would be my commands. But their crazy demands, no chance. And that sister/daughter arising "out of the blue," as we aviators say; I didn't know what to think about that—or her.

Despite the winning ruling, there remained what we lawyers call "housekeeping" matters to address. We waited for the court to call us in her chambers where she'd tell us what was next for the Ethan estate and its co-executors. The judge would order an accounting so that we could literally get a handle on the monies within the named family trust and begin administering those funds for the beneficiaries, some of whom just lost their bid for more, and the veterans, who just won big.

CHAPTER SIX

During the conference in chambers we received our marching orders, as expected. My attorney would prepare the court order reflecting the ruling dismissing the complaints filed against me and Warren's holographic will. I would no longer need an attorney to represent my interests, as I was now officially administering the estate with Thomas Beck. Though not admitted to practice in California, the court granted me permission to appear in the case under a special rule. Additionally, Thomas Beck and I would share the role of administrator, each as a co-trustee and co-executor. That way we had all the powers we needed to manage Warren's testament per his handwritten wishes. We were to meet with Warren's West Coast employee, the "trusted comptroller," Mr. William Chase, by Thursday, allowing me to fly back East that evening, as planned. Beck and I would file a report of our findings with the court and proceed from there.

The intervenor's lawyer, nearly silent till this point, spoke up. He informed the judge that he had taken this matter on pro bono (for free) and explained that his client, Ms. Lyndsey Taylor, lacked the resources to pay any of the estate's counsel fees. The judge responded reasonably, instructing Lyndsey's attorney to make a motion for relief and she'd rule on it. The lawyer seemed thankful for that opportunity. Rick's and Tiffany's and Tanya's lawyers listened glumly to it all.

Mr. Gensler and Mr. Beck were business-like leaving the chambers with me. I tried very hard to affect the same detachment and avoided gloating as we walked past Rick and Tiffany and Tanya. Rick was standing by himself while the women were standing close on the opposite side of the hallway perfectly insolent in a pouty, platinum L.A. fashion. I found myself most interested in Ms. Lyndsey Taylor, who was sitting all the way down the hall, far from the others, alone, waiting for her attorney. Upon closer scrutiny, it seemed to me that she could have been Warren's daughter. She looked nothing like Rick, who was his mother's son in every way: tall, dark, and thin with a narrow face and lanky limbs. Lyndsey, like Warren, was of average height and build. Her hair, though chemically highlighted, was naturally dark strawberry blonde complementing light eyes, like Warren's mix of gray and blue. Lyndsey had fair skin and a model-like face with strong cheek bones, a delineated jaw and chin, and a straight, prominent nose with a slightly aquiline bridge. Not a conventional beauty, but she was striking and uncommon in appearance. I would say Lyndsey had "presence." I made a mental note of my questions and observations.

Lunch with Mr. Beck and Mr. Gensler in Santa Monica would provide an opportunity to learn more about how we would marshal Warren's holdings. Our charge for the veterans was clear from the contents of the will, but its terms also gave us pure discretion over any future distributions to Warren's heirs, up to one million dollars each. In that sense, Mr. Beck and I became the bankers who would decide to grant or deny all Rick's and Tanya's future financial requests, if any were made. And, of course, human nature being what it is, they would be made. But what of the intervenor, Lyndsey Taylor? Though she lost her bid for a share of Warren's estate this morning, if she really was his biological daughter, she, too, would qualify as an heir under that discretionary bequest. Seemed to me, we co-executors had to consider her claim seriously, even if her attorney failed to file any proof of paternity.

The time had passed under California law for the intervenor, Lyndsey, to request support in the normal sense from Warren's estate. Like many states in the East, to advance a filiation claim and receive cash from the "so-called" father, either the mother or the child had to file papers claiming paternity by the time the child in question reached adulthood, or a reasonable time thereafter. If Lyndsey really was Rick's half-sister, they'd have different mitochondrial DNA ("mommy DNA"), but they'd share genes from Warren. Why didn't her lawyer ask for a genetic test? As co-executor, I would have to ascertain the proper class of beneficiaries and would entertain any serious requests for future distributions from Warren's rightful heirs including, perhaps, Ms. Taylor.

Besides, personally, I wanted to know if she was or was not Warren's daughter. I knew he had spent a lot of time in Las Vegas and Warren was still single when Lyndsey was conceived. I thought we'd learn more about this topic after reviewing Warren's financial history. Perhaps he'd paid Ms. Taylor or her mother, sub rosa; or maybe Ms. Taylor was simply an opportunist with a lawyer who'd read the obituary of a very rich man? But it didn't seem that way after listening to her counsel speak in the judge's chambers.

Michael's Restaurant was the setting for our post victory luncheon. Having secured my role as executor and trustee, as the day wore on I had gained a measure of respect from my Western colleagues. I described my interest in settling the class of heirs for this trust. Under law and equity, it was my duty to determine if Intervenor Lyndsey had a legitimate claim under Warren's will. My audience was unreceptive. No matter, I thought privately. I was the co-boss and I was nearly certain that the judge would break any ties between Thomas Beck and me in my favor, ruling for the daughter—of time: truth.

We discussed our obligations to file estate tax returns, manage money (or hire the right people to manage it for us) once we gathered it, and most rewarding of all, mete out the dollars for the veterans and maybe some of the heirs. Finally, my attorney changed the subject to payment for services we were to render for the foreseeable future. As the court noted, with all our responsibilities and fiduciary duties came compensation.

If no one objected within 30 days, Beck's firm and I would be paid both for serving as counsel and as trustees. That was fine with me, so long as the court approved it. And on that note, we were done. Lunch adjourned. Mr. Gensler and Mr. Beck picked up the tab and saw me off to my hired car. With a free afternoon, and feeling good about the morning's work and the mission ahead, I was chauffeured back to the Four Seasons, eager to catch up on my own case load and maybe a tan.

Yesterday I spent the sunny L.A. afternoon profitably by the pool, finishing briefs and preparing legal motions for my small New England practice. One of my cases was listed for a hearing next week in Barnstable and I was on the schedule to fly island turns on the weekend. It would be a busy week, but I was caught up for now.

Today in California, I was eager to meet with Warren's employee, Mr. William Chase, and learn all about the money I'd be co-controlling for the foreseeable future. I had worked with other people's money throughout my career, but not like this. I currently had some estate cases on the Cape, but none involved intrigue or philanthropy on a grand scale. I was looking forward to this most unexpected legal undertaking and its happy ending.

We were to meet at Warren's Westwood corporate building in West L.A., adjacent to UCLA's park-like campus. The Golden State was also the beautiful state. I'm not sure how those kids made it to class with the great weather and the gorgeous surroundings, people, and places. When we arrived at the office, I was formally introduced to Ethan Enterprises' comptroller, William Chase, but not for the first time. Warren had introduced us years ago and Mr. Chase was responsible for tabulating the Ethan assets and income that would never be mine once I signed that thirty-three page prenuptial prepared by Beck's firm, way back when.

Obviously, Mr. Beck and Mr. Chase had worked together and were on friendly terms. After cordialities, we—me, Mr. Beck and Mr. Chase—sat around a conference table with several large files. Although I shared my executor role with Beck, I intended to conduct my own due diligence with Mr. Chase, who, Warren himself wrote, held the keys to the financial kingdom and his charitable trust.

"Gentleman, I would like to ask a few questions." I said this as a statement, not a request.

"By all means." Chase responded.

"We've met, haven't we?" I thought this was a good opener, in case Mr. Chase had forgotten.

"Yes, we sure have." Chase replied.

"I don't recall, how long did you work for Warren before he died?"

"From the start. Since the New York days. Fifty some years. We were in the service together. We were just kids."

"Right. I remember now. Would you remind me of your professional background?"

"Nothing formal past high school, just like Warren."

"Mr. Chase, how did you learn to manage the finances of a large firm?"

"Call me Bill."

"All right. Bill, how did you handle the financial needs of a large commercial entity without formal training?"

"I was always good at math. I learned on the job and asked lots of questions if I didn't know the answers."

"I see." I responded, which typically prompts more information from the speaker.

"It's all a matter of keeping the numbers straight, recording everything in the proper place, meeting deadlines, and managing budgets."

"And did you manage Warren's investments as well?"

"No. I was just the comptroller. I kept the records for the managed investments, but I didn't manage the investments or assets. I paid the bills and prepared the tax returns."

"Do you know why you were singled out in the codicil?" I asked?

"No idea, except that I kept all the records. Let me show you everything I have and you'll see what I do—I mean did—here. "

Like so many very wealthy people, we saw from the registers Chase maintained that Warren rarely handled cash—that was Chase's job. He paid his boss's varied and monumental personal and business costs by drawing checks from Warren's various accounts, as and when required. When more cash was needed to cover the bills, Mr. Chase would tell Warren, who would contact the money managers in New York, who would deposit the required funds into the banks from which Mr. Chase wrote the checks supporting Warren's lavish West Coast lifestyle.

Fortunately, Chase kept scrupulous accounts of the money flows. He provided unlimited access to Warren's local bank accounts from the last five years, reflecting the many credits and debits of the Ethan family budget. From pages and pages of statements, we viewed exactly how Chase handled Warren's professional and personal obligations. These recent expense records reflected an enormous annual budget. Warren and his family lived large. L.A. was not a cheap place and frugality was not an aspirational virtue.

Chase also paid Tanya's stipend. For the months before Warren died, bank statements reflected corresponding withdrawals and deposits of one hundred thousand dollars. Some of that money, I assumed, was for the online gambling habit that Warren addressed in his written will. None of the statements that Bill produced for our inspection, however, revealed direct expenditures to Ms. Lyndsey

Taylor. Yet, that didn't resolve the issue of her possible biological tie to Warren. Maybe he paid her; maybe he didn't. Besides, in life as in business, some payments are off the books.

We did, however, find disbursements to various Las Vegas recipients; but none to anyone we recognized by name. Some were by check, some by wire transfer, and each in amounts less than ten thousand dollars. Chase guessed that the money went to bookies, but never confirmed his suspicion with his boss. Who would? Instead, Chase dutifully recorded the sums paid on a separate ledger, apart from the check registers.

While this was all very interesting to a fiscal voyeur, Mr. Beck and I were no closer to ascertaining the aggregate sum we had for the testamentary trust after this meeting than we were before. By the end of our review, we'd seen plenty of piles of paper with checks and ledger sheets and various local account statements, but nothing from the New York investment advisors.

"Why don't you have information about how much money Warren had on hand the day he died?"

Bill Chase shrugged his shoulders. "My job was to keep track of what was owed, remit payments, and file the taxes. Warren had all those New York statements delivered personally to him. He drew the line at some things."

"Meaning what?"

"I don't think he wanted me to know everything, like how much money he really had."

"I see." I said, urging him to continue speaking.

"Warren wanted me to pay the bills and file the right forms. Mr. B. Adlai Perkin runs the Epcot Fund and makes, or made, all the investment decisions for Warren. I was just the accountant, if you please."

I paused for thought and asked, "Did Warren keep the Epcot statements here?" I asked Chase.

"Not in my office."

"May I look in Warren's office?" I asked?

"That's not up to me. Tom, can she look in Warren's office?" Chase looked to Mr. Beck for advice.

"I think that I have copies of the statements in my office. I'll send them to Ms. Bergin." Beck replied, shutting us down.

Before dispersing, we agreed that Beck would share the statements he had. Meantime, Chase would ask Warren's secretary about the original Epcot statements that were sent to Warren directly. I said that I might pay Mr. Perkin a visit. In any case, once I had copies of the Epcot statements in hand, we could analyze whether Warren's assets were growing under Perkin's management—or not. Then we would make a decision to divest or keep the money where it was, to best fund the trust in keeping with Warren's final wishes. In the interim, Mr. Beck could carry on as needed in California and I would do all I could from the Cape and New York.

With the technology available today, our 3,000 miles separation didn't pose much of a challenge. We decided to prepare a spreadsheet to evaluate not only the California cash flow; but also the performance of the Manhattan money manager, once we had a handle on what kind of assets were available. We had to get our arms around Warren's assets before we could ensure their safe-keeping and fund the trust to fulfil Warren's last will. At the end of the meeting, Chase wished us well and offered his help if required. My hired car was waiting as I left Chase's office for the airport and a new monetary mission.

CHAPTER SEVEN

My red eye from LAX to Logan was unremarkable and arrived ahead of schedule, leaving lots of time to catch my puddle jumper from Boston to the Cape. When we approached Hyannis, the airport was shrouded by fog. Knowing the pilot in command allowed me to relax in the back of the plane and hope for the best. After just one go-around we landed on runway 24. I was looking forward to resuming my practice and my charter flying. I felt renewed by my California experience and my new role in Warren's life, or more accurately, death. I was now officially in co-charge of a substantial trust and able to do some measurable good for the most deserving among us. I decided on my own to visit that money manager in New York early next week.

After a short nap and a quick shower, I went to my office where Celeste awaited me this Friday afternoon. The fog had lifted and it was a lovely summer day.

"Welcome back, Ms. Kate, what have you brought us from California?"

"Nothing but sunshine, Sunshine." I smiled at Cel.

"Well, tell me everything, what did Rick's new wife look like in person?"

"Disappointed." I smiled, as Cel knew from my previous texts and phone calls that Warren's codicil and I prevailed.

"Oh come on, I need to know more than that."

"All right. She was very tall, very blonde, very skinny, and very, very disappointed." I complied with the request for more details.

Celeste smiled at me and we addressed the minutiae required to run a law firm when the only attorney on staff was across the continent for several days. After we reviewed my legal schedule and I signed some pleadings and correspondence, Celeste and I returned to the recent events in California, focusing on the posthumous appearance of Rick's putative half-sister, Lyndsey, and the previously unknown handwritten codicil to benefit veterans and their families. We agreed that a Hollywood script writer couldn't make this stuff up. Eager to get on with it, I excused myself from our frothy chat to call the Manhattan money manager, Mr. B. Adlai Perkin, before it got too late.

Mr. Perkin seemed to expect my call and invited me to his East Side office any time next week. We arranged to meet late Tuesday morning, allowing for weekend flying commitments, my Monday court appearances, and travel time to and from the Cape and New York the next day. I transcribed our polite conversation in a memo prepared for email transmission. As I clicked the "send" button, I pondered how Thomas Beck would receive it. I never saw a computer on his desk or any other electronic device in his hands. But the email address on his business card was valid. I figured his nice receptionist or his officious, pretty secretary had access to his account and printed out whatever was sent there and then probably typed up his verbal response. The process reminded me of twenty-first century dictation; but whatever. It gave people gainful employment. Besides, who was I to judge how people interacted with technology?

As I was thinking about my meeting in the City next week, I checked in at the charter company and was pleased to learn I'd be flying a turn to the Vineyard in the morning. But for now, it was all I could do to catch up on the documents piled high on my desk and in my computer. Lawyering is not for those who are averse to deadlines and words. Such are a lawyer's trade and craft.

Saturday brought a beautiful morning with a clear cerulean sky over Cape Cod. I was content and hoping that Mr. Philips might be on my plane to MVY—the Vineyard. Pleased with my progress and completing my preflight duties, I waited for the manifest. I was delighted to see Steven's name there, but was let down to see Lee's there, as well. After a moment's disappointment, I resumed normal attitude, but I did let my hair free from its bun. I was still in my uniform, but the loose hair does make a difference, in my mind anyway.

"Nice to see you again, Steven." I said with more than professional geniality.

"Good to see you, Captain."

"Welcome, on board the Cessna 402," I said helping Steven and Lee into the small cabin, using my strained friendly skies voice that I usually reserve for check rides.

"Sparkling water." Lee commanded me upon taking her seat, as if I were her servant.

"I'll see what we have." I said passively aggressively, an affect I was sure she'd recognize.

Still crouched in the cabin, I continued, "I would like to show you how to operate the door in case of an emergency requiring quick exit."

"Do you really think that's necessary?" Lee spoke condescendingly, emitting cigarette breath mingled with freshly applied Hermes Perfume 24 Faubourg—expensive and high sillage.

"Yes, FAA rules. Let me show you." I bent over her and reached over Steven's seat for the door handle on his side, placing the side of my jaw and neck just forward of his chest. While I am not perfect, I'm shrewd, attractive, and I smell good, like baby powder mixed with a whiff of citrus and a note of Downy fabric softener.

"What are you wearing?" Steven asked?

"Basic black, we pilots swear by it."

"No, I mean the fragrance, it's so fresh, and familiar, but I can't place it?" Steven seemed puzzled.

I looked directly at Lee and smiled, "Why Mr. Philips, you never commented before?" This was perhaps the over the line, but who'd complain? And if she did, so what? Sue me. I knew how to handle that.

"Where's my water?" Lee whined to me.

"I'm sure it'll be here soon. May I show you how to operate your seat belt?"

"No." She said.

To soothe his girlfriend, Steven interjected, assuring me that he'd buckle her up.

"Very well." I replied sweetly before I left the cabin. As I exited the aircraft, I flung my hair over my shoulder and did my final walkaround. I took comfort in the fact that I was in charge of this plane and it was going to be a bumpy flight. When Lee's sparkling water arrived, I entered the aircraft and handed it to her then headed to my seat in the cockpit. We taxied to runway 15 and took off travelling twenty-two nautical miles, southwest to Martha's Vineyard Airport.

I was enjoying flying the twin Cessna after my transcon rides in the Boeing 737. I wondered if there were any working lawyers who flew for a legacy airline, as I intended to do one day. I did know of a dentist who flew for Delta Airlines Fridays through Mondays and saw patients in his dental office Tuesdays through Thursday evenings. So it was possible to carve out two professions for yourself, but there was not much down time. We all have choices to make based on what's important to us. I had enough on my plate for now and concentrated on this short flight to MVY. Despite thinking about it, I did not fulfill my preflight intention to make the ride a turbulent one. It was smooth and I was a consummate professional.

After we taxied near the FBO entrance, I performed my normal pilot duties. When my final postflight checklist was completed, I helped Steven and Lee out of the plane and followed them into the reception area. As Lee left for the ladies room, Steven approached me and asked if I'd be flying them back to Hyannis on Tuesday. I shook my head, no, and explained that it would be a busy day for me. I'd be en route to New York City and meeting an investment professional.

Steven was curious and I saw no harm in explaining why I was Manhattan bound. I provided a brief distillation of my California trip, timed to end before Lee emerged from the lavatory. I was forthcoming, but excluded that fact that I was once related to the deceased testator/trust settlor. After all, how could that help me and what did that fact add to this story?

"And who are you meeting with?" Steven asked, as if he were genuinely interested.

"Mr. B. Adlai Perkin, know him?" I was forthright.

"Not personally."

"Have you heard of him?"

"Yes." Steven paused, "Kate, if you need any help, give me a call. You have my number."

Unsure of his sincerity, I thanked him just the same.

As Lee reemerged from the loo, the happy couple walked off hand-in-hand towards the parking lot to begin their Vineyard weekend. I prepared for the short return flight to HYA, wondering why Steven paused as he did and offered to help me.

On Tuesday morning, I had a trouble-free, scheduled flight to LaGuardia and effortlessly found my way to Mr. Perkin's Park

Avenue headquarters. I was on the twenty-third floor, well before our appointed meeting time. Perkin's receptionist greeted me and escorted me to a small, but plushly appointed space that seemed more like a lobby in a deluxe hotel than a finance professional's waiting area. After nearly an hour, a tall, thin, attractive dark-haired female appeared and asked me to follow her. As she led me toward what I guessed was the wizard's inner sanctum, a glass partition separated the hallway from a large interior space, partitioned by cubicles. Behind the pane I saw several men wearing headsets, sitting before multiple computer screens, seemingly monitoring numbers and executing trades from their individual stalls. I motioned up to the glass and asked the woman what those men behind the barrier were doing. "Making the magic happen," she coolly responded.

I followed the dark-haired woman into a conference room with a stunning twenty feet long, six feet wide, high-gloss Macassar ebony table surrounded by many leather chairs, but not much else. Urged by the staffer to take a seat on the near side of this magnificent slab of striped wood with my back to the door, I resisted. I preferred to be seated where I could see who was coming and going. She nodded and I sat where I wanted. She offered a beverage, which I declined. Again I waited.

Having practiced in Manhattan for as long as I did, I recognized what it meant when someone kept you waiting. Translation: you are unimportant. Given the extent of the Ethan holdings, and my status as co-executor and administrator of those holdings, I was important. Had I been here under other circumstances, say as an adversary or colleague, I would have reacted differently. Fifteen minutes late for a meeting and I walk unless notified or asked for forgiveness. But I was here to learn about Warren's holdings. Despite my bad reaction to this delay, an hour's wait would not prevent me from discharging my duty as Warren's co-executor.

Another fifteen minutes elapsed before a short, bearded figure who looked like a cross between a chubby bishop and a learned rabbi entered the room and took a seat at the head of the table, about four feet from the sumptuous black-dyed lambskin leather armchair that I occupied. Another lovely, tall, thin, dark-haired female joined us. She carried a large envelope and sat at Perkin's right side, across the expansive conference table from me.

"I'm Adlai Perkin, pleased to meet you, Miss, eh..." Perkin fumbled.

"Bergin." The female assistant uttered.

"Miss Bergin." Perkin completed his greeting, obviously unfamiliar with me or the nature of our meeting. He offered no apologies for making me wait 75 minutes.

I was irritated and wanted Perkin to understand the power dynamic between us. I was the client, after all.

"Adlai, were you detained somewhere in the outer boroughs?" I asked with a nice smile, using his first name, dispensing with the propriety I typically employ during an initial meeting.

"No, not at all." Was all he offered as an explanation.

I let it go. "Do you know why I'm here?" I wasn't sure and didn't want to waste any more of my time.

Adlai looked to his assistant for assistance, as he was clearly ignorant of me or Warren or the Ethan Family Foundation. The woman in her late twenties began to look inside the large envelope that she placed before her on the table. She removed some papers and handed them over to her boss.

"Some of my reports." Adlai said as he presented the documents to me without inspection and bragged, "I control over seven billion dollars. Epcot is very selective. Whomever we choose to allow into the fund is very special. We admit only the smallest number of applicants. You don't realize how fortunate you are to be here. So many called, but few were chosen."

I said nothing as I flipped through the thin stack of documents with Adlai's letterhead atop each page. The reports appeared more like letter opinions than numerical statements. My research revealed that Adlai was a Harvard-trained lawyer. Thus, his facility with words was no surprise; but he was famous for his financial wizardry, so I expected numbers, too. As I quickly scanned what lay before me, Adlai spoke in a manner suggesting that he was used to commanding a room with a captured audience, and enjoyed it.

"You'll see that Epcot reports are unlike generic bank account statements that people at your level are accustomed to seeing."

I glowered at him in response to the insult and condescension he had just flung at me.

Undaunted by my stare, Adlai continued, "For Epcot, I highlight strategy over balances and asset classes over interest rates; but bear in mind, simply knowing what Epcot's asset classes are, or even its strategies or positions, is not the whole story. Within each asset class, there can be, and often are, significant variations in risks that I, the manager, am prepared to make depending on kinds of returns I can achieve. So, you could say that risk is more important than asset class."

"So, do …"

"Please don't interrupt me while I speak. As I was saying, my goal right now is to help you understand risk, because I want you to understand what it means to be one of our investors. In fact, as you'll see in those statements, to our enduring chagrin, our reluctance at Epcot to take on more risk helped to suppress our returns over the years. The key is leverage, and the limits placed on position sizes. At Epcot we are primarily focused on risk arbitrage, investments in private debt claims and publicly traded securities of bankrupt and distressed companies. We also partake of indirect investments, including investment in mutual funds, private partnerships, closed-end funds, and other pooled investment vehicles that engage in similar investment strategies."

"What does that mean?" I demanded.

Unresponsive to my inquiry while relishing the role of Universe Master 2.0, Adlai waxed metaphoric on investment strategy.

"Wall Street no longer operates as a bull or bear, but as a shark. To survive in this environment you need to have a steady diet of deals as you swim through the water and live off the fees the deals create. Each position is a little business on its own. As on design runways, fashions in deals change frequently. It's like a parking lot. You don't want to leave a Lexus in the morning and return in the evening to find your spot is now occupied by a Ford Focus."

I drove a Ford SUV. I listened, not knowing where this soliloquy was headed and wondered who in the world would hand control of his fortune over to this man, then of course, I realized, Warren did.

Perkin continued.

"The Wall Street merry-go-round of deals keeps spinning. It's like when the Yankees got A-Rod from Texas,"

I interjected before he went off on the Yankees, which I found objectionable on so many different levels, not only because I'm from the Cape.

"Adlai, what does this have to do with the Ethan account?"

I didn't like this this grandiose, arrogant man, but I was not leaving his office without solid information as to what he did with

Warren's assets; how much was there on Warren's date of death, 2 June, and how much was available today.

"At our fund, as at many other hedge funds, we do not provide complete transparency, but we try to keep our partners informed of what we do and why we do it. It is so complex that complete transparency can be more confusing to clients than illuminating. I'm sure you understand."

"No, I don't." I protested.

"Well of course you don't. I'll try to help you. You see, in good times one can form capital by raising debt and retiring equity. In bad times, one forms capital by raising equity and retiring debt. The nature of deals is constantly changing, and not only on Wall Street. In sports, everywhere, everything. You must adapt. As Epcot's managing partner, I or my staff adopt a selective approach in evaluating potential investment situations. I generally concentrate on relatively fewer transactions that I can follow more closely. I might employ strategies involving derivative securities like options, futures and convertibles... I won't hesitate to use hedging devices and will engage in short sales."

I had heard enough from Adlai and put my concerns as bluntly as I could, "As co-executor of the Ethan estate, it is my fiduciary duty and legal obligation to know how much money is in the Warren Ethan Family Trust account and how and where it's invested. I don't care about anything else you do for other Epcot clients."

"But of course you do, everyone's interdependent, what's bad for one is bad for all and vice versa."

I could see I was not getting anywhere with this guy, so I demanded, "What is today's balance for the Warren Ethan Family Trust?"

"We've provided all the information requested, I certainly wouldn't know off hand." Perkin replied.

With that, I gathered the several Epcot statements on the shiny, black wood table and placed them back in the envelope, now in front of me. I told Perkin, "Once I analyze these statements, I'll get back to you about how we will proceed."

"Good. Please let my staff know if you need anything else," Perkin said as he rose from his seat and left.

As soon as he departed, I stood up and began to leave. His assistant sprung up and jumped ahead to lead me out of the conference room and down a different corridor decorated with multiple large Rothko canvasses hung on the walls. Not given time to admire or even look at these paintings, I was steered with steady, yet courteous haste, out of the Perkin headquarters into the hall towards the bank of elevators. Waiting for one of the cars to carry me down to the lobby, I was under the impression that Mr. B. Adlai Perkin thought that I had my one audience with him—and that was it. We'd see about that.

Knowing that I'd be in Manhattan for the day, I had called Mike Fortune, my former professional colleague at my New York law firm and my current friend and personal money manager. We had spoken regularly after I left the City, but had not seen each other since the day of my divorce when he served as my lawyer. Today, he invited me for lunch to discuss life, the pursuit of happiness, my own portfolio, and Warren's property. I sent him a text to let him know that my Perkin meeting was over. I was eager to see him again and pick his brain about finances and anything else that might help me now that I was co-executor of a substantial estate. Though I had practiced law in Manhattan and was generally familiar with what the super wealthy did with their money, I never had the opportunity before to meet with someone like Mr. Perkin. Maybe that was just as well. I needed Mike's professional feedback on what had just transpired before my eyes and ears through Perkin's Park Avenue looking glass.

Waiting for the car that Mike ordered to pick me up and take me cross town, I parked myself in a comfortable chair in the lobby of Perkin's Park Avenue building. Very nice, but no Rothko's down here. I decided to browse the Epcot "reports." Though not privy to Warren's financial matters, even while I was married to his son, I was naturally curious to see the outlines of the dynasty to which I willingly waived my rights all those years ago. As I began rummaging through the statements in the envelope, I noticed that the most recent two years were missing. I made a mental note to get them and tell Beck about this.

Besides the three years of older statements that I did possess, I found a document labelled, "Confidential Offering Memorandum for Epcot Partners, Limited Partnership" and began to read. It explained that Perkin was the managing partner of Epcot and that the investors were limited partners with, as I saw it, very limited rights. The offering explicitly stated in perfect Perkin Jabberwocky that he, for Epcot, would use whatever tools at his disposal to increase everyone's holdings. More than that, this document warned that the investment was not registered and not transferable. Withdrawals were limited by the investors, yet, Perkin, for Epcot, could kick you and your money to the curb at will. The fees were enormous. I didn't understand the attraction. Why did these wealthy clients stampede to Park Avenue to put their millions or billions in Epcot under Perkin's singular, unquestionable control?

During the ride from Park Avenue to Per Se, the still popular, if fading, multiple star restaurant at Columbus Circle, I thought about how Perkin managed all that money and made it so attractive to so many investors, though he spoke with the logic of a Lewis Carroll character. I was sure Mike could explain, firsthand, how financial managers for the super rich manipulated their clients' money in ways that were simply unavailable, and in a sense, unimaginable, to the ordinary person. I wanted Mike's reassurance that Epcot was a safe investment. Mostly, I needed to know whether Beck and I should retain Warren's estate in Perkin's high demand fund—or not.

Mike arrived a bit late at the restaurant and greeted me warmly. We exchanged updates on our professional lives. He sadly confirmed that my former law firm was fine without me. Though I was liked and respected there, I was replaced within a week. Nice to know that life goes on. No matter how crucial you thought you were to an organization, you weren't. I filled him in on my new role as co-executor. He found it ironic. I could see that point of view: woman waives great wealth in prenup, only to be placed in charge of great fortune after divorce when ex's dad dies several months later. Go figure. When we broached the subject of Warren's estate, I explained my utter dismay and confusion after meeting Mr. Perkin. I could not comprehend what he did with all the billions he managed or how he was as successful as he was. For a money guy, Perkin was verbose in the extreme, but not much on figures or confirmations from my recent experience with him.

Mike nodded and matter of factly told me in broad strokes what unregulated investment vehicles could do for the rich. I listened. I didn't interrupt or ask questions about something that I did not fully grasp. This was far out of my league. Not being a wealth investment specialist, I was no more familiar with these matters than the average man or woman on the street. Mike, however, was a tax expert and a sharp guy, comfortable in the world of global finance. What's more, he could tell when someone, like me, was lost in the weeds of hedge fund arcana. He took another tack.

"Kate, show me the statements you have."

I complied and handed over some of the older quarterly statements just provided by Mr. B. Adlai Perkin. After several minutes of silence, he focused on one of the documents I'd given him and tried to read it to me, while I looked on.

"This statement shows the value of Warren's account and the appreciation during the prior quarter."

Mike looked at another piece of paper. He appeared puzzled and that made me nervous.

"This is a letter report from Perkin describing his investment strategies for Epcot, but it doesn't provide the underlying positions, only the treasuries in Warren's account at the end of each quarter."

"What are you telling me, Mike?"

"It's interesting."

"Interesting bad or good?" I wondered.

"Not sure. Why would Perkin consistently exit the market at the end of every quarter and put his clients in treasuries?" Mike replied.

"Is there a problem? Aren't treasuries safe? Wasn't Perkin simply locking up his clients' gains?" I said urgently looking for reassurance.

"Not sure. Epcot's returns each quarter are solid; but I don't think I've seen anything like it before."

Mike pulled the phone out from his shirt pocket and began using the calculator function. He flipped through more statements as he tapped on his phone screen.

"What are you doing?" I asked.

"Looking for a trend." He shook his head. "Remarkable."

"In what way?" I demanded, calmly.

"The combination of low volatility and high returns—it's consistently good."

"And?" I needed to understand the ramifications of his findings.

"Perkin achieved a return from 17 to 11 percent each year, despite market performance. I don't know of any other firm that has shown this kind of steady success, not Bain Capital, not the Blackstone Group, not Cerberus, nobody."

My ears perked up at the sound of one word.

"Bain, you said." I was thinking of Steven Philips, my MVY passenger.

"Yes, and the others."

"Sounds like Perkin is doing a good job." I was beginning to feel relief from my anxiety.

"Could be. In private equity, the object is to maximize the return on your investment, or capital, but I've never seen returns this consistently good."

"So, what do you think, is the money safe there?" That was the heart of the matter.

"I'm not sure where 'there' is from these statements. Maybe Perkin has invested Mr. Ethan's money through an offshore partnership that works with another kind of fund to reduce taxation on his profits."

"Okay, and..." I needed more input.

"I can't tell you how safe Epcot is, because I can't see what Perkin is doing with the money; but that's not necessarily a bad thing. Many hedge fund managers keep a low profile. They don't want to attract attention; they want to maximize their returns. Most are not transparent."

"Mike, my immediate problem is deciding whether Epcot is a good place to keep Warren's fortune, so Beck and I can fund the charitable trust as the codicil mandates."

I was concerned because I lacked understanding and where there's ignorance on my part, there is a chance for great mayhem by others.

Mike put it plainly, "What you have is a fund whose returns are consistently good. Whatever Perkin is doing at Epcot is working. But I cannot assure you of the safety of the assets. It's just not clear from the statements Perkin gave you. Like he told you this morning, his goal is not transparency, and Epcot's investments are not transparent at all. I cannot tell from these reports what he's doing with the funds before they're placed into treasuries at the end of each quarter, which itself is strange to me. I wouldn't invest your divorce settlement like this."

"Fine. Thanks, I guess. But about Warren's money: What would you do if you were in my shoes?"

"Tell the court what you've found, that Perkin's returns are good, but the source of those returns is inscrutable and Perkin himself has exclusive control. That may—or may not—be best for a testamentary trust where you are the responsible fiduciary."

"Will you help me if I need you?"

"Of course."

I took a breath and paused to consider the ramifications of what Mike had just said. It wasn't all bad and it wasn't all reassuring either. I decided to change the topic.

"Mike, do you ever work with Bain?"

"Not directly, but I've worked with many private equity executives and I've been involved with Bain deals. Why?"

"I met a Bain guy from Boston on one of my runs to the Vineyard. Steven Philips, have you heard of him?"

"Yeah, smart. Cut throat. Count your fingers after you shake his hand."

"Really, tell me more."

"He's good at what he does, making money for Bain and his investors. But he's ruthless."

"Meaning?"

"Pure capitalist, a creative destructionist. All efficiency, no social utility. No heart."

"I see." Pure capitalist; cut throat; no heart? I was silent for a minute as I tried to align Mike's profile of the Steven Philips I knew, with his tousled hair, unassuming demeanor, and slight aroma of nicotine. It didn't fit.

I let it go and directed the conversation to our shared personal and professional ties, past and future, for auld lang syne and for all that and all that. When our lunch concluded the hostess called for a cab to take me to LaGuardia. The taxi arrived quickly and I thanked Mike for being a good friend and a decent man. We parted warmly with a hug and a promise to be in touch soon.

Though officially evening when I arrived on the Cape, there were enough hours left in the day to tend to my law practice and advise my clients. Celeste, still at the office, assured me that everything was under control and our schedule was in good shape. But there was a surprise. A woman by the name of Lyndsey Taylor had called wanting to speak with me. Ms. Taylor left a mobile number and an urgent request for a call back.

This message puzzled me. Ms. Taylor was, at least through last Tuesday, represented by counsel. That meant I, as a lawyer and trustee in involved in the Ethan estate case, could not call her back personally. To do so would violate about a dozen ethical cannons and possibly get me in trouble with the Bar and the Bench, not to mention Beck. Wanting to be responsive, I would call her lawyer, but I didn't have his contact information handy. Instead, I figured I'd call Beck, and give him a full briefing of Ms. Taylor's message to my office, while addressing my other concerns: my weird Park Avenue adventure with Perkin and securing an expert to help us determine if Warren's estate should remain in Epcot.

Sometimes that three hour West Coast time difference is a blessing. Still business hours in California, I placed the call to Beck in L.A. and immediately reached the receptionist. I held for a few minutes before Mr. Beck's personal secretary told me that her boss was busy, but would call me back soon. Surprised that I was not on his "put through" list, as in, no matter what I'm doing, put Ms. Bergin's call through to me; I left a detailed message: I reported Mike Fortune's findings; I thought we should hire someone to investigate whether Warren's money should remain at Epcot, or not; I was missing the Epcot statements for the last two years; and finally, the mysterious call from the failed intervenor, Ms. Lyndsey Taylor.

Nearly a minute later, Thomas Beck called back on my mobile phone.

"I received your lengthy message, Ms. Bergin."

"Good. I met with Perkin and I don't like him."

"Mr. Perkin manages one of the more desirable funds in the world." Beck was apparently pro Perkin.

"So he told me."

I changed the topic to the missing two years of statements, and Beck replied, "I will have them. Chase called and said he got copies directly from Perkin and is sending them to me."

"All right, so you'll have what we need?"

"Yes."

Beck was satisfied and that mollified me, for now. But there was another issue to address.

"I would like an expert to evaluate Epcot for the trust. I'd be more comfortable holding the money in an institution that is regulated and accountable. Mr. Perkin's fund is neither."

Silence from Thomas Beck. He was treating me like he was the lawyer in charge and I was a client, one he didn't like and who paid late.

I continued, "Since neither of us is an investment strategy professional, I think we need an expert, someone like my colleague, Mike Fortune, to help us decipher what's going on at Epcot before we decide to continue our relationship with Perkin—or not."

"I don't share your opinion but I will contact the court and provide the details of what you've found."

"No need, I'll do that myself. I don't need an interpreter."

"Ms. Bergin, you wanted to meet with Mr. Perkin in New York. You have done that. I will take care of the case in California, from here, in California."

"Not alone you won't. I am your equal in this case and I won't be told by you what I can and can't do. That's the court's prerogative." I paused. "Next, I need to discuss the intervenor, Lyndsey Taylor, remember her?"

"Vaguely." Beck answered coolly.

"Ms. Taylor called my Cape Cod office while I was in Manhattan. I know I can't call her back directly, but I'll call her attorney. Would you give me his name and number?"

"You are not authorized to contact her or her attorney. Her claims were dismissed and she has nothing to do with Warren's estate or the testamentary trust."

"That's not true. The court's current order doesn't limit me from returning phone calls to her counsel. And, if she's Warren's daughter, she has a claim to his estate."

"Ms. Bergin, if you persist with your demands, I will ask the court to remove you from your position."

"Mr. Beck, I am acting reasonably, diligently, and ethically. If you threaten me again, I'll take legal action against you. More information is better than less information, especially when we're supposed to be giving away Warren's millions, and they are at present, out of our reach." I was exasperated.

"I will report findings and your conduct to the court." Mr. Beck said.

"I'll save you the time. I'm calling the court now."

I was punching in the judge's law clerk's number on my touch tone office hard line while speaking to Mr. Beck on my mobile. He hung up. I guessed that his hard feelings resulted from being omitted from the will process at the last minute and that he didn't much like having to deal with me, an ex-spouse of Warren's adult son.

Beck's unceremoniously ending our call didn't resolve the issues raised during our conversation. Additionally, now I wanted to make the court aware that my newly appointed co-executor seemed unwilling to address my basic concerns about the status and safety of the Ethan estate. How could we work together if he refused to speak with me?

Within seconds, the California judge's law clerk was on the line. I related what had just happened and the need for a conference call with the judge in the Ethan estate case. The law clerk asked me to hold on and shortly thereafter, Mr. Beck, the judge, and the clerk were on the line with me. You had to love technology. The judge took charge—as judges do—and distilled the dispute between me and Mr. Beck succinctly and in numerical order.

The first point in contention was what to do about the fact that Mr. Perkin did not give me all the answers I wanted and failed to copy me on the last two years of statements for the Ethan estate. The second point: my plan to hire an expert consultant to evaluate the investment plans at Epcot. The third point: the intervenor reached out to me personally, seeking a reply. The fourth point: Beck's accusatory and uncooperative attitude.

The court asked for our respective positions on these items. I was similarly succinct. I needed all the Epcot statements. I wanted expert help to analyze them. I wanted to return Lyndsey's call, via her lawyer; and I wanted protection from Mr. Beck's baseless ethical violation charges and from his threat to remove me as executor in this case. I reminded the court that I alone was named executor in Warren's handwritten codicil and that it was Beck's firm that filed the request making us co-executors. And now that we were both in charge, it was our mutual duty, as co-executors, to learn as much as we could about Warren's money and his beneficiaries. In summary, I used Justice Brandeis's adage that sunshine was the best disinfectant and urged the court to let the light shine on this case and allow us to examine all aspects out in the open, with suitable assistance.

Mr. Beck's response was not concise or direct. He waxed on and on about my unusual role in this matter, given my personal history with the family and my divorce from the testator's son last November. He argued that I was officious and confused my role of co-trustee and co-executor with one of investigator. He finally accused me of inappropriate conduct relating to Intervenor Taylor, who, he said, I had been eager to contact ever since the court hearing.

At that point I interrupted, asking to respond to the last lie. First, Ms. Taylor called me, not vice versa. Next, the terms of the codicil were clear about grants to Warren's family members. If Ms. Taylor really was Warren's daughter, she'd be a member of that class of beneficiaries. I mentioned how a simple cheek swab from both the legitimate son, Richard, my ex-husband, and Ms. Taylor, the putative daughter, would put the matter to rest with 99.9998 percent certainty.

The court stopped me cold. Evidently, her law clerk had been working, looking up cases and writing memos as we held this impromptu telephone hearing. The judge sharply stated, "I have heard enough from you both. Here's my ruling."

The substance of her decision was terse and clear. Beck was to send me the Epcot statements from the last two years. I was to send the curriculum vitae of any proposed expert to the court, copied to Beck, who was permitted to have his own proposed experts. We trustees/executors could comment on the other's proposed financial experts before the judge would decide who would help us, and how much he would be paid. Until then, there would be no payment for any work performed by any expert before gaining official status from the court's imprimatur through an order and a formal, written letter of engagement.

In re Estate of Warren Ethan was not a sealed case and there was no gag order in place. Beck and I were free to discuss Epcot, Perkin, and anything else about the case with nonparties pending further court order. Finally, Mr. Beck could have possession of the original codicil and related envelopes—the one from Warren, which arrived sealed with the codicil inside, and the one transmitting it, from Warren's secretary, the day she learned of his death. The court had digital copies of all the documents and had no further use of the originals. The court clerk would provide more details on where Mr. Beck could retrieve these items.

The judge had recently granted Lyndsey's lawyer's motion to withdraw from the case. Ms. Taylor no longer had an attorney of record. There was no legal impediment to my contacting either Ms. Lyndsey Taylor or her former lawyer. The judge also found Ms. Taylor lacked sufficient financial resources (in legalese, she was IFP—in forma pauperis) and thus, was released from any obligation to pay legal fees and costs to the Ethan estate. Tanya, Rick, and Tiffany were not so lucky and their motions opposing the original fee award were still pending. Our reply papers were due next week.

My position as co-executor, co-trustee was safe. Unless I did something illegal or unethical, the court would not order me out of the case; same for Mr. Beck. After that brusque ruling, the judge declared us adjourned and told us to await further instruction from her law clerk.

Unlike the real world where very junior people in their careers have little to no power over more senior people; in the legal sphere, a law clerk—who might not have even received her bar examination results yet—wields improbable influence over every lawyer who appears before her judge. The law clerk, for as long as her term lasts, is the judge's deputy, gatekeeper, and sidekick. She might never have tried a case or met with a client. It doesn't matter. As the judge's clerk, she is the long arm of the law. When a law clerk speaks everybody, no matter how experienced or senior, listens—and basically, obeys.

Within seconds after the judge left the line, the law clerk assigned to Beck the task of drafting an order reflecting the judge's oral decision. If I approved, Beck would submit the proposed form of order to the court for execution and filing. The clerk confirmed that an audio recording of the preceding phone conference would be available upon request, if either Beck or I could not agree on the language for the order. Was she clear? She was to me. Beck remained silent.

The law clerk hung up, or more accurately, clicked off. We were dismissed, but remained on the line. I spoke first. "Mr. Beck, I hope to receive those Epcot statements soon and I plan to send those experts' CVs by the week's end, latest. I'll contact Ms. Taylor's former attorney tomorrow morning, as the court allowed."

"You do that, Ms. Bergin. The order will be in the court's chambers tomorrow."

"Don't forget to send it for my review and consent as to form, first." I heard a slam.

CHAPTER EIGHT

Not one to do tomorrow what I should do today, I got a copy of Mike Fortune's current CV and sent it to California. Next, I called Steven's office and asked for him. He was out and unable to be reached. Though I probably should have waited for Steven's return, time was of the essence and I didn't see the harm in acting without his express permission. After all, he did offer to help me last weekend. After a moment's deliberation on the propriety of what I was doing, I gave my name to the receptionist and asked to speak with Steven's assistant.

Within seconds, a pleasant voice answered and said she'd be pleased to comply with my request. In less than a minute, my in-box contained an electronic Bain Capital media kit, complete with the CVs of Mr. Steven Philips and the other Bain partners. I made a hard copy of Steven's CV for my records and forwarded the digital version to the court and Beck's office. Having ticked those tasks off my Ethan estate "to-do" list, I decided to call Lyndsey Taylor's former lawyer. Though no longer representing Ms. Taylor, I thought he could be helpful, giving me insight or a heads up on his former client. His name was in my notes from the telephone call with the court, so I easily got his number.

My call was dumped into an automated voice mail system and I left a message. Minutes later I was speaking to him. He didn't think Lyndsey was able to find another free lawyer and as far as he knew, Lyndsey was now pro per, representing her own interests in the estate suit despite her claims having been dismissed. He thought that Lyndsey had a compelling story, but he would not elaborate. I wasn't sure if that meant that he didn't really know Lyndsey well enough to tell me anything of interest; or that he couldn't tell me anything about a former client due to the attorney-client privilege. He did provide

Lyndsey's mobile phone number without condition or hesitation. It was the only phone contact he had for her and it matched the number she gave to Celeste, wanting a call back from me. According to her former attorney, Lyndsey lacked a landline—not so unusual these days—and her only official address was a POB in L.A. I would probe these facts when I spoke with the woman.

Just as I was reviewing my Ethan estate file, preparing to phone Lyndsey, Celeste buzzed me. A "Mr. Philips" was on the line. I eagerly picked up the receiver.

"Hi, Kate Bergin speaking."

"Captain Bergin, Steven Philips here"

"Thanks for calling me back, your secretary gave me your CV. I hope you don't mind." I said, nearly certain that no harm was done.

"She's been asked not to do that again."

"I didn't mean to get her into trouble."

"Captain Bergin ..."

"Remember, call me Kate." I interjected, trying to relieve any tension I caused.

"Right. Kate, I have a proposition."

"Do you?"

"I have no free time now, but I'll be flying to the Vineyard at the end of the week. I'll ask for you as my pilot and we can talk during the flight. Are you allowed to do that?"

This actually posed an interesting question because while I am allowed to speak during most segments of the flight, it's not supposed to be an absorbing, distracting kind of conversation. Rather, it's more like, "here's how to operate the door latch to exit in case of an aircraft emergency"; or "please don't touch that switch"; or "make sure your seatbelt is fastened." The kind of conference I wished to have with Steven Philips would require more of my head space than is supposed to be available during a commercial fight when I'm in command. After pausing to ponder all this, I replied.

"Well, I don't think this discussion should be on Cape Air Charter time. My boss wouldn't like it, the FAA wouldn't like it, and for a host of other reasons, I must decline."

"Understood. How about before or after the flight? If you're free."

"Hmmm. That's possible, depending on the schedule. Afterwards would be best."

"Terrific, I'll arrange it. We'll talk then."

"Sounds good. Thank you."

I paused and spoke again, "I didn't realize that CAC took pilot requests."

"Me neither, until I asked."

"When did you do that, Mr. Philips?"

"After our first trip, Captain Kate Bergin. We'll talk soon, gotta go."

And that was that. I called my air charter boss, Sean, to confirm that I was on the schedule for MVY turns this weekend and asked whether the company really did entertain passenger requests for specific pilots. Per Sean, I was and it did. Additionally, Sean informed me that the company retained a "NOT Fly" list because several customers let management know that they would "NOT fly" with certain pilots ever again. Sean refused to disclose if I made that list or not, citing some employee statute of some sort, so I let it go. I did ask Sean if Mr. Philips had requested me to fly him to the Vineyard this weekend. "Affirmative," Sean responded. I followed up by asking Sean if Mr. Philips had been requesting me since that first flight to MVY weeks ago. "Can't say," said Sean, who refused to confirm or deny. That was food for thought, too. Finally, Sean confirmed that I would have enough time for a postflight chat on the Vineyard with Steven Philips before operating my return segment to Hyannis later that evening. With that task complete, I returned my attention to my next undertaking: contacting Ms. Lyndsey Taylor, directly.

This assignment set my mind wandering backwards. When I began practicing law, I learned two things: (1) If it's not in writing—or somehow recorded—it never happened; and (2) Beware: Your current client is your potential adversary when or if things go astray. That is to say, when you lose the case for any reason, even if it's not due to anything you, the lawyer, did or did not do; get ready for some pushback. There are clients who will perceive the loss as your fault, quite apart from anything he or she did in the matter to contribute to the result. Then again, some people are just sore losers and will inflict pain upon those closest to them, often their lawyer, because no one else can stand to be near them by the time their case is over.

Though it seems obvious in a lawsuit that, in the end, one party will be the loser, and the other will win; some clients just don't view it like that. In fact, sometimes even the winner is a loser. Like Voltaire said, there were only two times in his life when he was financially ruined—once when he lost a lawsuit; and another, when he won one. But no one reads Voltaire anymore, and we are poorer for it.

Like I was taught, the best defense is a good recording. Long before the Ethan estate case, I invested in a gadget allowing me to preserve telephone conversations from my analog office landline, after obtaining the required consent from the recordee, as one should in New York, and must in Massachusetts. That way I was prepared when the "former" client filed an ethics complaint alleging that I did or said whatever they claimed. Then, when I received the complaint from the Bar, instead of mourning my fate and cursing the gods, I could simply search my computer for the audio files of my former client cursing at me and refusing to provide documents that were subpoenaed. When located, I would provide the Bar Investigators with this aural record of slurs, calumny, and assignations (the attorney – client privilege is waived on account of the complaint) and voila. I was spared years of misery trying to disprove a negative (that I didn't say what was alleged) and the case was dismissed.

All this in mind before calling Ms. Taylor, I dug around in my orphaned electronics drawer searching for my personal digital audio recorder among old cell phones, adapters, and chargers. Locating my trusty recorder, I plugged it into the handset jack of my desk phone and checked its voice activation function and time and date stamping. All systems were a go. I undertook a quick Internet search of the number that Ms. Taylor's ex-attorney provided. I learned that it belonged to a mobile phone issued by AT&T and that the area code was a fairly new one for Los Angeles. Now, I was ready to speak with Lyndsey, learn what she wanted from me, and what I could get from her.

"Hello," said a woman whose voice conveyed recent slumber.
"Ms. Taylor?"
"Yes."
"This is Kate Bergin, returning your call and recording as we speak."

I then asked her permission to continue this recorded conversation.

"Go ahead, Ms. Bergin. I have nothing to hide. Record away."
"You may call me Kate. May I call you Lyndsey?"
"Of course."
"Lyndsey, you reached out to me. What can I do for you?"
"I want to help you help me get my inheritance."

"What did you have in mind?" I asked.

"I want to help you with my dad's estate."

"Your dad's estate? The California superior court denied your motion to intervene, Lyndsey. What do you think I can do for you?"

"Prove I'm his daughter, like his will requires. That's why he changed it, or at least it's one of the reasons."

"I don't agree with your interpretation of what the codicil requires."

She harrumphed and stated slowly, "We need to get the court to order DNA tests showing that Richard Ethan and I are half brother and sister."

"I've thought about that. I don't think Richard will agree to submit to a sibling DNA test at this point, do you?"

"I don't know, but can't you can dig up our father if you have to."

"Actually, there's nothing to dig up. Warren Ethan was cremated and his remains were scattered off the coast of Malibu."

Lyndsey paused and replied, "That's because Richard knew I'd want this test."

"Maybe. I thought it's because Warren loved the Pacific Ocean." I paused, no reaction. People lose their senses of humor during financial battles over dead bodies, relatives or not. "What's your plan B?" I asked.

"It's your plan B, too, isn't it, Kate? I mean, don't you have to search for the truth?"

"I have to do what's best for the Ethan estate and the trust and its beneficiaries, not follow your agenda, Ms. Taylor."

I used her surname for effect. I would learn the truth to serve Warren's interests, not hers. Yet, if Lyndsey was his child, she was a lawful beneficiary and Warren would've known that and composed his will in such a way that she would partake.

Lyndsey spoke again, "Please get the DNA test and then I will help you."

"You are aware that that court will probably not grant that request as it already found that you were not a valid intervenor. As you were a party to the action, duly represented by counsel, you are bound by the court's ruling unless you file an appeal or seek reconsideration. If you do neither, you don't have any standing in the dispute. Speak to your former attorney about that."

"I don't understand. Why won't you help me?" Lyndsey sounded hurt.

"I don't represent you or your interests. If you want to revisit the court's order, there are ways to go about it. That's all I can say."

"What if I can get the DNA test results for you without an order?"

"I would address that when it happened. Is there anything else you would like to discuss?"

"What's going on with the money?"

"Right now that's not your concern."

"Yeah, but it will be."

"Maybe. Lyndsey, I understand what you want, and I've told you what you can do."

"We'll talk again, Kate."

With that, Ms. Taylor clicked off the line. I wondered why Lyndsey didn't ask for the DNA testing in her motion papers when she sought to intervene. I guess it's like they say, you don't want a cheap surgeon, dentist, or lawyer, because usually you'll get what you pay for. Had Lyndsey's attorney made the application for a buccal swab of Rick's cheek, the judge just might have granted it and ordered it performed then and there. That would've been something. Oh well.

I checked my digital recording for clarity and correct time and date stamping. Satisfied all was well, I compressed the large audio file into smaller ones for transmission to California via email. Given Mr. Beck's lack of computing skills—or a computer, for that matter—I wondered how he would extract these files for listening. In any case, that was NMP (not my problem). I fulfilled my duty to share with him as my co-trustee and was on to the next thing.

At some point during my Lyndsey call, Celeste left the office for the evening and all my files were in order. Tomorrow I'd be in court to argue a discovery motion on behalf of one of my clients. I spent time reviewing the materials, but couldn't delete the content and tone of Lyndsey's voice from my short term memory. Something about her unsettled me. She seemed too slick, but somehow earnest. Her former attorney was right, she was compelling, but I wasn't sure if that was so in a good way or bad. But I wouldn't worry about it, until I heard Beck's reaction to the conversation, if I ever did.

CHAPTER NINE

My legal adversary on the Cape, whose office was in Chatham—the Cape's elbow, or mid Cape—didn't believe in having his client answer interrogatories or produce documents or respond to requests for admissions, all of which made him vulnerable to my legal machinations. Today, I was seeking not only the material (i.e., "discovery") to which I was entitled; but also to impose monetary sanctions for this obstructionist behavior. Meanwhile, my poor client, who was not financially deprived, but emotionally bereaved, was left to face life without her beloved toy poodle, Touché, who with a teary eye (the poodle's) had gone to see the Chatham Veterinarian—now known as the defendant—and died. My client explained that Touché had suffered from too much tearing (epiphora) caused by an ingrown eyelash (distachiasis).

This painful and unsightly condition was supposed to have been resolved by a simple operation to clear the doggy's eye duct and remove the offending follicle. I suspected that the defendant vet overdid the 2,6-diisopropylphenol (propofol), but failed to intubate and ventilate the pooch, which would have enabled him to breathe again. Plus, I had a lawyer's hunch that this veterinarian forgot to give Touché an analgesic to go with the anesthesia. If true (and I would need answers to my discovery requests to find out for sure), it would mean that the poor poodle underwent surgery without a pain killer. Though unable to move once the scalpel made the first cut into his eyelid, Touché would have felt the knife and the restraints until he stopped breathing. No one wants to think about a beloved pet enduring that kind of pain and suffering, and I was hoping for a sensible settlement, once all the facts were assembled. I was entitled to receive the veterinarian's notes and other records, which he or his attorney, to date, refused to provide.

After righteous argument and a yeoman's effort, I won the right to obtain my requested documents from the defendant veterinarian, but not to have the poodle viewed, under the law of the Commonwealth of Massachusetts, as a special companion, who just happened to be canine. In a moment of sharing from the bench, the judge told my adversary and me that he was particularly fond of his twenty-year-old Titleist Blade putter, and would be utterly distraught if someone damaged it; but, like Touché, the putter was after all, just a thing—a chattel, not a companion chattel. I did, however, win the right to move forward on my wrongful doggy death and veterinary malpractice counts and seek damages equal to reimbursement for the costs of the eye surgery, as well as the loss of Touché, considering whatever distinctive value this pet might have had to his owner, my client. On account of this last part of the ruling, the judge had found that Touché (the putter-like chattel) was indeed special to my lady and that there was a higher price to pay for allowing this dog to die.

Since Touché's owner was not in court to witness the argument and hear the result firsthand, I called her to relate the news. While not exactly pleased, she understood the import of the judge's ruling and authorized me to proceed as I thought best. She needed some acknowledgment of the vet's wrongdoing and of the grief and loss he caused her to suffer. I understood and called the vet's lawyer with my opening demand, fifty grand. I was sure to hear back soon.

Celeste was next on my list of calls from court and I told her the news. It was a respectable showing, all things considered, in this dog eat dog peninsula cum island (ever since the canal was dug through what was a Pilgrim portage between Buzzards and Cape Cod Bays). I told Celeste that if I'd rubbed Mercy Otis Warren's petticoat, like I usually did before my court appearances, I probably would have gotten everything I'd asked for; but I didn't, and that was a lesson for the future. I assured Celeste that I'd be back to the office for a while to prepare some paperwork and then, off to fly. More hours in the left seat meant more time as PIC (pilot in command) and that brought me closer to the goal of a legacy carrier pilot, according to my career plan, part three.

Operating aircraft during the day, when the sky is clear enough for VFR (visual flight rules), is a straightforward task. You use your fishfinder (the automated traffic alert and collision avoidance system—T-CAS) and keep a keen eye out from the cockpit to avoid colliding into other aircraft. Even most amateur GA (general aviation) pilots can handle these conditions. But, when the visibility dwindles, you winnow the wheat from the chaff by relying on your instruments. Nearly fifty percent of the accidents involving weather are not because of thunderstorms or icing; but because someone—who's not instrument rated—flies into what pilots call marginal visual meteorological conditions (VMC) or IMC (instrument meteorological conditions), or what a passenger would call pea soup.

John Kennedy Jr.'s accident is a perfect example of this awful, but common, phenomenon. He was flying north towards the Vineyard from New Jersey at the worst time of the day, nautical twilight; during the trickiest season, summer. A clear July sunset in the New York Metro area with prevailing VMC (visual meteorological conditions) could trick you into thinking that you'll be able to see clearly when you arrive at the Cape or the islands; but you won't, because there are different factors at work. Down near the mid-Atlantic section of the Eastern Seaboard, the water is mild, affected by the warm and mighty Gulf Stream. As both the air and the water are tepid, there is less chance that blinding condensation will form; but as the water becomes colder up north from the frigid Canadian current, you can suddenly find yourself flying in the fog or heavy haze. If that happens, you must rely upon your instruments and observe IFR (instrument flight rules). If you are unable to do that, you lose situational awareness and often control of the airplane. When JFK Jr. approached Gayhead, he flew into marginal VMC (hazy night conditions) that confounded him because he was not proficient at controlling the aircraft on instruments. Without the use of his instruments, he lost clear view of the natural horizon, affecting his flight control inputs. He became disoriented with deadly consequences. As the NTSB said of the cause of the 1999 Kennedy crash, "the pilot's failure to maintain control of the airplane during a descent over water at night ... was a result of spatial disorientation."

When I'm planning a summer evening flight in New England, I'm focused. I decide the route I want to fly. Then, I get a good weather briefing for the departure, the climb out, en route, and the descent. I consider IFR departure and approach procedures. I review obstacle avoidance (trees, towers, tows) and as always, I do my normal preflight routines. As PIC (pilot in command) it's my aircraft and the PX (passengers) are in my charge. My life and honor are on the line each and every time I transport a living soul.

Years ago while visiting Pearl Harbor, on the decks of the Mighty Mo' or more formally, the USS Missouri, upon which the Japanese surrendered to the USA in 1945, I saw a plaque that hung outside the captain's quarters bearing a Joseph Conrad quote. From "Command at Sea," it described the ultimate responsibility of a captain for his ship, his crew, and his passengers. An air-faring captain is the progeny of the maritime kind. Transporting people via sky in my little metal tube is an awesome responsibility and I assume it with same solemn duty and integrity as the nautical captains who came before.

This Friday, I didn't give Steven Philips one thought until he showed up, alone, for the scheduled early evening trip to MVY (Vineyard Haven). I greeted him with a professional nod and continued my preflight duties. When it was time to board and give my safety briefing, I was friendly, but reserved. The takeoff was unremarkable, but en route the visibility at MVY deteriorated to 2,600 feet. If we wanted to make it to the Vineyard this evening—and not by way of New Bedford—I had to concentrate, and I did.

We had captured the glide slope and the Cessna settled into a stabilized approach. I glanced down from the instruments momentarily to review the MVY Runway 24 ILS missed approach procedure, and when I looked up, we had popped out of the weather into the clear, with the runway four miles ahead. The winds had picked up along with the chop that comes with gustier ground conditions. The bumpy ride and the clear view of the airport took Steven's attention away from his tablet.

With the strengthening crosswind, our crab increased to maintain the ground track toward the runway as we continued the approach. About a mile out I clicked off the autopilot. In the flare, Steven watched me kick in the rudder and lower the opposite wing, "cross controlling" and producing a decent slip to straighten out the Cessna. Still, the winds were blowing hard across the runway and caused us to touch down in a slight crab; but all was well, and we had "arrived."

We taxied close to the fence adjacent to the FBO where I was sure we'd see Ms. Lee waiting. We did. After I parked the plane, I led Steven down the airstair and stood close to the plane. He exited the Cessna and walked over to Lee. They appeared to speak to each other. I said nothing, but remained in the background, undetected, watching them closely. A lot can be learned from observing a person's nonverbal actions, warned my marital therapist back when I had a marriage. She said that as much as 80 percent of human communication was through body language, facial expression, and hand gestures. If true, Steven Philips was only 20 percent happy to see Lee. His words said "Hey there," but his body said nothing, in my view, anyway. No hands stretched out, his eyes did not narrow upwards, nor did his mouth form a smile. His affect was what my marital therapist would have called "flat," as she described Rick, who at the time was my husband.

Unlike the preppy and phlegmatic Steven, Lee was smoldering in her very unVineyard-like black, tight, short dress and five inch heels. For a high-end Boston-based interior decorator, I thought she lacked a sense of place and decorum. Just as I was smugly thinking that this Lee woman—barely wrapped in black spandex—was on borrowed Steven-time, I saw him smile and reach out to her, tenderly drawing her into his arms. They paused in an embrace and then he deeply kissed her. You didn't need a couples' therapist to recognize this full-body greeting between bonded lovers. Plainly, Lee and Steven were an intimate couple. Aristotle was right, there was no accounting for taste and bewitching was in the eye of the bewitched.

I cast my glance aside. I'd seen enough for now. I left my position on the ramp, checked my watch, and finished my paperwork for the trip just completed. My next leg departed in an hour and the weather conditions were deteriorating again. Eager to discuss my Ethan estate dilemma—as Steven promised—I waited until he and his woman unwrapped themselves. I approached them, still standing close together by the fence between the ramp and the GA terminal.

Steven saw me coming. "Lee," he said, "I need to speak with Captain Bergin for minute."

"My flight to Boston leaves in a few minutes, Steven," she replied tersely, obviously miffed.

Steven nodded. "Captain, would you mind waiting a few minutes, while I see Lee off?"

"Not at all. Have good flight."

Lee didn't respond.

"I'll meet you outside the pilot's lounge." I directed to Steven.

I made my way through the reception area of the terminal back to the pilots' lounge to check the weather on the computer. I was concerned that my next segment back to the Cape might have to cancel as runway visual range (RVR) continued to drop toward departure minimums. I called my base and spoke with flight ops to get its input. As I waited for feedback, I noticed Steven Philips standing in the doorway. I gave him a welcoming, but authoritative, captain-like nod to come inside the aviators' sanctuary. He did. Steven sat down next to me and listened while I engaged in pilot jargon with CAC's fight ops director. Apparently, my passenger/clients did not want to travel to Hyannis tonight because of the fog. They opted instead for a return trip tomorrow morning at 0800.

Since the trip back to Hyannis this evening would have been legal, and I was prepared for a departure, the passengers would pay for my overnight accommodations. I was directed to find lodging and report to the airfield at 0700 tomorrow, or 1100 Zulu. As I disconnected with my employer, I wondered if Steven would take me to dinner. In the midst of this happy contemplation, I heard Steven say something, but I wasn't paying attention, so I asked him to repeat it.

"Zulu time, remind me what that's about?" Steven asked.

"That's a compound question. Do you have two minutes for me to respond?"

"Sure, seems we both have some Zulu on our hands. Go on."

"Well, first the A, B, Cs of Aviation. Pilots use the standard ICAO (International Civil Aviation Organization) phonetic alphabet when they communicate in their aircraft with air traffic controllers. It helps to reduce errors in radiotelephony (RTF) that can be deadly. So, using the English alphabet, instead of saying "ESSSS" during a radio call, which can misheard as "EFFFF" depending on your native language, or the amount of static on the frequency, or the type of bourbon you drank..."

Steven looked horrified.

"That was a joke. As I was saying, we pilot use words instead, knowing that the first letter of the word is what's important. In the case of "S" ...

Steven interrupted, "You would use 'Steven.'"

"No, we'd say 'Sierra' pronounced, SEE-AIR-AH."

"What are the rest of the words?" Steven seemed interested.

"Alfa, Bravo, Charlie, Delta, Echo, Foxtrot, Golf, Hotel, India, Juliett, Kilo, Lima, Mike, November, Oscar, Papa, Quebec, Romeo, Sierra, Tango, Uniform, Victor, Whiskey, X-ray, Yankee, Zulu. Which brings us back to Zulu time, your original question."

"Right."

"Do you know about the Prime Meridian that runs through the British Naval Observatory in Greenwich, England and marks East longitude from West?"

"Yes. I'm familiar with that." Steven was slightly defensive.

"Well, in addition to being located at 0 degrees 0 minutes longitude, it's also zero time. Both the aviation and the military use it as their standard. It used to be called "Greenwich Mean Time," but now we refer to it as Universal Time Coordinated (UTC) or "Zulu" time, as the military expressed Greenwich Time by following it with a "Z" or "Zulu" and that stuck."

"I see."

"There's more. Zulu time is based upon a 24 hour clock, with the hours and minutes divided upon the rules of the Gregorian calendar. For instance, it's 6:18 p.m. now in Martha's Vineyard, E.D.T.; so it's 2218 Zulu time because we're -4 UTC. Do you understand?"

"Roger, that."

"I didn't teach you radio transmissions yet. You're getting ahead of yourself." I paused and smiled, then began again. "Steven, I want to discuss a financial matter with you, but I have to find a room for tonight. It's a summer weekend and the motel that CAC uses for crew rest is fully booked. Would you excuse me while I call the Vineyard's chamber of commerce for some help?"

"Don't do that, stay in my guest house."

"I don't know if that's appropriate."

"Of course it is. You can drive my car to the airport in the morning and Lee can drive it back when she returns tomorrow night."

Steven could see that I looked doubtful about this arrangement and he chimed in, "Don't worry Captain Kate, it's not a stick shift, you can handle it."

"Very funny." I hesitated and confirmed, "Sounds like a plan."

"I'll arrange for dinner and we can have our discussion then." Steven was direct, warm, and welcoming, or that's how I heard him.

He went to the parking lot to retrieve his car and said he'd be out front in ten minutes, but not to rush. That allowed me to change out of my uniform and into my civvies, which were my uniform without my stripped epaulets and tie. Before I left the FBO, I walked out to the ramp again. I was reassured by the sight of my Cessna 402's empennage outside the hangar, extending beyond the fuselage of a Citation that had parked beside it for the night.

When I emerged from the little airport structure housing the general aviation FBO, I was not surprised to find a late model, black Range Rover pull up to the curb. Steven got out, grabbed my brain bag and my rollabout and walked me around to the passenger side. I hopped in and noticed that this car was recently colonized by a woman. A make-up case was in the side pocket of the passenger door. There were Chanel sunglasses on the dash, and an umbrella of feminine design and fabric on the back floor mat. A faint scent of Hermes Perfume 24 Faubourg clung to the automobile's interior. I guessed that Lee, or another woman, left this detritus to make her mark on this territory. I might have done the same had I been in that position. A as mere a visitor heading to a guest house, I simply observed. Besides, I was interested in picking Steven's brain about the estate money, not his personal issues—for now.

We headed southeast towards Edgartown from MVY, leaving West Tisbury behind. As we drove down Herring Creek Road, I felt compelled to ask Steven why I never flew him to or from Katama Airpark Airport (1B2), a classic little field with three turf runways, open late spring through late summer and located right in the heart of his town. He explained that he preferred his airports with asphalt surfaces and more technology, so he could get to and from the Vineyard with fewer weather worries. I couldn't argue with that. Katama was literally a grassy "field." It was safe, but perhaps a little rough around the edges for most passengers. Its informal motto: "Life is short, fly your grass off," said it all. Still, there were good weather days in the Vineyard when Steven could fly within a few blocks of his backyard if he'd opted for Katama. Maybe we'd do that next time and enjoy an early coffee at The Right Fork Diner at the airfield.

We pulled into a very long driveway. Steven's island home was a waterfront estate off Forever Wild Way. Where else would it be located? We parked. Steven headed to the main house. "Candace will take your luggage and show you the way. See you soon."

Candace, a young woman in a short skirt and a sleeveless knit shirt escorted me from the car to the guesthouse near the eastern boundary of the property. The wood clad structure to which I'd been led had its own littoral access, yet didn't obstruct the spectacular water view of the main house.

"The fridge is stocked with fruit, yogurt, water, and juice. Please feel free to help yourself." She handed me a card with her name: Candace; her title: Personal Assistant; and mobile number. "Just call if you need anything. Mr. Philips will be by in an hour."

"Thanks."

When she departed, I looked about my quarters and gazed through the large picture window, admiring the neat green lawn and beyond that, a shoreline blurred by the dusky haze. From the outside, you'd never guess that this seashell of a cottage had the feeling of a small Buddhist temple at its core. Its interior was light and airy, even at dusk. Open and uncluttered, except for the cozy intimate corners, the space was perfect for contemplation and Zen acquisition. "O—M" I said to myself, out loud. The furnishings and accessories of deep wood and natural textures bore a soft island influence, but not Northern Atlantic. There were no navy blue stripes, ship wheels, or nautical themes found here. It was more subtle and exotic than that. Polynesian was my guess, with a few pieces of South Pacific indigenous sculpture, paintings, and prints displayed throughout. The Asian-styled bedroom and spa-like ensuite were appropriately private. Calming and restorative, I'd be fine staying in this space—for a few years—until Lee moved out of the main house.

By the time the knock came, I was dozing on the sofa in my new sanctuary. Steven was at the door dressed in shorts and a nice polo shirt.

I was wearing a fresh white blouse from my rollabout, but the same black pants I wore during the flight.

"Are you comfortable?"

"Yes, thanks. This is a lovely place."

"Lee redecorated it." Steven glanced towards the sea, "The sun won't set for a bit. Want to take a walk along the beach before dinner?"

"Yes, please. Lead the way."

And he did. As we strolled down the lawn, I asked Steven about Candace, the young woman who accompanied me from the car to the guest house. He said she was an Edgartown girl who Lee had hired to help with household chores and to run errands. Candace did not live-in, but was local, dependable, and took good care of the Philips Vineyard Manor and its occupants whenever they arrived. As we walked towards the water Steven explained that he didn't own all that much beach, maybe a few hundred feet or so, and after that, we'd be trespassing on his neighbor's shoreline.

It's a funny thing about Massachusetts littoral rights. Unlike most other states, the rich really can own the coast and keep the public from enjoying it. Under an old law enacted in Pilgrim times, the owner of waterfront land had title (or fee simple absolute) down to the mean low tide mark, where the ocean met the sand, soil, or rocks at the lowest ebb. That's a lot of Bay State seaside placed in private hands. But there's a catch: while you may own the underlying land (or sand or rock), you cannot own the "tide" above it. This legal quirk allows strangers to swim alongside a private beach so long as they continue swimming or treading water, keeping their toes from touching the private ground beneath the waves.

The Pilgrims, however, were apparently as pragmatic as they were didactic because their ordinance provided a narrow range of exceptions, allowing access to a private beach—bottom and all—for "fishing, fowling, or navigation."

Consequently, since the first Thanksgiving in 1621, sophisticated Bay State beach aficionados have armed themselves with any combination of poles, kayaks, or weapons (to shoot birds) whenever they sought to wade over another Massachusite's land and linger a while without being arrested or drowning. It's an amusing legal oddity and I wondered how many people tried accessing Steven's private beach in this way.

So I asked, "What do you do with your trespassers?"

"I don't have a trespasser problem." Steven. said.

"Oh, why not?"

"I have a pump action shotgun and chamber a round when someone's illegally on my sand."

"I see. So when the would-be bathers or water fowlers hear the unmistakable sound of your Remington, they swim off or escape through your neighbor's estate?" I couldn't help sounding sarcastic.

"Yes, but some fire off their own birdshot rounds in protest, and then leave. You have to respect that."

I was speechless for a moment not knowing exactly how to respond. Steven spoke up, "And that is why some have called me a Masshole—to this very day."

No doubt, I thought to myself, but remained silent, thinking about the wife and daughters he left for the interior decorator. Still I was curious about this waterfront after hearing how this urbane Harvard-trained lawyer and financier resolved simple property

trespass issues. I wanted to see more of this beach—"his beach"—
with permission of course.

During our walk, Steven asked how I came to live and practice
on the Cape. Withholding my Cape Cod roots, I deflected the question
with grace and then, asked him if he grew up in the area.

"Sort of, my sister and I spent summers at my dad's family's
compound."

I let it go at that. The word "compound" told me all I needed
to know about Steven's background. The sky grew dark as the sun
sank in the west and the damp air cooled as we walked along his strip
of ocean inlet. I was not dressed for the elements and was feeling
cold.

"It's getting a bit chilly," I said.

He nodded. "Let's get back," and we headed up from the
shore.

I'd been a guest at the Blue Heron Farm in my former life, and
Steven's house was a facsimile of that famous presidential vacation
spot, at least from the outside. We entered the clapboard sheathed
house through the solid wood door. Steven explained that while this
home was not old, it was constructed using lumber recovered from a
church that was demolished in western Massachusetts. Yet, this large
house was just as deceiving on the inside as the small cottage was.

I expected a luxurious New England coastal-style home like so
many in Nantucket and on the Vineyard. Instead, I entered an area of
Asian-inspired simplicity and straight lines. If the cottage was a little
temple of tranquility; this mansion was a monastery of infinite, yet
uncluttered abundance. Both interiors shared a minimalist vibe, but
this enormous house was built and decorated on a far grander scale
with higher walls, larger windows, and museum quality American
paintings displayed throughout and hung gallery-style. I had to give
Lee credit. She was good at what she did: home building; home
wrecking. Whatever. I wasn't the wife whose life she crashed and
stole.

While I preferred the artwork from the late nineteenth or early
twentieth centuries, Steven's, or Lee's, taste ran to mid-century
modern. This evening I bore witness to how a large orange square by
Josef Albers can be a thing of beauty and contemplation when placed
in the correct setting. That lustrous recycled wood on the floor and
those expansive warm-toned white walls provided the perfect
backdrop for the canvasses by Jasper Johns and Jackson Pollock.

There was no mistaking the money that a career in finance could generate when you looked at the material and contents of this island manse.

After our lobster and corn on the cob dinner—catered, not cooked, by my host—we sat for a while, nursing a bottle of good California cabernet sauvignon and speaking about New England. Steven was easy company, very smooth and rich, like the wine. Then, I got down to business and explained the situation concerning Epcot. He listened with interest.

"I have some statements that I received in Manhattan. May I show them to you?"

"Yes."

"They're in my rollabout in the cottage. I'll go get them."

"I'll go with you."

We walked from the main house to the cottage. Steven wanted to know how I became the executor of Warren Ethan's estate in a case venued in Los Angeles. Again, I graciously deflected the query and demurred, nursing whatever mystery I could generate. Instead of answering the unanswerable, I changed the topic and asked him about the interior decoration of the house and cottage.

"The Asian décor is elegant and tranquil, an inspired choice in nautical New England." I offered.

"Thanks, my wife and I spent several years in Hong Kong at the beginning of my financial career. We furnished the cottage with items we picked up in the Cook Islands."

"What about the main house?" I asked Steven.

"Getting just the right look and feel for the main house proved more of a challenge, so my wife hired an interior decorator that her best friend recommended."

"Lee?" I confirmed what he'd told me back in New Bedford.

"Yes."

Silence.

Then Steven spoke again, "Lee brokers artwork, too. She found the paintings you saw hanging on the walls."

"She found them?" I wanted to clarify the nature of that transaction.

"She thought they'd work well in the space and sold them to me—actually, to my trust in the Cayman Islands."

"I see." I replied while calculating in my head the enormous commissions that Lee must have made on the sale of those works to Steven's trust in a famous tax haven.

As we approached the cottage, the haze distorted the edges of the building—or it was the wine going to my head.

Steven opened the door, which we'd left unlocked.

"Shall we sit?" Steven suggested.

He started for a Japanese-inspired sofa with a low table before it. I left the living space to retrieve the envelope. When I returned from the bedroom, he was seated and wearing a pair of reading glasses that I'd not seen before. He reached out for the envelope and removed the documents. I remained standing as he read.

"Kate, this has nothing to do with my line of work. These are just hedge fund statements. I'm a private equity guy. I make deals. I don't do what Perkin does and have never worked with him or Epcot."

"So you can't help me?" I was disappointed.

"Only if you want to me to run the numbers. I don't mind taking a look.

"Please do. But I'm missing the last two years' worth. Warren's attorney, who represented him for most of his life, has them. Chase, the company comptroller, gave them to him."

"Do you think that was appropriate?"

"I didn't think it was inappropriate? Am I missing something?"

"Yes, two years of statements."

I nodded. "Obviously."

"Can I keep these statements over the weekend and get back to you?"

"Do you promise to keep them confidential?"

"No, I want to run them by my numbers guy. But he'll keep them confidential between us. Is that good enough?"

I hesitated.

"Kate, I'm trying to help you. If you don't feel comfortable, take them back." He handed them to me.

"No, you go ahead, I'm allowed to have you look, I just can't pay you until the court approves." I said, still standing. "I need to know if this fund is a safe place for the money or whether I should request a withdrawal now and place it in something more liquid— more transparent."

"We'll check it out. Here's a better number to reach me." He handed me another of his business cards with a different handwritten phone number on the back.

As I thanked him and took the card, I noticed Steven make the same gesture that President George H. W. Bush made during a 1992 town hall debate, which, some pundits speculated, led to his loss that November. Steven wasn't so smooth after all and I let him know it.

"Okay, I get it. We're done."

Steven looked up at me quizzically, saying nothing.

"Your actions shout more clearly than words." I told him.

"What are you talking about?"

"The surest way to end a conversation is to glance at your watch." I noted.

"You're good." Admittedly busted, Steven was slightly apologetic in tone.

"Subtle you are not. I bet you're all kinds of fun playing charades."

"Not great at charades, but I do like a game of poker."

"Who doesn't? I asked.

"Duly noted." Steven smiled in return.

Amused, we agreed it was past time for sleep. As he rose to leave with my envelope of Perkin statements, Steven's mobile phone rang and he took the call. It was Lee and he excused himself and said good night. We'd both had a full day and I had to fly early in the morning. I enjoyed myself and was confident that Steven would help me understand the nature of Perkin's Epcot fund, if he could. As for moving Lee out of the Vineyard Manse, I could not say when that would happen.

CHAPTER TEN

It was summer on the Cape, which meant you'd find mostly thick, gray haze in the air from dusk to dawn. Sure, we'd get a clear blue sky by the late morning burn off. Then, there'd be just enough brightness by midafternoon to lull everyone into forgetting what a temperate maritime climate produces after the warm Cape air meets the surrounding Atlantic Ocean in the evening, cooled by Canadian Labrador Current. The past weekend brought poor weather for flying but that didn't deter the crowds. The Cape and the islands were teeming with visitors. Your average American tourists remain on Cape Cod for their vacation; while the wealthy, new and old, leave for Nantucket or the Vineyard or even Block Island and fill the airplanes, which was good for CAC and good for me.

My flying career was not lucrative. When you consider the responsibility and the training costs, I earned a meager wage for those hours in the air, but I was gaining crucial experience. Working for CAC allowed me to accumulate more PIC (pilot in command) hours. Amassing this type of time was sin qua non to securing a position in the big leagues—the legacy carriers. Once I got my foot in one of their cockpits, I would have to serve time in the right seat for a while, yanking some captain's gear and listening to him go on and on during a four day trip or whatever it would be. I know this because my flying colleagues who've gone on to fly bigger and better aircraft have returned to tell these tales of FO (first officer) woe; when all you hear about is the captain's wives, his alimony, his child support, his children (emancipated and not) from the various moms (estranged and not); his girlfriends, and anything else that crosses his mind at about 33,000 feet. They say you know it's a long trip when on day five, the captain says to his long suffering FO, "Now, enough about me; let me tell you about my boat."

While it may sound amusing, my brethren assure me it's a bore, but a necessary part of the training. They endure these self-loving, insensitive captains until the day that they, too, can torment the next batch of long-suffering FOs coming up from the minors. Despite these complaints, the guys who are now flying for Delta or United, or what have you, clearly enjoy going to work. Flying in a small Cessna for short hops around New England, or New York every now and again, is certainly a different experience than getting in your new Boeing 737-900. I could hardly wait.

Meanwhile, my law office was as busy as ever and Celeste and I were swamped. I believed in a good wage for honest labor and that's what I got from Celeste, and then some. So what if sometimes I met payroll with my own divorce settlement money. We were making a difference in our clients' lives and that elevated our spirits and made our work meaningful, despite the costs. I now represented an accident victim, seriously injured when she fell off a deck of a local lobster shanty restaurant. Normally this kind of case would not generate a large settlement or verdict, but my client was a high profile ladies golf professional. Due to the permanence of the shoulder injury she sustained, she'd never return to the LPGA tour. She consequently lost not only her sport, but her vehicle for stardom and commercial success. I figured this injury cost her millions in lost pay and endorsement deals.

Within weeks of meeting her, I had secured her treating surgeon's report, the accident reconstruction report, an engineer's report concerning the condition of the wooden deck and the railing she fell through, a sports economist's report on her lost earnings, and the restaurant surveillance camera tape capturing that fateful moment when this woman's heel got stuck in that deck plank and she lost her balance. My legal ace in the hole was that my client, like me, was raised in Wellfleet and attended UMass. I was certain that by the end of the case, settled or tried, she'd be financially secure at age 32, despite her inability to swing a club like a pro ever again.

Looking forward to such worthy and rewarding litigation, I was in a good mood when Steven called my office. But he was all business and no pleasure. He explained in great detail what he and his quant (numbers guy) found poring over the Epcot statements, reports, and private offering documents I'd given him that night on the Vineyard. Initially, he sounded perplexed, explaining that although the reports and initial documents detailed an investing philosophy, he did not see it implemented. Plus, given the ROI (return on investment) reflected in the account, Steven wasn't able to verify the processes Perkin used to generate those consistently good, nonvolatile returns for Epcot's investors, year after year (noting that the most recent statements he'd inspected were now more than two years old).

Steven broke it down so I could understand the financial intricacies at hand. Instead of finding the highly variable returns that he and his expert expected with a fund that specialized in distressed debt and businesses undergoing restructuring and reorganization, Steven found a consistency that disturbed him and a ROR (rate of return) that neither he, nor his numbers guy, could ever replicate. No fund he'd reviewed for comparison had replicated it either, year after year. Unlike the reports claiming that the fund was growing from its diverse market investments, it seemed to Steven and his quant that Perkin was engaging in a scheme of a totally different stripe.

Given Perkin's boast of steady returns of over ten percent per year regardless of whether the market as a whole had advanced or declined, Steven spoke of a "split strike conversion" strategy in which a money manager would buy stocks of selected corporations that were included in the blue-chip Standard & Poor's 100 Index. Then, simultaneously, he'd buy put options below the current stock price to protect against large declines. He'd also sell call options above the current price to fund the purchase of put options. The call options, Steven explained, would also, to some degree, limit any gains that would be earned on the underlying stocks. (So much for clarity, I thought.) So far as he could figure, a split strike conversion executed perfectly could not generate the returns that were reflected on Warren's account statements. This phantom strategy made Steven suspicious; it made me feel stupid.

More disconcerting to Steven was that his confidential sources on the Street confirmed that Morgan Stanley was not the custodian for the securities Perkin managed, nor did Morgan Stanley clear Epcot trades—despite what was represented in the documents Perkin generated. That meant Perkin appeared to be running an operation where he was trading without a known broker and without a third party custodian for the funds. This one man shop style was verboten at the best funds because there was no way to track the trades in real time. The wealthy might trust someone like Perkin with their fortune, but generally not without a method to verify what he was doing.

There was even more evidence to raise the red flags according to Steven. As Mike noticed earlier, Epcot's quarterly statements, on Perkin's office stationery, disclosed only the value of Warren's account and the appreciation during the prior quarter. From these statements, Steven gathered that Perkin ostensibly exited the equities market at the end of each quarter and placed the proceeds into Treasuries. While there was nothing technically wrong with this approach, Steven viewed it dimly—as did Mike, I recalled.

Neither Steven nor his quant could conceive of any good reason for a trading strategy to consistently exit the market at the end of every quarter, unless it was to mask what was going on during the quarter. After all, at least some of the time, one could expect investment conditions and opportunities to span the days between the end of one quarter and the beginning of the next. What's more, there were no electronic trade confirmations provided in the documents Perkin gave me. In Steven's view, no one today would try to use an old-fashioned paper trail to report trades or account balances when there was universal access to electronic data—at least there should be.

Although I didn't understand everything he told me, I was clear on his tone. He didn't like what he saw and worse, Steven, a financial pro's pro, didn't understand what lie beneath the surface of what he read and calculated.

"Is it possible that Perkin was investing in private equity deals through Epcot?" Recalling what Mike Fortune said during our luncheon.

"No one I've checked with has done any deals with Perkin or Epcot, so I doubt it." Steven replied grimly.

"What should I do?" I was disturbed and eager to fix whatever problems I had, in a sense, inherited.

"Get the estate money out of there—like yesterday." He paused. "Kate, what you've got now is ... trouble. Trust me."

"Steven, I appreciate the time you've taken on this. It's a lot to digest."

"No problem. It's what I do. Tell me when you have the money out and I'll help you park it safely, if you want."

"I'll let you know. Thanks again."

"Okay. Bye." He hung up.

I was not quite panicked, but close. I felt I'd been warned that something wasn't right and that I had to do whatever was necessary to remove the money now. Time, according to Steven was not on my side, though he never explicitly stated why. I didn't relish the thought of calling the unbearable Thomas Beck and asking him to join my request for a court order to withdraw Warren's millions out of Perkin's fund, as Steven urged; but I felt I had no other option.

Using the same high tech technique as before—my landline from my storefront law office on Route 28 in Hyannis—I called the law clerk in beautiful southern California and asked for an emergent hearing by phone as soon as the judge could accommodate me. When she inquired into the nature of my emergency, since I couldn't think of any other way to state it, I blurted out: I have reason to believe that Warren Ethan's estate might be in jeopardy. The law clerk replied, "I see" and asked me to hold on.

Expressing earnest concern for the financial safety of an enormous estate seemed to be the magical incantation that opened the courthouse doors via phone line. I was told that the court would hear my order to show cause later that afternoon and to give my co-trustee telephone notice of the application. Meanwhile, I was to send any supporting documents to both Mr. Beck and the court. Sounded good, but Steven had my documents in his Bain office and Mr. Beck had possession of the most recent Perkin statements, so I'd call both men and ask each to cooperate, and why wouldn't they?

Each man apparently had his own reasons for obstinacy. First, I called the new number Steven gave me for his office and was put through immediately. Apparently I had been elevated to a higher status of contact. Even I was impressed and wandered if Lee received the same treatment. When I heard Steven's voice on the line I told him what I'd done in response to his analysis of Epcot and warning to get Warren's money out of the fund.

"Steven, it would help me if you would sign an affidavit that I've prepared from the detailed notes I took during our earlier phone call."

There was a pregnant pause.

"Kate, you're doing the right thing but I cannot serve in any official capacity in your estate case." Steven said politely, yet firmly,

"Is there any way to change your mind?"

"No."

"Then I need you to transmit to the court and to Mr. Beck's firm all the Epcot materials I've given you. You can use a 'blind' fax. That way, the statements will reach their targets in time for the telephonic return of my application, but there will be no way to tie them to you or to Bain."

Our conversation was direct and short. Steven appreciated my respecting his privacy—which I didn't, I simply wanted him to send the statements and sign my affidavit. I reminded him that I filed this emergent application because of his advice. Steven acknowledged my efforts by confirming that I was taking the correct action as the guardian of that money and the trust's beneficiaries; but that my duties as executor didn't change his mind. Steven didn't want the exposure and couldn't afford the time or commitment to become an expert or even a fact witness for me. He tried to make his denial easier to swallow by affirming he'd transmit the statements from his office and offering to guide me on the QT.

"Kate, I'll be here, deep in the background if you run into trouble or need additional assistance on financial matters. So long as you're discrete, I'm available to help. You can pick my brain, privately, for free; but not in any official or public position."

"Will you at least sign this affidavit based on what you told me earlier?"

"No. I offered to help you, personally, privately; not to be involved in litigation."

"I won't win without your affidavit explaining what you told me about Perkin. Please, sign it. You don't have to become the expert, just the guy who confirms that we should get the money out of Epcot." I pleaded with Steven.

"Kate, just tell the probate judge what you want and why."

I sighed. "You went to law school. You know as well as I do that I need evidence to support my application. No judge will just 'take my word for it.' Steven, I need you on the phone this afternoon or to sign the affidavit."

"I can't help you with that. Take what I've given you and do your job. Gotta go." Steven hung up and broke my heart.

My call to Thomas Beck was worse than expected. He sneered that I was out of my league and had no right interfering with the orderly administration of justice. Then, Beck arrogantly reminded me how he allowed me to remain in this case and didn't join my ex and the rest of Warren's rightful heirs who sought to remove me for cause. He ended the scolding by stating that Warren, if alive, would be disgusted and worse, disappointed by my conduct and lack of fundamental legal skill.

I reacted to this ad hominem attack by remaining calm and focused. I did not respond to contempt with the same. That hardly ever solved a problem and I saw no upside to escalating the disagreement with this disagreeable man. His comments about how poorly Warren would now view me pricked my heart for a minute. Generally, I didn't want to disgust or disappoint anyone and certainly not my former-father-in-law who overall, treated me kindly; but, I felt better recalling that it was this same man who, at the end of his life, secretly put me—and me alone—in charge of his charitable trust. Somewhat reinforced by my self-soothing internal dialogue, I emphatically informed Mr. Beck that we'd have to agree to disagree and that he should expect some paperwork via facsimile and a phone conference in a few hours per the court's directive. Then, we'd let her be judge, as it were.

The time between the calls to Steven and Thomas Beck was filled with my trying to get Mike on the phone to back up what Steven told me about Epcot. Unfortunately, Mike was in court and unavailable. I would be on my own, hoping that the Epcot statements Steven promised to send to Beck's office and the court's chambers would contain marginalia expressing the same disturbing findings and warnings that Steven's quant found and that Steven discussed with me earlier in the day.

At the appointed time, I called the law clerk as directed. Within seconds, Mr. Beck was on the line, too. The law clerk confirmed the caption of the case and repeated the stated reasons for my application for emergent relief. Over Mr. Beck's condescending remarks, the law clerk told us to remain on the line and the judge would join us when she was free.

After what seemed like forever, but was only five minutes, the silence was broken by the words, "Good afternoon, Counsel. It's late here, but it's very late for you on the East Coast. My law clerk has informed me, Ms. Bergin, that you seek an immediate order of withdrawal from the Epcot fund."

I responded in the affirmative. The judge read from a list of allegations I'd made and asked if it accurately reflected my concerns. I said it did and tried to argue once again, why Warren's money should not remain in Epcot with the inscrutable Mr. Perkin. Mr. Beck remained cordially mute when I was addressing the judge. Then, as I anticipated, he was seething when it was his turn to speak. In a pompous manner, he did not argue, but rather, advised the court that I was ignorant, unsophisticated, and above all, lacked evidence that the Epcot fund was anything but reliable and safe, as it had been for Warren and his money for many years.

In rebuttal, I reargued—without mentioning his name or his firm—what Steven's analysis revealed, perhaps not fully comprehending all that he'd imparted, but nearly reading from my verbatim notes, reemphasizing his final, ominous warning to get that money out of that fund. But there was no escaping what I lacked for today's application. I was not a fact or expert witness. The words of an advocate, without more, were not enough for victory. The court was sympathetic and articulated her desire to safeguard the corpus, but without testimony or proof that the funds were in danger, she was bound by law to deny my request, without prejudice. I could refile my application but would have to support it with corroborating evidence that a judge could hang her hat on; not mere argument, as she gently characterized today's effort.

After ruling against me, the judge expressed sympathy for my concern and swift action, albeit without the proper proofs. In consolation I thought, the judge confirmed that Mr. Beck was to provide me with copies of the most recent Epcot statements that he'd obtained from Chase after Warren's death. Meanwhile, I was to produce for Mr. Beck all the material acquired from my New York meeting with Perkin that was not already shared, and anything else I wanted to put before the court in this case. It all made sense and was a practical way forward.

Mr. Beck took exception to the court's sua sponte ("of one's own will") rulings and demanded a stay, warning the court that he'd file an appeal. The court, not cowed by Thomas Beck's imperious table pounding, promptly denied his request and reiterated that he and I both were to exchange the financial statements within a week or sanctions would apply.

Before the judge ended the conference she reminded Beck and me that we were working together, yet it seemed to her that we thought of ourselves as adversaries. It puzzled her. She urged us to review our common goal and do what we could to discharge our given duties under the will and testamentary trust. Her final comment was directed to my co-executor, co-trustee, "Mr. Beck, you had no official capacity in Mr. Ethan's final codicil as written. You filed an application to join Ms. Bergin as a co-administrator. I granted that motion on two grounds. The first, that Ms. Bergin did not oppose it. The second, based upon your proof of a forty-plus year professional relationship with the decedent. I am sure that Ms. Bergin expects you to work with her, not against her, or perhaps she'll make an application to remove you for cause? Good day."

In all, a mixed bag. I prevailed in the sense that the court understood my concerns about the safety of the corpus to fund the veterans' trust fund. I lost because the court denied my application for immediate relief and an order commanding Mr. Perkin to release the funds. To some extent my credibility had been tarnished for not backing up in filed papers what I said I could prove. In reflection, I was guilty of using bad judgment. I filed an emergency application thinking that I could rely upon Steven as a witness. I was wrong.

Despite my personal attraction to him and my professional interest in him, I guess there was something to Mike's warning that Steven Philips was not someone to take for granted. Lesson learned: Don't think you know someone when you don't—especially if he cheats on his wife with her interior decorator. I surmised that Steven liked me well enough to put me up in a guest house and spend a few hours reviewing a bunch of financial statements to show off his knowledge and power; but not enough to place himself in any discomfort, much less personal constraint or public position of support. The enigmatic Steven Philips disappointed me and there's almost nothing worse than that.

A long week had passed since Steven brought me to the brink of desperation by scaring me to death about Epcot, and then, in my view, letting me down by refusing to back me up when I asked the court to grant me the relief that he said I sorely needed. Fortunately, Perkin and Epcot were status quo, and as far as I knew, Warren's wealth was safe and sound.

I was looking forward to receiving the most recent account statements from L.A. by the end of the day. My being on the East Coast cost Beck three hours to produce these documents. But I couldn't figure, why the secrecy? Why was Mr. Beck so irascible? Most people found me good company with an easy, if not slightly quirky, temperament. When I was Rick's wife, Mr. Beck was respectful and well-mannered, if not warm. Why the transition to beast? Isn't life hard enough when there's no money to fund a trust?

Here we had millions and millions to give away, but not to the recipients that Beck expected. What was it to him? Why would he care? Mr. Beck was never a beneficiary—was he? Now I wondered, maybe he was and that's why he was cantankerous. I wasn't sure what his problem was. Whatever. Life goes on, except, of course for Warren.

So, in loss there is always the consolation of philosophy. One can contemplate that the only constant in life is change and that one's character is one's destiny—and the like. There are also the comforts of the material world. My practice was becoming healthier, if not outright robust, considering its location and small staff: me and Celeste. The winter was impossible and the spring was tough. Our receivables had declined in the previous months and our collectibles increased. Yet, summer was looking green. Though my golf pro case was puttering along, my dog malpractice case settled quickly and generously, providing an unexpected windfall, proving what one of my favorite jurists said to me many years ago: You win your case in the pretrial phase by getting good evidentiary rulings and gathering excellent discovery. Surely, rubbing fellow Cape girl, Mercy Otis Warren's petticoat also helped.

Overall, I've found that sometimes simply asking the right questions, letting the other side know that you know what you want— and what they've got—is good enough to commence serious settlement discussions. I paid attention, Celeste typed her heart out, and between us two, the fees we generated were collected. I could pay the rent, Celeste's salary with a bit of a bonus, and all the other expenses for my office without spending my own money. Plus, for the first time in a long while, I allowed myself a draw. This was no small feat as I had been underwriting the practice from my personal divorce savings for some time. By the end of the spring, my bank account was nearly depleted after the lean months of barely getting by. These summer gains were welcome and necessary. Today we'd deposit a new two thousand dollar retainer, money out of the blue—literally.

"Ms. Bergin, your ten o'clock appointment is here." Celeste let me know at 9:06 a.m. I guess he or she was anxious to see me and showed up nearly an hour too soon for the appointment made this morning at eight. I try never to be late, but I am definitely not one to meet with a new client early, especially someone who calls that same day for an appointment, lest I seem desperate or too eager for the business—regardless of retainer size or how much I might need the money. One must maintain a certain distance and reserve—and it begins with how you handle time—yours and another person's. Both Perkin and Beck applied this time strategy when dealing with me to communicate their self-perceived superior status. I learned this game.

Another Celeste alarm arrived on my phone at the quarter hour, warning me to wrap it up. As bidden, I completed the memo I prepared for the lady golf pro case and printed it out for filing. I still like a hard copy of some things. It's easier for me to glance at a piece of paper quickly as I take a deposition or argue a motion, than it is for me to open the file, scroll down, and find whatever it is that I want on a screen. I'm old-fashioned like that. Besides, Celeste likes to read all the details of the cases we handle, though she's sworn to secrecy to keep them safe.

At the top of the hour it was time to leave my office and walk down the hallway towards the "meet and greet" space in the front. As I approached the closed door to the sound-proofed conference room containing the client, I asked Celeste if she had a completed case information statement ready for my review. She did. I looked at her and asked why she was trying not to laugh. Uncharacteristically of Cel, she wouldn't say. She was turning purple and her cheeks were about to burst, but she remained mum. I took the intake sheet from her hands and saw two names.

"Cel, there are two new clients in there?"

Still unable to speak without uncovering her mouth, she nodded.

Not knowing what to expect, I let myself in and found two attractive people in their mid-twenties looking uncomfortable and embarrassed. I sat down and introduced myself and, as usual, glanced at the contents of my form. Seeing enough, I stopped in my tracks and before uttering a legal word of advice or inquiry I told them that each would have to sign a release waiving any conflicts of interest that might arise in my representing both of them. If they didn't agree, I would refund the retainer and they could decide how they wished to proceed, with another lawyer.

"I don't understand." Said the man.

I explained, I wouldn't entertain a dual representation role in most criminal cases, but given the unique nature of what I'd read so far in the intake form, I was confident I could handle their cases in tandem, working out a good deal for both of them. But they'd have to agree to a waiver. It was their choice.

"Wait here, I have something for you to read and review very carefully." I counseled them.

I left the room and asked Celeste to print out two "Consent for Dual Representation" forms. She did and entered the conference room giving a copy each to the man and woman. They read it. In less than ten minutes, the man emerged and said that they'd agree to my representing them both. I nodded and asked Celeste to grab her notary gear to attest the signing, and be a witness as I performed a voir dire on the knowing and voluntary nature of the form they were about to execute, confirming that each was of sound mind and free from duress or coercion.

Celeste left the room after providing her jurat on the waiver forms, and taking them with her to copy and place in the file. When the three of us were alone, I began asking them typical lawyer/client intake questions. He ("Paul") was a pilot with a local little airline operating under the umbrella of United Express. She ("Cheryl") was a flight attendant for the same little airline. He flew a Bombardier Dash 8; she flung coffees and cokes—her words—at the thirty or so passengers they carried above and around New England. During a flight scheduled yesterday from GON (Groton-New London Airport) to BTV (Burlington International Airport) bad weather required a diversion to HYA (Barnstable Municipal Airport). And that unfortunately, brought us to the troubles of today.

They called me because of my favorable hangar report. The aviation word was that I was decent with the stick and rudder—for a woman who was a late-in-life pilot—and a former New York City lawyer. (Faint praise I thought.) My professional reputation among local law enforcement was at least as good. After Pilot Paul and Flight Attendant Cheryl were booked at BPD (Barnstable Police Headquarters), one of the officers suggested they call the "flying lawyer" to help them with their "situation." From what I learned, I would say that Paul and Cheryl had more of a predicament, but then semantics have always been my thing.

Generally, one diverts an aircraft due to bad weather, or mechanical problems, or a fuel issue (too little), or a bomb scare, or even a passenger emergency (medical issue or unruly conduct). So, having an HYA diversion on route to BTV is neither unusual nor an automatic pathway to misfortune. Crews divert all the time, no problem, just some paperwork. But having the crew diverted to a local lawyer for a last minute, emergent meeting is rare. According to Paul and Cheryl their personal diversion to BPD late last evening and the need for my professional services early this morning was a saga of poor judgment, drunkenness, and regret. And who among us hasn't had one or two of these in her life?

Their tale of woe began yesterday after they landed safely in HYA, and were released from duty until show time (at noon today) and reached the hotel. Paul and Cheryl—who are married, but not to each other—decided to enjoy this unscheduled Cape Cod layover by dining together at their hotel's restaurant, located near a secluded golf course and residential area just outside Hyannis proper. One thing led to another. There was clam chowder. There was lobster. There was beer and so much more.

"I had a Slippery Nipple and a Buttery Nipple, followed by a Screaming Orgasm." Said Cheryl.

"I had at least two Blow Jobs and a Screaming Orgasm, too, I think. It's hard to say, I don't remember that much." Admitted pilot Paul.

We all knew that they were taking about shooters, and various combinations of liqueurs, but I was smiling as I imagined the police officers drafting their reports for this dynamic duo. Not wanting to insinuate myself into the story, but eager to draw out the nuances of my new case, I relied on my time honored direct examination practice and asked, "And what happened next?"

In response, Paul offered a synopsis of the evening. As he spoke, I listened, urged him on, and took notes by hand.

"We left the hotel restaurant after dark. Cheryl was not walking very well and I held her up, sort of. Next thing I know we've walked into some woods and Cheryl tells me how attractive I was. And then, I don't remember much until the helicopter flew above and the dogs came after us. Cheryl tried to hide behind a tree. I tried to hide behind Cheryl. It's all a blur. Here's the police report."

Before I read it, I asked Cheryl if she agreed with what Paul said so far, and if not, what had she to say about the events of last night.

Cheryl didn't remember much either, besides being naked, wearing only her wristwatch and sandals, and later, the police blanket given her in the patrol car. She confirmed that Paul was naked, too, but wearing flip flops. She recalled him taking a flashlight from a parked car at some point before their frisky walk in the woods.

Paul chimed in, "She's right. I did borrow a flashlight, but I never meant to keep it."

"I see." I was nonchalant. "Give me a minute to review the report."

The official version of the evening was summarized by Officer Donohue as: "The neighbors behind the golf course alerted police to the sound of animal noises that were unusual and disturbing. BPD sent out a helicopter, equipped with heat seeking capability and we located two bodies in the woods on top of each other. We sent out our K-9 unit and the dogs led us to an area where we could detect a naked man and a naked woman, apparently intoxicated, engaging in various and sundry lewd and sexual acts. After approximately a half hour of surveillance to make sure none of our residents was endangered and to secure evidence of the crimes, we approached the couple and arrested them. The male was holding a flashlight that he removed from a car parked in the restaurant lot. We gave them blankets for cover and brought them to headquarters to be processed. Collectively, they were arrested and charged for an array of crimes: indecent exposure, lewdness, theft from an automobile, public drunkenness, loitering, and prowling at night.

While not amused as Celeste had been, I tried not to shake my head in disapproval at everyone involved. I wasn't hired to judge. I was hired to make this go away. I was certain that my colleague, the Barnstable County prosecutor, would see things my way, given that his police officers were voyeurs, as opposed to peace keepers, during that half hour of so-called surveillance. I wondered if that spying included more than eye witnessing. The phrase, "secure evidence of the crimes" gave me pause since I didn't see any references to sobriety tests or BAC (blood-alcohol content)—so exactly what evidence were they gathering? If those officers made any electronic recordings of my clients in flagrante delicto, I would have to get hold of the material and safeguard it. Then, I'd hammer out a deal, after which the "e-Evidence" would be destroyed.

I told Paul and Cheryl where they stood.

"I can help you with the criminal case, but I suggest you contact your unions immediately, if you haven't already, and ask how to save your jobs."

Both nodded. I continued.

"You did something dumb, but both of you were clearly drunk, so I think we can negate intent and get the criminal charges dismissed. I can probably work out a deal with a steep fine. I'll know more after I speak with the prosecutor. Saving your jobs, though, is another matter. I'm not sure how the FAA or the airline will view your conduct. I assume you're both suspended without pay pending an investigation?"

"Yes," both answered.

"How did your families react to this news?"

"I didn't tell my wife." Paul said sheepishly.

"I haven't told my husband either." Cheryl followed.

"You won't be able to keep this a secret. Once your arrests are posted on the Barnstable Police Blotter Website, your adventure will be carried on all the newswires, UPI, Reuters, AP, you name it. It's too late for me to try and stop that. Unfortunately, what happened in Hyannis will not stay in Hyannis. But be thankful that they didn't put you in the pillory and stocks downtown, stark naked but for the sandals, watch, and flip flops."

"They still do that?" Cheryl looked concerned.

"No, they stopped that, like in the 60s." Pilot Paul tried to reassure her.

Under my breath I muttered, yeah, the 1660s. Audibly I was reassuring, "Let me make a few calls and I'll get back to you by the end of the week. Call if you need me."

Released on their own recognizance, they were, ironically, I thought, not flight risks, just senseless.

Paul and Cheryl left my office looking more relaxed than when I first saw them, but probably not as relaxed as when the officers first laid eyes on them—and then hung around for half an hour to watch the show. I called Celeste and asked her to arrange a telephone conference as soon as possible with the County Prosecutor. Waiting for the logistics for this conference, I checked my calendar to coordinate my flying and my lawyering, as both had brought me this interesting case I was sure to ameliorate.

I confirmed that my next trip for CAC was a charter to Nantucket; then, a leg to the Vineyard for my final segment from MVY to HYA. I was happily building my hours and counting the days till I worked for the majors. Professionally, I'd fly whatever I could. Personally, as a passenger, I prefer Boeing. As they say, "if it's not Boeing, I'm not going." As for Airbus, they float better than they fly—an homage to Sully's US Airways watercraft, A320-214, fortuitously equipped with forward slide/rafts.

Celeste buzzed my phone and let me know that while I was in conference, Ms. Taylor called and left a message. She said that she was representing herself and asked if I—as an officer of the court, sworn to uphold the law and seek justice—would ask the judge to order a DNA test proving her relationship to Rick and Warren, or "Dad" as she now called him. Lyndsey promised to keep in touch and shared an observation that didn't come as much of a surprise: Beck didn't like me anymore than he liked her. I made a mental note to ask her how she knew what Thomas Beck liked—or didn't—when I returned her call.

Thomas Beck failed to produce the documents he was ordered to share by Monday, close of business, East Coast time. I should not have been surprised, but I was. When the documents had still not arrived by 7 p.m. on their due date, I called his L.A. office, noting that it was only 4 p.m. his time and if something had happened, or he forgot, his staff could scan the documents and send them electronically or even fax them, like in the old days. But it was not to be. Not only was I unable to speak with Mr. Beck himself, as he was out of the office; his secretary told me that she had nothing on her desk for me, nor had she been instructed to send any documents. I'd have to wait till Mr. Beck returned to the office later in the week.

When you're given a kiss off like that from your co-trustee you know that something must be done. Unfortunately, orders are not self-executing. If a person, even a lawyer, doesn't do what he or she was ordered to do, it's up to the person wronged (or as we say, "aggrieved") to go back to that same court and seek relief or enforce a prior order. Usually you'll get your wish and the judge, who doesn't like being ignored, will grant the request and impose sanctions—typically attorneys fees or costs. Even so, it doesn't expedite the process or transform an obstinate party—or in my case, co-trustee—into someone civil and accommodating.

I was in the office early the next morning to prepare my paperwork. I would not be caught without supporting documents again, so I took care to detail my calls, my efforts, and my entreaties to play nice with Thomas Beck and to administer Warren's last will as he, Warren wanted, and Mr. Beck apparently did not. When the pleadings were ready to file, I called the court as soon as I could,

123

noting the three hour time difference. The law clerk was cordial. After a brief recitation of why I was again requesting the court's time and resources, the clerk scheduled me for another order to show cause by phone after lunch, California time. As ordered, I sent all the documents to my co-trustee's office across the continent and put him on notice that I sought his removal from the Ethan estate matter. I added a request for a DNA test to reveal whether Ms. Lyndsey Taylor really was Warren's daughter. Since this part of the application pertained to Rick, I had to give notice to Rick's attorney of my pending application to swab the inside of his client's mouth and see if he had a sister.

While I waited for these pleading bombs to detonate in beautiful southern California, I finally got down to business in Barnstable. The County prosecutor was a friend of a friend. I've been around long enough to know that an ear lent with a predisposition inclined towards kindness, at the very least, is helpful. Even if you don't get what you want, you've established a rapport, maybe built a bit of trust and made a bridge of your own to cross the next time.

But friend or foe, unlike the world of civil litigation where the defendant often hides the truth until a determined plaintiff reveals it through precise discovery requests and court orders enforcing prior orders; working in the criminal part of the law brings a different set of rules. Not only is the burden of proof higher for the prosecution—beyond a reasonable doubt, as opposed to the infinitely easier "more likely than not" (that is to say, by a preponderance of the evidence); as the state's lawyer, the prosecutor must provide me—the defense attorney—with whatever exculpatory or impeachment evidence he possesses that bears upon my client's lack of guilt, or even innocence. The last items, i.e., "not guilty" and "innocent" are two related; but alas, different, concepts.

In the matter of Paul and Cheryl, this duty to share material was helpful, but in an unexpected manner. While it might have proved the state's case; it also gave me grounds to file a big old civil suit, and thereby, leverage to work out an amicable solution. The prosecutor admitted that the officers had videotaped the various Paul and Cheryl permutations that they encountered for nearly forty minutes in those golf course woods. More than that, they had shared these digital files with others on the force, a big department no-no. Glaringly, no one bothered to collect samples from the two arrestees' blood or breath to determine their blood-alcohol content. The cops were too busy recording the hijinks on the links.

The prosecutor and I knew this was a case to resolve. So we began negotiations. He'd dismiss all charges and impose no fines or penalties. My clients would agree to waive their rights to file a civil suit against the department on account of the sex tapes and file sharing, violating Massachusetts law. If the prosecutor would give his imprimatur to my clients resuming their careers in aviation, I thought we could find our way to "yes." But I'd have to discuss it with Paul and Cheryl and get back to him. Part of the deal would have to be a return of the recordings of the sex acts and their deletion by hard drive destruction. As an aside, I asked why the police would flout basic police standard operating procedure (SOP) and make multiple and lengthy recordings of a couple having sex, as if they'd never seen it before?

My learned, literary colleague at Massachusetts Bar replied, "Kate, after viewing all four versions of the evidence collected in this case from distinctly different angles, I can confirm that the variety of shapes which your clients could assume was endless and mesmerizing. At one point that stewardess, a wealth of bloom and bough, lay across your pilot's upright knee like a great overturned basket of fruit, captivating all who beheld her."

"Oh my. How do I rid myself of that image?"

"I don't know, but since I showed those tapes to my wife, we've never been happier."

"Excuse me?"

"That is a joke, Kate. Let me know if we have a deal."

I summoned Paul and Cheryl to my office. I explained the proposed deal's pros (no official evidence of what happened, no more publicity) and cons (giving up the civil case and possible money damages). Fight or settle—it was their call. I would do whichever they thought best and would allow them to move forward from their brazenly bad drunken behavior. Weighing the alternatives and eager to put this mess behind them, Paul and Cheryl accepted the offer, which I immediately relayed to my colleague. For public consumption, the prosecutor offered an official closing statement, "The people of Barnstable are protected from those who suffer from the prostration of their faculties. Justice has been done, and the property at issue has been returned, with new batteries." And that, was that.

I was just about ready for the California court conference when I received a conciliatory call from Mr. Beck explaining that he'd been sick, and that just this morning he'd sent those Epcot statements from the last two years. They'd be delivered to my office tomorrow evening. He was sorry for any confusion he might have caused. I replied that he should tell it to the judge during our conference call in about an hour. He hung up.

During the judicial phone conference, as she was wont to do, the probate judge expediently ruled on my application with orderly dispatch, first reciting the issue, then the facts, and finally, her ruling, in quick succession. If Mr. Beck didn't provide those recent Epcot Partnership Fund statements to me by the end of the week, he would be facing contempt and possible jail time. Better yet, he had to show cause why he should not be removed as co-trustee of the Ethan estate.

Next, my application for a sibling DNA test was granted to the extent that Rick consented, as the court did not have the power under these circumstances to compel him to undergo any physical procedure, no matter how minimally invasive. Finally, the parties were to pay all costs for any genetic testing, and with that, she bid us a good afternoon and hung up. Mr. Beck and Rick's lawyer remained on the line. I asked the latter when I could expect a response about the buccal swab for the genetic testing. He replied, "Never."

So I tried another tack. What lab would Rick like to use? It was a very easy procedure. He'd receive a kit in the mail, follow the instructions, and return the big Q-tip to the lab for processing as directed in the stamped, addressed shipping envelope. He'd have the results in about two weeks—we all would. Rick's attorney was duty-bound to convey my message, but warned me not to expect submission. Rick had only to lose if Lyndsey were found to be his sister and if she were not, he'd be in the same situation that he was in now. There was nothing in it for Rick. I thanked the attorney for his time and everyone hung up.

Next call on the list: Ms. Lyndsey Taylor. But before I could bring myself to speak with another truculent Californian, I needed to fortify myself with coffee. I left my office for a short walk to the kitchenette, not far from my conference room. As I waited the ten seconds for my small coffee pod to brew, I brought Celeste up to speed on the Ethan estate, ending with Rick's certain refusal to agree to the DNA sibling test. Just as I was about to complain about the unfairness of it all, Celeste said something that made all the difference—as she often does.

"Kate, do you still have the letter?"

"What letter?"

"The letter you got from Mr. Ethan, when you were divorced."

"Yes, of course." I replied.

"Did you save the envelope?"

"Yes, it's with the letter."

"So you have your saliva from Warren Ethan."

"Can you get DNA from an envelope months after it was sealed?

"According to 'CSI: L.A.' you can. Let's check."

With that, Celeste logged on to her computer and searched. She read from the web site text of several AABB (American Association of Blood Banks) accredited labs and provided an overview of DNA testing and extraction procedures. If Warren actually licked the envelope himself, we could probably prove a match—or not. DNA collection and quality depended upon the kind of glue on the back of the envelope and the amount of saliva applied. Whether Warren was a liberal or parsimonious licker would affect the kind of DNA a lab could extract from my envelope's glue strip. The test cost five hundred dollars. Nearly seven out of ten efforts to extract DNA from these sources were successful. No one could give odds on a match, but chances were decent the test could be performed on a valid sample. With nothing else to go on, this method sounded good to me. I reattached my phone recorder to my office handset and placed a call to Lyndsey.

When she answered, I greeted her with a gracious, but professional tone, delivering the bad news first: Rick would likely not agree to undergo testing. Then, I gave her the better news. We had a chance to extract Warren's DNA from an item in my possession. No guarantees, but it was the best we could hope for now. Ms. Taylor was encouraged and agreed to cooperate, but warned that it would take a week to gather the fee, unless I paid for her. I explained that I could not personally pay for her lab test, and if the estate were to pay, I'd have to make another application and get Mr. Beck to sign on. To expedite matters and maintain privacy, I suggested she do whatever she must to gather the funds. Once that was accomplished, we'd be on our way to discovering whether Lyndsey was the sister-in-law I never had. Before we ended our recorded phone conference I asked what she meant by her message telling me that Mr. Beck didn't like me either.

"Isn't it obvious?" She said matter of factly.

"I guess so." I replied and ended the call on a cordial note.

We had a plan of action. Whenever we received Lyndsey's payment, Celeste would order the test. Assuming there was enough spit on the envelope, and Lyndsey followed her specimen collection instructions, we expected conclusive results. The lab we selected would continue testing the samples until it could prove that Warren was either not Lyndsey's biological father or it could certify with a 99.99 percent probability that Warren was Lyndsey's dad. This was a case where a mere 99 percent probability of parentage was not good enough. We needed that extra .99 percent, or "near scientific certainty" for the court to admit the lab results—no matter the outcome—into evidence.

Encouraged by the chance at finding the truth about Warren's heirs—all of them—through an old envelope, I got to thinking about the Epcot account statements for the last two years. Why was I digging in the same hole (bothering with Thomas Beck) when it was getting me nowhere? Sometimes my "lateral thinking" is flawed and I fail to recognize the simplest solutions. I had to dig in a new hole.

Why wait for Beck's copies to arrive? What was to prevent me—the co-trustee, co-executor, co-administrator of the Warren Ethan estate—from calling Mr. Perkin and asking for duplicate copies today? Nothing. So I called the Park Avenue office and asked for help. Not surprisingly, Mr. Perkin himself didn't speak with me; but one of his minions was happy to accommodate my request. I simply provided Warren's account number, which she put in her system. Finding it quickly, this woman asked if I'd be satisfied if the materials she'd just printed were dispatched in the evening's mail? Sure, I told her. I'd waited this long, what was the rush? Now, no matter what Mr. Beck did or did not do, I'd get the missing Epcot statements in three days from Manhattan to Hyannis. Another problem solved—slowly, but solved none the less.

CHAPTER ELEVEN

After a hard day's lawyering in Barnstable, it was an early night for me. No flying, just an evening at home in South Yarmouth, relaxing beside the scenic Bass River in my little cape on the Cape. Surrounded by Nantucket beadboard and New England coastal décor, I felt peaceful near the water as I defrosted a quahog, made myself a nice vodka-free cape codder spritz (seltzer, a splash of cranberry juice and a lime), and turned on the local news.

Except for a couple of great white sharks spotted near Chatham stalking the abundant (and apparently delicious) seals and sea bathers, it had been a beautiful summer's day on the Cape. This week, the Cape's weather was just a bit better than normal and everyone loved it, despite the nocturnal fog. The local TV weatherman was sunburned and ebullient conveying a forecast for more of the same—sun and sharks—that was sure to please all but the furry pinnipeds gathering along the Cape's coast and a few hominids wading in the ocean between Chatham and Nauset beaches.

Feeling pretty good myself, I defrosted another quahog and dug in. It's nice to have some quiet time for dining, reflecting, and reviewing your mail, new and old. When I finished my meal, I secured Warren's "Dear Kate" letter from last November and placed it where I'd see it in the morning. Tomorrow I'd bring it to the office to retain in the safe till the DNA testing kit arrived.

That done, I attended to the domestic chores required when you live alone. Taking the laundry out of the dryer, my mind wandered to Steven Philips. I wondered if he was the passenger I'd be flying from the Vineyard to Hyannis tomorrow late afternoon. If he were, it would be interesting to see how he related to me after his investigation in the Ethan trust funds.

I felt let down, but understood his desire not to be involved. Still, I thought we had a nice chemistry, or understanding, and if he'd asked me to help him in a similar manner, I would have. But he and I were not alike. I'd deal with it. I had repair mechanisms in my psychic repertoire. Besides, what was Steven Philips to me? Just another one of hundreds of passengers I encounter each season. When we next met at the airport I would fly him safely from point A to point B, maintaining my professional decorum all the while. I might not like what he did, but he didn't have to know that.

By the time I was folding laundry, a breaking news bulletin from the Boston channel that I'd flipped to after dinner caught my ear. I listened carefully. A prominent New York money manager, a former Chairman of NASDAQ, and a well-known and well-liked social maven by the name of Ernest ("Ernie") Schuttauf, was just arrested for securities fraud. I did not recognize the name but the billions that were invested with him and his wealth management business were apparently lost. The first reports were sketchy but mentioned something about a Ponzi scheme.

When the ten o'clock news began, I sat in front of the screen and listened carefully. I'd never heard this man's name before, Ernie Schuttauf. It was definitely not B. Adlai Perkin or the Epcot Partnership. Though I felt relieved for myself and Warren's millions, many people—charities, foundations, and even endowments for colleges and hospitals—had reportedly lost everything they'd invested with this well-respected, well-connected, and by all accounts, charming Wall Street veteran.

Ernie Schuttauf's photo flashed on the screen. No wonder people trusted him, he reminded me of George Washington: similar jaw, nose, and hair. Next, a live video feed from New York City revealed desperate men and woman reacting to this unexpected and shocking news. Their money was gone. This morning they possessed the security and privilege only those with millions of dollars knew. When darkness fell, they were penniless, wiped out by fraud and deception. According to their own standards, they were worthless— they were nothings.

Turning away from the TV, an image of the East Side rich appeared in my mind. These victims were likely my former colleagues and neighbors and clients. I wondered how they would cope with sudden poverty, invisibility, and powerlessness. I thought of Bob Dylan's song, "Like a Rolling Stone," a spontaneous mental allusion giving expression to my sordid curiosity: how did it feel—to go from riches to rags in a matter of hours? Would they have to take their diamond rings and pawn them? Would they live out on the street?

As the news unfolded, I checked my smart phone for activity. Nothing for me personally or professionally, that was reassuring; but the financial sites were ablaze with this story. Shockwaves were rippling throughout the plutocracy of Manhattan; Southampton; Greenwich; Westport; and Palm Beach. This calamity of pain and penury was real and it was earthshaking, if not entirely heartbreaking. I mean, these were not exactly the kindest, most unpretentious people you would ever meet; but I would leave the schadenfreude for another, more appropriate time. Now, I was simply watching the train wreck from the side lines, glad I was not on board with the Ethan estate money.

The more I watched the news, the happier I felt by comparison, and this is nothing to be proud of. I could barely contain my utter relief at not having any connection to this financial meltdown of epic proportion. My fear of a catastrophe of this scale was exactly the motivation I had for seeking a court order last week to withdraw Warren's money from Wall Street and place it into something that I could understood and evaluate, not take on faith or the word of Mr. B. Adlai Perkin, the wily Wizard of Epcot. Given my recent failure to secure a quick redemption of Warren's fortune from Perkin's Epcot Limited Partnership, I felt immensely lucky, like I missed a doomed plane because I was running late and it left without me, never to land. Though I failed, I succeeded, in a sense. All was fine, and not thanks to me, or the disappointing Steven Philips.

When I next saw the man from Bain I would mention Ernie Schuttauf's multi-billion dollar securities fraud and remind Mr. Philips that there, but for the grace of God, went the Ethan estate and all the money earmarked to help our veterans per Warren's handwritten codicil. As a pilot who never had one, but always feared it, a "near miss" (a barely evaded collision in the air or "runway incursion" on the ground) can be as terrifying as it is re-energizing and useful for refocusing the mind. But I was too tired for any productive thought tonight. I needed a good eight hours of sleep and in the morning would call Mike Fortune, my friend, former colleague, and my legal connection to upper echelons of New York's money-based society. I wanted to know the inside scoop. Did he know anyone who was affected by this debacle? Was he aware of any Upper East Side apartments soon to be listed at fire sale prices?

Weather, especially adverse weather, is unpredictable and can change drastically aloft, virtually without notice, until it's too late. Despite what the flying public might think, our weather information in the cockpit of a small plane is not perfect, at least not in my Cessna. It tells you where the storms were when the radar last scanned the area and transmitted the data to the satellite, which then bounced it to the receiver. But as a pilot, I want to know where the TRW (thunderstorms) are right now, to avoid them and the serious trouble they can cause a plane. Yet sometimes, knowing where the storms were—about eight minutes ago—is the best you can do and you simply try to navigate around what you cannot foresee.

My home phone rang and roused me from a pleasant REM cycle. I was landing a B-737-900 at BOS (Logan), runway 27, and it was beautiful.

"Kate, have you heard?" a familiar male voice asked.

I was not at all awake and couldn't comprehend how my bedroom phone rang as I rolled my aircraft on the asphalt, landing in smooth air, right sneaker (tire) touching first, one wing low.

"Mike, why are you calling me this early?"

"Kate, I'm sorry. Your estate, it's all gone."

I sat up, yawning. "I saw the news. Warren didn't invest with that man. He had his money with Adlai Perkin, in that Epcot fund, remember?"

"Perkin's Epcot Partnership was a feeder fund for Ernie Schuttauf's investment company."

"I don't understand."

"Perkin handed over all the money invested in Epcot to Ernie Schuttauf and his investment firm, which turned out to be a massive sixty five billion dollar Ponzi scheme. There's nothing left of Epcot."

I couldn't breathe, much less speak. Mike resumed the conversation with compassion and at slower speed, as if I were having difficulty comprehending speech, which I was.

After a few seconds, I managed a response. "How do you know?"

"It's all over the street." It took him nearly ten minutes to explain a simple concept: there was no more Ethan money. I was now the co-executor of an estate with nothing, of nothing. I had presided over the greatest failure of my personal and professional life. I had to alert the court, Rick, and the other Ethan heirs, and of course, Thomas Beck. I thought about my meeting with Mr. Perkin and his arrogant dismissal of my questions and concerns; but none of that mattered now if what Mike said was true.

I turned on the TV news and switched my mobile phone "on," from its nightly "do not disturb" setting. I immediately saw that I had multiple calls beginning shortly after I turned in for the evening. The first message was from Steven Philips just before midnight. He knew before Mike did that Warren's Epcot money was intertwined with Schuttauf's firm. The next calls were from Mike beginning at four in the morning. Bad news certainly travelled fast. It would be many hours before I could reach the probate court, but this news was worth calling Mr. Beck and waking him. I tried but did not get through.

Like a robot, I went through my morning routine to get out the door, but I was numb. My memory reverted to law school, was this abatement or ademption? One describes the estate being depleted before the testator dies; the other, after. Ah, I recalled, it was abatement. This badness was about to go from awful to ugly and worse, and I was in the middle of it, along with Beck.

I arrived at my law office long before the official opening at 9 a.m. There was a parcel waiting for me from California. These were the Epcot statements from Mr. Beck's office. Terrific, timing is everything. Now I had the recent statements to show me what no longer existed. Distraught and still not fully understanding how something of this magnitude could have happened; I ripped the package open and saw the 25 months of statements for Warren Ethan's account with Epcot. These pages were nearly identical to those I had in my possession for the years before, except there was more money according to these documents. The last statement was from 30 June, not quite a month ago, and revealed a balance, in treasuries, of just over 184 million dollars. I nearly choked as I remembered that the money wasn't invested at all. It was handed off by a fake, Perkin, to a fraudster, Schuttauf, only to be paid out to more senior investors until the arrangement fell apart, as Ponzi Schemes always will, when the balance tips to more redemptions than deposits.

The numbers involved in this Schuttauf fraud were scandalous and shocking. As of 30 June, when the victims received their last statements—such as the one I'd just glanced at, 73.1 billion dollars of people's perceived money and gains had vanished. When one reduced that figure for the fake investments and returns, the 64.8 billion dollars or so owed to Schuttauf client/victims still boggled the mind. I didn't think it was possible to lose so much money, but when the Federal Bureau of Investigation called my office, the reality of it all began to sink in. This was not a nightmare, this was a severe TRW that I'd flown into and consequently suffered a catastrophic in air failure—my wings ripped apart from my fuselage.

According to the news, updated by the minute, my pitiful Ethan estate mayday was drowned out by the unfolding tsunami of financial distress among the wealthy of a certain social class. Warren's multiple millions were barely a drop in this bucket of billions of lost dollars. I found myself glued to the Internet reading about this Schuttauf character and how he and his "investment firm" operated. It was a Grimm Fairytale indeed, only scarier and far more disturbing than anything those German brothers could imagine.

I learned that Mr. Ernie Schuttauf ran his "business" under cover of his own family and the SEC, which seemed to defer to him despite warnings of impossible returns. Since Ernie was well known on "the Street," no one questioned him. So long as the money flowed, really, no one cared. Customers thought Ernie and his firm were serving as investment advisors and custodians of the securities they held and traded for their patrons; but none of that was so.

The "market making" and "proprietary trading" units of the Schuttauf firm were really just cover for the fraudulent "investment advisory" unit, as it was known until last evening. This Ponzi portion of the business was lucrative and kept far apart from the real business entities that lost money. Unlike the market making and proprietary trading sections, which used real time computer trading and engaged in risk management and registration, the IA ("investment advisory") unit did none of that. Isolated in a separate floor of the Schuttauf office, a handful of long time employees had access to the IA accounts and an ancient IBM computer system, unconnected to the Internet or any third parties. This old system harbored a special program that generated fake statements for Schuttauf's direct customers since the scheme commenced nearly two decades ago.

Still not believing how this massive fraud could continue under the nose of Wall Street cognoscenti and securities regulators, I scrutinized the mechanics of the plan. Though Ponzi schemes were not new or original, Ernie's brand was unique and blossomed in the rarefied world of the wealthy erudite. Schuttauf stoked demand for his advisory services by flagrantly restricting availability. He actually denied people the opportunity to give their money to him and his "firm."

When you were admitted to Ernie's world, you felt privileged as you gained access to a special club—after all, there were many he'd rejected and turned away—poor schmucks. A keen student of the psyche of his target audience, Schuttauf knew they'd be flattered by his coveted invitation—inclusion amongst the exclusive. At Manhattan charity balls, Southampton dinners, and Greenwich clubs, his marks vied for the chance to hand over their riches for Ernie's absolute control. In return, Schuttauf promised, and they expected, a steady 10 to 17 percent return on their investments, year after year after year, regardless of what was happening in the world at large or the markets in particular. For this kind of result you had to be special, a friend of Ernie, and everyone who was anyone, knew it.

While his marketing methodology might have been unusual, the mechanics of the Schuttauf swindle were classic Ponzi all the way. Ernie, like the Ponzi schemers before him, simply used new customer deposits (funds that were *supposed to be* invested and grown, earning steady returns in the meanwhile) to "pay out" the returns or redemptions for other "investors." There was no trading activity or investments made. Simply, money came in, money went out; and so long as the former was greater than the latter, the scheme could continue.

New "investments" were paid out as "returns" for the previous "investors." There never were real returns generated or profits earned because there never was any legitimate trading or investing, just the flow of funds from one poor sucker to another until the music stopped and thousands were left without a chair, or their fortunes—or nest eggs, in the case of the lowest level investors. For Ponzi victims, a buy and hold strategy was the worst possible choice because the money was gone shortly after it was handed over for "investment." If you never redeemed a dime, you didn't benefit from the next chump investing with Schuttauf, you were merely fleeced and fed fabricated paper statements in the mail.

I drank more coffee and steeled myself for what lie ahead in the Ethan matter. I glossed over the newly arrived statements from California for the Epcot feeder fund. I wondered how Ernie, the master of Wall Street and markets managed his fakery for so long and attracted so much money, while escaping detection. Centering my searches on Ernie Schuttauf's internal operation, I learned that, unlike Perkin's clients who received "newsletters," Ernie's investors' statements actually bore a list of trades—complete with prices and dates—that never occurred, but looked real on paper.

My research revealed that producing such fakes was not so hard to accomplish. Ernie's elite clientele lost their wealth to low level clerks who knew one thing and did it very well: how to punch in fabricated numbers using an ancient IBM AS/400 computer system, circa early 1990s. A custom software program allowed Ernie's miscreant elves to store investor information into segregated accounts and then, input fake transactions and market positions in a fictitious basket of stocks and funds. The program would turn this work into customer statements that were perfectly reasonable upon inspection, and utterly fictitious.

The genius of the old Schuttauf software program was to actually carry the false trades and compound the fake profits over the life of the account, for each customer, consistently, and in proportion to his or her initial investment. The Ernie Schuttauf investor received paper statements reflecting returns that were steady and favorable, until they weren't. No one seemed to care that he or she could not check his or her account balances in real time, electronically. Instead, all "trade confirmations" were sent by mail, with a lag time of many days and sometimes more than a week, depending upon where the investor resided and how far it was from Ernie's Manhattan office.

Quarterly Schuttauf statements showed all the supposed equity trades had been liquidated into treasuries, just like the Epcot statements in my hands, reflecting increased, accrued values. Looking back, it seems preposterous, because it was. The power of denial or the suspension of reality can be a defense mechanism, or a tool of self-destruction, depending on the arena. So while Schuttauf's direct investors received statements reflecting trades in the prior months, there never were any actual trades or transactions completed.

The entire "basket" of stocks was all nonsense, entirely fabricated by a few employees who knew how to run the software on old computers that allowed them to insert fictional data. Meantime, a huge, legitimate Wall Street brokerage, JP Morgan served as the repository for the Ernie Schuttauf slush fund, identified as the "307" account, for the last three identifying numbers assigned to it. Everyone's money was either deposited in, or withdrawn from, the

Morgan "307" account, depending on investor demand. Every day, Ernie's trusted, devious elves would tabulate reports reflecting deposits and withdrawals from "307."

When the market closed, the cash in "307" was transferred to overnight investment accounts at another large institution, Chase Bank, where Ernie purchased United States Treasuries or money market securities until the next time he needed cash—to fulfill customers' withdrawal requests or "interest" payments or satisfy any whim or acquire any object that Ernie or his family ever dreamt of or desired. I was brought to the brink of nausea. Instead of more fretting, I gathered myself for the demands of the day ahead. Whatever it would bring, I would try and do my best.

After contacting Mr. Beck again and leaving a message, I decided there was no need to wait for normal business hours. Under the circumstances, I had a responsibility to reach out to my West Coast counterparts immediately. Plus, from internet news accounts, I surmised that the Schuttauf fraud was already a big story in L.A. among a certain crowd. A prominent Hollywood financier and philanthropist began his own hedge fund several years ago, but like Perkin, fed all the money to Ernie. Now that money was all gone and the effects were felt from Malibu's Carbon Beach to Marina del Rey, where the earth was quaking, but not from a geological fault. I deliberated about what I should say as I left these phone messages, confirming the Ethan estate catastrophe, care of Mr. B. Adlai Perkin.

Knowing that I'd be unable to reach a human at this hour, I decided to prepare a script. As I sat there, thinking of what to write and then say, my stomach was upset and I was woozy. I reflected on my experiences with wake turbulence. Depending on the size of the aircraft that created it, this roiling air can create havoc. For a time, the pilot in the following plane has limited control over his aircraft's flight path as it's buffeted by the vertical and horizontal forces inside that wake. When something unusual occurs in the air, the pilot's goal is to maintain SOP (standard operating procedure) and follow the relevant checklists. But until control is recovered, everyone, from the PIC (pilot in command) to the last passenger on the airplane, must exercise negative capability. As Keats would say, "Capable of being in uncertainties, mysteries, doubts, without any irritable reaching after fact and reason." You don't ask why. You don't complain. You remain calm and get the situation underhand, ASAP.

For most people, the unknown and uncertain is difficult to tolerate, making them nervous and upset. As the pilot in command (PIC), I try to prevent this distress from escalating by keeping passengers as informed and as comfortable as I can. I will make PAs telling them what's going on, assuring them that I am on top of the matter. It usually makes a huge difference for them to know the captain is doing all that can be done and communicating as much as possible given PIC priorities: aviate, navigate, communicate. I'd nearly mastered "negative capability" from both my legal training and flying experience, and believed my West Coast colleagues would benefit from it now. Unfortunately, after all my thinking and reflecting about it, sudden turbulence, maintaining calm, and regaining control, I failed to find the words that would make what I had to say less alarming. Instead, I reverted to another section of my flight manual. My message to the West Coast contingent of the Ethan estate litigation was, "Mayday, Mayday, Mayday. Call me. Kate."

Considering my Schuttauf shock this morning, I was fortunate to be cast in a fairly passive role—what we lawyers call, "baby sitting"—at my LPGA pro's deposition for most of the day. As my adversary verbally probed my client to help his case and hurt mine, I was stationed beside her as a guardian of the legal process, to ensure that the rules of discovery were scrupulously obeyed and to object on the record when necessary. My adversary could be rude and irritating. That conduct was allowed. Yet, should he cross the line into abuse or vulgarity, I would—and legally could—stop him.

For hours, I sat at the conference table, ready to pounce as needed, while the defense attorney tried through leading question after leading question—allowed during a deposition—to catch my client in a lie, under oath. He failed because she's the ideal personal injury plaintiff with the perfect narrative. No matter what he said to throw her off—"didn't you injure this same shoulder muscle during your second year on the tour?" and "haven't you received treatment for this shoulder spasm before visiting my client's restaurant?"—my lady golfer, prepped and ready for the attack, remained calm and focused, repeating the same facts in response to same query, phrased just a bit differently each time. She testified that she was healthy before, but permanently injured after the lobster restaurant's deck failed and she fell, right shoulder first, through the rotted, wooden railing.

This day-long deposition was a common defense attorney ploy. While there was still some plausible billable time to squeeze from a case, he would wring out his last dollars—I mean hours—of attorney time, before this case settled, as it would, eventually. Welcome to civil litigation in America, early twenty-first century where nearly 98 percent of all filed cases are settled or dismissed. While the injured party's attorney doesn't receive a penny in fees from a client unless and until a verdict or settlement is reached; the defense attorney, working for an insurance company in charge of the defendant's case, is paid by the hour, no matter what happens: win, lose, or settle.

Like Charles Dickens paid by the word, the longer a defense attorney works on a case, the more money he earns. Oddly, the more I worked on a case, the more money a defense attorney earned, too. But plaintiffs' lawyers know this and accept it. We don't mind waiting for the money. Personally, I enjoy the challenge of outthinking the defense and staying at least two steps ahead, if I can. My aviation training taught me the value of patience (pilots, by and large a persevering bunch, will say, "time to spare, go by air") and of always being "in front" of the aircraft or "never letting an airplane take you somewhere your brain didn't get to five minutes earlier." A pilot flies her airplane with her head, not her hands. You must know where you're going, because you're traveling too fast for regret. In my legal work I'm patient and anticipate future obstacles, except of course when I don't—or can't. It was still hard for me to comprehend, much less accept, the loss of Warren's 184 million dollars, or whatever it was, minus the fake Ponzi returns.

I was relieved when the deposition finally ended. My client was unscathed, and the defense attorney promised to speak to "his carrier" about a settlement offer. Ka-ching. Having failed to "break" my client, he had finally come to see the case my way: his restaurant client was liable and my homegrown lady golf pro was a jury-lovable plaintiff with permanent damages—a disaster for him if this case were ever tried. I told my adversary I'd await his offer and in the meantime, confirmed the pretrial status conference with the court. Sometime during the interminable deposition, Celeste took the message that I was to be available for a conference call at 4:30 p.m. E.D.T., with the California probate court and my West Coast counterparts on the line, including, with permission of the court, Ms. Lyndsey Taylor, now pro per, representing herself.

Free from my own legal duties after the deposition, I joined the meeting from the beginning. After briefly addressing the devastation of Warren's charitable trust monies and the frustration of its purpose, the court scheduled a hearing next week in California. No Skype, no "face time," no magic jack; instead, I was to appear, personally, on my own dime, as the co-administrator in open court. We would all go forward from there, doing what the law required when the worst that could happen, happened to an estate. Until then, I was to report any new information I obtained from the East Coast. Thomas Beck would report any West Coast news from his Beverly Hills, Bel Air, and Brentwood bailiwick.

While things can get pretty somber in a probate court with its steady docket of death and fighting heirs, I can conclusively say that the conference today, discussing the now defunct estate of the late Warren Ethan, was as depressing as any formal court proceeding I'd encountered. Ever. Poor pro per, Lyndsey Taylor took it the worst. Her only hope for financial independence was gone, regardless of lab results, which were yet to be sent. It's like we say, you cannot get blood out of a stone, even if it's a genetic match. In consolation, I told Ms. Taylor she could call my office anytime and I'd speak with her, recording our conversation, as always.

When the conference call concluded, the skies over my storefront office grew overcast and it was raining in my soul. I was itching for the sky. I recalled another favorite passage from *Moby-Dick*, which I personalized: "Whenever I find myself growing grim about the mouth; whenever it is a damp, drizzly November in my soul... I account it high time to get to [the sky] as soon as I can."

Luckily I was scheduled for a flight later that afternoon. By the time I arrived at the Barnstable County Airport the clouds were thickening, but still flyable. My schedule had changed. No trips to the islands, no chance to see Steven Philips, just a short hop to Marstons Mills (2B1) to pick up a puppy and then back to Hyannis, to deliver the doggy safely to its owner. Officially called "Cape Cod Airport," Marstons Mills was an old-fashioned, family-managed, county-owned turf airfield and a five minute turn from HYA. Ask any pilot and she'll confirm that avoiding obstacles of all manner at 2B1 is always a concern, be they fixed and terrestrial or moving and aerial. When the jumpers are jumping, the drones are swarming, the banners are flying, and the trees are standing, I'm on high alert. It was too late in the day for the radio controlled (RC) quadcopters, parachute jumpers, and banner towers to confound me; but the trees were still standing tall over Runway 35 and I was careful to drop in at the correct angle and the proper speed.

My landing was uneventful. There were no tree clippings, no drift, and I was within 50 feet of the touchdown sweet spot on the center line. As I taxied off the grass runway, I could see that my canine passenger and his handler were waiting for me. I maneuvered the Cessna towards the tie downs and stopped the plane a safe distance away. When I disembarked, I saw a small white poodle-like dog wrapped up in a towel and nestled in his carry-crate, fast asleep. After securing the pup in the back of the plane, the handler left and I closed the door. I started the engine upon completing my checklist. I let my sleeping dog lie. He was utterly undisturbed by the noise and vibration, still groggy from whatever happened to him today. I recalled my Chatham veterinarian case and my client's beloved, dead poodle, Touché, and thought this doggy lucky to be in Marston Mills. I hadn't heard a bad word about the vet who practiced in this village and never had the opportunity to sue her.

As soon as the Cessna and I were ready, we rolled on to runway 35 and climbed towards home. The micro trip was less than ten minutes, but for that time, I'd slipped the surly bonds of worry, free from the Schuttauf debacle and the decimation of my Ethan estate. The clouds broke open for my final approach to HYA and I was grateful for the chance to fly, even as a puppy charter pilot. After conducting my postflight checklist, I got the dog out of the back of my aircraft and remained beside the plane with my canine passenger, kind of like a UNAM (unaccompanied minor), only a bit furrier and much less trouble, being confined to a crate and all. I wondered to whom this pooch belonged and why on earth, or in heaven, was he flown a distance of seven miles?

No sooner had I completed that thought when Lee, the decorator, appeared, approaching my aircraft with a leash. Steven Philips was nowhere in sight, so I surmised she was here for the dog. Lee seemed more subdued than the last time we crossed paths at MVY. Dressed in a simple ivory-colored knit shirt, khaki capri pants, and sandals, I wondered if she fell into an Ann Taylor store and couldn't get up until someone tastefully dressed her. But Lee's sartorial adventures were not my business; ferrying her little dog around, well, sadly, that was my concern. But I did it well. Not a hair was shed, and the dog looked good, too. At this point, my estate was insolvent, but my "poodle hopper" was a success. I had nothing left to lose. Why not be nice?

"Hi, Lee. Is he your poodle?"

"Bolognese." Laconic Lee emphasized my mistake with one word and a snide edge to her voice.

"Is that his name or his breed?" I remained professional and civil as I was ignorant of dogs.

"Her (emphasis supplied by Lee) name is Barkley and she is not a poodle, she's a purebred Bolognese. Catherine the Great, Madame De Pompadour, and Empress Maria Theresa owned one."

"Did they share it or did they each get their own?" I returned, so much for being nice.

This effort at humor was met with silence, so I tried another approach. "What happened to Barkley in Marston Mills?"

"Surgery." Lee replied, again, with one word.

"Well, Barkley flew like a pro—on Ambien; but a pro none the less. Let me help you bring her to your car."

"Thank you." Lee accepted my offer of assistance, surprising me.

As we de-carted and unwrapped Barkley, I could see that this fluffy white Bolognese was the focus of Lee's lavish attention. So that's why this creature was flown a few miles after her veterinary procedure. Or, maybe this was an example of passively and aggressively spending your boyfriend's money? I wasn't sure and my curiosity was piqued. When this happens, I probe, as lawyers do. And as luck would have it, Lee answered, as most lay people will when not represented by counsel in everyday life.

We talked as we walked from the airfield through the terminal and out towards Lee's parked ivory-colored Audi, which matched her outfit. She carried the still groggy Barkley and her leash in her arms. I carried the empty dog carrier. I learned that no expense was spared on Barkley, the "love dog" of the union of Steven Philips and Lee. And speaking of love, Barkley had just been artificially inseminated with the sperm of another purebred Bolognese. Apparently, Bologneses don't do it doggy style very often and prefer sex by test tube—like who doesn't these days?

I gathered from this procedure that Steven denied neither Lee, nor Barkley, anything that money could buy; including canine ART (assisted reproductive technology) and private charter flights for what would have been a fifteen minute drive, if there were traffic. Lee seemed appeased, if not pleased with the arrangement—Steven had money; she would spend it, regardless of their physical proximity. In the end, I believed that Steven would be paying dearly for this woman and their dog, but it was his money and he should have his fun. Besides, how else to get another purebred Bolognese puppy?

As we approached her car, I asked Lee why I hadn't seen her or Barkley on my recent trips to the Vineyard. Lee explained that Steven was very busy traveling for work. He'd been to London, Jersey—off the coast of Brittany, Switzerland, Singapore, Hong Kong, and the Cook Islands. Today he was in the Caribbean, returning tonight. I wondered why Lee wasn't along. Dog sitters are everywhere and I'd certainly seen her plenty of times without Barkley, the poodle-looking Bolognese. Sometimes asking a question obliquely is your best shot to gain an answer; other times, the direct method is most effective. I listen and adjust as my subject reacts by either responding or evading my queries.

Bit by bit, I learned that Steven's itinerary was full of business meetings and very little down time. Lee would not have seen much more of Mr. Philips if she'd accompanied him, as she did remaining at her house on the Cape with the soon to be pregnant Barkley and Skyping or face-timing Steven. Lee didn't offer any additional facts about her or Steven or the Vineyard and I wondered if I detected a note of sadness or anxiety in her voice. After securing Barkley in her crate once more and putting her in the Audi's back seat, I watched Lee drive off.

As I made my way back to the pilot's lounge, my cell rang. It was an unfamiliar number. Usually, I ignore calls from unknown numbers, but given what had happened today, I didn't know who might be trying to reach me, so I answered with a formal "Hello."

"Kate, Steven Philips here. I am calling about Perkin and Schuttauf and your estate case."

"It's a mess. I'm appearing in probate court next week in L.A."

"Sorry. Maybe there's something I can do?"

"Unlikely, but thanks anyway. Where are you?"

"About 32,000 feet somewhere over the Atlantic."

"You're using a satcom handset?" My interest was purely technical, as there are no cell towers in the oceans.

"Yeah, Iridium."

"Good choice. They have 66 satellites at low level polar orbit, so you have worldwide coverage, versus the Inmarsat, which fails at about 82 degrees polar north and south."

"My partner has nothing but the best on this G-V."

"Evidently." I paused. "You'll be relieved to know that Barkley is back home, safe with Lee."

"Barkley, Lee's dog?"

"Yours, too, I thought. But yeah, I just flew Barkley from Marstons Mills to Hyannis. Both canine patient and Lee seem fine."

"I'm sorry. I'm not sure I heard you correctly. You did what?"

"I picked up the dog up at Marston Hills and flew her back to Hyannis after her insemination. Lee told me all about it."

"She had you fly the dog home from the vet?"

"She did." Silence, then he continued, "Thanks for the up-date."

"Anytime. By the way, Lee said that you're about to have purebred Bolognese puppies."

"I guess so."

"I thought Barkley was a poodle."

"Me too." Steven laughed.

"What would you get if you mated Barkley with a poodle? A Bolonoodle?"

"I suppose."

"When you do that, put me down for a puppy." I meant it.

"Done. I'll be in Boston tomorrow. I'll call you if I hear anything helpful."

"I appreciate it. Thanks. Bye." I was friendly with a cool undertone, wondering why the show of concern now? When I needed him, he refused to sign the affidavit, which made me feel abandoned; which in turn, pushed my emotional buttons, said my former New York therapist, who continues to provide telephonic tune ups, time to time, as my psyche requires.

I wouldn't hold my breath waiting for Steven Philips to give me a Bolonoodle puppy or to help now that Warren's money was lost in Perkin's fund; but if it made him feel better to call and promise some kind of future support, fine. Plus, I surmised that my doggy airlift this evening was an example of a relationship suffering from, at the very least, communication issues. Good luck to them both. I wondered who'd obtain custody of Barkley and the grandpuppies when Lee and Steven split.

It was late when I returned home. I turned on the news and zoned out, half paying attention and half ruminating on the day's events. Schuttauf was still big news. Though the Securities and Exchange Commission blew it by allowing Ernie to operate his Ponzi scheme under its nose for all those years, it was now, apparently, on the job. The TV news reader confirmed that a federal court in New York granted the SEC relief under SIPA (Securities Investor Protection Act) to halt further fraud; prevent the destruction of evidence; and freeze and preserve assets for victims. Gee, just in the nick of time. The court also appointed a trustee to pursue the case against Schuttauf on behalf of the (now) poor investors. I noted the trustee's name as the California probate court would surely order me and Beck to file for restitution with this man.

Since mid-adulthood, I've enjoyed reading the New England Transcendentalists and some of their unusual progeny (like Ralph Waldo Emerson's unlikely German admirer, Nietzsche). I will re-read Thoreau and his well-worn essays during bad weather days or when I'm on layovers or simply in need of practical American philosophy. From "Walking" I recall the phrase, "Eastward I go only by force; but westward I go free." You hear that line quoted when people discuss the character of the Western Americans and their descendants. Those pioneers who travelled to stake their claims to new land, or escape the ties or laws that bound them to—or in—the settled East. And while I understand the conceptual lure of the "West," I've never personally felt the pull. I like the land scraped by glaciers and boulders and worn by the customs of my forefathers and my faith. I favor a white church steeple anchored by a New England clapboard church on town green more than the sprouting giant sequoias in Mariposa Grove that could tickle the belly of an airplane flown at 300 feet above ground level (AGL).

And it's not that I don't appreciate the beauty of the western landscape. I admit that California, from sea to the Sierra, is objectively more dazzling than anything to be found in New England; yet, it's the latter that I choose as home. I am an East Coaster. It's a state of mind, I've heard it sung. So when the court called my office to reschedule the Warren Ethan hearing for this Friday, there was no joy or frisson of excitement for westward escape. Like it or not, I was flying to LAX on Thursday, where, in the elided words of Thoreau, "Thither business leads me."

I called and asked my CAC boss, Sean, to take me off the schedule for the next week or so. I felt bad about this absence without notice. Late July is the highest of the high seasons, and the worst time for my company to lose a pilot. He responded by repeating verbatim the dates that I said I needed off, thus acknowledging my request and his acceptance. Sean was pure pilot meat. No emotion, no questions, just a verified two way transmission of verbal information. This is what happens when you speak mainly with other pilots and ATC (air traffic control). A pilot could be forgiven for losing the gift of small talk when this was the customary mode of conversation. I thanked Sean for the time off and promised to return to flying as soon as possible. I closed with a comment about the local airport case and how it was progressing slowly, as expected. Sean confirmed receipt of my information and hung up.

I wrapped things up at the office by making a recorded call to poor Lyndsey Taylor. It was a short chat. She seemed sadder than when I first met her in that California courthouse; but she remained determined to prove her paternity. Even if the estate was insolvent, Lyndsey wanted to show the world that Warren was her father and I was her means of proof, but for all the reasons, she just couldn't gather the money needed for the DNA test. I understood. She needed cash and parental attachment, even at this late time. I promised to do what I could, now that all else was really lost. I would ask the court to reconsider compelling Rick to swab the inside of his check and check his DNA's against Lyndsey's. Plus, I would request that Bill Chase pay for these tests using whatever funds remained at his disposal to pay recurring and ordinary Ethan estate expenses.

If denied again, I promised Ms. Taylor that we'd proceed with plan B—with my "Dear Kate" envelope and—if the court wouldn't allow Bill Chase to pay this invoice, I would ask for permission to lend Lyndsey the money. As the administrator of Warren's estate, I didn't want to be accused of champerty, so I needed clearance from the court to advance lab fees from my own pocket. After what had just happened in Manhattan, I didn't think anyone would care if I fronted a few hundred dollars in the quest for truth; it usually costs so much more.

Celeste confirmed that she could handle all professional emergencies in my absence and reminded me that there were phones and the Internet, and even faxes just in case. No matter what, we could remain in touch. She reviewed my trial calendar to make sure we didn't overlook a hearing or a conference. Last, we double-checked my paper notes on top of my physical files for the final "all clear." Celeste remembered that during the afternoon of the day the evening news broke the story of Ernie Schuttauf's massive fraud; I'd called Perkin's office and asked for the statements that I had yet to receive from Beck. My notes confirmed that someone from Perkin's office promised to send them.

In all the excitement, I'd lost track. Besides, I received those same statements from California the very next morning. Now, Perkin's documents would be duplicates. I told Celeste that unless I were to auction the statements on eBay as mementos of financial devastation, featuring the date and time stamped metered postage on the envelope, that they'd be worthless to me; just another set of papers telling me how much money I no longer had to administer in Warren's trust.

"I'll look out for the Perkin envelope just the same and I'll let you know when it arrives." Celeste was cheerful as ever, even during a financial crisis.

"Well, Cel, it might be a while because Perkin, while not quite as evil as Ernie Schuttauf, was still a horrible person and those statements of his were mailed straight from hell—and you know how bad the mail service is between the Cape and Hell."

Celeste smiled and wished me safe travels. I was free to pack that evening and set off the next morning to begin my air trek.

As neither the estate, nor Mr. Beck, was paying for my airline ticket to the West Coast, I decided to try my hand at using a CAC travel pass to fly from BOS to LAX. Usage of one's travel passes involved unavoidable boarding ambiguity that exercised a pilot's previously described negative capability. Yet, it made it possible for someone like me—a low seniority pilot, from a small airline—to fly standby on another airline, at a popular hub, and pay nothing. The catch: I remained uncertain of a seat until the cabin door closed, and even after that sometimes, you could be escorted off the plane if a person with a ticket appeared at the gate before the plane departed.

And so it is, "load factors" are published to airline employees for a reason. They allow jumpseaters and non-revs to analyze the flight and perhaps, catch a bit of luck and hitch a ride every so often, even on the most popular routes. Conventional hangar wisdom teaches the pass traveler to check in early and arrive at the gate in time to take the first scheduled flight of the day to the desired destination. Even if the early flight is booked full or over capacity, you can typically count on a few no shows. No matter what, some full Y fare revenue passengers (the ones who pay the most for their coach tickets and support the industry) will hit their snooze buttons and miss their planes, secure in the knowledge that the carrier will accommodate them by "rolling them over" to the next flight or by booking them on another airline to the same destination. As in life, as in the airline industry, there's always an escape valve for those who pay top dollar.

But every pass traveler knows, there are no pretentions of kindness or customer service when you seek the jumpseat or are listed as a non-rev in a revenue world. Once experienced, you never forget the ignominy of settling into your seat, pulling out your digital reader or paper magazine, only to be tapped on the shoulder by an officious flight attendant who tells you to pack your things—you're off the plane because a pilot senior to you (or a revenue passenger) who was stuck over in Terminal A, just made it to the jetway and the captain has decided to reopen the cabin door to admit her. When that happens, your soul grows callous, your heart hardens, and your once keen sense of compassion and empathy for your fellow traveler diminishes. There are no friends on a "stand by" day.

This is why the jumpseat rider and his kissing cousin, the cabin seat non-rev (as in non-revenue passenger, including everyone who works for an airline, pilot or not, and their immediate family members) flock to the very earliest flights on any given day. My plan was to give myself the best chance for takeoff. I would aim for the five a.m. departure from Boston. I hoped for a seat in the cabin; but listed myself for the cockpit jumpseat, as it's always a better bet you'll be seated in the flightdeck (cockpit) versus the cabin (where everyone else sits) when the destination is popular and the loads are high (planes are full).

Unlike other aviation employees, when you are a certified ATP (Airline Transport Pilot), with the necessary credentials—a valid airline ID, current medical certificate, and your FAA license confirming your current aircrew status—you can ride on the jumpseat in the cockpit of another carrier's plane under reciprocal privilege agreements in place between the carriers who use the post 9/11 CASS (Cockpit Access Security System). So long as there's no one more senior, or from that airline, ahead of you—and the captain approves, it's a pretty good way to travel. But it's always up to the captain to say "yes" or "no," despite your documentation. So introducing yourself when you arrive at his gate, and explaining that you are listed on his jumpseat, is more than just an example of politeness; it's the only way for you to sit in his cockpit.

The morning of my BOS departure grew darker and stormier by the hour. As a standby pass rider, I had enough uncertainty on my plate that I decided to drive. Little planes are never a sure bet in very bad weather, as they will often be delayed or canceled for practical reasons. But if thunderstorms and foul weather are awful for small plane operators and passengers; they're great for jumpseat riders and cabin non-revs alike—so long as it's just bad enough that the paying passengers have difficulty getting to the airport. When that happens, we travel pass riders thank these "misconnects" and wish them safe and easy travels—later in the day, on another flight—as we gratefully take their seats, made empty by bad planning, the acts of God, or even the TSA (Transportation Security Administration) imposed delays at security check points.

So, I was feeling pretty lucky and drove to Logan with an open mind and a small prayer that a decent sized storm would park itself just beyond the airport. It's a delicate balance. If the storms are directly over the airport, it's no good, because while the connectors might be late; your plane is stuck at the airport as well, so it usually works out that everyone's delayed, but then everyone's put on the aircraft that they're scheduled for. This does not help the jumpseat rider or the non-rev hoping for a place on that plane. No, the ideal situation is the TRW (thunderstorm, in METAR-Meteorological Terminal Aviation Routine Weather Report-ese) just ten miles off property. That prevents the arrivals, but allows departures.

I know that wishing for foul weather seems harsh; but traveling for free on industry passes is not for the meek or those who shrink from competition or the willingness to think a bad thought or hope for a certain inconvenience to befall others—without harming them of course. While that seems cruel to the uninitiated, just imagine what it's like to sit around an airport for hours, or days, being turned away, gate after gate, at the last moment because the more senior pilots or revenue passengers—or both—all show up at the last minute.

I was relieved that on this auspicious day for non-rev travel, my worries were for naught. Though I introduced myself to the captain and his crew—mandatory jumpseat courtesy—I made it to

LAX on the first try, in the cabin, in the regular economy section. Just as well, the cabin seats are more comfortable and I could stretch out a bit on the empty seat next to me (another no show). In six hours we'd touchdown in LAX and shortly after, I'd be at my cheap, last minute, luxury hotel preparing for the next day's hearing.

The California probate court hearing commenced promptly at nine. Lyndsey was there by herself, so was Warren's trusted comptroller, Mr. William Chase. I was there present the same complement of attorneys and beneficiaries as the first court date, seemingly so long ago. It would have been a glorious day—if there were any money in the estate. Rarely is an attorney greeted by a judge with the words, "You were absolutely right." Her Honor followed that statement by reviewing her notes and regretting that I was unable to persuade her, based upon my advocacy alone, that Warren's money was in peril with Perkin and his Epcot Fund. But, she recited how under California law, I'd failed to meet my burden of proof when I made that naked application, unsupported by affidavit or evidence, and so she was required to rule against me. (I preferred her telling me that I was right, not that she was even more right.) The judge inquired whether Mr. Beck had produced the decedent's recent Epcot statements. I dolefully reported that they arrived from California in Cape Cod the morning that I'd learned of Perkin's role as a feeder fund for Ernie Schuttauf. I added that I'd not had the time to pore over them in detail; but yes, those statements were finally produced and seemed to be copied to the court, too.

The court also asked Thomas Beck why he hadn't filed papers to show her why he should not be removed as the co-administrator in this estate. Beck's reply shocked me. He didn't think it was necessary after he'd sent those Epcot statements to my office as the judge had ordered. With this nearly contumacious response, the court put him on notice that if he didn't file papers stating why he should not be removed from the estate, that she'd enter an order to that effect by next week. Beck appeared unperturbed. I guessed that this calamity of misfortune was okay with him, or maybe, with no money left, he didn't care to remain in a position of responsibility for his now poor, dead ex-client.

We learned from Mr. Chase that Warren's real estate was encumbered by debt and all properties were in default. But of course, why should anything go right? After nearly an hour of court time, we left the room with a case management order full of deadlines for the accounting that California requires when an estate becomes insolvent during the probate process. All property, real and personal, encumbered or not, would be marshaled and itemized and sold. After paying the brokers, the transactional lawyers, and the creditors, I doubted there'd be enough money left to cover the bill for my ex's favorite dinner wine. No matter what in the past I thought of Rick or his wife, I felt bad for them now. No one expected this sudden fall from affluence. As a couple, they were probably least capable of coping with this type of calamity.

Before the session ended, I made a special request to revisit the DNA test issue. The court indulged my entreaty, hearing my argument and then promptly denied my request for Rick to provide a buccal swab. I was, however, as co-trustee, granted permission to personally advance funds for Ms. Taylor's own DNA testing, albeit without a court order compelling Rick's cooperation. I was ordered to disclose the amount paid and the lab results within 24 hours of receipt. The judge reiterated that now especially, the estate was not in the position to be spending money.

Ms. Taylor heard it all in court and remained in the hallway to speak with me once the proceeding ended. As Ms. Taylor was sanctioned to be at this hearing, I felt safe speaking with her without a recording device.

"Kate, thanks for being my advocate." Lyndsey seemed sincere.

"I'm not your lawyer. I do what's best for the trust."

"Well, I've got something for you." Lyndsey reached into her pocketbook and took out a package that I recognized.

"Your saliva sample, I presume?" I said, nicely.

"Yup. You'll front the money?"

"Yes, I will. When I'm back in my office I'll complete the paperwork and send the money to the lab. We'll have a result in two weeks or so."

"You're a good person, no matter what they say about you." Lyndsey was full of goodwill towards me now.

"Well, don't let anyone else know or it'll wreck my street cred." I smiled and took the envelope from her hand and placed it in my own satchel.

"You'll call me when you know something?" Lyndsey asked.

"Of course."

151

"Is it really true, that Warren's money is gone?" Lyndsey seemed hopeful that I had a better answer.

"It's true. Warren was in good company, some of the richest people in the world were fleeced by Schuttauf." I was heartsick, still.

"Poor rich people. Just my luck."

"Let's see what happens. At least you'll know if Warren was your father."

"Either way, I was cheated."

I wasn't about to take on that topic.

"Lyndsey, I'll be in touch. Take care of yourself."

As I left the courthouse, I felt a near compulsion to walk over to a dejected Rick and Tiffany, but when their daggers nearly blinded me I decided it was best to move along. As a pilot, my eyes are my livelihood. I did nod graciously in their direction, but as their backs were turned to me, they missed my gesture. Maybe that was just as well.

CHAPTER TWELVE

After the court hearing, I went directly to the airport. LAX is interesting because it's one of the few places in the world, along with JFK and LHR (London Heathrow), where the masses mix with the famous who don't fly in their own or chartered private planes. So, hoi polloi can be on a security line with the beautiful and the celebrated, before the latter depart for private VIP lounges that the airlines secretly reserve for them. But, as an airline captain, even for a small operation, I have credentials that allow me to bypass most of the strict screening measures that TSA places before the flying public. I whizzed by Heidi Klum and Nicole Kidman in the security queues, traveling separately, removing their respective shoes; but that was where my special treatment ended.

Though my trip to the West Coast went perfectly (I was boarded on the very first flight I attempted to take from Logan to LAX); my return travel plans today were not running as smoothly. It was early afternoon and the delays and cancellations of the morning were mounting, wreaking havoc on my itinerary. Despite listing myself as both a non-rev passenger and a jumpseat rider with pilot credentials, I watched from gate after gate as plane after plane departed for Boston without me. I came close once, but an employee from the airline on which I attempted travel appeared at the last minute, flashed her ID, and took my seat in that plane.

Finally, after watching several more flights depart for the East Coast during the SoCal afternoon and evening, I was granted access to a cabin seat on narrow body nighthawk from LAX to JFK. I took it happily, and would get myself from New York up to Boston somehow despite the all night leg during my WOCL (window of circadian low). My immediate goal was to reach the Atlantic Coast of the country and work out the details, north or south, after debarkation.

According to the "airshow" display, I slept away the hours over Nevada to Pennsylvania despite my uncomfortable crouch in a middle seat of the last row next to the lav. Still, you couldn't beat the price, if you didn't factor in the last twelve hours at the airport watching, waiting, and hoping to board a plane home. But that's the non-rev experience; it's always hit or miss. When we landed in New York, I was lucky. My own airline had a commuter flight serving the JFK to BOS route. The timing was right and as an employee, I had rights to any vacant seat: my employer's metal, my dibs. For those forty minutes up the coastline between Long Island and New England, seated across from a paying passenger, I let go my worries and enjoyed the scenery. For now, I was relieved to be in a familiar and reliable propjet heading towards home.

I was exhausted when we landed at Logan, but determined to send Lyndsey's DNA to the lab along with Warren's envelope flap saliva sample today. I gathered my reserves and drove from Boston to Hyannis, hoping I'd get there before the post office closed. The summer traffic, however, made the seventy mile trip nearly three hours long and I reached my office on Route 28 past noon. I ran in and fired up the computer to quickly prepare the transmittal letter to the lab enclosing Lyndsey's sample, Warren's envelope flap, and my law firm's check. As soon as I placed everything in a mailing packet, I drove to the post office only to find it closed. I missed it by minutes. Disappointed, but undaunted, I returned to my office with my special DNA package that would have to be dispatched Monday morning.

In my absence, Celeste had organized the mail and set it on my desk ready for my review. Jetlagged but wired, I dove into the pile. One large, white padded mailer immediately caught my eye. It was posted from Manhattan late in the afternoon of the day that the Schuttauf debacle unfolded on the evening newscasts. It came from Perkin's office. I knew what it held, the last two years' statements of doom. Why bother reading that again? I set the Perkin envelope aside and decided to call it a night for the day. I figured sleeping in my bed would do me a world of good.

"Good morning, Ms. Kate." Celeste was in the office earlier than I on the Monday morning after my lost weekend.

"Hi, Cel," I answered at half past nine, having just personally gone to the post office to mail the lab's envelope containing Lyndsey's saliva swab and Warren's "Dear Kate" divorce envelope.

"Are we on summer time?" Cel asked me, warmly.

"Why no, we're in summer time, so dock me." I was slightly impudent.

"You're a bear this morning. Did you wake up on the wrong side of your cave?" Cel was sassy, too.

"Sorry, slept in. Depression, I think."

"Make some coffee, the caffeine will help."

"Sure, Cel, how do you want it?"

"Not for me, for you. But if you're there, I'll take it light with cream and sugar."

I nodded and headed to the coffee machine. As the water warmed, I filled Cel in on the events in California. The accounting, the encumbered assets, the insolvent estate, Lyndsey's saliva, and the court's permission for me to forward the lab fee to test her DNA, although we never did disclose that we were testing against a dead man's tongue, so to speak. I wondered if that mattered and decided under the circumstances that it didn't. The court refused to order Rick to stick a Q-tip in his mouth. So what did the judge think I'd be paying for when I, the co-trustee, asked permission to advance the lab fee? I was satisfied that paying to test Lyndsey's relationship to Warren—using something that just happened to belong to me—was permissible. The court did not limit the DNA testing; it just avoided ordering Rick to cooperate. Celeste nodded attentively, like a concerned sibling, or aunt, maybe, though our age difference was not that great.

After I made us both the coffees that were supposed to make me feel better, we moved to my office. Celeste and I reviewed the work calendar, determining what had to be done today, versus what should be accomplished in the coming week, given my obligation to CAC and my promise to fly my little heart out to make up for my sudden and unplanned absence. Sitting across from me, Celeste noticed the unopened white mailer on my desk with the Manhattan return address.

"Ms. Kate, you didn't open this?"

"No, why bother. I know what's in there."

"I want to see the cover letter." Celeste was serious.

"Why?"

"Because."

"Well then, by all means, here's my letter opener and my receipt stamp. Go for it."

I began riffling through a file while Celeste opened the big white envelope.

"Very nice. High PQ."

"What?"

"The paper, high petting quality. Feel the linen, it's like a dollar bill."

"If only. What period do the statements cover?"

"Here, see for yourself."

Celeste put the cover letter back in the opened envelope and handed the package over my desk and into my outstretched hands. I set the mailer aside and closed the file I'd been working on. Celeste remained in the chair and exhaled loudly in disapproval over my delay. When I didn't immediately respond to her breathy protest, she sipped her coffee and stared at the package. I knew that she wanted me to do something with this material so she could file the statements and touch the pretty stationery again.

When I was good and ready, I grabbed the mailer, slid the documents out, and laid them across my desk. I noticed that Perkin's office sent statements for the last three years, with the most current statements at the bottom of the stack. I'd seen the first four statements before. They were among the quarterly reports that Perkin handed me back when I was in his office. I already shared these with Mike and Steven. Next, I found the statements that Mr. Beck was so late to produce, spanning backwards two years to the present. It was nearly too painful to review that sudden swoop from the multi-millions of dollars in June of this year to nothing as of now; but I persevered and read on. And then I reread the statements from the last two years, twice more.

There was a mistake. Perkin must have mixed up his accounts, yet the statements bore Warren's personal information. I must have looked alarmed because Celeste asked what happened and why my face went white and my jaw dropped.

"Something's not right here." I said with unease.

"What do you mean?"

"These statements show that all but one hundred thousand dollars was withdrawn over a period of eighteen months. Most of Warren's money was withdrawn from the Epcot account six months before the Schuttauf news broke."

"So you have the wrong statements?"

"I don't know. I just don't know."

"Call Perkin's office." Celeste seemed unfazed and eager to help me resolve this simple mix-up.

"Okay."

That wasn't about to help because there was no one from Epcot at the Park Avenue office to speak with me. Perkin's operation was shuttered, save the federal investigators doing their work. Then it dawned on me to call the feds. Since I'd learned that the Perkin-Schuttauf arrangement was a fraud, it seemed appropriate to ask an FBI agent if my statements were mixed up with someone else's, or whether something even more sinister was afoot? Did Perkin fabricate these documents on that fateful day as part of plan to continue the charade? I looked for the message from the FBI agent who'd reached out to me after the news broke last week. I made the call to the number he left and was relieved when the same agent answered the line and heard me out. He was assigned to this case and his staff had compiled a list for the federal prosecutors of who had lost what, when, and how much. He told me to wait while he accessed his records. It wasn't long before he came back on the line.

"A hundred grand and change was in the account according to Perkin's files." The agent was nonchalant.

"Do you have the correct account for Warren Ethan?"

To verify, I promptly furnished the FBI agent with Warren's date of birth, address, and even his social security number. Warren was, after all, dead. What more could happen, identity theft?

"Correct. Reports verified, amount on last day of operation in the account of Warren Ethan, 100,219.58 dollars" The FBI agent was matter of fact.

For the next twenty minutes the agent indulged me as I read the account summaries on the last pages for each of eight most recent quarterly reports, going back two years. Everything matched. Every number, every entry, and every multi-million dollar withdrawal, which I now hoped represented real money that I or law enforcement could locate. I attempted to gain more information from this agent: Did this mean Perkin stole from Warren's account? Where was Perkin? Did the feds have his assets frozen? Could I get my hands on that money for the trust? The agent listened for several minutes before confirming the 100,219.58 dollar sum again, and that was all. He suggested that I contact the Department of Justice. He'd done all he could for me. I thanked him and hung up.

Celeste, riveted by my part of the dialogue with the FBI agent over the Perkin statements from Manhattan, remained seated in the chair on the opposite side of my desk throughout the call.

"I will get the number for the federal prosecutor?" Celeste asked.

"Yes, and we have to call the California judge after I speak with the federal prosecutor. I must advise the court of this discrepancy."

"And the parties, too?" Celeste asked.

"First the judge, and then I'll take her direction." I paused.

"What do you think happened?" Celeste inquired.

"I have no idea, but, maybe, just maybe, if Perkin siphoned off that money, I could file a suit against him and get a judgment for the 184 million dollars that was withdrawn from Warren's account a full six months before the scam was discovered."

"Won't everyone who lost money be going after Perkin's assets?" Celeste wondered.

"Probably, but I'd try to attach his assets first, like, real estate—or all those Rothkos that perhaps were still hanging in his office."

I explained that this would not be easy and there would be obstacles to recovering every dollar lost to Schuttauf through Perkin; but at the least I had solid legal ground to file a claim to the 164 million that Warren had initially invested in Epcot, if not the 20 million in paper gains that were fake. I could certainly fulfill my role as trustee by recovering a good portion of that original money.

I recalled Emerson's journal entry, "I am Defeated all the time; yet to Victory I am born," and for this moment, I believed it applied to me, too. I was nearly giddy, imagining myself in the gallery watching as Sotheby's global auctions garnered gazillions from the sale of the Marc Rothko canvasses that the sheriff would have seized from the Perkin Park Avenue offices due to my legal work. But of course, it would never happen like that. This was a criminal matter and the federal and state prosecutors would be in charge of those paintings and any other assets they could get their hands on. After I thought it through, I told Celeste that she was correct. I would have to get in line with the rest of the victims and creditors to collect anything.

I called the probate court. Though it was still early for the West Coast, my news could not wait. This unexpected discovery gave me a glimmer of hope, though I had no idea what Perkin did with those withdrawals, or exactly how I would be allowed to proceed on behalf of Warren's estate. I needed help and thought that maybe an injunction against Perkin and his assets would be helpful, even if Warren's estate was in a long queue of theft victims. After leaving my message on the automated court voice mail system, I phoned Mike Fortune. He had friends working in the SEC and the DOJ and the state's Office of Attorney General. Mike could learn from them if Perkin had stolen money from other clients—and what I could do to maximize recovery for Warren's trust. Waiting for Mike's assistant to patch him through, I felt a twinge of optimism that maybe though awful, this catastrophe could have a satisfactory, if not exactly happy, ending.

"Kate, what's going on?" Mike sounded concerned.

"I just opened the statements from Perkin and they're different from the ones I got from Warren's attorney in California."

I explained the differences as Mike listened quietly. When I finished the tale, Mike informed me that he'd not heard about any other cases in which Perkin had stolen from clients, other than the obvious high fees his feeder fund charged simply to place his clients' money into Schuttauf's fraudulent scheme. But he promised to make some calls and report back. Meantime, I'd send him copies of these new statements and we'd go from there.

Times of confusion can create peril—or not; depending on how you react, in or out of an airplane. Regaining control after a disruption is critical to a good outcome. For instance, every pilot is taught how to fly the plane straight and level by checking one's position in reference to the horizon and making necessary corrections. Aircraft control requires mastery over the ailerons, elevators, and rudders to adjust airspeed, power, pitch (up and down motion), and yaw (side to side motion), as required. Besides the physical elements of safe flying, aviators rely upon other aids—checklists and data collections protocols, i.e., flight operational quality assurance reports (FOQAs), aviation safety action programs (ASAPs), and line observation safety audits (LOSAs)—to help them analyze their performance and eliminate errors and hazards. I try to think along these lines when I run into any situation that throws me, aviation or not. I take a step back, regain control, review the data, assess my reactions, and strive for a better outcome in the future. The contents of the Perkin statements differing from what Mr. Beck had provided last week

159

caused a brief disturbance; but I was regaining control and aimed to maintain a steady course.

In the midst of my Warren trust audit, Celeste, who'd gone back to her own desk out front, buzzed me.

"What's up?"

"A Mr. Philips is on the line for you."

"Okay, give me a minute."

I took his call when I was ready.

"Steven, it's Kate. What can I do for you?" I said in my medium friendly voice.

"I've been busy at work but wanted you to know that I requested you to fly me to the Vineyard this weekend."

"Thanks, I look forward to it."

"Right. How are you doing with Schuttauf matter?"

I paused.

"Kate, are you there?"

"Funny you should ask." I muttered.

"How do you mean?"

I made a tactical decision and told Steven what I'd just seen and that now I was dealing with possible larceny by Mr. Perkin. Steven listened, much as Mike did. When I finished the briefing, Steven asked if he could stop by. He was at Lee's house on the Cape and wanted to have a look at the statements from Perkin and review what I'd received from California, to compare them for himself.

Having nothing to lose by seeking Steven's judgment, I agreed. Come over, have a look, what's the harm, none of which I verbalized—but thought. My spoken words to him were, "I'm free at noon."

He arrived at two.

"Hi, Captain." Steven greeted me as I walked from my office towards the reception area.

"Welcome. The statements are on my desk. Follow me."

Once we were in my private office and I sat in my chair, I motioned for Steven to sit across from me. I watched as he surveyed the décor and the setting.

"Nice place," he said. "Cozy."

"Thanks. We like it." I was referring to Celeste and me, as none of my Cape Cod clients ever commented on my office space.

As I handed him both packets of statements, I noticed Steven's eyes fixed upon the two framed photographs on the bookcase beside my desk.

"Your parents?"

"Yes, may they rest in peace." I said.

"Sorry to hear that. Recent?"

"No." I hesitated. "They were killed soon after I was graduated from law school."

"Oh."

Steven appeared surprised, yet was polite enough not to ask what happened if I didn't offer an explanation. So after a still moment, I did.

"Both my mom and dad were pilots. One day they were out in their Piper Cub, my dad was in command, when another pilot training for his instrument flight rating and wearing a hood, misread his instruments. He flew outside his stated path and into my parents' plane just slightly above their altitude. They were flying VFR, with flight following. They never saw what hit them from behind. He sheared their plane in half in midair."

Silence.

"My condolences. Is that why you're a pilot?" Steven's voice was sympathetic.

"Maybe. My therapist and I still are working on that one." I managed a trace of a grin.

"Did you sue the pilot responsible?"

"The estate hired a lawyer and sued. I couldn't handle the case emotionally or professionally. I was traumatized and didn't even have my bar results yet. I was what you would call a 'degreed law clerk.'"

"Did the estate win?"

"Yes, the lawyers and I established a trust to help the Audubon Society maintain the Wellfleet Bay Wildlife Sanctuary and honor my parents. I was the trustee. Warren knew about it."

"How's that?"

"How what?"

"How would a man like Warren Ethan living in California know about your parents' trust?"

At that point I realized I never told Steven that I was Warren's daughter-in-law.

"I was married to Warren's only child, Richard Ethan, for more than a decade."

"Oh." Steven hesitated. "And you're involved in your former husband's father's trust—after the divorce?"

"Yes. Strange but true. My therapist and my lawyer are helping me solve that puzzle." I paused. "Just kidding, I don't have a lawyer. It's just my therapist." I smiled and lightened the tone that I'd just darkened by my sad tale of sudden and horrific parental death; ditto, litigation.

"You look so much like your mom." Steven was alternatively examining the photo of my parents and, in person, my face.

"Yes, except the eyes are different." I nodded in agreement.

"I can see that."

Having exhausted that topic, Steven directed his attention to the other frame. A memento from my married days, taken somewhere in Colorado, this photo displayed the pinky-tangerine alpenglow on the snow-covered Rockies captured after a long day on the slopes. Despite an undercurrent of melancholy, the images of my lost parents and those marmalade peaks from long ago brought me both peace and comfort when I needed a boost in times of sorrow or worse.

"Do you ski much?" he asked.

"Used to. Not now. Do you?"

"Not since I blew out my ACL on a double black trail in Utah a decade ago. Glop caught my ski and kept it during a hop turn." He answered, removing the statements from their envelopes.

"Oh." Was my response. I wasn't interested.

I continued, "You'll see one set of statements shows that there was barely one hundred thousand dollars in the Perkin's Epcot partnership when news broke of Schuttauf's fraud; the other set of statements shows that a 184 million dollar fortune was with Perkin at the end of June, and lost.

"Hmmm." Steven uttered in response.

Moments passed. I sat watching Steven pore over the papers, comparing each page from each package, side by side, on the edge of my desk.

"The L.A. papers are slightly different." Steven opined.

We spent the next hour comparing the documents and inspecting the similarities and differences in paper quality, text, ink tone, spacing, and format.

"Did Beck have a power of attorney for Warren?" Steven asked.

"Don't know."

162

"Is he still in the country?"

"I think so."

I couldn't imagine Beck stealing from his longtime client and friend. Plus, Beck was a man of means and connections. He didn't have to do this.

"What do you suggest I do now?"

"Did you alert the authorities?" He replied.

"Of course. An FBI agent called me after the Schuttauf fraud was discovered. We were in touch again after I saw Perkin's statements. I've also called the Department of Justice and the state and federal Attorneys General offices."

"Do you know who you spoke to?" Steven asked.

"I don't recall, but I have the details in my notes. Why?"

"Curious, I've had to work with the authorities on occasion."

"Oh." I said and paused. "Did you have funds in a Ponzi scheme, too?" I asked.

"No." Was Steven's taciturn reply.

We were silent for a moment, and then I asked, "What else should I do?"

"Be alert and keep your ears and eyes open."

"Where do you think that money is?"

"No telling."

Steven then explained how money can move around the world without detection till years later, if ever. He told me about Taiwanese billionaire Y.C. Wang, who died without a will in Short Hills, New Jersey in 2008.

"What happened?" I asked, unsure of why this was relevant to my situation. After all, Warren had a will; but not the one people were expecting.

"Years after the estate was divided in Taiwan, Winston, a son of the billionaire, discovered that some of his dad's trusted financial advisors were involved in hiding about fifteen billion dollars of the dad's wealth."

"How did they do that?"

"By creating several secret offshore trusts and then transferring assets into them. Winston wants courts in the U.S., Hong Kong, and Bermuda to set aside those transfers and return the misappropriated assets to the estate for the heirs' to inherit."

"Gee, Hong Kong, Bermuda, U.S., sounds like your recent itinerary."

"Yes, it does." Steven, unaffected, refused the bait.

"Will the son win?" I was eager to hear that someone would find a happy ending after losing so much estate money.

"The lawsuits are ongoing, search www.offshorealert.com and 'Formosa Plastics Group' and see for yourself. At least Winston traced the assets out of Taiwan and was named the administrator for his dad's estate. That's a start."

"I guess. Steven, are you telling me that Beck took the money?"

Steven looked up from one particular statement that had caught his eye. "I don't know. What I see are statements that show something unusual happened. I'm giving you one scenario."

"Right..." I trailed off in thought.

"Warren himself might have orchestrated this caper to escape estate taxes or a lawsuit. You never know."

"Would he go through all this trouble to create a holographic will, establish a trust for veterans, and then secret away his own money not to pay the government or face creditors? I don't think so." I said with an edge.

"Kate, you don't know."

I stopped for a moment to reflect on what I knew and offered, "Maybe Warren wasn't aware of the details of his holdings. As long as Chase paid his bills and money was available to him, why would Warren care or have reason to suspect anything was amiss? Beck could have used a power of attorney to withdraw the money from Epcot without anyone noticing."

"Maybe. Except whoever got the statements would have seen those withdrawals." Steven paused. "Did the statements go to Beck?"

"No, according to Chase, Warren's comptroller, Warren made it a point to have those statements sent directly to him, not even allowing Chase to see them."

"Kate, you just don't have enough information to know what happened. But where there's paper, there's generally a trail, same for transactions on computers."

I remained silent.

Steven glanced down at his watch, as he'd done before while I was his at his house on the Vineyard, confirming that our time was up. He rose from the chair in which he'd sat for the last hour plus and issued a final, friendly directive, "Kate, do the best you can. It's not your fault. Someone who understands global finance, hot money, and tax havens should be digging into this."

"Are you volunteering to help?" I said hopefully.

"Not at all."

"Can you suggest anyone?" I queried.

"Not right now." He paused and then said, "I'll see you later in the week at the airport."

While waiting for the California probate court to call back, I recalled a trip to Europe with Rick in my old life. Travelling through Switzerland I heard someone joke about the quaint Swiss city where we lodged for the evening. "Zug is like Zurich, where the streets are clean and the money is dirty." It got me thinking about offshore funds, tax havens, and hiding money in trusts. Many countries like Liechtenstein, Bermuda, Singapore, Hong Kong, Liberia, and the Cook, the Marshall, and the Channel Islands excelled at hiding assets to shield them from taxes.

I recalled Warren visiting the Caymans in the distant past. "The Caymans" were several islands: Little Cayman, Cayman Brac, and the biggest, Grand Cayman, had a decent airport (Owen Roberts International Airport MWCR/GCM) with an exclusive and secluded terminal to accommodate all those corporate G-Vs and their clandestine comings and goings—no stamps on passports; no records kept of landings. Bankers were stationed there to service their tax evading patrons. There was even one building, Ugland House, in George Town on Grand Cayman Island that served as the official headquarters of more than 15,000 shell corporations. I mused, "The Grand Cayman Islands, where the shells are corporate and the climate is nonregulatory," but I had no idea if that was where the Ethan money trail led.

My own cyber search of Beck's name and the Caymans revealed nothing. No surprise there. Generally, if you hide money, you don't use your real name; but it was all I could think of to do. I needed a professional asset tracer—or hider—under the theory that it takes a thief to catch one. The situation brought to mind a biblical phrase, "Behold, I send you forth as sheep in the midst of wolves: be ye therefore wise as serpents, and harmless as doves." I wondered if that were possible and hoped it was.

Celeste buzzed me, "Kate, California is on the line."

165

I picked up, announced my name over a speaker, and barely heard the law clerk instruct me to remain on the line for the judge and the other attorneys and the want-to-be heir, Lyndsey Taylor, who were standing by. After what seemed like hours, but was barely a minute, the judge greeted each of us by name, assuring that we could hear her voice and vice versa. She recited the contents of my message—how I'd discovered the discrepancy between the statements from Perkin and those supplied by Thomas Beck. The court wanted to know what else I could add to this breaking news. I filled everyone in on what I'd done and who I'd spoken with to confirm that most of the Ethan estate was not in the Epcot fund when it collapsed. Instead, per the FBI, only a hundred thousand and change was lost. The rest of Warren's assets, about 184 million dollars, were withdrawn, bit by bit, over a course of about eighteen months, beginning two years ago.

Silence dominated, then the judge spoke.

"What do you know about this, Mr. Beck?" She demanded.

"Nothing, Your Honor. I'm shocked by this disclosure."

The judge asked if anyone had anything to add—I spoke up.

"I will need help from someone (I looked at my notes from my meeting with Steven an hour ago) who understands global finance, hot money, and tax havens."

"By that do you mean a forensic accountant, Ms. Bergin? Do you have anyone in mind?" The judge seemed interested.

"Yes, Your Honor. I'm working on that."

"Mr. Beck? Before I rule on the motion to remove you, what have you to say?"

"With all due respect, Your Honor, without having an opportunity to see the statements that so alarmed Ms. Bergin, I rather think she misread them. And while I understand her motivation to find a glimmer of hope to recover the money that Perkin lost in the Schuttauf Ponzi scheme, I doubt if her account of events is correct."

The judge ruled quickly, as she always did.

"Ms. Bergin, you are to furnish the court and counsel with copies of the documents from Perkin's office by the end of the day, California time, scanned and sent electronically."

"I will do that." I affirmed.

The court continued, "Upon receipt, I will entertain the names of proposed forensic accounting experts to investigate the difference between the statements from Mr. Beck and Mr. Perkin."

A pause.

"Mr. Beck, if I don't have papers from you explaining why you should not be released from your position as co-trustee and co-administrator by tomorrow, I will entertain an order to show cause from Ms. Bergin to dismiss you from this case."

Finally, the court noted, "Ms. Taylor, you are on this call due to the appeal you filed and the stay of dismissal granted. Unless the appellate court rules otherwise, you will not receive the financial documents discussed today."

"That's not fair." Lyndsey protested, without using the obligatory address, "Your Honor."

"Good luck on your appeal, Ms. Taylor." The court coldly replied.

Beck piped up predictably and pompously. "Your Honor, I ask that I receive hard copies of these new documents. My secretary will be out of the office for the next few days and I don't have access to whatever comes through on the computer without her assistance."

"Would faxing suffice for you, Mr. Beck?" The judge was accommodating.

"I would prefer copies sent by overnight delivery, I'll pay the costs."

The judge asked, "Ms. Bergin, can you do that by tomorrow, to ensure his receipt of the hard copies the following day?"

"Yes, Your Honor, I'll send the copies both ways, electronically and for next day hand delivery, charged to Mr. Beck's firm."

"Good, it's so ordered, with Mr. Beck reimbursing Ms. Bergin costs. Ms. Bergin, you supply the form of order. This matter is adjourned."

CHAPTER THIRTEEN

Celeste helped me scan and transmit, then copy and send, the sets of statements as the court directed. The package for Mr. Beck would leave the Cape in the morning. I was also searching for a forensic accountant. I called Mike and left a message asking for the name of an expert who was familiar with tax havens and all the intrigues that Steven described. Waiting for Mike's reply I grew anxious. With the passing of each day, whoever had taken Warren's 184 million dollars was closer to keeping his ill-gotten gains. I was out of my depth and I didn't like being ignorant and blind, unable to fly clear.

I recalled my early flight training. My certified flight instructor (CFI) would warn, once a pilot is in a dangerous circumstance, escape can be harder than you'd expect. He would tell me how he'd lost several student pilots within 250 hours of gaining their certificates because of bad judgment and overrating their aviation skills. These fatalities commonly occurred when the new pilots flew into marginal visibility conditions or instrument meteorological conditions (IMC)—for which they were not trained and could not handle. If you cannot read your instruments and you can't see outside the cockpit, you are in trouble when you find yourself "popeye" in the goo.

Rookie pilots will resort to dangerous maneuvers to fly out of the muck and into what they think are safer visual (VFR) conditions. Some will "scud run" under the weather in an effort escape the soup and to find visual contact with the ground. Unfortunately, many fail to avoid physical contact with it. We call that controlled flight into terrain (CFIT) and it kills amateurs and professionals alike because flying low means flying where obstructions and terrain are found.

Each month the NTSB accident reports http://www.ntsb.gov/aviationquery/ reveal pilots who've flown into a low ridge or a cell phone tower or power wires in the ironic effort to get below the low ceilings where they could see—but didn't. Other pilots fare just as poorly by trying to climb above the milky sky. Instead of reaching the visual flight rule (VFR) conditions they need, they lose control, becoming spatially disoriented by the poor visibility.

My CFI would tell me how to recognize and avoid these traps; but if I ignored his advice and found myself in a perilous situation in the cockpit, I could regain control by thinking it through and remaining calm, always maintaining SA (situational awareness)—noting where I was, where I was headed, and where the weather (WX) and obstructions (planes, towers, terrain, and high tension wires) were—and never being afraid to ask for help. Many a pilot who's flown over paygrade in experience has been saved by ATC's becoming his eyes and ears, and then talking him out of the pall and into the clear, where safe flying and landing were possible. I needed eyes and ears in California. I knew one person who'd be interested in helping me help her.

I told Celeste that I'd be in my office for a while, recording a call to my soon-to-be collaborator, Ms. Lyndsey Taylor. After confirming my actions on her behalf—yes, I mailed the DNA test; yes, I would tell her the moment I received the results—I enlisted her services. Would I pay her? No. The estate was insolvent, but she could help herself by helping me learn what was happening three-thousand miles away. Lyndsay didn't immediately grasp the implications of the differences in the Perkin statements versus the ones I received from California, so I drew her a picture, in words, of the nub of the issue.

"Lyndsey, as you know from the court conference, we have proof that something is wrong. It looks like someone secretly took control of Warren's assets and depleted the Epcot account months before it went bust."

"How does this help me, or you?" Lyndsey, always the charitable one, queried.

"If we can find out who withdrew money from the Epcot fund and where he deposited it, we can restore the estate and the trust with whatever amount we can identify and recover."

I was clear and calm reporting our position.

"But if the DNA test doesn't prove I'm Warren's daughter, what good does his money do me?" Lyndsey, showing her true, "what's in it for me" colors.

"But you are his daughter, right? Besides, something from nothing is nothing. But with the DNA coming out as you predict, your nothing status can turn into something after all, with a good lawyer, like me, helping you." I told her in my friendly but formal attorney voice, as persuasive as it was stern.

"What do you want?" Lyndsey whined.

"Your help. Learn what you can about Thomas Beck. I suspect he's behind this."

"And how am I supposed to do that?" Lyndsey was not yet on board.

"You are in L.A.; I am on Cape Cod. Use your location and the talents that God gave you. Focus. Be resourceful. Pretend your future depends on finding out what Beck did with Warren's money, because, it probably does."

"You mean, like, spy on him?" Lyndsey caught the gist, but was unsure how to execute the plan.

"Do what you can within the limits of the law and propriety." I said, after all, I was recording this.

"I'll think about it."

"Lyndsey, who filed that appeal for you and got that stay from the court's dismissal order?"

"I did. I got the form off the court web site and followed the filing instructions. It wasn't hard. You lawyers are overpaid."

"Not in this case, at least not now." I promptly replied.

"You know, I have my father's brain." Lyndsey responded.

"Then put it to good use. Make him proud. Meantime, take care and call when you can." I said I as disconnected and stopped recording, to protect us both.

With hours to go before my evening CAC flight, and no legal clients on the office schedule this afternoon, I fired up the old PC and commenced a search for information at a web site that Steven recommended about money hiders. When I browsed its material, I decided it was too sophisticated for someone at my level and that I needed a primer on tax havens. Recalling that Al Capone was convicted on tax evasion charges, I read up on the topic and learned that Meyer Lansky, the "Mob's Accountant," was the father of the offshore account, American ingenuity at its most fiscally harmful. Lansky originated the "loan-back" scheme whereby assets would be changed into cash or bearer bonds and deposited into unnamed (but numbered) Swiss or Caribbean bank accounts. Then, the cash would come back to the owner via "a loan," with interest due, claimed as a legitimate, deductible business expense. Many American companies continue to use a variation of the Mob ploy to this very day.

Mining this cyber vein, I found references to the "Dutch sandwich"—a clever, if not erotic, technique for moving corporate profits through Ireland, the Netherlands, and Bermuda to evade U.S. corporate tax rates. More web pages revealed, in easy to follow text and diagrams, how Swiss banks had been serving the financial needs of drug dealers and crooks—including the Cali and Medellin cartels and the Russian and Sicilian Mafias—for decades, or at least since Lansky taught the villains and their bankers how to hide cash from the tax man.

Indignant over foreign jurisdictions encouraging tax evasion, money laundering, and corruption, a few more clicks exposed a surprise. Delaware has welcomed thousands of shell companies to its little shores and reputedly holds an estimated five trillion dollars' worth of sheltered or "undeclared" assets within its diminutive borders. I wondered, could Warren's money be just down the U.S. coast?

More Internet digging revealed more dirt on the various island nations. Thinking about Steven's own recent worldwide trip, and his Cook Islands decor, I conducted a deeper search using Rarotonga's major city, "Avarua," as a term, along with the words "offshore" and "trust" and "financial secrecy." And it was just like Emerson wrote in one of his essays, sometimes the one book you need appears before your very eyes at just the right time; same thing happens with web pages.

My computer screen bore the mother lode of tax haven information. A link to a site, http://www.icij.org/ operated and owned by the International Consortium of Investigative Journalists (ICIJ) appeared at the top of my search results. I clicked and read with rapt attention about worldwide corruption, "Secrecy for Sale," and the "Global Offshore Money Maze." I searched the comprehensive ICIJ "Offshore Leaks Database" containing the actual names behind secret companies, trusts, and directorships. I was hopeful, but found nothing familiar or related to Thomas Beck, Warren Ethan, or his fortune. Still, what I did read astonished—and appalled.

"Offshore operatives" like Singapore-based Portcullis TrustNet (PNT) and British Virgin Island-based Commonwealth Trust Limited (CTL) helped their wily and wealthy customers "weave elaborate financial structures" that spanned "countries, continents and hemispheres." One-stop-shops for high net worth (HNW) entities and individuals seeking "asset management activities," PNT and CTL buried trillions of treasure under multiple layers of trusts, foundations, insurance products, and other corporate entities (with "nominee" shareholders and directors) tailor-made for anonymously hiding cash and assets offshore.

The rich who were motivated to hide their assets could do so, easily, with a sophisticated battery of experts at their disposal. Within a few clicks, http://www.icij.org/offshore/who-uses-offshore-world one could find the "how-to's," hard facts, and shocking accounts of such misdeeds. Each story was supported by copies of the actual documents proving how teams of lawyers, financial advisors, and accountants secretly moved money around the globe, free of tax and beyond the reach of most laws—and divorcing spouses. I read about Tony Merchant, a famous Canadian lawyer, married to a Canadian Senator, who hid from taxing authorities more than a million dollars in a Cook Island trust. Using third party names (not his own) as shareholders and directors of his companies, he cloaked his identity until someone leaked the paperwork to the ICIJ, who shared it with the world.

According to this site, former U.S. citizen and Friend of Bill Clinton (FOB), Denise Rich, the ex-wife of the presidentially pardoned felon, Marc Rich, used offshore accounts to avoid U.S. taxes. So did many, many others including James R. Mellon and Mit Romney—who favored Bermuda, Ireland, Luxembourg, the Cayman Islands, and until 2010, Switzerland. Even the Crocodile Dundee actor, Paul Hogan, tried his luck at the offshore game; but it backfired on him. In the mid-naughts, Hogan's lawyers and financial advisors structured secret offshore trusts—Quatre Saison and Carthage—to shield the actor's Crocodile Dundee income from the Australian taxing authority. Only problem for Paul, they hid it from him, too.

As the ICIJ site reported: "It was 'a sordid tale of wayward fiduciaries and international fraudsters supposedly absconding with millions of dollars in funds from a Swiss bank account'... Hogan's 34 million dollars 'has been lying for almost 20 years in account number 379865 at the Corner Bank in Lausanne' run by the Geneva firm Strachans. But Hogan cannot get his hands on it." Talk about Karma kissing fate? I took note that Hogan's trusted attorney and business advisor was the suspected architect of this treachery. I was now nearly certain Thomas Beck, attorney at law, had stolen Warren's money. Warren probably never suspected that Beck was a thief, or did he? Could that be why my ex's dad secretly wrote his own will and kept Beck at bay?

With a little more time on my hands, and residing in Massachusetts, I dove deeper into the former Governor's offshore holdings. My search was interrupted by a call from my adversary in the lady golf pro case. He said he had an offer and I listened. I was soon disappointed to learn that the carrier didn't think much of me or my client, offering a mere twenty thousand dollars to settle.

After formally rejecting the insult out of hand, as I'd already spent more than that on court reporters and experts fees, I told the restaurant's attorney to prepare for trial and I'd see him in the Barnstable County Courthouse in September. Some cases, like this one, cried out for adept jury selection—the most crucial step in a trial—and a big, juicy verdict. I was ready. I said he and his client (the insurance company) would regret this missed opportunity. My adversary remained silent. He knew I was right and hung up. I asked Celeste to draft a letter to the client, updating her on the lowball offer, and I closed up the law shop to move on to my night job.

The WX (weather) looked good this early summer evening in Hyannis as I drove to the airport for my evening turn to PVC (Provincetown Airport). En route, the radio played an old Simon and Garfunkel song that made my spirits soar to about 4,200 MSL (mean sea level). I cranked up the volume to what became in my car, the "Only living girl on Cape Cod." I could be forgiven for singing my own lyrics—"Kate, get your plane right on time." And that was the plan.

Gliding in the building to my boss's office, all seemed right with the world, minus the fact that the millions under my control had vanished somewhere, somehow, months ago. Still, one was responsible for cultivating joy and I took it from whence it came—the radio, the workplace, wherever. Sean was glad to have me back on the CAC schedule. We were busy and the WX was finally cooperating, causing fewer delays and cancellations (CX) than normal for this time of year, except possibly for this evening. I checked my V-file and the latest METARs, TAFs and NOTAMs (weather forecasts) for my destination and overflight area. Several features caught my eye. I could deal with the scattered cloud layer at 2,500 feet, but my attention focused on 2200 Zulu, when there would be thunderstorms in the vicinity, and when a broken layer at 5,000 feet could include cumulonimbus clouds. The winds and broken clouds posed no problem, but it described moderate cumulus clouds to the east off P-town. That could be risky.

Cumulus clouds can be benign or not, depending upon whether they develop vertically beyond what meteorologists call "fair-weather cumulus"—what I call "summer puffies." Summer puffies can cause a bumpy ride if you are caught beneath them in the up-drafts, but they are not considered dangerous or threatening. My concern deepens when these clouds begin to grow vertically. That's a sign that the thermals are intensifying and thunderstorms, which do pose a danger, could be brewing. I'd wait for the freshest information available before heading out at six for the lower cape with my passengers in my Cessna 402.

I took a look at the radar and PIREPs (current pilot reports) and decided we'd be fine. It wasn't the best possible flying weather— CAVU (Ceiling and Visibility Unlimited); but it wasn't the worst either. I knew where the WX was, what it was forecast to be, and I was satisfied we'd be safe for the ten minute flight from HYA to PVC, Runway 7/25, via air—and that I'd be able to return to HYA without drama or trauma or as we pilots say euphemistically, "buying the farm."

My turn to P-town was uneventful, if a bit bumpy, as predicted. Same thing could be said for my local law practice. But it wasn't all dire. Being a solo practitioner offered multiple opportunities for charity, if not riches. Sometimes, I took on matters, knowing that I would never be compensated for my efforts or results, just to do a good deed for someone. I find myself in these positions because I cannot turn away a worthy client for whom I hold sympathy or empathy, or both. Generally, these people have been wronged in some way that cries out for redress; yet they lack the means to hire a lawyer to set things right, as required in twenty-first century America. Most of these folks find me because they've heard, somewhere, that I'll give credit or accept items other than legal tender as payment in full for the professional services I render.

Most recently, I filed an adversary proceeding in the federal bankruptcy court because a trusting soul in Bourne was rolled by an unscrupulous "design professional" from Boston, who was not Steven's Lee. When the trusting soul realized this man had taken her money under false pretenses, she demanded a refund in full. He refused and told her that she's lucky he didn't bill her for more money, as he'd apparently prepared a new invoice, retroactively, showing that she owed him another five thousand dollars for the forty-some hours he said he spent over the last six months cleaning her house at his rate of 225 dollars/hour, allegedly while waiting for furniture deliveries. The lovely, resourceful New England lady responded to his backdated bill-padding by filing a complaint in small claims court, as a pro se (on her own), claiming consumer fraud and treble damages.

Instead of answering her detailed and well-drafted pleading, on the day his answer was due in the state court, this designing scoundrel/defendant filed a "no asset" Chapter Seven bankruptcy petition, adding the word "debtor" to his name. Honest he was not; shrewd, he or his attorney was. Filing a bankruptcy petition has several critical effects.

First and most important for the debtor and his creditors, a legitimately filed petition for bankruptcy results in an automatic stay of all proceedings of any manner, except for family support payments and a few other exceptions. Therefore, in most cases, all litigation and collection efforts levied against the debtor must stop—at once—or the creditor may have sanctions imposed against her by the bankruptcy court. Second, a lawful bankruptcy petition has the potential of legitimately wiping out the most deserving of creditors on account of the statute's "fresh start" rationale; one of the reasons the U.S. has a robust entrepreneurial economy. Instead of debtor's prisons, American law provides the debtor the chance to start anew, so long as the debts to be discharged were not a result of deliberate fraud or a few other specific exceptions.

In this case, my lovely Bourne client was defrauded of her cash. She knew it, her "design professional" knew it, and after the adversary complaint I filed for her, the bankruptcy judge knew it, too. Having survived the dastardly designer's second attorney's motion to dismiss, we were in the thick of discovery. So far, the devious designer produced nothing and I was preparing a motion to compel the production of his answers to interrogatories; requests to produce documents; and my favorite, and the most useful of the bunch—requests for admissions.

In the correct hands, the drafter of the request for admissions can streamline a trial by hours or even days, simply by forcing the other party to "admit" facts that, when pushed, simply cannot be contested or denied. Though useful, drafting detailed requests for admissions takes time and for most lawyers, time is money, or as A. Lincoln said: a lawyer's time and advice are her stock in trade. But not for me. At least not in this case. In this latest act for sainthood, my time was an offering to the worthy. Perhaps my Bourne lady would pay my fee from a portion of whatever she recovered, though I think I heard her say she was knitting me an afghan—a coverlet, not a dog. I told her my favorite color was headset green, if she had choice of yarn available. I figured, I might as well enjoy my hard earned blanket and have it match my bedspread.

In addition to opportunities for altruism, sometimes the life of a solo lawyer is frenetic and sometimes it's eerily calm, especially as high summer arrives on the Cape and many of the judges and lawyers are away on vacation. In the old days, long before I practiced, the courts would close for the season, or at least August, but that's no longer the case. Now, you can still have a trial scheduled for the dog days of July and August, but in reality, the hard core business of civil justice—as opposed to criminal justice, which knows no holiday—occurs from mid-September through June, nearly mirroring the docket of SCOTUS—the Supreme Court of the United States, which runs from the first Monday in October to the last week in June.

I planned to use the lighter summertime court schedule to catch up on my office housekeeping matters like billing—regardless of whether my transcribed time sheets would result in collectibles or receivables; reviewing vendor contracts; and purchasing hardware and software upgrades and the like. I would fly as much as I could, building my PIC time, hour by hour, which moved me closer to my dream of flying for the majors.

Mike called back with the names of financial experts, but none of them was interested in working with me on a contingency basis. Instead, each professional economist and accountant that I spoke with suggested relying upon the criminal prosecution of the federal fraud case against Schuttauf and his pals and hope for some kind of restitution. When I related this feedback to Mike, he was sorry for me;

but wasn't surprised. Despite his name as the referral source, no one worked for free, except attorneys, he admitted. Thus so far, went my search for a forensic wizard to trace and recover Warren's missing millions.

I had not heard from Lyndsey in two days and decided to give her until the beginning of next week before reaching out. Until I could find an expert willing for work for nothing, pending discovery of the missing funds, Lyndsey was my means of intelligence and I needed her "boots on the ground." I had a message from Mr. Beck's office that he filed his papers to remain my co-trustee. His office received the documents I sent and would be sending me a check to cover my costs.

While settling in my office chair to pay some law firm bills, Sean called my cell. Was I available for a last minute charter to the islands? Sure I was. I'd be there in twenty minutes. Celeste assured me that she could handle everything scheduled for today, and I went off to Hyannis, lucky that my flight bag and pilot accessories were in my car. The weather was severe clear and I looked forward to a nice ride to wherever and with whomever I'd be flying.

Arriving at the CAC base, I learned that a couple with a dog had requested that I fly them to MVY. Don't tell me. I thought to myself, it must be Lee, Barkley, and Steven. I said to my boss, "Is there a crate for the woman and a harness for the dog?"

Sean looked at me as if my chiastic phrases were unintentional. (They weren't.)

"There's a crate for the dog and the woman is free to fly with normal restraints per FAA rules."

"May I see the manifest?"

Sean nodded and showed me the paper. Sure enough, I saw the list bearing the names of Steven, Lee, and Barkley, who by this time, I assumed was with puppy.

In preparation for the hop to the Vineyard, I kicked the tires, checked the lights, and put some avgas in the plane. Pilots don't always fill the tank before a trip. But we do assess what fuel we need by flight distance, weight, and the forecast. The better the weather, the less gas I need for reserve because I'm not likely to encounter a delay or diversion. A good rule of pilot thumb: the longer the weather report, the more fuel goes on board. For each typed line of forecast, I add another ten minutes worth of av (aviation) gas.

Assured that my aircraft was sound after all systems checked out, I looked over my shoulder and saw that my passengers had arrived on the ramp. I stood at plane's door and waited. As the couple and a crate approached, I greeted them in a kind, but professional, pilot-way giving my canine PX, Barkley, nestled in her carrier, special attention.

"How's she doing after her procedure?" I asked the non-furry ones.

The female non-furry one ignored me, as Lee had done before, particularly in Steven's presence.

Steven replied, "She's pregnant. She's expecting four puppies."

"The dog or the woman?" I said when Lee wondered out of ear shot. To this, Steven laughed, which could not bode well for his relationship with the non-furry female.

"Counselor, or Captain..."

"Kate." I interjected.

"Right, Kate, that was harsh, don't you think?"

"At least I didn't ask how your bitch was, you wouldn't know how to answer, would you?"

He glanced down and shook his head, either in disgust or in agreement, I couldn't tell.

"May we speak about something after we land?" I asked Steven, earnestly.

"About your missing money?"

"Yes, and about Bain."

"Yes, to the first; maybe to the second."

"Thanks." I nodded and walked away.

I loaded Lee and Barkley into the backseat and put Steven beside me in the front of the Cessna. I explained that weight and balance were critical and that this was the best configuration for safety. Who could argue with the captain?

The fifteen minute flight was smooth as you'd expect with good flying conditions and as silent, given the seating arrangement. I could have yanked and banked just for fun, but I wouldn't do that with pregnant Barkley on board. If she became airsick and vomited, I would be the one to clean it up, same for the humans, so there was no incentive to produce turbulence by successive steep climbs and banking turns with high G loading and unloading. I'd save that E-ticket ride for a Barkley-free trip.

Still, my passengers had no idea how close they came, in my mind, to having a very, very rough ride. When a pilot has a bad thought, she doesn't have to act on it, or reproach herself for thinking it. So, instead of making my passengers nauseated, I consciously adhered to a set of repeatable, consistent steps that I created to stabilize my approach and descent. When I follow my routine, without weather or traffic distractions, I find my touchdown and rollout are nearly perfect, if I do say so myself. My Cessna kissed the asphalt on MVY's runway 24, one wing low, right sneaker down first, slightly noticeable in the absence of a cross wind on this late afternoon in early August.

As Lee disembarked and took the carrier containing Barkley into the terminal lounge, Steven wandered off to inspect some of the impressive hardware (Citation Jet, Gulfstream V) parked on the ramp near us. This was my opportunity, so I walked up to him and began to speak.

"Steven, I read Nicholas Shaxson's article in *Vanity Fair* about Bain and our former Governor's offshore accounts..."

"I'm not discussing proprietary information. I'm sure you appreciate that, Counsellor. And I'm not a Shaxson fan." Steven was abrupt.

I was cordial and unrelenting as I continued the interrogation of my passenger under duress—Steven's, not mine.

"Isn't it true that Bain's been shifting money offshore for decades?"

Steven was silent.

I continued. "You've been doing this for years at Bain."

No response, so I explained my problem.

"There's a big world out there, and I'm just a solo attorney in Cape Cod—'big sky, little plane.' I have no money to pay someone and no one is agreeing to come on board as a forensic accountant without a huge retainer paid in advance. I need to find out what happened to Warren's fortune, but I don't have any money to hire someone. So, you're the perfect person to help me find it."

"What do you want, exactly?" Steven was edgy.

"As a Bain man, you know what I need better than I do."

"I will do what I can, just keep my name out of this." Steven was adamant.

"Thanks, I knew you'd help me with the trust. Both sets of Epcot statements marked 'personal and confidential' are at your

Boston office now. I didn't know I'd be flying you to MVY this afternoon."

"I'll have my office send them to me here. I'll see what I can do." Steven mollified me.

"Thank you. There is a bunch of worthy people who would have benefited from Warren's charitable trust."

"I said I'd help. Anything else?" Steven had enough of me.

I shook my head no and said, "Thank you."

Steven walked off to meet Lee who was now talking on her mobile by the gate adjacent to the ramp. I checked my plane, got in, and rolled towards the runway for the fifteen minute ferry leg home, just me and my Cessna; big sky, little plane.

I landed at Hyannis and reviewed my updated schedule. I was flying as much as the FAA regulations permitted. I owed that much time to Sean, who appreciated my reliability, given the legal demands on my time. Steven Philips, on the other hand, had what we aviators called a "high drift factor." If you have a high one, you aren't reliable. In my mind (but not in his), he'd let me down when he wouldn't sign that affidavit. I hoped he wouldn't do it again. I wondered what, if anything, Steven would do after receiving the statements I'd just sent him. I recalled a phrase attributed to Ralph Waldo Emerson. "What You Do Speaks So Loudly I Cannot Hear What You Are Saying." But, what Emerson really said was, "Don't say things. What you are stands over you the while, and thunders so that I cannot hear what you say to the contrary." And it's true. Actions speak louder than words. I would wait for Steven's acts to match his promise to help me, or the thunder of his refusal—again.

CHAPTER FOURTEEN

A new work week brings renewed hope—at least it does for me. Most of the time. An email confirmed that the California judge entered an order last week, allowing Beck to remain my co-trustee in the case, but admonishing him and his law firm to share all documents relevant to the Ethan estate, electronically or otherwise, with me and any expert of my choosing, whether or not court appointed. She knew there was no money to hire a forensic accountant and encouraged us to do the best we could to carry out our fiduciary duties to the estate and the trust, given our extraordinary circumstances. I reviewed the order and thought of Lyndsey. I called her. The judge's new order explicitly acknowledged the stay granted by the appellate court and thus, pending her appeal, Lyndsey had standing to be a pro per party of the estate proceeding. I decided that I would not record this conversation. Sue me, I thought, if Mr. Beck objected.

"Hi Lyndsey, is this good time to speak?"

"It's as good as any. What's new Kate? Is the blood work back?"

I paused, "No, but I will follow up on that."

I addressed the heart of my concern, "Lyndsey, I want to hire you as my paralegal, in L.A. That way, whatever you learn is cloaked by my attorney privilege and work product. Are you willing to work for me?"

"Depends, how much do you pay?" Lyndsey, ever calculating, asked without a trace of irony.

"We'll work that out. I have a new court order in the case and want you to take it to Beck's office. Say you are my proxy in California and that you must have access to all the electronically stored information concerning Warren and his affairs. Bring the order and get yourself on a computer if you can and see what you find."

"I'll try."

"I'm sending you a PDF of the scanned order now. Check your phone."

After a few seconds, Lyndsey confirmed, "Got it."

"If you are given access to Warren's records, download all data—everything, including documents, excel files, jpegs, videos, and texts—on a thumb drive with a large capacity and fast transfer speed. Better take several, to be safe."

"I can do that." Lyndsey was electronically fluent and assured me that she could find her way to any USB port in a storm, or a law office.

She paused and spoke again, "I need money to buy the drives and some cash to hold me over."

"I will give you five hundred dollars as an advance against your paralegal billing. I'll pay you twenty dollars an hour, no benefits, sorry. Try Obamacare."

"When will I get the money?" Lyndsey was always direct.

"Tomorrow morning. I'm transferring you now to Celeste. She'll need your bank information. Let me know what you find."

As Celeste obtained Lyndsey's routing number for a wire transfer, I wondered if I had just committed an ethical faux pas having a party, who was a putative heir, with an active appeal, work for me in a case in which she sought money. I gave it a moment's consideration and dismissed my concern. I was certain that hiring Lyndsey was an effective, legitimate means to reach into Beck's dark secrets and maybe, if we were lucky, trace Warren's money to wherever it went over the last year and a half. As the co-trustee of Warren's will and trust, my duty was to find that money and put it to its rightful use. Lyndsey was my tool, in a good way; as I was hers.

Reminiscing about times past spent within the Ethan family made me sad. Maybe tonight I'd open another one of those bottles of magnificent, complex, red wine that Warren gave me and Rick so many years ago. I'd offer a toast to my dead ex-father-in-law and ask for help from above, or below, or wherever his spirit now resided. Just as I was musing how the wise heart seeks knowledge from whatever source may hold it, Celeste buzzed in, jolting me from my rescue reverie.

My new client, Helene, had arrived and was waiting for me. She was a thirty-something year-old woman who wanted to confirm her status as an heir, given the unusual circumstances of a will executed by her recently deceased, maiden Great-grandaunt Millie. I was to review the document and determine Helene's standing, if any. Before I looked at the will, I asked general questions about the size of the estate, the quality of the assets, and the nature of Helene's claim.

Helene explained that her New England-frugal Great-grandaunt Millie Aldridge mastered the Internet as an octogenarian. Sometime after that, Millie downloaded a preprinted form from a web site that promised E-Z legal documents. Both of Great-grandaunt Millie's named beneficiaries, two very old siblings, had predeceased her. They had no children who survived them, nor did their children have live children. As we say in the business, Great-grandaunt Millie's sibling beneficiaries died without surviving "issue" or lineal descendants. Naturally, their parents (ascendants) were dead, too. This Aldridge line had ended, except for my client, Helene—an astute, second great-grand daughter of another dead sibling that Millie long ago renounced. Helene explained that one of Millie's beneficiaries became her benefactor. Great-granduncle Albert, Millie's brother, died two years earlier at age 93, leaving Millie a chunk of beautiful Madequecham waterfront property on New South Road, worth about three million dollars. I asked a question about the devise from Albert.

"Is this Nantucket property located near the bunker built for JFK during the 1960s on the Tom Nevers Sub Base?"

"Yes." Helene answered, "It's on the southeast side. It's been in the family forever, and now I think it's mine."

Helene was self-assured as she pulled the two-page, preprinted document from her purse and unfolded it, describing the will's provenance as she placed it before me on the conference table.

I saw that the document was simple and straight-forward, printed clearly and written in language any high school graduate could understand. I instantly recognized the potential threat posed to small law firms and solo practitioners like me if anyone could prepare her own legal documents by logging onto a web site, paying a small fee, and pressing the print button. Without sharing my private thoughts on the approaching obsolescence of my profession and fearing the same fate as the buggy whip makers and cathode ray tube manufacturers of years gone by, I read the text of plainly stated bequests and listed devises.

I parsed the will again, slowly and carefully, not quite believing what my eyes did not see. This E-Z will, for all its ease and simplicity, lacked the saving clauses that no attorney would dare omit: a residuary clause and a general bequest clause that would encompass property accumulated after 2007, when Millie executed the will. From my review, Millie's cheap last will and testament was far too narrowly drafted to be useful now, as her named beneficiaries had predeceased her without issue and the bulk of her estate was "after acquired." Great-grandaunt Millie's estate would pass to Helene, the only living Aldridge heir, however distant, under the Massachusetts laws of intestacy—49.95 dollar Internet will, notwithstanding.

After an hour of my time spent checking the intestacy statutes and the recent case law interpreting them, I was able to deliver the good news to Helene, a "laughing heir" in the eyes of the law—too distant to be bereaved by the loss, but close enough kin to happily qualify for the inheritance. So, lawyers remained a value-added service after all. At least we could review "canned" do-it-yourself documents that were sometimes worth just what you paid for them.

Reviewing Great-grandaunt Millie's flawed will was only a small portion of the legal work that was necessary before title to Millie's property could pass to Helene. There were pleadings to file, letters to issue, notices to send, and searches to conduct before Helene could begin redecorating the estate house. Naturally, Helene was free to hire another attorney to perform these tasks, but she selected me to finish the job. This Monday was turning out to be very good indeed.

While the nearly ecstatic, if not laughing heir, Helene, waited in my conference room for Celeste to print the retainer agreement, I excused myself to check my email. Walking to my office, my mind wandered back in time to my law school T&E (Trusts and Estates) professor. I recalled one class when his goal was not to teach us the rule against perpetuities, nor the nature of nonprobate assets; but rather, to address the realities of practicing law, including the ultimate monetary value of do-it-yourselfers.

Though he warned that we'd forego the fees from drafting their wills at the outset, as lawyers, we'd have the opportunity to earn so much more—from so many—when these flawed, self-drawn, documents failed to withstand probate. At the end of this lecture, our professor gave each student a handout bearing an old verse by the early nineteenth century Scottish judge, writer, and wit, Lord Charles Neaves:

Ye lawyers who live upon litigants' fees,

And who need a good many to live at your ease,
Grave or gay, wise or witty, what'er your degree,
Plain stuff or Queen's counsel, take counsel of me.
When a festive occasion your spirit unbends,
You should never forget the profession's best friends;
So we'll send round the wine and a light bumper fill
To the jolly testator who makes his own will

He premises his wish and his purpose to save
All dispute among friends when he's laid in the grave;
Then he straightaway proceeds more disputes to create
Than a long summer's day would give time to relate.
He writes and erases, he blunders and blots,
He produces such puzzles and Gordian knots,
That a lawyer, intending to frame the thing ill,
Couldn't match the testator who makes his own will.

Of course, Warren had done just this with his self-drafted codicil and that warranted some reflection. Meanwhile, I offered a silent moment of prayer for the peaceful repose of the soul of the dearly departed, newly-adapting, do-it-yourselfer, Great-grandaunt Millie.

As the day wore on I wondered why I wasn't assigned to fly Steven, Lee, and Barkley back to the Cape. I hadn't heard from him, so I decided to call his mobile.

"Steven, it's Kate, is this a good time to speak?"

"Yes. I've reviewed your statements. I've made a few inquiries."

So long as I kept his name out of court documents and the public eye and ear, Steven assured me that he would help, in his own way. I decided to accept his clandestine assistance and not try to control the process or complain about the undisclosed terms. After all, he wasn't charging the estate and the secrecy I could deal with.

"Oh, there's something else." I added.

"More good news?" Steven was sarcastic but pleasant.

"I hired Lyndsey, the would-be daughter, to help me gather information in California."

"Hmmm." Steven uttered, nearly nonverbally.

185

"Should I take that sound as a sign of disapproval or disbelief?"

"Sometimes a 'hmmm' is just a 'hmmm'."

"Steven, I'm stuck. I think Beck did this and I need Lyndsey, who's in California, to help find out for sure."

"And this is ethical and you trust her?" Steven was dead serious.

"It is, I think, and I do. Besides, I've hired her and I have the court's imprimatur to do what I can with my limited resources."

"I see."

"Would Bain like to subsidize my hiring of a top shelf forensic accountant for the depleted Ethan estate?"

"No." Steven was adamant.

"Then don't judge me."

"Okay."

There was a pause, then, unable to resist, I asked Steven why he was still in the Vineyard. He demurred and changed the subject, wishing me a good afternoon and telling me he'd be in touch.

Steven Philips piqued my interest from the first time I saw him on the ramp at Hyannis late last spring. Though I thought he'd let me down, truth was, he never owed me any duty of care or cooperation. I had simply projected my feelings towards him—on him—and he didn't reciprocate. That's how life goes. You win some, you lose some. But now, Steven's charitable streak or whatever it was, was engaged.

I was still drawn to him without any hope or indication that he had any interest in me personally, other than as the vessel of Warren's largesse for the veterans. I was mindful to reject my intruding thoughts of what he was still doing on the Vineyard, and with whom, or what he thought of me and why he was with that awful woman having puppies. Instead I pondered, as a detached professional, having Steven as my wingman as I searched for Warren's missing millions. Steven Philips, man from Bain, would, as we pilots say, watch my six (directly behind the "twelve" on the clock).

Funny thing about pilots, we are used to cooperation. We call it cockpit resource management (CRM). Hard-wired and trained to play nice with the other pilots when we report for duty; we have no choice but to work as a team. When the cockpit—or to be more politically correct, flightdeck—is built for more than one of us, we work as an cohesive team to operate the aircraft as it was meant to be flown. Even if employed by Delta or American, we are an united crew.

How is this harmony of avionics accomplished between strangers? Flying requires exact, predictable inputs and reactions. Our flying routines are really repeatable rituals—tombstone tested, standardized, and religiously followed. They are holy and sanctified and built for safety. Like orchestrated players, the pilots look perfectly organized as they perform their complementary tasks. Even an experienced observer can be fooled into thinking they've been paired together for ages. Most people are shocked to learn that normally pilots don't know each other and have never flown together before they show up for a trip. Think of this fact when you take your next commercial flight to Florida or wherever. Those pilots in the front, who hold your lives in their hands, work in perfect harmony to ensure your wellbeing, though they are usually meeting and working together for the first time during your flight.

I made a mental note to tell Steven that I thought of him as my co-pilot on this matter and would explain what I meant, and how I expected him to behave—or maybe it would be smarter to stay quiet and let him be and do whatever he would, however he would. Meantime, I'd schedule a telephonic session with my therapist and work on my control issues.

The next morning I was still on the Cape, but decided to travel to the West Coast, again. Too much was at stake and there were some things that required a personal touch. This was one. I would make this absence up to Sean, somehow. Eventually, I'd tell Lyndsey of my travel plans, but not yet. It seemed to me that Steven didn't trust her, but I didn't trust him, entirely, either. Favoring immediate action, I reached for my phone and placed a call to Lyndsey from my office, just to touch base, not to share my recent decision to fly west.

Lyndsey was more accommodating than ever and eagerly informed me that she'd already achieved some success investigating what she still perceived as her missing inheritance. Yesterday afternoon, she visited 801 South Figueroa Street in Los Angeles, and talked her way up to the offices of Beck, Stein, and LaMer. When she arrived at the reception floor, Lyndsey struck up a conversation with the firm's summer receptionist/model/actress, Brigitte. When flattered, Brigitte called the temporary secretary assigned to work for Mr. Beck.

This temp, Gail, emerged from the inner office sanctum to meet Lyndsey in the reception area. They shared a brief chat based upon the court order Lyndsey held in her hand. Lyndsey learned that the law firm hired Gail because Mr. Beck's late midcentury, beautiful blonde secretary had taken ill quite suddenly and was placed on a temporary leave of absence. No one seemed concerned for her health. Instead, Gail, the stand-in, assumed the secretary had scheduled a bit of "maintenance" during the L.A. summer lull. Mr. Beck, Lyndsey learned, was also under the weather. Perhaps he was indulging in a bit of plastic surgery himself, but she couldn't say for sure.

Though Lyndsey wasn't able to record any data yet, she made a date with Gail to return to the office later in the week to review the contents of what she described as "her" file. It wasn't my fault that Mr. Beck and his secretary decided to take a concurrent leave of absence, allowing my desert fox into their den. Whatever Lyndsey missed, I'd try to find on my own flash drive, as soon as I made the trip to the coast. Given the mistrust among my crew (Lyndsey and Steven), my California excursion would be a secret kept from Lyndsey—for now—and would include a house call with Beck, if possible. I had his personal address from long ago when my last name was Ethan. I bet that Beck had not moved since my divorce and I'd be able to knock on the door and see how he was doing, all friendly and nice. I'd use the shock effect to my advantage, till I managed to grab his cell phone and download its contents.

CHAPTER FIFTEEN

There are many odd things about the aviation culture besides the lingo and our apparently different view of risk and what is natural for a human to do in a tiny metal cylinder powered through the air at great speeds—though not so great if you're in a single engine plane, I grant you. One of the unique pilot idioms is "flying west," which I was about to do, yet again, since I was served with notice of Warren's death on Cape Cod, seemingly so long ago. To a pilot, "flying west" means D-E-A-D. Physically, I was not sick or compromised in any way. My first class medical certificate was intact and not endangered, but I was growing worried and weary.

When I told Sean that I was flying west, he looked at me and it appeared as if he wished it were true, in the pilot sense. Here I was leaving him in August, when he needed me so much. I explained that going to California was a matter of duty and honor and involved forces greater than him and I and CAC combined. Sean was not a verbal guy and nodded me off, dismissing me. I had attained a high drift factor in his eyes. I had become, admittedly, unreliable. I felt bad about it, but I would make it up to him.

As I drove from the Cape to Logan, I called Celeste and asked her to book me a room in L.A., as cheap and as luxurious as any ultra-last minute Internet request could render. Meanwhile, as she clicked, I discussed the status of each open and recently closed case. The synopsis completed, Celeste assured me she understood where everything stood and reassured me that I was in good shape to leave the law office in her hands. It was August after all, an historically slow month for litigation. Celeste could handle whatever popped up, or would contact me as needed. Before the call ended, I'd received a text with a hotel reservation and confirmation number. Satisfied that my work was done on the Cape, I completed the drive north on Route

93 to Logan. My clients were in good hands and my practice protected by good karma. Approaching the long term parking area, I hoped some of my non-rev mojo would be with me now, allowing a quick and easy escape from Massachusetts.

My journey west was propitious. I made it out of BOS, runway 15R care of Delta, on the first try. The non-rev gods were with me, aware, no doubt, that my mission was one of mercy and justice. The non-rev gods always liked that, along with a good offering, which, of course, I made by placing my pilot job in jeopardy from all the estate fussing and flying back and forth across the country. As I landed in LAX, my mind shuffled multiple and simultaneous "what if" plans, driven by anxiety, the least tolerable of human sensations. That which awaited in California filled me with angst.

In the slough of despond, I wondered what if Beck was gone? What if I was unable to obtain any information? What if Warren's fortune was never to be found? The last "what if" was unacceptable, so I concentrated on a course of action that might lead to success. You know what they say in California: change your intention and you change your reality. I intended to rent a car straight away and drive from LAX to Beck's last known address, the Wilshire House. If Beck hadn't left the country, and really was unwell, I should be able to coax him into granting me entry and an opportunity to grab his phone. Meanwhile, I would take notice if he had a computer, mobile device, or tablet at home, meaning he was computer literate after all.

Yea, as I left the National Rental Office of LAX, I would fear no evil, for Thou wert with me; thy rod and my GPS—or so I thought—as I drove off in my shiny, nearly new Malibu with 876 miles on it, northbound on the 405. I found the Wilshire Boulevard exit easily and swiftly, given the unusually light freeway traffic. Old address book in hand, I found Beck's home and drove up the short, private driveway towards the Wilshire House. The white setback decks wrapped around each of the building's twenty floors gave the impression of a giant cruise ship moored amidst the concrete.

After leaving my rental with the valet attendant, I entered the opulently appointed lobby, complete with a falling water feature against the far wall. The occupants of this building had a full range of amenities available, all the time. I asked the concierge for Mr. Thomas Beck, giving my name and his floor and apartment number as listed in my old address book. I figured, if Beck hadn't escaped to the Cook Islands, he'd be wise to see me, lest I grow more suspicious of him.

I waited near the reception desk, hoping for white smoke to rise from the phone receiver, reflecting the decision allowing me upstairs to Beck's apartment. As I stood, I recalled the distant past, restaurants, not far from this spot on the Wilshire Corridor, where Rick and I'd dined with Warren and Beck and his wife, Patricia, now dead several years. After a few seconds, the doorman waived me over and admitted me to an elevator headed to the seventh floor.

Once it reached its target, the elevator door opened to a semi-private landing that was shared with only one other unit. All mirrored and marble, the space reminded me of Beck's downtown law office lobby. Without my having to knock, an apartment door opened and a tiny housekeeper greeted me. She ushered me through a formal entry hall to a sofa in the living room, where she invited me to sit and wait for her boss. This was the first time I'd been in Beck's home and I used the opportunity to survey the surroundings.

Beck's apartment was on the back side of the building, away from the heavy Wilshire Boulevard traffic below. His living room was serene and elegantly decorated in a subtle, but rich combination of natural materials, tones, colors, and textures. I was certain that this lovely space reflected Mrs. Beck's taste and was sorry she was gone.

Seated among her furnishings and accessories—ivory and sand-toned silk and sisal and wood and onyx—I was mesmerized by the twelve foot floor-to-ceiling windows providing panoramic views of L.A. and the mountains beyond. Though not a penthouse, the seventh floor was elevated far enough above the ground to be stately and peaceful, but not so high as to feel unsafely suspended above the Puente Hills thrust fault. The PHTF, as it's known among seismologists, runs underfoot from the San Gabriel Valley through the Los Angeles basin, which, unfortunately, is filled with fine sediments that amplify shaking when stirred by seismic forces. It's the fault that could, say the pros, "eat L.A." So seven floors up was just enough for me, as I'm sure it was for the Becks, glass walls notwithstanding.

Once my eyes left the expansive glass exterior, they fixed on an interior partition featuring a large, framed wedding photo, circa 1966. As I gazed at the beautiful bride in the picture, the housekeeper approached me with a glass of cold water laced with fresh lemon, explaining that Mr. Beck would be several more minutes. When more than ten minutes passed, I pulled my phone out from my pocketbook and, unable to connect to Wi-Fi, checked my mail and voice messages via the cell network. Satisfied that there were no East Coast emergencies, I patiently sat and contemplated my personal journey back to L.A., feeling utterly isolated in this splendid room. Mr. Beck made me wait forty minutes in all, but I wasn't on a schedule. I was on a mission and I had the time it would take.

"Ms. Bergin, I'm sorry to keep you waiting. I was on a conference call that ran later than expected and you, Madam, were not at all expected."

Beck's manner, to which I'd grown accustomed, was formal, but now cordial. Wanting to change the tone and reestablish us as more than colleagues, I decided to use his dead wife as a wedge into his memory of a time when I was once an Ethan.

"Your home is lovely. It bears Patricia's touch. I was sorry to learn of her death."

"Thank you."

"This room reminds me of her, elegant and refined. Is that your wedding photo?" I wanted him to understand that I truly liked his late wife.

Beck loved his dead wife much more than he resented me, a mere nuisance and painful witness to the loss of his lifetime client, Warren. Beck and Patsy moved to L.A. from the East many years ago to follow Warren and his riches. The wedding photo query led to many more questions, with surprisingly forthcoming answers. And so I learned of Beck's recently diagnosed atrial fibrillation, causing his doctor's concern and Beck's unexpected absence from work. I learned that Warren's companion, Tanya, remained in the mansion, when she wasn't traveling and living her unfunded high life. Meanwhile, Rick and Tiffany were despondent and deep in debt, just down the road in Westwood.

I asked for, and received, a tour of his beautiful 2,368 square foot condo with two bedrooms and three bathrooms. There was no electronica to be seen. No wires, no routers, not even a flat screen TV. This place had not been touched by technology in years. After a brief discussion about the apartment, I felt I'd seen and done all I could here at the Wilshire House. I was intent on visiting Beck's L.A. law office, to learn what I could on site. Before taking my leave, I asked if I could connect my phone to his Wi-Fi network. He apologized for not knowing exactly what that meant. I accepted that response as honest and moved on. I suggested that Beck join me in asking the court for a status conference as soon as possible. Since I was here, I wanted to see, first hand, the fine points of managing estate insolvency in California. Beck agreed and said he'd arrange it. I asked him if he'd been in contact with his office today and he said, yes.

It reminded him, he had to follow up on a matter. With no landline in sight, he used an old flip phone that was in his pocket. I remained where I was and listened. When the call ended we had a court time tomorrow afternoon. Before replacing the phone in his pocket, I asked Beck if I could see the clam-shaped, silver object. He handed it to me, explaining that he resisted carrying a mobile phone, but it became necessary several years ago. This model, he said, was easy for him to operate and the audio quality was excellent. So, he kept it, never trading up as the technology moved on. I didn't have the heart to stick the old phone in my pocket and run, and I didn't think it would help if I did. If he stole Warren's fortune, Beck didn't do it via his Motorola E815 dumbphone. We parted as colleagues and past friends. I declined to tell him that his office was the next stop on my itinerary. I figured he'd learn soon enough and so what of it?

Even with traffic, it took only thirty minutes to drive from Beck's home to his downtown office. Parking was easy, if expensive, and I anticipated no entry problems when I arrived. After receiving approval from someone at the firm, the lobby gatekeeper allowed me past to the bank of elevators. Quickly, I rose up through the building's core. When the doors opened, I walked towards the reception area of Beck, Stein, and LaMer. Beautiful Brigitte sat behind a grand marble façade to greet me and was delighted to call Mr. Beck's extension.

In minutes, Gail, the temporary secretary, appeared to escort me to Mr. Beck's section of the law firm. I'd been here before, back when I first saw and read Warren's will. Nothing had changed since then, except for Beck's absence and Gail's presence. After a brief chat, I learned that my "paralegal," Lyndsey, was due to arrive the following day. Gail wondered if there was anything she could get me?

She granted my request to access the expanding redrope wallets and bankers boxes containing the files for Warren's estate. Gail seated me in the conference room where the documents were kept.

"Where would I find the original codicil and envelope that Mr. Beck received from the court?"

"I have no idea, I'm a temp. Have a look and if you need help, call." Gail was cooperative and accommodating. "If you don't mind, I'll leave you here. I'm just down the hall."

I thanked her. As soon as she left, I closed the door and began riffling through the files in one of the bankers boxes. I found documents that I'd already seen or had copies of in my possession. I did the same for two more boxes till I began rummaging in the fourth box. There I found a large manila envelope that contained the original handwritten codicil Warren wrote in February, along with the original typed will that Beck's firm had drafted and believed controlled Warren's estate; but didn't.

With anticipation and some sadness I pulled the manila envelope out of the box and removed the codicil. Two different envelops were carefully clipped (not stapled) to its upper left side. One was a large, white folded outer envelope that Warren's secretary used to send the codicil to the court on 2 June. The other was a normal letter size envelope from Warren's ivory-colored stationery that contained the codicil. The outside of this envelope bore Warren's script instructing: "To be sent directly to the court upon my death. WE, 2 Feb."

The original handwritten codicil was one page, written on both sides, as I knew; but nothing prepared me for touching the genuine article. The copy that I held in Beck's office, back when this case started, was a poor facsimile of this original.

Touching Warren's elegant stationery, I could nearly feel his presence. Holding his original codicil in my hand and reading his last wishes sent a frisson of energy down my spine, like his spirit was in the room with me. I closely inspected Warren's writing. I was so very sorry how this turned out. I wanted to serve him better than I had. Before returning the objects to Beck's firm's manila envelope, I laid them out on the table and snapped photos of the bunch using my phone. I wanted a record of these documents—the codicil and the two envelopes—intact, as I found them.

After a moment of personal reflection—of the past, my present, and whatever the future held for me and for Warren's estate; I restored the items to the way I found them in the envelope, clipped just so, and put them back in the bankers box, exactly where and how I found them. I was done here. I left the room and walked down the hallway to Gail's cubicle outside Beck's corner office. Interrupting her politely as she appeared to be transcribing a document, I asked if I could enter Beck's personal office to look at the photographs displayed there. I was wondering if I could gain any insight from the images he chose to exhibit.

Sensing that Gail might say "no," I decided to share some of my personal history with her. I told her that Warren, at one time, was my father-in-law. Gail seemed surprised and after a moment's hesitation, she relented and allowed me in Beck's sanctuary as she followed me. I entered the chamber with Gail on my heels. I remarked that it seemed odd that Beck didn't use a computer. Gail explained that most lawyers of a certain age did not touch technology, save the telephone. She'd worked as a temp for many men of that era and their reliance on her typing and computing skills was, for her, a good thing. I saw her point and rephrased my inquiry to be more explicit.

"So he never uses a computer or tablet or a smart phone?"
"Never."

"What can you tell me about his secretary, the pretty lady who's out sick?" I asked, innocently, as if the answer were insignificant.

"You mean Sharon? She's been with Mr. Beck forever. She's his right arm."

"Where is her computer?" I asked, innocently, again.

"Here, it's the one I'm using." Gail pointed to the desktop PC at her workstation just outside Beck's office, where Sharon sat and which still bore all of Sharon's travel photos, but none of her family, that I could see.

We exited Beck's office and walked towards Gail's cubby. I didn't want her to see me insert my own flash drive and copy the Ethan files from this computer, so I made a simple request for aspirin and water that sent Gail away for a few minutes. The second she disappeared from view, my thumb drive plumbed that computer and quickly copied everything pertaining to Warren Ethan, Ethan Enterprises, and the Warren Ethan Family (WEF) Trust, just as I believed my court order authorized. Gail returned minutes later, a bottle of Advil in one hand, a bottle of water in the other, and apologized for not finding any aspirin. I acknowledged her kindness and accepted both offerings. After ingesting a pill and chasing it with a chug of water, I asked Gail if the law firm had issued her a cell phone or tablet in the course of her assignment. It hadn't. I asked if

Gail knew where Sharon lived. No, she didn't; but could find that information quickly. I thanked her and waited for it.

When she returned with the address, I told Gail that, "something unavoidable had come up that required my immediate attention," and said that I must leave but would return soon. I waved goodbye, and walked myself out of the law firm.

On my drive to Sharon's apartment on Westholme Avenue—not far from Beck's place, but a million miles away in terms of real estate values—I called Lyndsey to announce my presence in California and to offer her dinner this evening. She was surprised, but pleasantly. I promised her that I would explain, in part, why I'd flown more than three-thousand miles on no notice. I decided to use the meal as an opportunity to assess Lyndsey's progress and her credibility, given the seeds of doubt that Steven Philips had subtly planted in my head.

While located in a perfectly fine and quiet residential neighborhood, Sharon's building was no Hollywood cruise ship. I parked on the street. As I approached the low slung concrete building, I called Sharon, using the number Gail provided. Instead of ringing through, my call went straight to voice mail. Sharon, however, had nothing to fear from me or my visit, unless she had secretly siphoned Warren's money away. After another try with the same result, I decided to go directly to her apartment.

I rang the doorbell and waited. I repeated. Still nothing. Next, I went low tech and knocked on her door. Silence. After several minutes, a tall, slim, attractive woman walked by me and placed a key in a door down the hallway. I asked this woman if she'd seen Sharon. She had not. Slam. With nothing left to do, I wrote a friendly note and stuck it under Sharon's door explaining that I was in California and hoped to hear from her. I did not explicitly state that I wanted her phone and her personal computers for a few hours to copy their contents and scrutinize what she'd been doing the last two years. I didn't think that approach would be fruitful. I left her apartment wondering where I was going with this scavenger hunt and how I could be more effective at it.

Bumper-to-bumper traffic on the "10" (Santa Monica Freeway) made the ten mile drive from Sharon's place to my last minute, deeply discounted, deluxe hotel on West Olympic Boulevard, take more than an hour. Located close to the Staples Center, the Ritz-Carlton was within easy walking distance to Beck's law firm, even for a pedestrian averse Angelino, which I obviously was not. After valet parking via Georgia Street, checking in, and unpacking I was eager for a SoCal respite.

I tried to relax as I set up my mobile office in my room on the eighteenth floor. From my purse, I removed the thumb drive that I used on Sharon's—now Gail's—computer. I stared at this small item that I'd hoped would contain so much. I plugged it into my laptop with great expectation. I perused the list of files quickly, but nothing jumped out at me. I would read everything later. I could hardly keep my eyes open. My East Coast body was in desperate need of a West Coast nap. As I was preparing to lay down on the California king bed and place my weary head on the perfectly fluffy, non-allergenic, down-substitute pillows encased in high-count, luxury linens, Celeste phoned.

"The results from the lab are in." Celeste was excited.

"Well, what are they?" I was adamant.

"I didn't open the envelope; it was just delivered this evening by UPS."

I looked at my watch; it was 3 p.m. on the West Coast, 6 p.m. back East.

"Open it." I was more than eager and forgot my manners, so added, "Sorry Celeste. Please, for the love of God, open it."

After what seemed like forever, but was probably five seconds, Celeste read the pertinent sentence, "The results are inclusive due to poor quality DNA on paternal sample."

"Damn." Was all I could say.

"What a disappointment." Celeste said, feeling as bad as I did about this. She added, "There's a number for you to call for more information. I'll scan the letter and send it to you via email."

"Okay. Thanks, Cel. I'll inform Lyndsey tonight."

Trying to be upbeat, though both of us were crestfallen with the test results, Celeste asked, "How is California?"

"Sunny...Beck is suffering from Afib, has an ancient cell phone, and doesn't use computers. Nothing conclusive yet on what he knows or doesn't. On the bright side, I was able to copy the Ethan files from the secretary's work station."

"And she let you do that? I'd defend mine—yours—with my life." Celeste meant it, too.

"Well, the usual secretary is out on leave and her temporary replacement allowed it, sort of." I tailed off at the end.

"What do you mean by 'sort of'?" Celeste demanded.

"I did it while she was kind enough to fetch me some headache relief, and I certainly felt better afterwards."

"I see, Ms. Kate. How would you like it if someone did that to me?"

"Oh, Celeste, come on. You're from New York, no one could do that to you and live to tell the tale." I chuckled.

"You have a point. So where is the real secretary?"

"Unknown." I was tired and sounded so.

"Kate, you'll feel better after some rest. Let me know how to help."

"Okay, bye."

I felt refreshed after the hour of sleep I managed to gain. With Lyndsey due for dinner soon, I had just enough time to hop through the shower, dress, and refresh. I was meeting with someone who was soon to be very disappointed, and that was never a good thing, as I knew from both personal and professional experience.

CHAPTER SIXTEEN

In honor of Warren, I decided that we'd dine at the posh Asian fusion restaurant on the twenty-fourth floor of the hotel. When I stepped off the elevator, I was surprised to see Lyndsey standing across the vestibule, staring out the window, watching and waiting. Nearly fragile-looking in silhouette, she was thinner than when I last saw her in court. She wore a dark gray crepe sleeveless sheath dress, a medium length string of white pearls and matching earrings. Her legs were bare. Her classic mushroom-colored leather pumps complemented the taupe leather satchel that she carried. Unable to see me from where she stood, I inspected Lyndsey's face in three quarter profile. Besides a neutral lip gloss and eyeliner, I detected no make-up.

Her cheekbones were more prominent on account of the weight loss. Her nose and jawline were Warren's—in a finer, feminine form.

"Hi Lyndsey." I was warm and welcoming, no harm in being nice.

"Thank you for the invite." Lyndsey was polite, but guarded.

"Shall we sit?" I offered as the evening's host.

"Sure." Lyndsey cordially accepted.

We walked through the lounge area and were seated at a table by a window overlooking downtown L.A. To start us off, I selected the 2007 Darioush Estate Caravan, a dark and powerful, reasonably priced Napa cab cherry bomb with relatively high alcohol content.

"Why are you in L.A. now?" Lyndsey was direct.

"Urgent times call for urgent measures."

"Right. Did you receive the lab results?"

"Yes."

199

"So you know I'm Warren's daughter." Lyndsey said convincingly.

"No. I don't. The results were inconclusive on account of the poor quality of the sample from the envelope."

"So we'll try something else."

"Like what?" I asked.

"Rick's dental floss." Lyndsey was unfazed and onto plan B.

"I don't remember him as a flosser." I told her honestly, "Besides, how would you get hold of that?"

"Garbage." Lyndsey was matter of fact.

"Ah, dumpster diving. Well, I guess one could go that route." I paused and changed the topic. "Let's look at the menu."

After selecting our meals the server took our order. I entertained Lyndsey's questions about my experiences as an Ethan by marriage; if not by blood, as she claimed. I told her as much as I wanted to about my married life with Rick—and Warren as a semi-father figure—then turned my attention to her.

"Why should anyone believe that Warren is your dad?"

"Because he is—and because my mother said so."

"Tell me about her." I asked.

"She was beautiful, smart, talented, and working class poor. From Swansea—that would be Wales, in case you were wondering."

"I'm Welsh, Lyndsey, thanks." I stated without the sarcasm that Lyndsey deserved.

"My mom wanted to be a ballerina, but when she was seventeen years old, she became pregnant. She married the eighteen-year-old father. Soon after, she miscarried."

"I'm sorry." I whispered.

"No. Mom saw it as a sign from God to escape. She knew if she got to America, she'd have a chance for a better life. She left home after high school and never looked back; but never got divorced either. She arrived in California after crossing the Canadian border travelling south. When she ran out of money, she went to Las Vegas where she hoped to use her dancing talent."

"And then what happened?"

"Yes. She became a showgirl at the Stardust Resort and Casino."

"Is that like a stripper?" I was honestly not sure.

"Not at all. She was Bluebell Girl. By the time she was nineteen years old, a jubilee was built around her. After Warren saw her show, he attended every night."

"How do you know this?"

"My mom told me. They were nearly married."

"Really?" This surprised me, if true.

"Yes. My mom became pregnant with me and Warren was supposed to arrange a quickie Nevada divorce from her Welsh husband. But he never did."

"What happened?" I asked.

"I think he insisted that she get an abortion, but she refused. Not long after I was born, Warren married my half brother's mother."

"So what did your mom do?"

"She had me and we got by as best we could. When she needed money, Mom would call Bill."

"Bill?" I asked.

"Yes, Bill Chase, he worked for Warren. Bill would send cash or wire money, whatever my mom needed, but it never could be traced back to Warren. That's how Warren wanted it.

"Oh. How long did that arrangement last?"

"Until my mom began living with another man. I was about five years old."

I paused. My review of Warren's finances did not include the time when Lyndsey was a little girl.

"So Bill Chase knows you?"

"No, he knows of me; he knows my mom, but would never admit it."

"Have you tried to speak to him?"

"Yes, several times. He sent me away. He's a terrible man."

"Did Warren ever reach out to you?"

"Not that I can remember."

"Did you ever reach out to him?" I asked.

"No, my mom asked me not to. I think she was trying to protect me, in case he rejected me in person, like he did to her."

"I see." I was sad for Lyndsey, if this were true.

"Mom suffered many setbacks, none of which would have happened if Warren married her, like he promised. Yet she talked about him until she died."

"When did she die?"

"Thirteen years ago."

"I'm sorry." I didn't ask how the mom died and Lyndsey didn't offer.

"I still miss her. Would you like to see a photo when she was with my dad?" Lyndsey was eager to show me.

"Of course."

Lyndsey dug into her large purse. She removed two phones, a beat up looking iPhone that she placed on the table, and a brand new Droid that she kept in her hands and fiddled with for a few seconds until she found what she was looking for. Then she handed me the Droid and urged me to look at the screen. The image displayed an elegant, tall blonde beauty on a stage wearing an elaborate, body length headdress of purply-pink plumage, a glittering bra encrusted with rhinestones, and a shiny silver G-string that barely covered her bikini area. High heeled dancer shoes and fishnet stockings on her long legs perfected the costume.

"Wow." I paused. "Where's Warren?"

"In the audience, front row center. He took that picture, even though it wasn't allowed. My mom always kept it near. I scanned it and now I keep it with me."

"She's incredibly beautiful and very tall. Gorgeous, really. She looks like Julie Christie. What was your mom's name?"

"Linda Seymour Taylor—that's why she named me "L Y N D S E Y", it combines her names: Linda and Seymour, only she changed the "i" in Linda to a "y" for me. Taylor was the Welsh husband's name."

"That's an incredible story."

"Yes. Sad, too, life took its toll on my mom."

"I think you look like your mom." I was honest.

"A bit, but I've got my dad's face. My mom said I was his daughter in every way."

"How did you learn of Warren's death?"

"Everybody in Vegas knew Warren. News spread quickly through Las Vegas."

"I see." I muttered.

"Kate, you should know that my dad never stopped gambling, he never stopped going to Vegas, and he never stopped loving my mom."

"How would you know?"

"I grew up in Las Vegas. I work there ..."

I interrupted, "What do you do?"

202

"Casino security." Lyndsey said without expanding.

"What does that entail?" I asked, typical lawyer and all.

"Anything and everything to stop the cheats from stealing."

"I see." I responded.

"As I was saying, I knew when Warren was in town and you know what?"

"What?" I was playing into her hand.

"He'd visit my mom's grave before returning to L.A. and leave her a single pink rose each time."

"You saw him do this?"

"No, I had him tailed."

"You mean you put him under surveillance?"

She nodded.

Through dessert, lest I had any doubt, Lyndsey confirmed—between forkfuls of cherry blossom cake—her resolve to prove her heritage and find her rightful branch in the Ethan family tree—whether money was hanging from it, or not. By the meal's end, I was nearly convinced that she could've been Rick's half-sister—or that Lyndsey was a gifted actress. Who really knew? L.A. was full of emotionally wounded and beautiful women who parlayed that precarious combination into something lucrative.

Lyndsey had become teary-eyed speaking about her dead, beloved mom and how Warren allegedly let her down. She'd downed nearly three large tulip-shaped goblets of the chocolaty, cherry wine to my half-glass. Before we were ready to leave the restaurant, Lyndsey took her purse and excused herself to use the ladies room. She could walk, but not pass a sobriety test. Her gait was unsteady and guided by the chairs and tables she grabbed to balance herself as she ambled towards the restrooms. Not one to overlook fate when it presented itself—I surreptitiously took the iPhone that she left on the table and placed it onto my lap. When the phone was safely covered by a napkin, I inserted a flash drive with a micro USB port into it to download as much as I could, as fast as I could.

Lyndsey returned to our table, long after I did the deed, totally unaware of what occurred. The iPhone was placed right where she'd left it. The server brought me the check. I added a generous tip and charged it to my room. I asked Lyndsey where she was staying.

"I have a Vegas friend who moved to L.A. last year. I'm staying with her in a Silver Lake bungalow."

"Would you mind giving me the address, so I can get you a cab home?" And, I thought privately, to know where to find you.

"Sure." Lyndsey complied and with effort, wrote the Silver Lake address with a wobbly hand.

Before we left the restaurant, I motioned to the worn looking iPhone that was semi hidden behind her napkin, on the window side of the table.

She looked flustered and grabbed the phone.

"Thanks, I didn't see it there."

"No problem. Let's go."

We departed and took the elevator down to the lobby and said goodbye. I made sure Lyndsey was safely placed in a taxi. I paid the driver and waved as she headed to the Silver Lake address I'd asked her to write down for the driver—and for me. I walked back into the lobby and towards the elevators that would carry me up to my room. I was sorely tired, in dire need of sleep and restoration.

The next morning, with a body still on Cape Cod Pilgrim Time, I rose very, very early. Having hours to consume before the afternoon conference, I ordered some coffee and breakfast and planned to read whatever I captured on my flash drives yesterday. Looking at the index copied from the law firm computer, I found nothing alarming or surprising. Most items were estate documents that I'd seen before, plus some memos about the case that I hadn't. The drive bearing the contents of Lyndsey's phone revealed a ton of tweets, texts, videos, photos and Facebook posts, but nothing jumped out at me. In the absence of recognizable smoking guns, I wanted help with these drives to make sure I wasn't missing anything. Though it was still very early in the east, I reached out to Steven. I knew he followed the global markets and was probably up hours by now. After all, the globe never slept.

He answered right away. I told him of my dilemma and asked for a computer guy in L.A. that I could afford. In a business tone Steven told me that his assistant would get back to me with the name of someone to help me. In less than five minutes, a young woman called with a name and a number and the instruction that I should use Steven's name as a referral. I followed her, really Steven's, directions.

Whatever I said was enough for Fred—no last name—to help me, quickly. Over the phone, Fred confirmed that most information created and stored on computers and mobile devices (laptops, tablets, smartphones and their like) is readily available, if you have access to the system, know how to look for it, and employ the proper programs. What most people think of as ephemera—emails, social network communications, SMS text messages, call logs, pictures, videos, documents, applications, audio recordings, blog postings, and website searches—is easily recovered and analyzed, if not wiped clean by a program designed to destroy files and directories.

For the most part, he explained that one's use of the delete key is meaningless to a computer forensics expert—both a blessing and a curse, if you ask me. Fred suggested that we meet this morning. He promised to discuss my case in greater detail to determine how he could help me, or how I could better help myself. We agreed to hold this meeting poolside, 10 a.m. on the 26th-floor of my hotel. It was, after all, L.A.

I was East Coast early, but L.A. Fred was already waiting for me as I exited the elevator. I thought it a little creepy, to find him standing there with a piece in his ear, a phone on his belt, and a tablet in his hands; but we were in a safe place, he was highly recommended, and I needed his expertise to locate Warren's lost fortune. After exchanging greetings, we sat down at a table in the shade. Fred asked me open-ended questions about my involvement in the Ethan estate. For a tech guy, he seemed pretty interested in context or "background," none of which would help me read any hidden data on my thumb drives.

When I finished my narrative, hitting all the highs and lows of my Ethan estate saga, it was his turn. I listened as Fred began to discuss the general points of disk imaging, data retrieval, and perhaps most useful, and most questionable for a lawyer to consider, remote control, also known as electronic hijacking. I learned how a complete stranger with access, know-how, and nimble fingers could secretly plant spyware on my electronic gadget and turn it into a computer, camera, recorder, and GPS device rolled into one, that he could control and tap at will.

Call it malware, call it active electronic interception, call it what you will. My immediate reaction was horror. My second was fear. I followed the diagnostic steps Fred demonstrated and found my phone was clear. Fred asked to check my work. I agreed and, reluctantly, gave my phone to him. He manipulated it for several seconds, checking settings and clearing caches, and returned it to me, saying, "You're good to go." He could see I was amazed. Fred noticed and told me that even someone at my lowly electronic level could place what amounted to a wiretap-tracking device on any phone that was "on" and in my hands. I told Fred that I couldn't bring myself to infect someone's stuff with spyware. I thought of it as criminal behavior. Fred nodded and smiled. He said he understood and admired my restraint. In what I perceived as a gallant act, Fred offered to hack a few phones for me, I'd just have to get him the phone or tablet or whatever. Then he laughed. I couldn't get a read on this guy, so I wasn't sure if he was serious or humorous, or just mocking me.

He next offered to help me delve into the thumb drives I brought with me to the meeting. Fred wanted to know why I was interested in Lyndsey's phone. I explained that our mutual friend, Steven, seemed wary of her. Plus, as Lyndsey was now working for me, I wanted to know if she was who she said she was. Fred asked if I thought what I did was any worse than hacking her phone? I looked at him—electronic peeping tom-for-hire that he was—and responded: "Well, you raise a good point. She can sue me and we'll both find out."

"All right, calm down." Fred offered.

"I'm only trying to find Warren's money." I nearly whined.

Fred nodded, silently, keeping his comments to himself, which was just as well. He excused himself from the table and made a call. He returned and stood next to my chair, arm outstretched, and handing me his mobile said, "We have a mutual friend who'd like to speak with you." Figuring it was Steven, I took the call.

"Kate Bergin here, L.A. Law."

"Relax. Fred is friend, not foe. Let him help you."

"What do you suggest?"

"Listen to him. I would."

"Thank you." I said and added, "You're a fine first officer."

Steven responded, "You're not the captain now, Kate and I'm not one of your crew..."

He paused a moment and added, "I'm more like your belayer."

"A what?" I had never heard the word before and wasn't ashamed to say so.

"A belayer keeps a lead climber safe by handling the ropes below. If the lead climber falls, the belayer takes up the slack to slow the climber's descent. But keeping the rope too tight prevents the lead climber from reaching the heights. So, it's a position requiring constant attention and fine tuning. When the lead climber reaches the summit, he becomes the belayer for the second climber. It's a balancing act for both belayer and climber; they have to trust each other." Steven spoke metaphorically, I think.

"I see. Anything else?"

"Kate, don't look for zebras when you hear hoofbeats."

"Excuse me?"

"Like Occam's razor, often the simplest explanation is the best. If you hear hoofbeats, think horse first."

"And applied to my estate case you mean...?"

"Don't deny the obvious—oh, and sometimes the butler really did do it."

"Mary Roberts Rinehart, aside; most often you'll find that 'the butler' was framed."

"You think? Tell that to William Marsh Rice."

"Who's that?" I asked.

"Look him up. Anyway, as a lawyer, remind yourself who had the means, the motive, and the opportunity to divert funds from the Warren Ethan Family Trust before Warren died, however he died."

"Are you suggesting Warren was murdered?"

"No, but keep your eyes open to whatever Fred helps you discover."

"Okay. I'll call if we find Swiss bank account numbers in Beck's briefcase."

"Look forward to it."

I handed the cell phone back to Fred, who spoke with Steven, the belayer from Bain, for another ten minutes. Steven was right; I needed whatever help Fred could offer. Change your mind, change your approach, or as we say in the aviation business, it was time to "go around." As a pilot, you "go around" when your first approach is lousy and you must gain altitude quickly before something bad happens. Let's say you're off the glide slope or likely to overshoot the runway because of a sudden, unexpected tail wind. You must take decisive action. Put flaps at twenty; check thrust; positive rate; gear up; check missed approach altitude; and then, with the correct lateral mode engaged, and up and off you go. After the "go around," you shoot your approach again, and hopefully, successfully, stick the landing—not to be confused with a dead-stick landing, which is when you land with a "dead stick"—from the days of wooden propellers, when you lost your propulsion power, you had a "dead stick." No pilot, male or female, wants one of those.

More receptive to Fred's suggestions, I listened as he explained that many of his clients would exploit every avenue of digital technology—high and low—to obtain whatever information was required to solve the problem at hand. So, why not have a look around L.A. literally, and take advantage of the surveillance cameras in places of interest to see if any of "my suspects" were caught on candid camera doing anything suspicious or illegal. An L.A. native, Fred claimed contacts who would give him access to these closed circuit security cameras planted all over the cityscape, no questions asked. I was impressed at his connections, in addition to knowing my Steven of Bain.

I gave Fred the addresses I had for the putative heir, Lyndsey; the disinherited, gambling girlfriend, Tanya; and my ex, Rick, and his wife, Tiffany; and Beck and Sharon—all the people that I thought would have access and a motive to take what they thought was rightfully theirs, but wasn't. From that list, Fred promised to map out of web of other probable "go to" places like banks, coffee shops, gyms, yoga studios, restaurants, hair salons, hotel elevators and lobbies, gas stations, airports, and any other establishments with videos that could capture my people of interest, doing something of interest. But it would have to be recent activity, as he explained most security cameras rerecorded after 60 days. Since I had recently learned of the missing money, I was hoping we'd get lucky. Before forgetting, I handed Fred the plastic hotel bag that contained both thumb drives I'd used. Fred promised to analyze them for hidden data that could help in my quest for Warren's 184 million dollars.

When our poolside conference ended, there was just an hour remaining before court time. Fred and I had covered a lot of theoretical L.A. ground and I had a nice copper glow. Fred joked that he was ready for a green smoothie and a Pilates workout; but from his appearance, skinny and pale, he didn't look like he'd enjoyed much of either. Fred seemed confident he'd be able to copy some security tapes by this evening for my viewing. He'd also work on the flash drives and be available by phone should I need him. I thanked him again and offered to pay him now for the time he'd spent so far on my estate case. He declined, preferring to bill me later for the entire job. When I asked why he was so willing to extend credit and help a stranger under these stressful circumstances Fred was blunt. He wasn't poor or stressed and Steven, our mutual friend, took excellent care of him—I assumed for business referrals and the like. Besides, Fred said, he liked working for the good guys. Then he was gone.

I wondered if Steven was a good or bad guy, but whichever, I liked Fred's literal "look and see" approach much more than hacking someone's phone. Whatever hidden security cameras caught, they did so in places where one was out and about. The fact that you might not expect to be captured on video wasn't the point. The public space was a free for all. A person had no legitimate expectation of privacy outside his home in these days of ubiquitous digital cameras, also known as "phones." As for furtively copying the contents of Lyndsey's phone on a micro drive, so be it. I concluded that my quest to recover a stolen fortune was an honorable one. If I found the missing money and was able to return it to the trust for distribution per Warren's will, many worthy people would benefit, or so I rationalized my behavior.

I looked up "William Marsh Rice" to learn he was born in Massachusetts; made a fortune in Texas; lived for a while in New Jersey; founded Rice University; and, in the year 1900, was notoriously killed by his butler (valet) in New York City at the behest of his Texas lawyer who forged Rice's "Last Will" in an effort to gain control of the estate. Now more than ever, Beck seemed suspect to me.

After heading through security at the L.A. County Courthouse, I found Department 29 easily. I waited upstairs, seated on a wood bench in the airy wide hallway outside courtroom 240, upon confirming that the Estate of Warren Ethan was listed first for the afternoon session. This court conference promised little drama. It was merely one more step in a straight-forward accounting of another gloriously insolvent estate. Nothing exotic, except for perhaps the sums of money lost and assets depleted. I understood from temp Gail that Warren was not the only client affected by the Schuttauf Ponzi scheme. Other trusts were decimated, leading to all kinds of heartache for the families involved and intricate legal work for Beck's firm. I didn't discuss how Warren's matter was special because I had two sets of statements that showed different amounts in the account before the money was lost through Perkin to Schuttauf. I kept that information to myself, as she apparently wasn't familiar with the details.

Considering my chat with Steven this morning and my meeting with the inscrutable Fred, I was eager to see my suspects again in the flesh and parse their deeds and words for clues. Lyndsey was the first to appear. She sat down beside me and complained. I told her I had a plan, which sparked her up a bit, but not for long. Beck was second to arrive; followed by Rick and Tiffany and their attorney. Tanya's attorney showed up, but not with his client. Just before the hour, the bailiff opened the door to admit us. The judge conducted the conference in open court, with all parties at counsel table. Lyndsey was welcomed to sit with the other parties' attorneys at the bar. The judge noted everyone's appearance and the absence of Mr. William Chase.

I realized then, as I reviewed my notes from the last court date, that neither Beck nor I had received any new financial information from Chase. At least as far as I knew. I made a note to myself to request this material. When asked if anyone knew where Mr. Chase was, Beck spoke up. He said that his office received a notice that Mr. Chase was on vacation till next week and couldn't return for this hearing on such short notice. Chase, he said, was available via phone if the court needed him today.

With that bit of housekeeping completed, the judge ran down the list of items received, items outstanding, and requested their status. She inquired of my search for information on the different sets of Perkin statements that I'd discovered and brought to her attention. I reported that despite many hours of effort, I'd been unable to find an expert who would take this matter on without a substantial retainer. I confirmed that was I doing all I could within my budget of zero. My broke and broken hearted co-litigants and counsel looked on. My response did not satisfy the court.

"Mr. Beck, I want Mr. Chase on the line. Give the number he furnished you to my court clerk. I will see you all back here in half an hour."

Mr. Beck did as ordered and we all left the courtroom for a break.

We returned early and resumed our places in the courtroom. The clerk had Mr. Chase on the line. The judge conducted the proceeding.

"Mr. Chase, I see that I'm calling a mobile phone with an Southern California area code and a L.A. exchange, where are you physically?

"On vacation, Your Honor." Mr. Chase sheepishly replied.

"Where?"

"Avalon, Catalina, Your Honor."

"When will you return?"

"Next week, Your Honor."

"What can you tell me about the funds in Perkin's control on behalf of Mr. Ethan or Ethan Enterprises?" The judge asked.

"Nothing. I had nothing to do with investments, as I explained to Ms. Bergin and Mr. Beck." Mr. Chase was defensive, or offended, I wasn't sure which.

"Where are the Ethan Enterprises files?" The judge asked Chase.

"What type of files? I think Mr. Beck has all the files." Mr. Chase seemed unsure of what the court wanted.

"What about the statements from Perkin, where are those?"

"I've never seen them. Warren had them sent directly to him. I never saw the statements that Perkin issued."

"Where would Mr. Ethan have kept those statements?"

"I don't know, Your Honor, ask Mr. Beck or Warren's secretary." Chase replied.

The Judge addressed us in open court and asked if anyone had knowledge of where the decedent would keep those statements.

No one answered.

"Very well. Mr. Chase, can you hear me?"

"Yes, Your Honor."

"We will have a hearing on short notice next week. I order you, Mr. Chase, to appear with whatever documents you have for all of Mr. Ethan's interests, personal and corporate, including Ethan Enterprises Incorporated and the Warren Ethan Family Trust from the last two years."

"Yes, Your Honor." Mr. Chase responded.

"I want the decedent's secretary here to testify, as well. Mr. Beck and Ms. Bergin, draft the order, consenting as to form. Ms. Bergin, you may appear telephonically. I am aiming to find enough cash from this estate to allow the co-executors to hire a forensic accountant to explore what's going on this case. We are adjourned."

The judge clicked the speaker phone off. Everyone rose and she left the bench. We were free to leave, too; but I lingered until Beck exited. I followed him out the door and asked if I could meet him at his office later. He cordially declined, explaining that he had a previous, unbreakable engagement. He promised to meet me tomorrow, if I wanted. I nodded, feeling nearly friendly towards him now.

Walking outside the courthouse, I could understand the allure of L.A., if you were a person fond of perfect weather. This afternoon in early August was delightful, 72 degrees, hazy sun, and low humidity. Having walked here, I was planning to walk back to my hotel, but with a detour to Beck's office about 1.15 miles away. I headed toward South Figueroa and entered the lobby of 801.

The building's receptionist recognized me, but called up to the firm anyway to assure I was still welcome. After gaining entry to the elevator, I arrived at the law firm reception area where beautiful Brigitte greeted me kindly, once again, and called for Gail the temp.

When Gail appeared, I explained that I was here once more to review the Ethan files. She was welcoming and allowed me back in the same conference room, with the same boxes stacked in the corner from yesterday's review. Once alone in the room, I searched for the box containing the envelope with Warren's holographic will. I located it easily, and removed the large envelope. Once in my hands, I opened it and lifted its contents out and on my lap. As the codicil and its two attached envelopes lay there, I ripped a small portion from the flap of Warren's original envelope and put it in my shirt pocket. Once I'd secured the smidgeon of fresher Warren saliva for further DNA testing, I replaced everything, as I found it, nearly. I left the room and walked out to Gail's work station.

"Gail, may I enter Mr. Beck's office, I think I left my lucky Mont Blanc pen in there yesterday?"

"Certainly, go right in."

This time Gail did not follow me. I was free to look around. My eye caught a large framed photograph of Beck and Governor Pete Wilson, circa 1994, propped up on his credenza, near Beck's chair and phone. There were several more politically powerful figures standing next to Beck, along with several of him and Patricia. There were no longer any photos of Beck with Warren, as I recalled from my first visit. I left after several minutes, satisfied that this man had no hidden equipment, save perhaps a tape recorder, circa 1972, like Nixon's, under the desk. I was done here. As I left Beck's office, Gail politely offered to fetch me water or coffee or Advil. I declined each and respectfully requested copies of any reports that she'd be receiving from Mr. Chase. Gail promised she would send them. I gave my thanks and said adieu.

When I arrived at my hotel I went straight to my room and called Celeste. I told her in brief terms what had happened in the morning by the pool and afternoon in court and, later, at Beck's firm. I wouldn't be back to Cape Cod till sometime next week. Cel assured me that the languid summer time had arrived in full force and my clients and adversaries were away on vacation, cancelling appointments, and postponing meetings daily. I was not to worry. If she needed me, she'd call.

Relieved that all was well in the east, I phoned the DNA lab and asked for help. Explaining that this was a matter of urgent importance (isn't it always?); I requested and received a promise that this new piece of evidence that I would send for testing would be completed within fourteen days of receipt. As I was gathering my thoughts and preparing a memo to the file on my laptop, my phone rang. Fred had news and I should get to his "office" in Santa Monica as soon as I could.

It was a straight shot west on the "10" as they say, and then, ever so slightly north for a stretch on the "1" or Pacific Coast Highway. I reached his address and parked in his driveway. Fred's "office" was a three floor row house on what was known locally as Palisades Beach Road, but was also called the Pacific Coast Highway. As I entered the multi-million dollar home, I saw numerous large monitors set up on what should have been an elegant dining room table, but was serving as a work desk for this electronic detective. I was impressed with the panoramic view through the picture windows of the beach beyond, from Malibu to the pier. Fred, now seated at his cockpit, called me over to view one of the screens set before him.

"Nice house."

Fred did not respond.

"So, you were able to get hold of the security tapes?" I offered.

"That's what I do." Fred was very matter of fact.

I wanted to know how he did that. I had worked with many different types of investigative professionals in my career, but I didn't understand how he was able to get his hands on these recordings so quickly and without any trouble.

Fred explained a facet of his handiwork, "Most people don't know where to look."

"Ah, that's the problem." I said sarcastically.

"True. The recorders and hard drives for these digital security systems are often located far away from the cameras, sometimes off the premises entirely."

"That never occurred to me." I was truly surprised

Fred told me that a real estate investment trust (REIT) owned the downtown office building where Beck's firm was located and had a security team devoted to monitoring screens with live video feeds. Another team maintained the offsite recording equipment and hard drives full of archived digital images, as required by the various insurance contracts covering the building. All the images were scanned and kept in the cloud. Security employees, whether on or off site, logged on to the proprietary security system by signing in on a computer screen, using a username and password, much like that required for access to any private network.

"So a staffer gave you the credentials to enter the security system for the building at 801 S. Fig?" I asked.

"No, I did this myself, by remotely logging in."

"How?"

"Many installers never change the factory setting for log in information." Fred was matter of fact.

"So the user ID was 'userID' and the password was 'password'?" I said incredulously.

"Something like that." Fred was patient but not forthcoming.

"Were these digital images legally retrieved?" I was concerned.

"They look good to me, see for yourself."

Fred ignored my question as he clicked on his keyboard. He had the last sixty days' worth of high resolution, black and white digital security videos from 801 South Figueroa Street, as well as the last thirty days from The Wilshire House and Sharon's building on Westholme Avenue.

I sat down and we decided to examine the law firm videos first. From oldest to newest, beginning two months ago, we selected the view from the camera near the front street entrance and scrolled through quickly, slowing enough when I caught a glimpse of the faces I'd come to know. It took nearly an hour to scan the first twenty days. I saw Sharon and Beck, many times, and William Chase, far fewer. None of this was suspicious as they each had valid reasons to be there. Mr. Chase was helping with the estate's accounting on behalf of Ethan Enterprises and Sharon was working in the building with Beck, who was leading part of the estate administration.

Fred prepared the next batch of days for my viewing. As I hunkered down before the screen and monitored the images, Fred asked me what I thought about Tanya. I told him "not much."

"Their relationship was based on mutual attraction no doubt." Said Fred.

"No doubt. That's what the habitation agreement was for." I replied.

"She's got a body to die for." Fred commented.

"Yeah, and a face to protect it." I snarked, as it was quite untrue, but sometimes I'll say anything for a laugh.

"And here she is." I pointed Tanya out.

I wondered why she'd be going to Beck's office. Her attorney was not in that building; but I wasn't sure what to make of it either. I said to Fred, "It is a big building with lots of tenants; maybe her bookie has an office there?"

"Bookie, really? With an office, in L.A.?" Fred was at last amused.

"Yeah, she's a big online gambler, so I hear."

"I'll make a note of it." Fred said in his low key, SoCal style.

Still not certain if this meant anything important, I asked Fred to help me scrutinize the security video of 801 S. Fig for the most recent thirty days, including the date when I discovered the difference in statements and that next day when I let everyone in California know that there was a problem.

Fred complied and during this newer collection of images we watched Sharon and Beck come and go, no surprise there; and then, Lyndsey, before I hired her to work for me; and meanwhile, more of Mr. Chase and some of Tanya. Yet all of these people conceivably had reason to be in that building. Lyndsey could have been begging Beck for recognition and money. Tanya and Chase had legitimate reasons to meet with Beck. Even if Tanya had an attorney elsewhere, she was Warren's live-in companion, and was occupying the house Beck was ordered to sell. Maybe there were some things she had to discuss with him personally.

Needing a break and something else to focus on, I asked about the thumb drives. Fred said they were at a facility being analyzed. I was disappointed, thinking he'd have something for me now. Fred didn't react to my upset. Instead, he calmly said that I was a lucky lady. Aside from the obvious—that I was alive and in fairly good health, minus my recent anxiety—I wanted to know what made him say such a thing?

"Because your friend was using an old iPhone we were able to exploit its weaknesses."

"How's that?" I wondered.

"It's not encrypted and you obtained maximal data extraction."

"Did I? Purely accidental, I'm sure. What exactly did I extract?" I earnestly asked the stoic tech guru.

"You copied resident data, as well as data that she may have purposefully or inadvertently deleted." Fred seemed genuinely pleased to report.

He continued, "Would you like to view more of the security videos I've got?" Fred pointed to yet another monitor that'd escaped my attention when I first entered the house.

For the rest of the evening I viewed the security images for Sharon's and Beck's apartment buildings. When I finished viewing what he'd brought to show me, I asked Fred for his preliminary take on the information on the drives I gave him. Fred looked at me with the coldest eyes and said, "I could tell you now, but then I'd have to kill you."

Seeing my reaction, he quickly relented and said, "Difficult can be done right now, the impossible will take a little while. You'll see."

"At least tell me what you found on those drives that I couldn't see on my laptop."

"Can't." Was all he said.

"Those drives are mine." I complained.

"Now they're mine. Possession is 9/10ths of the law, right counsellor? I'll see you poolside tomorrow. Do you know the way back to your hotel?"

I said I did, thanked him and left, confused and unsure why he stole my drives. Admittedly, I did not understand most L.A. people. They seemed to vibrate to a frequency that I did not receive and could not capture with my East Coast mindset.

I arrived safely at my hotel just before midnight. The valet welcomed me like an old friend, like everyone does in L.A., but doesn't mean it, unless you can do something for them. I tipped the man generously and the gesture made us both genuinely happy for a moment or two.

As I entered the hotel lobby, my mind's eye was reviewing the surveillance tapes—which of course were not "tape" at all, but a series of digital images stored on a hard drive and exported on a disk for viewing in a gorgeous, but strangely decorated row house overlooking the Pacific. I pondered why Lyndsey would be visiting Beck's secretary, Sharon, multiple times at her home in West L.A. last month. I realized that Lyndsey felt cheated and upset, but I didn't understand this link.

Perhaps when I was ineffective establishing her connection to the Ethan family, Lyndsey thought Sharon was her second best shot at reaching or influencing Beck, whose residential hallways she did not darken—at least not within the thirty days of tape that I saw. Sharon and Beck, however, seemed to be an item, or very close working partners, with each going to the other's house regularly, but not remaining overnight. These were relatively short visits, just enough to go upstairs for a nightcap after an evening at dinner or the theatre.

Not once did I see Tanya or Rick or Tiffany cross either Sharon's or Beck's thresholds in those thirty days of video recordings. I wasn't sure what this meant, but wanted to share it with Mike and Steven, who were probably sleeping at this hour. So, instead of calling my support team, at eight past midnight, Pacific Daylight Time (PDT), or in pilot speak 0708 Zulu (UTC/GMT), I performed the one business function I could without disturbing anyone's slumber.

To alleviate my rising angst and move my little ball forward along the field, I went to my room to retrieve the DNA sample that I secretly and naughtily tore from the envelope enclosing Warren's handwritten codicil. While at the desk in my room, I used my nice Mont Blanc pen and Ritz-Carlton stationery to compose a cover letter to send with the small piece of envelope flap that I had poached for a higher cause. Fred scared me off computers for life. The hotel provided a FedEx overnight, insured mailer that would be picked up first thing in the morning from my hand, from my room—not the desk. Within two weeks, as long as Warren's saliva was on my new sample, we'd know for sure whether Lyndsey and Warren were related—or not. By this time my interest was as personal as it was professional.

Sleep proved elusive. When slumber fails me, I try to read something boring but required, like a flight manual or a law journal. This evening, however, in honor of my host town, I read an issue of *Variety* left in my room. There was no better publication to initiate one to the mysteries of the local culture, customs, heroes, and villains. Ignoring the physical repercussions I was sure to suffer from this voyeuristic Hollywood indulgence, I read until the wee hours of the morning.

This was a mistake. Any pilot will tell you, your body is set on a certain circadian rhythm that regulates your sleep/wake cycle, as well as other daily actions like eating, elimination, cell regeneration, hormone production, and even phases of brain wave activity. Deprived of natural daylight, we humans tend towards a 25 hour cycle. When exposed to normal earthly life, things like daylight, temperature, social contact, physical activity, and even meal times (so-called "zeitgebers") work with our suprachiasmatic nuclei to set our bodies to our customary time zone—which in my case was EDT or -0400 Zulu. And while it's easier on the body to fly west and gain time than fly east and lose time; hard as I try to sleep in—I can't in California. No matter how great the bedding and effective the dark out shades, by 5 a.m. on the West Coast, my body thinks it's 8 a.m.— and I must GET UP.

As an aviator, I try to avoid circadian rhythm disruption (CRD) if possible, so I arose at 4:30 a.m. as my suprachiasmatic nuclei insisted. It was morning in New York and I placed a call to Mike that went straight to voice mail. Next, I called Steven's cell. This time I was not shunted off to an assistant, and Steven was about as friendly he ever got. I told him what had happened, what I saw, and that I thought Fred was a strange character, though he did manage to get hold of the security videos he promised.

I didn't understand how he got them; but that didn't matter. I knew that private investigators were often connected to law enforcement and enjoyed the kind of network that only cops and their ilk can maintain and use. Still, Fred was a riddle wrapped in a mystery inside an enigma, I reported to his referral source. To lighten the mood, or aggravate me, or just change the subject, Steven offered a joke.

"Kate, what do you get when you cross 'The Godfather' with a lawyer?"

"What?" I responded, semi-annoyed at this dumb riddle.

"An offer you can't understand." Steven chuckled.

"Okay, Steven, what have you got when you have two Bain investment bankers up to their necks in sand?"

"Not enough sand." Steven had apparently heard this before as a lawyer joke, as I did.

"What do you make of Lyndsey visiting Sharon; and Beck and Sharon visiting each other?"

"Is this a riddle?"

"No." I said, curtly.

"Well, not much. What do you make out of it?" Steven asked.

"Me? I want to sue everybody involved, issue subpoenas, get bank records, and recover Warren's money." I said impatiently.

"Maybe it's not a lawsuit kind of thing." Steven was calm and detached. He continued, "Wasn't it Abraham Maslow who said, 'If you only have a hammer, you tend to see every problem as a nail'?"

"Meaning?" I was miffed now that Steven was impugning my judgment or ability or both.

"Kate, you're a good lawyer and I'll bet you're great during a deposition and cross examination and all that; but you might be in a bit over your head now."

I didn't know exactly what to say next but I strongly concurred with Steven. I was in over my head. With nothing left to say, I changed the topic and asked about Barkley's impending motherhood. With no news on that front, we ended the conversation and said we'd keep in touch.

I pondered Steven's observation that my mind was set in a lawyerly way, with the implication that perhaps it wasn't serving me well in this instance. Maybe I should widen the lens, and change my perspective when confronting new circumstances. But as a lawyer and a pilot I was trained to do what works, over and over, varying the application of my hard-won skills by degrees, depending on the context. In times of distress I resorted to the tried and true: what I knew well and learned best. It's the law of primacy. In the air, when you find yourself in times of upset—say a deep stall or inverted spin—your basic stick and rudder skills are automatically available to restore your straight and level.

In my view, the Ethan estate was in a spin, but I couldn't determine for sure if it was a steep, nose-down spin or flat spin. To save yourself from the first—contrary to natural instincts—you learn to apply full rudder opposite from the direction of the spin's rotation and then put the nose down. The second type—the flat spin—was usually deadly. There is little a pilot can do to recover or remediate from it. Generally, you need a parachute to escape with your life.

After the FedEx lady arrived at my room to retrieve my package, I was able to relax and drink some coffee, also known as pilot fuel; but lawyers, of course use it, too. I had several hours before meeting Fred poolside, so I called my office and got good news. My bankrupt designer case had an unexpected turn for the extraordinary. The bankrupt's rich older brother, averse to my subpoenas, decided it was best to put an end to the conflict and simply pay my lady client what she demanded, and a bit more for her trouble. In exchange for that settlement, I would dismiss the adversary complaint and the brother would also pay my fees and costs. My Lady of Bourne was thrilled with the result and told Celeste that my afghan was finished. She would personally deliver it to the office next week, in all it's 90" x 95" glory of sea green bobbles and honeycomb blocks coupled with strips of Aran braid.

These tidings from Hyannis brought me intense joy and I tried to hold on to it, but could not sustain it. Like most other humans, I was always searching for the new and the next. Having checked that box as a "win," my mind focused on the challenge at hand: the Ethan estate, the difference between the Epcot statements, the impenetrable Fred, and the sphinx-like Lyndsey. I was worrying and generally wasting my time, waiting in my room till it was time for Fred to arrive, when my room phone rang. I picked up the receiver, thinking Fred was early. Instead, the operator informed me that my meeting at ten today was cancelled. I would be given more information after 4 p.m. It was only 6:45 a.m. When I asked for an explanation, I was told none was given. No one left a number or a name. No one had asked to be put through to my room to speak with me directly. This woman on the phone knew only what she read on the piece of paper in front of her. There was no name or date or other identifying information on the sheet, just that "meeting at ten today cancelled. More information provided after 4 p.m."

I had just been foiled by my own private investigator. Now what? I called Fred's number, provided by Steven. It still worked but went straight to voice mail. I called Celeste again and told her what just happened. She suggested that I call Steven, the origin of this contact, and tell him that I'd been conned by his referral. When I reached Steven on his cell, he was calm and almost reassuring. He told me to be patient and suggested that I head up to the pool, relax, and read a good book, unrelated to the law or aviation, and perhaps have a Swedish massage or a manicure and pedicure, or do all those things at once. Is that what he told Lee to do? I wondered (but did not ask). Instead, I remained silent. Confused and condescended to at the same time, there was not much more to say or think. Steven excused himself explaining that he was busy and had to get off the phone. I heard, "Bye" and then a click.

Next, I called Lyndsey, but her phone went straight to voice mail. I called Gail to see if she'd seen Lyndsey, but Gail wasn't in the office yet; neither was Beck. The law firm answering service offered to put me through to his voice mail. I declined with well-mannered thanks, not overt panic. It was not even seven a.m. in L.A. and already I felt doomed. It was like my aircraft was yawing round its vertical axis with a pitch altitude approximately level with the horizon and none of my control surfaces (ailerons, elevators, rudder) was working. In the dreaded and deadly flat spin, I could no longer save myself. Having abandoned all hope for a good outcome in my Ethan matter, I decided I would go to the pool and search for an allegorical parachute.

I eschewed the massage and the mani/pedi, but decided to head up to the pool with a few magazines that I'd packed for the trip. Besides my own literature, I would study my fellow poolside patrons. I had no idea that so many things could be accomplished in such comfort and sunshine. Ideas for movies and TV shows and what have you pitched beside the water as I watched in awe and envy. This was *Variety* writ large, though I understood that this was second or third tier, with the big guys at the Polo Lounge at the Beverly Hills Hotel or Peninsula's pool cabanas. But I was here, and there was plenty to behold.

Celeste called several times, more to check on me, than to provide a status. I appreciated her concern. I'd come out here to save Warren's estate and instead became entangled in a film noir. I could kick myself for ignoring my normal due diligence just because Fred had Mr. Bain's seal of approval. I deserved what happened. But believe me, I wouldn't make that same mistake three times, no sir.

As I watched very young, thin, pretty people with their very sophisticated, thin electronica interact with each other, I felt like a stranger in very strange land. I reflected on my Massachusetts home, and my East Coast roots, and how different it all was from California and Californians—native or aspirational.

I once heard someone say that what made the Western section of the country different from the East was not only the pioneer spirit and the so-called rugged individualism of its inhabitants; but also, that these folks choose, every day, to live in a locale where the earth and weather could kill them in an instant. Back East, you might get the occasionally bad hurricane or snowstorm, but generally speaking, mudslides, earthquakes, and fires were not omnipresent fatal hazards. Out here, they were. Such hair-trigger danger prompted them to live for the day and take more risks, for tomorrow they could all fall into the ocean or what have you.

So, when you live with the chance of dying every day among such scenic beauty on an epic scale, you see the world differently. Or maybe it was the consistently great weather and sushi? I wasn't sure. By lunchtime, I had my financial friend and colleague, Mike Fortune, on the phone; but just for a minute. He was on trial and would call me this evening. Next, I phoned Fred. Again, straight to voice mail. I called Steven and I got the same. Ditto Lyndsey. Gail, however spoke to me and apologized for not having sent Mr. Chase's reports to me at the hotel. Regrettably, Mr. Beck must have been working with these very same reports because they weren't located in the place where she was told they were filed. I responded graciously, as one who has accepted her powerlessness over the situation and fate in general, and confirmed that next week would be fine.

By midafternoon, I was nearly beside myself with anxiety and boredom. Poolside life was not for me. I needed clouds and cold and rain to know I was alive and well, just like the Pilgrims and their close relatives, the Puritans. When the strain of ennui grew too much for me, I laid my head back and napped on the chaise lounge, SPF 70 slathered all over my mostly pasty white body.

CHAPTER SEVENTEEN

I'm not sure how long I was sleeping, but a handsome actor/pool attendant awakened me by leaning over my chaise lounge and discreetly whispering, "Ms. Bergin, Ms. Bergin, wake up. Wake up." And it worked. I awoke, a bit startled and disoriented.

I was deep in delta wave sleep and was not sure where I was when my eyes opened, which is a little scary at first. When I gained my bearings and composure the attendant apologized and explained that I was summoned to the TV near the bar. Too dazed to question, I just covered myself with a robe and followed him. When I was seated before the TV, the attendant called on walkie-talkie-looking device and confirmed, "She's here and it's on."

I looked at my watch and it was nearly 5:30 p.m., long past my expected briefing time. I asked for a glass of water and remained in my seat. The attendant had returned to my lounge to pick up my belongings and bring them over to me, confounding me. Why all the fuss?

My eyes wondered off in the distance at the surrounding panorama of L.A. and the mountains and the ocean. I wasn't sure if I was in a semi-sleep state, still. When the attendant returned with my things he stood in back of me, waiting for something, or so it appeared. I asked if there was something else. He nodded no, but that he was directed to make sure I was all right and could see the screen. I decided that this concern was an instance of the Ritz-Carlton putting on the Ritz for one of its patrons, even one with a deeply discounted last-minute rack rate.

The early evening news was about to be broadcast on the large LCD Samsung TV before me. I remained still, regaining full awareness and stability. As I reached down for my purse, and looked for my phone, I heard a news bulletin. BREAKING NEWS. Local man arrested for embezzling millions, story up next. My eyes popped up to the TV and saw a commercial. I resumed my purse phone search and began to check my email when I heard the voice over, "Man nabbed by FBI for forging documents and faking statements." I looked up to see a video of Fred with William Chase in custody. Story at six.

Nearly paralyzed by shock, I had difficulty answering my phone when it rang. It was Fred's number.

"Who is this?" I answered.

"Did you see?" Fred asked.

"Sort of, what's going on?"

"There's more, but I'll say that your drive of Lyndsey's phone helped with phase two now in progress."

"I don't know anything about this, start from the beginning."

"We've concluded phase one. Now we're wrapping up phase two. I'll be there later to explain."

"Did Beck have anything to do with this?"

"We'll talk in person."

"So you're an FBI agent?"

"Yes, and my name's not Fred, sorry."

"Of course. Does Steven know about this?"

"Can't answer that. I'll see you this evening. Keep the news on."

I called Celeste and told her what just happened. She couldn't speak either at first, and then wanted to know all the details that I didn't possess: what happened and how did they catch him? I explained that I knew nothing and was promised a visit tonight; but of course, I'd been stood up before, so who knew? I really was in shock, too, and wanted to watch more of the news. Celeste understood and made me promise to call back as soon I could with the full scoop. I could barely wait until the full story at six, so I called Gail. Voice mail. I called Beck. Same. I was on my own. I searched my phone for more details on the Internet, but found only the skimpy fragments that I'd already heard broadcast on TV.

Eternity passed until it was 6 p.m. Another voice over the same video tape that ran at 5:30 p.m. announced: "William Chase, accountant for Ethan Enterprises and confident of the late L.A. entrepreneur, Warren Ethan, admits stealing millions from his late boss and his company."

That was the tease. After three more minutes of commercials, the story ran and I could barely believe what I was hearing and seeing for the shock of it.

"Federal Prosecutors charged Mr. William Chase with embezzling millions in private and corporate funds in a scheme that began nearly two years ago when he started to siphon Ethan money into bank accounts he controlled in an island called Tortola, in the British Virgin Islands. He is expected to plead guilty after an investigation that broke open based upon evidence recently collected."

The reporter continued: "Prosecutors launched an investigation into Chase last month after the Schuttauf Ponzi Scheme unraveled. Documents in the Ethan probate case in L.A. County helped prosecutors focus their investigation on Chase and a co-conspirator whose name is being withheld."

Then it was back to the anchor: "Chase is charged with having transferred funds into bank accounts that he controlled. The FBI, also working the case, said that all of the money had been systematically withdrawn from various Ethan accounts and deposited into Chase's personal bank account located in Tortola, which was depleted of funds by a co-conspirator, whose identity remains under seal. If convicted of all counts, the maximum penalty for Chase is nearly ninety years in prison."

And back to the reporter: "According to prosecution documents, Chase, initially offered several false explanations, when confronted with evidence collected, but ultimately admitted to the theft. He told the FBI agent in charge of the investigation that he would gladly turn over the remaining funds, but couldn't because the money was stolen from him. Authorities apprehended Chase this morning at LAX with a one way ticket to Tortola (EIS) by way of Atlanta and San Juan, Puerto Rico."

I ordered bourbon, neat. Why not? The reporter continued after another commercial break: "Chase was able to evade detection by creating false statements and false accounting entries making it appear that the money was where it belonged, when, according to the complaint, Chase was regularly transferring the money to his offshore account. Without detection, Chase used the money to fund a lavish lifestyle, purchasing luxury automobiles including a Ferrari and Maserati, and properties in Napa, Sausalito, and Manhattan Beach under his limited liability corporation called ChaseBillLLC, said a special agent with the Federal Bureau of Investigation."

That's when the TV changed to another story. My phone rang, it was Steven.

"I told you to relax by the pool." He was smug and self-satisfied, I could tell by the tone of his voice, his normal tone.

"Where are you?" I demanded.

"In Boston, working."

"For whom?"

"For the man. But I did help you."

"How?" Again, I demanded.

"Making sure the case went to the right guys. Frank should be there in a while—or Fred, as you know him." Steven had the nerve to laugh.

"You, Mr. Philips, can go right from the gates of CPH for AY666 straight to HEL."

"Funny you say that. I've taken that Finnair flight to Helsinki. I saved the boarding pass, flight 666 to HEL, it's a classic."

I paused, exasperated and then spoke, "I don't know what to say to you." I was bewildered.

"Thanks would be a good start." Steven was serious.

"I need to know what happened and why I'm finding out like this, like everybody else with a TV." I was beyond upset, but relieved and tired.

"I don't know more than you do right now, except that they didn't recover the money until you gave them one of those drives."

"Which one, from Beck's firm or from Lyndsey's phone?"

"Not sure, Frank will fill you in, but congratulations, you were the missing link."

"How do I get the money back in the trust?"

"Frank will explain."

"Okay. Thank you."

"Now that wasn't so hard, was it, now say it like you mean it."

"Good bye, Steven."

Mike called next and I told him everything I knew. He wanted to know how he could help, while admitting he was in the midst of a criminal tax case in federal court and could not fly out to California until next week. I assured him I was okay and would keep him apprised of all that I learned.

I wandered back to my chaise lounge, ordered club soda and reclined. I thought about what had just transpired. I wondered where the money was and who'd stolen it from Chase.

Fred or Frank called me at nearly 9 p.m. We agreed to meet in the hotel club, to which he assured us access. I met him at the elevator on the twenty-third floor and we walked to the club entrance. Admitted without question, we sat at an empty table surrounded by no one. Instead of speaking, Frank/Fred laid before me the confession that Chase signed earlier today. The other culprit was in custody and being questioned as we spoke. I lifted the document from the table and read the short affidavit by William Chase. It stated:

1. I have committed fraud. Through a scheme of using false bank statements and forged deeds, I have been able to steal title to real property and embezzle many millions of dollars from the accounts of my former boss and friend, the late Warren Ethan, and his company, Ethan Enterprise, Inc., the Warren Ethan Family (WEF) Trust, as well as several other entities he owned or controlled. My transfers and forgeries continued undetected until last month.

2. My forgeries began nearly two years ago, shortly after I learned that Mr. Ethan had been diagnosed with lung cancer that had spread to his spine and brain. His doctors told him he had months to live. He told only me of this news. I had seen the will his attorney prepared at that time and saw no provision for me.

3. Approximately eight months ago I successfully transferred out of the country most of the funds, which by that time were managed by Mr. B. Adlai Perkin, who I've never met, and have never spoken to directly.

4. I was able to conceal my crime of forgeries by being the sole individual with access to the accounts held by Mr. Ethan and all his entities. Ethan Enterprises was essentially a one man shop. Mr. Warren Ethan trusted me from the time we met in service until his death from cancer. Everyone knew I was the guy in charge of all Ethan financial matters. If anyone questioned my authority I would simply point out that I was with Warren from the beginning and I was the sole person he trusted.

5. Using this authority, which was unquestioned due to my long history with Warren, I established rules and procedures as each new situation arose. I ordered that all financial statements were to be delivered directly to me unopened, to make sure no one was able to

examine an actual statement. I was also the only person with online access to all of Warren's accounts using the various online portals bearing log in credentials only available to me.

6. For the money with Perkin, there was no such portal and his statements were the easiest to forge. As for the banks and the financial institutions, I told representatives that I was the only person they should interface with at Ethan Enterprises and that Warren was too busy and or unwell to be dealing with petty finances. No one questioned me.

7. No one else ever saw an actual bank or investment statement. The financial statements were always delivered directly to me when they arrived in the mail. I made counterfeit statements within a few hours of receiving the actual statements and filed the forgeries, providing copies of them to Mr. Ethan's lawyer as needed or requested. Using a combination of Photo Shop, Excel, scanners, and both laser and ink jet printers, I was able to make very convincing forgeries of nearly every document that came to me. The few I could not convincingly replicate, I destroyed.

8. I also made forgeries of official letters and correspondence from the banks and various financial institutions, as needed to conceal my activities.

9. I could create forgeries very quickly so no one suspected that my forgeries were not the real thing that had just arrived in the mail. With careful concealment and blunt authority I was able to hide my fraud from others. I learned how to falsify online bank statements and everyone who ever asked for them accepted my forgeries without question. All the statements in Beck's possession were copies of my forgeries.

10. This fraud was completed many months before the Schuttauf Ponzi fraud was discovered. Mr. Perkin's office staff complied with my redemption requests, but was not a party to my embezzlement. I called Perkin's office and asked for the last two years of copies to be sent to me and not be available to Ms. Bergin. Perkin's staff complied and asked no questions. My deception was unrelated to Schuttauf's scheme and it turns out that my fraud was fortunate, preserving the Ethan estate. If the estate trustee had not asked for Perkin's statements directly, no one would have detected my fraud until I was out of the country and the money untraceable.

And that was the end. So I asked Frank, where was the Ethan fortune now? He explained that he could not provide an answer yet;

and that the second part of this saga was unfolding as we spoke. The FBI would not release more information pending the completion of this phase of the investigation. The next new announcement would be given to me directly, before sharing with the wire services or local news reporters. I persuaded Frank I was entitled to an outline of what had occurred so far, if not currently, in the case I'd helped him break.

Frank obliged and began, "The case commenced when you called the FBI about the different statements. Subsequent calls by your office to the attorney general, and to law enforcement by two of your colleagues..."

"Mike and maybe Steven?" I interrupted.

"Who will remain unnamed, sharpened our focus."

"Last month, a judge approved our request to tap Chase's phone in what was termed, "Operation BillChase." That tap revealed his part in this case. The phone you handled and copied the other night was secretly registered under an assumed name, but the texts on that device led us down another path and we're investigating it now."

"What does Lyndsey's phone have to do with Chase's embezzlement?"

"I can't give you details now; but I'll tell you what we knew before you gave us the micro drive."

"Okay." I said.

"Sometime after the probate denied her request for money, Ms. Taylor visited Chase's office in West L.A. There, Ms. Taylor planted a self-activated recorder during her first visit.

"Where did she come up with that approach?" I was curious.

"From you, in part. She told us that you recorded her conversations from beginning to end..."

"Yes, I did." I interrupted.

"When she retrieved it, she heard him speaking to bankers in the BVI."

"How does that make her a co-conspirator?" I didn't see it.

"She threatened to turn him in. Instead he offered her a cut; but it looks like she might have acted on her own.

"Meaning?"

"It appears that she forged a power of attorney and some other legal documents and correspondence and transferred the money Chase stole from the BVI to another location. We're working in this part now."

229

I asked when the case would be wrapped up. Fred/Frank informed me that it would end when it was over. No time line offered. I asked if I should remain in California. I was informed that the decision was mine. I wasn't needed for the investigation and the FBI knew where I was if it needed me. I thanked Frank for his time. He parted telling me that I'd done a good job.

"You mean Bravo Zulu."

"Do I?" Frank asked.

"It's a naval signal for a task well performed."

"Oh." Frank said.

"I work with a couple of NFOs. Ironically, the naval aviators are technically better fliers than the Airforce pilots, go figure." I tried to explain, realizing as I spoke that Frank could care less.

"Right." Frank nodded and then uttered, "Have to go." And he took his leave

I decided to depart L.A. tomorrow. No need to remain out here. We knew the identity of the initial culprit, but I wasn't any closer to recovering the money. Approaching my window of circadian low (WOCL), I needed sleep.

I rose early, rested but restive in a holding pattern. I planned to checkout this afternoon, and didn't have much to do but wait for developments out of my control. I looked at the loads for the flights from LAX to BOS and my best hope to depart was two days from now. No matter what I planned, I'd be in California for a few more hours, at the least.

I had the local news on, but learned nothing new. In the meantime, no one called, no one wrote—not even my Celeste; but it was a weekend in high summer. Cel could be forgiven for forsaking me. I felt that I'd done enough pool time during the trip and decided to occupy a new venue. Today: the lobby. Soon after making that crucial decision, my cell rang. I didn't recognize the number. Having nothing more to lose, I answered. An unrecognized woman's voice in a pleasant, yet formal tone, asked if she was speaking with Attorney Kate Bergin. I responded uncharacteristically, "Who wants to know?"

Agent Margaret Andrews identified herself and said there was news that she'd like to share with me in person. Could I come down to the FBI headquarters this morning? I said okay and packed. I checked out of my hotel, figuring I'd leave for the airport directly from the FBI field office later today.

Like most pilots, my primary navigational tool in a plane remains a short-ranged radio-based system called VHF omnidirectional range, known more commonly as "VOR." In a car, however, I rely upon GPS. When you're in an unfamiliar city whose ways and roads you don't know well, a GPS device alerts you to the best routes and lets you concentrate on the driving. As you negotiate the traffic, your GPS warns of imminent lane changes and exit proximity. Should you miss a turn, it'll reroute you without shaming you.

Plus, I'm always pleased to hear Ms. Garmin announce, in her upbeat computer accent, "Your destination is on the right"—or whatever. As I followed Ms. Garmin's directions this morning from downtown to the FBI field office on Wilshire, I was almost certain that she'd reduced my travel time by half an hour. I don't think I would have opted for the freeways, but that was the correct choice this morning. Ms. Garmin made me happy as she "talked me in" and with barely any traffic, my trip duration was merely 15 minutes.

Despite the relatively early hour on a Saturday, I was admitted to the modern building as soon as the receptionist heard me mention Agent Andrews and checked my photo ID. In seconds, a petite woman with light skin and shoulder-length, straight, dark hair pulled back in a ponytail approached from behind glass doors. She held out her hand and introduced herself, "Hello, I am a Special Agent Margaret Andrews. Please follow me."

I followed Agent Andrews to a conference room. She told me to have a seat and asked if I would like some coffee. I declined. I learned that Special Agent Andrews was an attorney who formerly worked in the California Department of Justice. She was currently assigned to the FBI Los Angeles Anti-Fraud Team, where she investigated all manner of financial fraud and money laundering, both within the United States and overseas. She was in charge of phase two of the Ethan investigation.

"Attorney Bergin, your copy of the contents of Ms. Taylor's iPhone was crucial to the case's resolution."

"How so?" I asked.

"I have a superb team and we uncovered a staggering amount of material from your download. A megabyte of storage space is the equivalent of 500 double-spaced pages of text; and just one gigabyte of storage space—or 1,000 megabytes—is the equivalent of 500,000 double-spaced pages of text. You captured 1.6 gigs on the micro flash drive and gave it to our agent, Frank."

"Wow." Was my learned response.

"Once my team and I had access to the material that you captured I prepared an affidavit to support a search warrant that issued."

"And you seized Lyndsey's phone?" I was catching on.

"Yes, her phone and other electronic devices. We've been examining them for evidence leading to the funds missing from Mr. Chase's Tortola account."

"I see.

"When an individual wants to move money from an offshore account to another account, she will often turn to the Internet—generally browsers, email, and texts—to research potential new depositories, plan transfers, and communicate with others about intentions and activities."

"Are you speaking about Lyndsey in this case?" I asked?

"No, I'm giving you general information." Said Agent Andrews.

"Thank you." I replied and listened intently, realizing I had nothing to say.

"When an individual does any of these things, we can recover a footprint of some—or all—of this research, planning, and communications activity from devices capable of accessing the Internet."

"Good to know." I said, not adding much to this conversation.

"In my experience, even when most communications are by email or social media—individuals will follow up with telephone contact with the persons or entities that they searched and with whom they've established some kind of relationship to carry out their enterprise or plan."

"Excuse me, Agent Andrews, but did you locate the missing money?"

"Most of it."

"Well that's a relief." I said, relieved.

"I invited you here as a professional courtesy. I wanted you to know the results of my team's investigation before we released it to the public and the newswires, as you are implicated."

The word "implicated" made me nearly choke, yet I appeared calm and did what any lawyer hearing that word would do. I remained silent and focused the attention elsewhere for now.

"Where is Lyndsey?" I asked Agent Andrews.

"With us."

"Is she represented by counsel?" I asked.

"She said you were her lawyer."

"That is not accurate." I thought for a moment and spoke up, "So that's why I'm implicated?" I was relieved, now that I understood my link to the investigation.

"No." Agent Andrews replied, again.

"How am I involved in this?" I importuned.

"I'll tell you what we know. Ms. Taylor confronted William Chase with her recordings of him speaking with his Tortola banker. Without arousing Chase's suspicion, Ms. Taylor accepted his demand for silence in exchange for some of the Ethan fortune he'd amassed."

"I had nothing to do with that." I protested.

"We know. Under the guise of keeping Chase's secret Ms. Taylor elicited the bank information, while she continued telephone contact and surveillance by a hidden recorder that she could remotely control."

"That's not legal in California." I noted.

"Since we have Chase's confession, it doesn't matter."

"It will for Lyndsey."

"Maybe. Shall I continue?"

"Yes, sorry."

"When Ms. Taylor learned that Chase was about to leave the country and double cross her, she decided she had to move quickly. She took matters into her own hands. She bought a phone off the Internet using a straw buyer."

"The old iPhone that I copied?

"Yes." Agent Andrews confirmed. "And was seized under the warrant."

"Good, what did you find?"

"Ms. Taylor used her contacts get a durable power of attorney, a simple trust, and guardianship papers. These documents looked professional. They were on law firm stationery, witnessed, and notarized."

"How would she do this, or even know how to do this?"

"Do you know what Ms. Taylor does for a living?" Agent Andrews asked.

"Yes, she told me casino security."

"Her title is Senior Vice President, Corporate Security at Wynn Resorts Limited. She oversees the global security and investigative operations for Wynn Resorts Limited. She had many resources to draw from and lots of people did her favors."

"Funny, I didn't find anything about her when I looked her up."

"She uses a different name professionally."

"Of course, and what name is that?" I wondered if it ended in "Ethan."

"You'd have to ask her."

"Understood." I replied.

"She's street wise and very, very smart. If she's not convicted, I'd like to hire her."

"Interesting. So what happened after she got a power of attorney?" I asked.

"Ms. Taylor strategically deployed these documents to gain control over William Chase's assets and with the guardianship order, even Chase himself."

"Brilliant; don't think it was legal, but brilliant in a diabolical kind of way."

"I won't comment on that. Once Ms. Taylor got control of the Ethan assets and the funds Chase had diverted and converted, she hired the Tortola branch of Commonwealth Trust Limited to incorporate a new Tortola trust.

"So that's where the money is?" I hoped.

"No. Ms. Taylor transferred all assets and cash she could find into this new trust and, using this new trust as a vehicle, opened another nonresident account in a different tax haven jurisdiction. My team and I had great difficulty locating the new country until we translated some of the data found in Ms. Taylor's iPhone."

"Where did you eventually find the money?" I asked eagerly.

"Jersey."

"Have we gotten to the point that Californians require a translator to understand a person from New Jersey?" I asked, half astonished; half joking.

"No, Ms. Taylor transferred the trust to old Jersey, as in cows and fabric and the Channel Islands off the coast of Normandy. The data we found wasn't in English; it was in Legal French, a different language even from French. "

"Oh. Why Jersey?"

"Jersey banks guarantee complete secrecy for accounts and account holders. Without that iPhone, we'd still be analyzing where she put the money."

"I see. But how does any of this involve me?"

"Ms. Taylor stipulates that all her actions were done to protect her father's trust and not for personal gain. To prove this, she signed documents transferring all ownership and authority of this trust and its corpus to you and the probate judge who's been handling the estate case."

"No." I couldn't believe it.

"Yes." Was Agent Andrews' reply.

"I had no knowledge of her actions." I proclaimed.

She ignored my statement.

"Ms. Taylor alleges that she mailed two letters after she transferred the money from Chase's account to the Jersey trust—one sent to the judge and one to you, explaining her actions and her conduct."

"When was this?"

"We're not sure. We don't have the letters yet. We're tracing them through mail covers and the USPS Mail Isolation Control and Tracking program."

"I see." I was still stunned and astonished.

"Ms. Taylor stipulates that she did what she did to honor her mother's memory and to prove her ability to solve a problem that no one else could. Plus, she knew that you and the judge were probably well documented, busy people and could confirm that you had nothing to do with forming this shell entity, which she named, 'Charitable Trust.'"

"What will happen to Lyndsey?" I asked.

"The investigation is ongoing."

"Unbelievable."

Agent Andrews stared at me quizzically, silently.

"Do I have something caught between my teeth?" I couldn't figure why she gave me that look.

"No, don't you want to know how much money you and the judge have at your disposal, sort of?" Agent Andrews laughed.

"I certainly do. How much?" I asked

"Of the nearly 260 million dollars that Chase embezzled over the course of nearly two years, including all of the Perkin account– minus the 100,219.58 dollars that remained, but was lost to Schuttauf; and the other properties and accounts that existed before Warren died; you have 197 million dollars, minus the real and personal property that Chase purchased with stolen funds."

"What will happen to those things?"

"Eventually, all will be returned to the Ethan estate."

"And what's that worth?"

"An additional 15 million, depending upon the market values of the items."

"How do I get that money back in Warren's trust?" I asked with hope and awe.

"I'll give you a guide for federal forfeiture and restitution procedures."

"Ah, yes, forfeiture, that's how you law enforcement types get all the good stuff."

"You're right; you enjoyed one of our seized assets with Frank the other night."

"You mean that Santa Monica beach house?" I was stunned again.

"Yes. Owner and son caught dealing drugs in that house. Both charged and convicted. They got time; we got the house."

"You got a good deal, pardon the pun." I paused. "Agent Andrews, I don't think Lyndsey's a bad person, her heart was in the right place. I hope she can get by with a lesson and not much more."

"Not up to us. She's allegedly forged documents, laundered money, used false pretenses, and used the mail to execute her plan. There's long list of federal crimes committed. It's up to the federal prosecutor to charge her or not."

"Yes, but we both know that Chase is the bad one. Lyndsey saw an opportunity to do something great and good and she took it. It's actually kind of amazing and the result is nothing short of miraculous."

"She should have called us."

"Sure, but the system has never worked for her."

"Tell it to the judge—not the one who she named on the account with you—rather, the federal judge who'll be assigned to Lyndsey's case."

"I will, not as her lawyer, but as a witness. I would testify on her behalf."

"You can see Ms. Taylor now." Agent Andrews offered.

"Will you bring her here?"

"No. I said you could see her, not meet with her. My boss released the phase two results to the wires a few minutes ago. See for yourself."

It was nearly 9 a.m. Agent Andrews turned the TV on and tuned it to the local news. We watched the breaking news banner featuring the story. Next we watched a video showing Lyndsey Taylor in a perp march towards the federal jail, with Frank holding her by the arm, walking beside her.

I asked Agent Andrews if Beck or my ex and his wife or Tanya had anything to do with this missing money. No, she assured. Nothing. They were checked and cleared. So much for my intuition about Beck. I asked Agent Andrews about Beck and Sharon, since Frank had probably taped and tapped them together, I wanted to know, were they an item?

Agent Andrews replied, "No. Just friends, really. Sharon is, how I shall say it, 'kept' by a little, old Japanese man who likes tall, beautiful blonde women from L.A. Beck is just lonely and likes Sharon's company when she's not on call. That's all."

"Where was Sharon now?" I asked Agent Andrews?

"According to my sources, she's in Palm Springs, doing her duty with her special friend—eating sushi and being mounted by a tortoise without a shell."

"What?" I exclaimed.

"So say my scout's notes, verbatim." Agent Andrews smirked ever so slightly.

I scolded myself for misjudging Beck completely. I recalled Steven telling me to think horses not zebras and that sometimes the butler did do it. Though Chase wasn't the butler per se, he was Warren's financial manservant, in a way, with the singular access and motivation to steal the money that he coveted and that his sick boss would not soon need. Sure, it all made sense if you were a thief and didn't believe in the laws of succession, or any laws for that matter.

I asked if I could visit Lyndsey, and was told not today, not for a while.

"How many people worked on this case?" I asked.

"As many as we needed." She replied generally.

"Give me a ball park." I requested.

"A few Assistant U.S. Attorneys; a few special FBI agents; a few inspectors of the U.S. Postal Inspection Service; several professionals from the U.S. Attorney's Office Economic Crimes Unit and the Office's Asset Forfeiture and Money Laundering Unit."

"And I thought I'd solve the problem with a few subpoenas." I was shaking my head.

"On behalf of the President's Financial Fraud Enforcement Task Force, I like to say you're welcome and we're at your service." Replied Agent Andrews.

"Is that task force number listed, in case I run into this kind of problem again?" I said with friendly humor.

"Ms. Bergin, I suggest that you use the web site, www.stopfraud.gov. It'd be easier for you since the task force involves more than 20 federal agencies, 94 U.S. Attorneys' offices, and state and local partners."

"You don't say?" I was not kidding.

"Results speak for themselves. This task force represents the broadest coalition of law enforcement, investigatory, and regulatory agencies ever assembled to combat fraud. Over the past three fiscal years, the Justice Department has filed nearly 10,000 financial fraud cases against nearly 15,000 defendants."

"Okay, I'm sold." And I was. I never messed with the federal government.

Although this evening I'd hoped to depart as a passenger; as a pilot, flying in or out of Los Angeles International Airport (LAX) could be tricky. The STARs and SIDs are demanding and unyielding, but not as you'd expect. In aviation, a "STAR" is not a celebrity, but a standard terminal arrival route; while "SID" stands for standard instrument departure. Both STARs and SIDs describe specific air traffic control (ATC) direction sequences published in charts (or "plates") bearing diagrams and lists of instructions that pilots must follow to arrive at, or depart from, certain airports. My flight instructor told me to think of STARs and SIDs simply as mandatory welcome maps with directions leading to and from an airport.

But despite that easy analogy, sometimes STARS and SIDs were confusing, even to the most experienced pilots out there. Consider the LOOP7 SID at LAX. It's the seventh revision of a plan that requires aircraft to take off to the west towards the Pacific, and then, at a specified point, turn back nearly 180-degrees, towards the mainland. Thus the SID name: "loop." These sorts of departure procedures are supposed to reduce noise over inhabited areas near the airport, enhance safety, and help ATC arrange and direct traffic.

Before this trip, I'd read an FAA bulletin emphasizing the necessary turn soon after planes departed LAX from the south runway complex using certain SIDs. Around LAX, that necessary turn is based on a radial crossing rather than a named fix, so many flight management systems (FMS) won't automatically identify when it's time to turn. As a result, pilots leaving LAX from all airlines—and all fleets—were missing the required SID turn, and the FAA was irked. Generally, when the FAA says turn, we pilots ask how high. But because these SID "turns" arise shortly after takeoff during an intense, high-workload phase of flight; too many pilots were missing them. Being on a busman's holiday, I was eager, from my non-rev seat at 27A, to see how this flight crew did the SID.

The LOOP7 SID was executed perfectly. Feeling safe behind this crew's yoke, I put my seat back one and one quarter inches and relaxed. While waiting to board this flight, I had purchased and downloaded a book whose title now appealed to me, *Treasure Islands: Uncovering the Damage of Offshore Banking and Tax Havens*. Firing up my electronic reader, making sure to mind FAA regulations, I began to read Nicholas Shaxson's account of the Channel Islands and understood why Lyndsey selected Jersey, a small, quirky, Norman island, west of France's Cotentin Peninsula for her offshore discretionary trust.

A "peculiar possession" of the English crown with its own parliament and currency, Jersey's primary purpose seemed to be hiding and hoarding a large chunk of the world's wealth from tax or accountability. Apparently, some 85 billion dollars in assets were shielded from tax within Jersey Trusts. Disheartened by the avarice of the rich and too weary to read how they buried their treasure on this island, I turned my switch off and slept as we flew for hours eastwards through the deepening night sky, where the stars twinkle and pilots drink lots of coffee.

We landed in Boston early Sunday morning. All was quiet and my drive to the Cape uneventful. I went straight home and rested. Tonight I intended to open another of those bottles of wine that Warren had given to Rick and me to celebrate life's happy occasions,

239

though I think he meant together, not as divorced individuals. While Warren might not have foreseen this circumstance, certainly the tracing and eventual recovery of his fortune would qualify as reason to pop the cork. I would pour a glass of wine that reminded me of roasted nuts and coffee with overtones of big, deep, dense, chewy, black fruit and make a toast, alone over dinner—a defrosted, perfectly reheated quahog before me—to the memory of Warren and his many, many millions that will help those he intended to serve through the terms of his secret will, written in his crooked little cursive hand.

Apart from my appreciation of, and occasional indulgence in, an exceptional gift of rare wine; as a returning New Englander, especially from Cape Cod, I was slowly readjusting to the local culture and its fundamental and founding ideals. Frugality, self-reliance, enterprise, cooperation, and perseverance were common; but for me, still aspirational. Even if God's grace and wisdom eluded me now, I was a pilgrim in progress, like everyone else. Being from the Cape was just a bonus.

I reflected upon the joys and sorrows of my recent journey to L.A. and the habits of one's heart, whether it leaned towards betrayal or loyalty or nobility. I called Celeste and gave her the *Cliff's Notes* version of the last week: trusted, life-long friend cheats other trusted life-long friend; long lost and angry daughter nabs cheat, confronts him, and when given the chance, swindles him and saves the money and the day from ruin, restoring all through her own charitable trust. It was bizarre, but true.

As a fiduciary whose assets had been recovered, I was grateful for the support of friends and colleagues; the President's Task Force; and the U.S. government's robust remission and restoration programs that promised to return Warren's money to where it belonged, in due course.

I called Sean at CAC to tell him I needed an evening off, but would be available to fly tomorrow and thereafter. Even Sean sounded happy to hear from me, signing off with an uncharacteristically enthusiastic, "Roger that." I was free for the remains of the day to do laundry and contemplate life's unpredictability.

CHAPTER EIGHTEEN

Air transport pilots are the mariner's modern children. Many of aviation's words and customs derive from those used on the high seas. That's why your pilot in command (PIC) is a "captain"; your jet's inside is a "cabin"; and the whole thing is an "aircraft." And much like our seafaring ancestors, aviators are always plotting and charting. Pilots will chart a course—a planned line between point A and B; meanwhile, they "track," or actually fly, according to winds and other conditions. Put another way: you plan a course; but you fly a track. But even then, your track can change with magnetic variation; much as your course will vary with great circle navigation. In the end, life itself can have the feel of a great circle, I decided as I sat in my little storefront office on the Cape, near the place I was born and not far from the patch of sky where my parents were killed.

Everyday routine regained its appeal and pleasures, large and small. By Tuesday of August's last week, I was pushing as much paper as I could manage between turns to the islands and the popular local attractions—Plymouth, Provincetown, and even day trips to Boston for tourists to walk the Freedom Trail and return to the Cape by night. The Land Division ruled in our favor. The Hyannis airport would expand and that bode well for everyone's future, if not the Kowalski Brothers' fast-food joint. As I promised Sean, I was flying as many hours as the FAA would permit. In between flights, I tried to tie up as many loose ends in my law practice as possible before Labor Day.

I knew that my lady golf pro case would not settle before the trial date, but that didn't stop my adversary from churning the file. This afternoon I received a hand-delivered motion seeking summary judgment in his client's favor and a dismissal of my lady pro's case. I read these papers with an equal measure of interest and disgust. My adversary argued that discovery in this case confirmed that his client, the defendant restaurant owner, had no prior notice that the wooden deck or its railing was defective or weak. Thus, his client bore no responsibility for what happened to the plaintiff—my client, the lady golf pro. Therefore and henceforth, in my adversary's learned opinion—which he greatly valued—his client should win and my case dismissed.

Celeste looked at the ream of text in my hands and asked what I thought of this motion. Not much. It was a pitiful and desperate effort to milk a cash cow client until voir dire started in the local courthouse this fall. Then, the insurance carrier—the real client, not the restaurant owner—would insist on settling this matter, lest a Cape Cod jury hear how the restaurant-chain owning defendant from Florida failed to care for his wooden deck and railings in New England, causing the rails to became weak and dangerous from warps, splits, rot, and splinters.

No, my adversary would not prevail. But I was ticked that his filing would waste my time, as it required a response to his sixty pages of rubbish. Even more irritating, my response to his motion would require his reply, which would just generate more fees for him as he charged by the hour. I soothed myself by imagining an enormous jury verdict that neither he, nor his insurance carrier, would ever forget. That's what I thought about the motion.

"So we'll win?" Celeste was a bottom line kind of woman. And while I could never guarantee a result, I assured Cel that we sure weren't going to lose on this flimsy, yet voluminous, motion for summary judgment and dismissal filed ten weeks before trial.

As I retrieved the golf lady's case file from my computer's directory to begin responding to the silly motion for summary judgment, my electronic "to do" list popped up. It bore an item that had nearly slipped my attention: follow up on Lyndsey's DNA test. The overall excitement of tracing the money and knowing that it would, eventually, be returned to fund the trust established in Warren's codicil had eclipsed my interest in Lyndsey. I never received her letter, either; but figured it was intercepted by the mail programs that Agent Andrews mentioned.

I decided I would call the lab today for the DNA results from the snippet of Warren's codicil envelope that I took from Beck's firm. It wasn't that the results weren't important to me. They were. It's just that I had about 197 million other things on my mind since returning to the Cape—flying and lawyering. Beck—still my co-trustee—and I were working closely with agents to repatriate the assets from Lyndsey's trust in Jersey. Thanks mostly to Beck and his L.A. team the process of restoration had begun; but would not be completed until the disposition of Lyndsey's federal case. I was not given scheduling details for this prosecution, and not surprisingly, Lyndsey didn't call me, though I was hoping she would.

Thomas Beck and I had become more collegial. He reported that the news of Chase's arrest, and Lyndsey's unusual involvement, thawed Rick's and Tiffany's cold front towards her. Beck, who finally asked me to call him "Tom," relayed that Rick and Tiffany appreciated my efforts, as well. They came to realize that without my getting those original statements from Perkin when I did, Chase would not have been identified as quickly as he was. A few more days and William Chase would have left the country and the money he embezzled, forever gone. So that was something, but so was Lyndsey. In a strange way, without Lyndsey's actions and temerity, we wouldn't be recovering anything, let alone 197 million dollars.

Celeste peeked in my office and saw that I was busy beginning to gather my thoughts to draft a response to the bogus motion to dismiss my golf pro case. She kindly offered to call the lab for me— right now. She did and the lab confirmed that we'd receive the updated results very soon.

Just like Lyndsey fell off the face of the earth since my return to Massachusetts, so did my on again, off again, unrequited potential romantic interest, Steven Philips—belayer, not crew member. I must have flown eight turns to the Vineyard in the last eight days and not one of them included Steven, Lee, or Barkley. But that was about to change. Sean contacted me and asked if I could fill in for a pilot who'd called in sick on short notice. Of course I could, I said, attempting to regain my reliability factor. "Good," Sean tersely replied, adding that me show time at Hyannis was 3 p.m.; wheels up by 4 p.m. for a turn with just one outbound passenger.

Did this passenger have a name? Yes, Mr. Steven Philips. He had requested me. Well hallelujah. Finally. After all that we'd been through—especially me—Steven and I would have a chance to debrief and maybe bond at about 2,000 MSL (mean sea level), or so I'd hoped.

I wasn't due back to HYA till the next morning when I would fly a family of three from the Vineyard home to the Cape. Though

Sean confirmed the airline reserved a room for me for the night, I thought perhaps Steven and I would make it another evening at Casa Philips down Forever Wild Way. I would definitely pack another pair of pants, sandals, and a nice sweater to wear as we walked along his private beach discussing off shore tax havens and what I learned from Nicholas Shaxson's book.

The weather was nearly L.A.-like perfection: 72 degrees and clear with a brisk, cleansing breeze out of the southwest. It was an extraordinary New England afternoon. I drove to the airport through traffic dense with tourists and locals. The town sidewalks were thick with crowds and the merchants appeared happy and busy. The enchantment and magic of summertime on old Cape Cod caught me in a strong updraft, but not in a dangerous way. Instead, a microburst of contentment made my spirits soar. My happiness meter was pegged. I was grateful for these gifts and the joyous sense that for this moment, on this sliver of Massachusetts, all was on the verge of well. My soul, nearly at peace.

Once in the terminal, I did all the things I do as a preflight pilot. I checked my V-file. I checked the route paperwork. I checked the weather, and I was about to check the plane. All looked good and my mood was bright. Then, I saw Steven. His bearing was distinctly remote. I was nonplussed by his distant demeanor. After all we'd been through together—in a sense, though we were never together in another sense—it seemed to me, he and I should be friends by now. But, it was obvious today that we weren't. I wanted to fix that.

"Good Morning Steven."

"Hi Kate, are we on time?"

"Ahead of schedule, the plane is good, the weather's good, I'm good."

"That's what I pay for." Steven nearly barked at me.

"While we can't control the weather, we try to keep the planes running and the pilots flying." I said, stunned and hurt by both his words and tone.

"Thanks." Steven replied as he was reading something on his iPad.

As he rebuffed my effort at chit chat, I decided that he was more distracted than rude. I was, however, surprised that he didn't congratulate me on the honorable work and excellent results for the Ethan matter. This last omission I found strange and sad, considering his involvement. I excused myself to barely a nod of his head.

After making final preparations for the short flight, I noticed Steven was not on the ramp, but was in the lounge. I went inside and announced that his flying chariot awaited him. Steven gave no verbal response, but finished whatever he was doing on his phone and followed me outside.

"Kate, I have some important documents to review and I'd prefer to sit in the back today."

"Fine." I replied and made sure he had plenty of space, metaphorically and otherwise.

I lowered the airstairs and invited Steven onboard.

When he was comfortably seated in the cabin I gave him the routine safety briefing. With nothing more to say, I headed for the cockpit and tended to my checklists. Soon we were airborne in silence, except for the engine noise and the radio calls, which only I, wearing a headset, could hear.

The flight was so smooth it felt as if we weren't in motion. In fact, I felt like we'd gone backwards. We landed in MVY 18 minutes later than expected due to traffic and a couple of vectors on approach.

Before Steven exited the aircraft, he spoke, "Sorry not to chat. I've got lots on my mind today. By the way, good job on the estate."

"Thanks. Maybe we can debrief sometime." I replied nonchalantly.

"Sure, but not now. Sorry, too busy at work."

"I see." I said, hoping he'd say more, and he did.

"By the way, Lee and I have ended our relationship."

"Oh, I'm sorry." I paused and then inquired, "What about Barkley?"

"She's due to give birth soon. Lee's on vigil. I'll let her keep the dog and the puppies." Steven answered flatly.

"Is Lee at your Vineyard house with the dog?" I was curious about my lodging arrangements for the evening.

"No, she moved her things out a few days ago and took the ferry to the Cape. Barkley's with her, she has what you'd call sole custody."

"I see. Are you selling the Edgartown house?" I wondered where he; and I; and our relationship—such as it was, were going now that Lee was gone.

"No. My wife and I will keep it. She selected the property to begin with and the girls will enjoy it."

"Oh." Was all I could say to him; to myself I wondered whether his wife would redecorate—herself this time.

"I owe my girls my time and attention." Steven was a man with far away eyes. He was not in MYV with me, and it was a good thing I had a room for the night.

"Well, that's very good news. I wish you and your family all the best." I tried to sound convincing, but I didn't see this end coming in quite this way.

"Thank you. I appreciate it." Steven was nearly friendly now. Perfect timing, that.

"I never cared for Lee, too much drama." I figured it didn't matter anymore what I said about that woman.

"Yes; that and other problems." He said.

"Reminds me of a Keats line, 'There is nothing stable in her world: uproar's her only music.'" I said in a companionable, calming tone.

"Careful Kate, someone could say that about you, if they only knew you the last few months, as I have." Steven smirked as he broke my heart and hurt my feelings.

I didn't respond at all to him and several slow, awkward seconds passed silently. Steven seemed to recognize that his words wounded me.

"Come on, Kate. You're a woman who's about to administer a trust of nearly two hundred million dollars. You shouldn't look so glum."

At last I learned what was meaningful to Steven, the money.

"Kate, I'm sorry—for everything." This utterance seemed heartfelt.

"No apology required. It was a complicated situation. I'm just glad it's over." I was referring to both my one-sided emotional involvement with Steven and the Ethan estate roller coaster ride.

"I'd like to introduce you to a friend of mine."

"Oh?" I said, not knowing what he meant by this.

"Someone I know from Wall Street. He's a bit older than you are, much older, actually; but he doesn't look it. He's recently widowed. He has young children. I think you're the perfect person for him and his family when he flies to Nantucket and eastern Long Island."

"You mean as his pilot, right?" Unsure of Steven's intention.

"Yes, of course." Steven replied.

"What's this widower's name?"

"David Luskin."

"Oh, I've heard of him; and his brokerage firm. He is old."

"And you're older than his wife by a year or two; She was blonde and beautiful."

I said nothing.

"Kate, you're attractive, in a *Stepford Wives* kind of way." At this, Steven smiled.

I remained silent.

"Can I tell him to call CAC and ask for you?"

"Sure. I'd be pleased to fly him and his family to ACK or FOK or wherever else they would like to go."

Steven broke the next moments of silence. "I'll see you, Kate."

"Farewell, Steven. Thank you."

And that was it. Steven walked off to resume his former life with his wife and children. I stowed the plane and waited for my cab to the motel.

Even this fourth rate Vineyard motel, near a strip mall and not much else, was busy during this time of year. I arrived at the old-styled drive-in, two-story building just as "blissful hour" was in full swing at the little bar and restaurant attached to the office with the old-fashioned front desk. The chalk board menu displayed in the dining area featured limited fare, basically what you could put on a grill or in a fryer and cook in less than five minutes. My room was ready, but there was no space for me in the restaurant. I would have to wait an hour for a table. My thoughts wondered back to my stay at Steven's guest cottage off Forever Wild Way and how this dive was a world away from that. Feeling deflated for all the reasons one would suspect after that flight with Steven, and without a car, I had nowhere to go but upstairs. Ahead, an evening of solitude in the dinky crew motel on this crowded piece of summer heaven in the Sound. I'd check my messages and see what else could disappoint me.

When I arrived at my law office later the next afternoon, my response to the motion in the lady golfer case was ready for my review and filing. The balance of my day was free for catching up and meeting with clients who were in the mood to conduct business before the holiday weekend. The mail had arrived before noon and was waiting for me on my desk. I saw the envelope from the lab and called

Cel into my office. She sat across from me in her favorite chair for such events.

I opened the envelope, using my letter opener shaped like a caduceus—a gift from a doctor/client—and removed the sheet of paper from within. I read aloud the pertinent parts:

"With paternity testing it is possible to exclude a possible father with 100% certainty. To include someone as the biological father with 100% certainty, however, would require testing the individual's genome—the entire DNA sequence. Such extensive testing is not feasible for most people to undertake. That is why standard paternity tests use certain markers which can produce probabilities up to 99.99%, meaning the tested individual is "not excluded." Putting it another way, the paternity test results are 99.99% confident that subject is the biological parent, if the subject is not excluded.

RESULTS FOR TEST # 8DJEJKD:
Subject is excluded.
Subject is not the father of child tested."

I gulped. I reread the results to make sure that I'd not inserted an extra word or syllable. No, I wasn't guilty of misreading. Lyndsey was not Warren's daughter.

"Now what?" Celeste asked.

"I'm not sure. It doesn't make a difference to me; except that she's not a beneficiary of the trust; yet I wonder who she really is and why she said she belonged to Warren?"

"Can we call someone to help us find out?" Celeste offered.

"I think we can. Give me a moment."

I picked up my mobile and looked up the phone number for Agent Margaret Andrews. She was in L.A. so it was prime morning time to reach her.

I dialed her direct line but was transferred to her voice mail. I left a message asking for a call and hoping all was well. In the meantime, Celeste asked to see the results for herself, so I handed her the piece of paper bearing the news. I looked around my office, content with what Celeste and I were able to build from scratch and not much money. The David Clark headset-green colored afghan from my Bourne lady client was folded on the armrest of my office sofa. I would make a point to bring the gift home with me this evening and place it in my bedroom. I watched Celeste read the lab results and mouth out the words as she read the page for the second time.

A blocked number was making my mobile ring and shake. I took the call.

"Attorney Bergin, Agent Andrews returning your call."

"Thank you. I have a bit of information I'd like to share. Perhaps you can help me interpret it?"

"All right."

"Are we being recorded, I thought I should ask under the circumstances."

"Not now, should I fix that?" Agent Andrews was accommodating.

"No, thanks, just checking."

"Do you want my news first?"

"Sure." I calmly replied.

"You've been cleared by the Bar, by the state prosecutor, and by the federal prosecutor."

"I had no idea I was in potential trouble."

"You could've been, but the investigators concluded that your actions were sanctioned by the California probate court order compelling you to try to trace the funds, given your special circumstances. Plus, Ms. Taylor's iPhone was deemed abandoned on the table when she left it and went to the ladies' room at the hotel restaurant."

"That's really good to hear."

"I thought you'd be pleased. What's your news?"

"I have the lab results excluding Warren as Lyndsey's biological father. What do you make of that?"

"Ms. Taylor is not Mr. Ethan's daughter."

"Agreed. What else can you tell me about her? Why did she insist that she was Warren's rightful heir?"

"I can't read her mind but I can tell you that she is from Las Vegas. Her mother was a dancer who later became a pute de luxe."

"A what?" I asked.

"A high-priced call girl. We have confirmed that Warren did have a relationship with the mom at the time of the girl's conception."

"Would that mom be Linda Seymour Taylor, originally from Swansea?" I asked.

"Yes and no. That was her stage name, but her real name is Norma Dockery. She was born and raised in Nebraska."

"Are you sure?"

"Yes."

"Did she die years ago?"

"No. The mother, who is not well, resides in a small home outside of Las Vegas. Lyndsey supports her."

"What is Lyndsey's real name?"

"Angelica Dockery, but she does use the alias 'Lyndsey Taylor.'"

"What else was true?"

"She does work for Wynn, or I should say, she did work for him, and she believed that Mr. Ethan was her dad."

"And the connection to Chase?"

"Affirmative. In custody, William Chase confirmed that Warren and Norma dated and that a little girl, Angelica, was born to the mom. Warren never thought the baby was his and wanted Norma to abort the child. She refused and Warren lost interest, but for many years, Warren would send money as Norma needed through Chase. Norma led Lyndsey to believe that Warren was her father."

I listened for the next ten minutes, Celeste still sitting across from me in silence, listening to one half the conversation.

In aviation, it generally takes several little things going wrong before something catastrophic occurs. In the law, it's different. Under a legal analysis, one big thing—the "sine qua non"—can make all the difference. That is to say, but for the one thing, whatever happened would not have occurred.

The Ethan estate matter was a hybrid, it took a lot of little things (the many undetected thefts and forgeries of William Chase; the Schuttauf Ponzi Scheme; and my request for Epcot statements while waiting for those two years of records to come from California); but the big thing for rescuing the money, the sine qua non, was that old iPhone that Lyndsey, or Angelica, left on that dinner table in L.A., for just enough time for me to capture the data and discover what she did to Chase and where she transferred the embezzled funds.

Lyndsey had no intention of sharing at first. When she learned that Chase had double-crossed her, she reacted. She was smarter, more sophisticated, and even more devious than he was. Her charitable impulses arose when she and I were about to leave the restaurant and I pointed out the iPhone that she'd left on the table. At that moment she figured that I'd gained access to it, somehow. After all, that's what she would have done to me. Working out the odds, Lyndsey thought her chance for a good outcome was a clever act. Once she left the hotel after dinner with me in L.A., she executed the documents that gave the probate judge and I control over the Jersey trust she'd created. Then, she wrote those letters to me and the judge.

During this time, as far as she knew, the DNA paternity test was inclusive. A fact Lyndsey believed broke her way. Plus, Lyndsey did believe that Warren was her dad; though she was never sure because her mother never pushed the issue with a test or a court action. So, for someone like Lyndsey, it was worth the effort to file a lawsuit and use her talents at surveillance and deception. She had nothing to lose by filing her motion and suit as an intervenor in the estate case and everything to gain by contacting Chase and secretly recording him.

Lyndsey had recently hired an excellent attorney to mount a defense against the federal criminal charges pending against her. Agent Andrews believed that with a decent deal, Lyndsey could enter a plea and serve about four years; maybe less. She could even be eligible for parole in eighteen months, depending on the prosecutor and the judge.

The California State charges were more of a problem, however. Lyndsey could get fifteen years just for the illegal recordings she made of Chase. Yet, her attorney was experienced. He'd file all the proper defense motions and if that failed, he'd take his chances on a trial and hope for jury nullification and a not guilty verdict, meaning really, we're not going to punish you for what you did because of the result. After all, when all was said and done, Lyndsey's deeds, or misdeeds, saved the day.

Whatever happened in the state court proceedings were of no concern to the Ethan estate. Warren's millions would be released to Beck and me for placement in Warren's testamentary trust upon resolution of the federal charges, not the state's.

"I don't believe it." Celeste remarked after listening to me repeat what Agent Andrews recounted.

"Me neither. If truth is the daughter of time, then we discovered Warren's daughter after all."

"Maybe trust is the daughter of time."

"Maybe Cel, a charitable trust."

EPILOGUE

While the state case against Lyndsey was still pending, in mid-December Lyndsey pleaded guilty in federal court. Under her deal, as a first time, nonviolent offender, she'd serve a three year sentence in a federal prison for forgery, only. By early January, Warren's money was transferred from the Bailiwick of Jersey back to L.A. and parked temporarily in short term U.S. Treasury Bills, for real this time. Tom and I are working well together to establish a procedure for the veterans and their families to access these funds per the terms of Warren's codicil. Taking Mike Fortune's advice, we plan to invest the trust money conservatively and safely. That means NO HEDGE FUNDS, but perhaps some staggered treasury notes; a few international money market funds; some high-grade tax exempt municipal bonds; a bunch of high quality corporate bonds; and some old-fashioned dividend paying stocks—so that the good works Warren intended can continue for many future generations.

Tom and I agreed that Rick and Tiffany will be given their respective shares of their inheritance, along with Tanya, who finally vacated the Beverly Hills estate after legal action was commenced against her. The property will be sold and the proceeds placed in the trust. Mr. William Chase pleaded guilty in federal court and will be serving what remains of his life in a federal penitentiary in Colorado for bank fraud, forgery, and embezzlement. The state was prosecuting him, too. As Chase sat in jail, Tom and I began the work of recovering all the real property Chase purchased, mortgaged, or illegally transferred into in his LLC's name through use of forged deeds.

Meanwhile, with Celeste's help, I engage in the practice of law—and life, on this sandy fragment of Massachusetts where, "A man may stand ... and put all America behind him," doing what I can to help others in need of tender legal care, while I fly my way to higher PIC time and an eventual position at one of the legacy carriers. Personally, I've learned that a new life is possible for most of us, at any age, with a bit of grace and patience and sometimes the unexpected kindness of friends, acquaintances, and even strangers. Steven introduced me to widower David and his three young children. I have flown this bereaved family to and from Southampton and other East Coast destinations several times since meeting them in late September of last year. David and his little ones have channeled their grief to good use by helping the helpless among us, human and animal. These young, motherless children are transcending their special loss by focusing their attention and energy on rescuing abandoned dogs and cats, and finding them fosters till permanent, new parents take them home, forever.

Having given up on dogs, I have adopted one of the tiny rescue kittens. She's an adorable tabby that bears the marking of a pure Sokoke parent. I call the kitty "Going Boeing"—"Gaby," for short. David and his children will be visiting my home in this new year to see how Gaby and I are getting on together. The children want me to teach them to fly. David wants me to help them as I can in the wake of their mother's loss. I will do my best on all accounts.

Now, when I awake at dawn in my little cape on the Cape, with "Gaby" sheltered and safe beside me, I rejoice in the sun rising on a new day; America in back of me, the future in front, the sky and its blue wideness beckoning above.

THE END

www.ingramcontent.com/pod-product-compliance
Lightning Source LLC
Chambersburg PA
CBHW070550130626
46556CB00001B/94